His name shall be Cymrych,
and he will bear that sword.
His destiny will carry him many places.
He shall fly above the earth,
Even as he delves its depths.
Wind and fire, earth and sea
All shall fight for him,
When it is time for him to claim his throne.

THE MOONSHAE ISLANDS

N

Sea
Of
Moonshae

Caer Callidyrr

Doncastle — ALARON

OMAN'S
ISLE

MORAY

Llewellyn

GWYNNETH

Caer Allisynn

Caer Corwell

SNOWDOWN

Kingsbay

FANTASY ADVENTURE

BLACK WIZARDS

by Douglas Niles

Cover Art by
KEITH PARKINSON

TSR, Inc.
PRODUCTS OF YOUR IMAGINATION™

For my mother and father

BLACK WIZARDS

This book is protected under the copyright laws of the United States of America. Any reproduction or other unauthorized use of the material or artwork contained herein is prohibited without the express written permission of TSR, Inc.

Distributed to the book trade in the United States by Random House, Inc. and in Canada by Random House of Canada, Ltd.

Distributed in the United Kingdom by TSR UK Ltd.

Distributed to the toy and hobby trade by regional distributors.

FORGOTTEN REALMS, PRODUCTS OF YOUR IMAGINATION, AD&D, and the TSR logo are trademarks owned by TSR, Inc.

First Printing, April 1988
Printed in the United States of America.
Library of Congress Catalog Card Number: 87-51258

9 8 7 6 5 4 3 2 1

ISBN: 0-88038-563-4
All characters in this book are fictitious. Any resemblance to actual persons, living or dead, is purely coincidental.

TSR, Inc.
P.O. Box 756
Lake Geneva,
WI 53147 U.S.A.

TSR UK Ltd.
The Mill, Rathmore Road
Cambridge CB14AD
United Kingdom

What has
gone before. . . .

King Kendrick of Corwell was one of the four kings of the Ffolk who dwelled upon the Moonshae Islands. Corwell, along with the Kingdoms of Moray and Snowdown, owed fealty to Callidyrr, for Callidyrr was home to the king of Callidyrr, who was the titular High King of all the Ffolk.

Tristan Kendrick, Prince of Corwell, had studied some of the arts of kingship very diligently, swordfighting and military science in particular. However, he was less interested in the more mundane aspects of rulership, such as economics and agriculture.

Robyn, the king's ward, had been raised as his own daughter, but her interests lay beyond the castle. She showed a proclivity toward the woodlands and all things natural.

In the twentieth year of the prince's life, Kazgoroth the Beast rose from its fetid bog to threaten the kingdom of Corwell. Walking the land in a number of guises, it recruited allies and sought its one goal: the disruption of the Balance so crucial to the Ffolk—and the very isles themselves.

Forced into battle, Robyn found herself wielding potent druidic magic—earthmagic that was the legacy of the mother she had never known. Tristan fought the Beast and created an army to defeat Kazgoroth's minions. In the process, he found the Sword of Cymrych Hugh. This legendary weapon, lost for centuries, allowed him to slay the Beast and served as a symbol of the lost unity of his people.

At the same time, Tristan and Robyn found their relationship changing, growing as a long-dormant love for each other awakened inside them.

But Robyn could not ignore her legacy, and so she went to study under her aunt, Genna Moonsinger, the Great Druid of all the Moonshaes. Tristan remained in Corwell, enjoying the accolades of victory, and swiftly growing bored.

We resume their story one year after the death of the Beast. . . .

Prelude

The plane of Gehenna was a bleak and oppressive realm, hostile to mortal life. It was a world built upon a vast, unending mountainside, sloping steeply always, never reaching a bottom or a summit. Gouts of steam erupted from the mountainside, and rivers of lava flowed across it, sizzling through long cataracts, collecting in bubbling pools.

Such was the domain of Bhaal, murderous god of death.

A seething, angry god, Bhaal thrived on bloody, violent acts. He grew in strength as his worshippers spread across the worlds, slaying in his horrible name.

Bhaal sought vengeance.

A minion of the god had been killed nearly one mortal year ago, but an eyeblink to the god. Kazgoroth was neither Bhaal's most powerful servant, nor his most favored. But he was slain by a mortal, and the man who dared strike a minion of Bhaal's might as well strike at the god himself.

The bloodlust of the god began as a simple hatred—a desire to see this mortal, and those who aided the man, slain. Bhaal anticipated their deaths with grisly pleasure.

But the man was a prince. And he was the beloved of a druid. His woman carried her own power, and she served a goddess who was foreign—and thus, hateful—to Bhaal.

And so Bhaal's need for vengeance evolved and grew into something far more terrible than any plot for murder. The prince was a leader of his land, and the druid was a caretaker of that land. It seemed fitting to Bhaal that not only the mortals, but their land itself, should die.

The god had a powerful tool for wreaking this vengeance. Bhaal's minion, Kazgoroth, though slain, was not entirely gone. One fragment of the Beast—its heart—remained, clutched desperately by one of its former servants. Bhaal *took careful note of the Heart of Kazgoroth. He would have a use for it soon.*

Yes, he decided. The land of these mortals would become a land of death—a nation ruled by the dead, over the dead. No living thing would mar it.

Thus was dealt the vengeance of Bhaal.

* * * * *

"Enter."

The assassin looked around sharply but could not see the source of the hissing voice. Nevertheless, the stone wall before him slipped open, revealing a corridor even blacker than the surrounding night.

Muttering a curse, the assassin entered and disappeared into inky darkness. In his silk shirt and trousers he slipped along without a whisper, his soft leather boots gliding silently over the smooth stone floor. All around him the sprawling vastness of Caer Callidyrr lay dark and slumbering.

The assassin walked cautiously into one of the castle's towers. He saw blackness, a deep and unnatural gloom. Then he heard a soft snapping of fingers, and the darkness dissipated. But it did not exactly grow light; the effect was more a relief of blackness. Faint rays of moonlight spilled through narrow windows high in the walls, and he could vaguely make out the council.

The Seven sat around a long, U-shaped table. They faced the assassin, their table open before him like the jaws of some beast. Deep, cowled hoods concealed the faces. The assassin looked up at them and clamped his teeth together. He could scarcely repress a shudder of revulsion.

The one in the center, he knew, was Cyndre.

The master of the wizards confirmed his identity, his gentle voice belying the terrible powers at his command.

"You were careless about that task in Moray. King Dynnegall's daughter survived long enough to provide a description of your men."

The assassin sniffed loudly through his broad nose. "The guards were more numerous than you led me to expect. We had to kill several dozen of them. And the nursemaid hid the baby in an attic—it took us hours to dig out the little

brat. I lost two good men, and the mission was a success—
the Dynnegall line is ended—as I ended the royal line of
Snowdown for you last year." The assassin punctuated his
statement with a low, inhuman growl.

"I do not expect such sloppiness, for the coin I am paying,"
said the great wizard quietly. "Even your mother, the orc,
could have done better."

The insult was too much. A dagger flashed from the assassin's sleeve. Faster than the eye could follow, it flicked
toward the wizard's unarmored breast.

The others gasped in surprise, flinching at the sudden
attack, but Cyndre merely raised a finger and quietly spoke
a word. Instantly, only a foot from its target, the dagger was
transformed. In its place, a large bat fluttered upward,
turning to lunge at the assassin's throat.

Another dagger flashed, but this one remained in the
assassin's hand. He casually spitted the bat upon the thin
blade and flicked the carcass to the tabletop before Cyndre.
He could sense Cyndre's eyes upon him, boring from the
depths of his hood.

For a moment the room remained frozen, the wizards
intent upon their leader. The assassin stood stock-still
before the table. The black wizard gestured casually, and
the dead bat instantly disappeared. A smooth, amused
chuckle emerged from the dark hood, and the tension in the
room slowly drained away.

"Now, Razfallow," continued the wizard, his voice as
pleasant as ever, "you will soon be free to return to Calimshan. However, one more king upon the Moonshaes threat-
ens the dominance of our . . . liege.

"You will take your band to Caer Corwell. The prince of
that realm is something of a local hero, and he is a menace to
our ambitions. The cleric, Hobarth, has warned us that we
must act quickly, for the prince has a beloved who is equally
dangerous.

"You are to kill them, and the king, as well. The fee will be
twice your usual—thrice if you can return the prince's
sword to Caer Callidyrr. Above all else, this prince must die."

❧ 1 ❧

A Druid of Myrloch Vale

"Let's go swimming now! Can't we, Robyn? It's so hot, and we've been working so hard. . . ."

"You mean *I've* been working so hard!" said the young woman, pausing to push a sweat-soaked strand of black hair back from her face. "All you've done is get in the way!"

Her companion, a two-foot-long orange dragon that buzzed like a hummingbird around her, turned his scaly snout away in momentary indignation.

"Besides, Newt," Robyn continued, "I've got to sort out this tangle of vines before we do anything else. They seem to grow thicker every day! I don't know how Genna tended this entire grove by herself." Once again, she pried the vines away from the trunk with a heavy stick, grasping one and pulling it free from the ground. She tossed the vine onto a pile of its fellows, destined for an evening fire.

"Why do you have to sort these stupid old vines anyway?" the dragon sulked. "Let them grow the way they want to—and let us go swimming the way we want to."

"I've told you a hundred times, Newt. This is the sacred grove of the Great Druid of Gwynneth, and she is training me in the ways of our order. Part of my training is to obey her instructions and to aid in caring for the grove."

The explanation sounded a little hollow even to Robyn, who had, for nearly a year, dutifully followed the instructions of her aunt and tutor, Genna Moonsinger. Today was not the first time the Great Druid had rested peacefully in the shady comfort of the cottage while her erstwhile student toiled away in the summer heat.

Still, Robyn was a devout pupil. She paused and drew a

deep breath, relaxing as she exhaled. She repeated the process as her teacher had shown her, and soon she felt the annoyance pass away. Robyn turned again to the thick vines that threatened to strangle the trunk of an ancient oak. She even felt guilty about her doubts. Genna always works so hard, she reminded herself. She certainly deserves the rest.

Robyn's job was near the periphery of the enchanted area that was the Great Druid's grove. Near her were the tall hedges that bordered much of the grove, and she was surrounded by massive oaks. Closer to the heart of the grove sprawled a wondrous garden and its placid pond, and within these areas stood Genna's simple cottage.

Behind the cottage stood the grove's dominant physical feature, and also its spiritual heart: the Moonwell. The deep pool was surrounded by a ring of tall stone columns covered in bright green moss. The tops of several pairs of pillars were capped with stone crosspieces, raised by the earthpower of great druids in ages past.

It was to learn the secrets of this earthpower that Robyn studied her craft so diligently. She had proven, both to herself and to her teacher, that she had the innate talent to perform druid magic. This was the legacy of the mother she had never known. Inherited power was one thing; it was another matter to learn the skills and discipline necessary to control that power.

Robyn pulled on a thick root, bending it away from the trunk until it snapped free. She tossed it onto the pile and grasped another tendril with a hand that had grown strong and calloused during her training. That vine, too, came reluctantly away from the oak tree, but it required most of her strength to pull against the tension of the plant.

"Well, I'll help too, if that's what it'll take to get done with this. Here—I'll pull on this one and you grab that—"

"No!" cried Robyn, but before she could stop him, the little dragon had seized a loose end of vine and pulled it with a strength that belied his small size. The vines she had so carefully untangled burst free and instantly twisted back around the tree trunk.

The springing mass of vines caught the faerie dragon in their coils, pinning him against the tree. A short, wriggling stretch of red tail and a tiny, clawed foot stuck from the tangle of vines.

"That serves you right!" she chided him as she began to pull the vines from the tree once again. "You should pay attention to what you're doing!"

Newt finally forced his head from the tangle and shook it quickly. "That's the last time I try to help you," he huffed as he crawled free. Flexing his gossamer wings, he buzzed into the air and hovered before her.

"Why don't you just use your magic on these vines and be done with the job?" he asked, eying the tree belligerently.

"The tending of the grove is a matter for a druid's hands and heart," replied Robyn, reciting one of her lessons. "The grove is the source of her magic, and thus cannot be maintained with it, or the magic would lose its potency."

"I should think it would be very boring to do all these studies and silly jobs, day after day, forever and ever. Don't you miss Tristan? And don't you ever want to go home?"

Robyn caught her breath sharply, for the questions were painful ones. She had come to the Vale nearly a year before and had had no contact with her previous home. Genna insisted that such diligence was the only way Robyn could properly develop her skills. She thought carefully before answering, more for her own benefit than Newt's.

"I miss him very much—more, each day, it seems. And I want to be with him. Perhaps, someday, I will be. But for now, I must learn what I can of the order of the druids— find out for myself if I am destined to serve, as my mother did and my aunt does, as a druid of the isles. This is something I have to do, and if Genna tells me that the only way I will learn is by performing mundane tasks around her grove, then so be it."

"Of course," Newt said nonchalantly. "Tristan's probably got plenty to do at Caer Corwell, anyway. Festivals and hunts . . . all those pretty country lasses and barmaids. I don't imagine for a minute that a prince of the Ffolk would waste his hot summer afternoons in a cool alehouse, of course, but just supposing he. . . ."

"Oh, shut up!" exclaimed Robyn, more harshly than she intended. Newt had an uncanny ability to aggravate her.

She did miss Tristan. But, she reminded herself, she was doing the right thing by following in the footsteps of the mother she had never known—the mother that had left her a book and a staff as proof of her druidic legacy.

Wasn't she?

She remembered the sense of awe and wonder with which she had opened her mother's book, only a year ago. It had been given to her by her stepfather, King Kendrick of Corwell—Tristan's father. Through its pages, Robyn had begun to understand the nature of the work she was capable of doing. She saw that she had the power to serve the goddess, Earthmother, and to use druidic magic to maintain the balance of nature in the islands that were her home.

Now she recalled the smooth ashwood staff, plain and unadorned, that had nonetheless become her most treasured possession. Crafted by her mother's own hands, it was both a receptacle and a tool for the earthpower of druidic magic. Not only had it saved her life, but it had been instrumental in rescuing the kingdom itself from the terror of the Darkwalker. Now it stayed safely within the Great Druid's cottage, awaiting her need.

Wistfully, she wondered about her mother—as she did so often. Her Aunt Genna had described her to Robyn in such detail that she now seemed completely familiar. Sometimes Robyn felt as though she had indeed known her mother. As always, a great sadness washed over her at the thought that she would never truly know the woman who had brought her into the world.

A sudden sound—the snapping of a dry twig—cracked through her thoughts, and Robyn froze. She knew every creature that visited the grove, and none of them would make such a careless noise. Even Grunt, the cantankerous brown bear who lived with them in the grove, moved his bulk silently among the plants.

The cracking was repeated, and Robyn located its source in a clump of bushes behind her. A sharp prickle of fear ran along her spine, and she reached for the stout stick leaning against a nearby stump. Slowly, she turned.

The bushes rustled, indicating that a large creature was moving toward her. Suddenly, they parted to reveal the staggering figure of a man. At least, she thought it was a man—the shaggy, matted hair and beard, the filthy, spindly limbs, and the dazed, sunken eyes looked more beastly than human. The creature shuffled forward like an ape, clad only in a tattered rag tied with a crude belt.

But a sound croaked from an unmistakably human throat as the figure collapsed on the ground at her feet.

* * * * *

The boat's slim prow slipped through the black waters of Corwell Firth. The boat blended perfectly into the moonless night, as did the eight cloaked figures within. Each of them used a narrow paddle to move the craft away from a huge galleon that sat quietly in Corwell Harbor.

The port was silent, for the hour was past midnight. No splashing disturbed the boat's graceful movement as it glided slowly toward the overhanging protection of a high pier. Here, six paddles were withdrawn into the boat, while the remaining two pushed the narrow craft carefully between the pilings.

The shadowy figures lashed the boat to the pilings. One after another, they sprang to the pier and slipped quietly onto shore.

The figures moved carefully up the street of Corwell Town, darting from building to building with perfect stealth. The leader of the group, taller and stockier than the rest, paused to let the others pass while he watched for any sign of danger.

A silken black mask concealed the face of each of them, but this one pulled his aside to peer more effectively through the darkness. While manlike, he was not a man. A broad nose with wide, flared nostrils spread across his face, and his teeth were gleaming and sharp. Quickly, he pulled his mask into place and slipped after his band.

* * * * *

Tristan Kendrick, Prince of Corwell, was a little drunk. Perhaps more than a little, he decided, as a swelling of nausea rose within his stomach. His head hurt, and he wanted to go to bed—all of which made this argument seem that much more unpleasant.

"You don't act like a prince! You don't look like a prince! You'll never be fit to be a king of the Ffolk!" His father's harsh voice boomed behind him and cut through Tristan's weariness. The prince whirled to face the king.

"A year ago I routed an army of Northmen from these very walls!" he growled, resisting the urge to shout. "I fought the Beast that stood within our courtyard. Father, I even found the Sword of Cymrych Hugh!"

Tristan gestured at the mighty weapon, hanging in its place of honor above the hearth, crossed with his father's favorite boar spear. The sword was a treasured relic of his people and had been missing for centuries—until he and his friends had discovered it in the depths of a firbolg lair.

"All deeds very fine and heroic—and dramatic," the king sneered. "You've enjoyed the adulation of the ladies and the drinks of the aleman on those merits.

"But there is more to being a king than heroism. What do you know of our law—of the administration of this realm? Could you sit in judgement over shepherds who argued about a shared pasture, or fishermen who quarreled over rights to a berth? Until you change this, you are not fit to rule. You know the customs—you can only be granted the kingship if a majority of the lords think you capable! I doubt they would, were the vote taken tomorrow!"

Tristan clenched his hands into fists, and for a moment he was so angry he could scarcely keep from striking his father. He walked away in frustration, finally flopping heavily into the largest chair in the study. Already the fog of alcohol was dissipating.

But his father would not abandon the attack. "It's amazing that the houndmaster even got you home," he said scornfully. "And where is Daryth now?"

"Probably in bed—but leave Daryth out of this! He's my friend, and I will not allow you to insult him!"

"Ever since Robyn left to study with her aunt, you've been acting like a brooding puppy one minute, and a drunken buffoon the next!"

"I love her! She's gone, and nothing seems to matter except the next time I can see her face. By the goddess, I miss her! I don't even know if she'll ever come back—what if she decides to spend her life in the woods, tending some Moonwell of the Vale?"

The king stalked around the chair to face his son, and the prince forced himself to meet his father's gaze.

"And what if she does? That is her privilege—and perhaps her responsibility. But you wouldn't know about that, would you? Responsibility has never—"

"Father, I have decided to go to Myrloch Vale and visit Robyn. I will leave as soon as I can prepare," Tristan interrupted bluntly. He had contemplated the idea several days earlier, but had not had the courage to tell the king. At least, he thought, this argument had given him that fortitude.

"That is exactly what I mean! You—"

"Perhaps you're right about me," Tristan interrupted, leaning back to look at his father. "After the adventures of last summer, the thought of spending my days cooped up—"

Suddenly, the door to the study crashed inward with a wood-splintering slam. Tristan saw his father's eyes focus on the door, and then the king pushed wildly at the back of Tristan's chair.

The prince heard several "clicks" and felt some sort of missile whir past his head before his chair crashed backward onto the floor. The wind exploded from his lungs, and a cold shock of panic washed over him, driving the last vestiges of alcohol from his mind.

Instantly Tristan rolled from the chair, watching a silver dagger flash over his head from where he lay on the floor. He saw his father pluck a slender dart from his own shoulder, then pick up a wooden chair to block the attack of a charging black figure.

Tristan sprang to his feet in time to meet another black figure face-to-face. The face was covered by a terrifying black mask, and the body was cloaked all over in black silk, but Tristan's eyes focused on the gleaming dagger that seemed to reach forward, questing for his blood. Desperately the prince looked around for a weapon, at the same time remembering his sword hanging ten feet away. A low table separated him from the hearth.

Tristan feinted a lunge at his attacker and then dropped

prone to roll under the table and spring to his feet. The attacker leaped over the table at the same time, and his dagger cut a bloody nick in the prince's ear. Tristan drew the weapon and continued the motion through a full turn, driving the point deep into the attacker's chest before the intruder could strike again.

Tristan saw his father stumble backward as another black-cloaked figure burst through the door. Behind that one were several others. The prince kicked a chair into the path of his new attacker, slowing him enough that he could pull the king's boar spear from its place above the mantle.

"Father!" he cried, tossing the stout weapon sideways across the room.

Tristan leaped over the chair he had toppled, certain that the figure before him, armed with two daggers, was no match for the gleaming Sword of Cymrych Hugh.

But one of those daggers clashed into his blade, nearly knocking it from his hand. Only by stumbling backward did the prince prevent the weapons from driving into his bowels. As it was, a dagger cut a burning streak across his abdomen.

Even more frightening than the nearly fatal blow was the deep, rumbling growl that emerged from behind the silken mask. Although the other attackers had seemed human, the one before him was stockier and smellier than a man. The creature attacked with savage intensity, forcing Tristan back against the fireplace with a dazzling series of blows. Each slash and thrust was accompanied by a bestial snarl. The prince found himself desperately wanting a look behind the black mask, to assure himself that this creature was indeed flesh and blood and not some demon conjured from a drunken nightmare.

Grimacing, Tristan drove his sword against the foe, struggling to gain room to maneuver. Once again the intruder forced him off balance with lightning-fast cuts and lunges.

The prince whirled away from the hearth, catching his breath as he saw his father driving the boar spear into the chest of the other attacker. The king fell on top of the enemy, and the pair lay motionless on the floor.

Tristan's attacker surprised him by suddenly dropping to

the floor. In a flash the prince remembered the men at the door, and in the same instant he fell prone, sensing the whirring passage of deadly missiles over his head.

Then Tristan scrambled to his feet and sprang toward the foe. At the same time, he heard a scream of pain from the doorway. Apparently the growling attacker was equally startled, for his masked face turned to the door in surprise. The prince almost caught the creature with the point of his sword, but he looked back at the last minute and sprang to his feet with catlike speed. Even so, the tip of Tristan's blade struck a glancing blow against the thing's head, tearing the silken mask away in the process.

The prince stared for a second at the snarling face. The creature looked like a cross between a man and a beast—his body and features were humanlike, but his widespread maw was studded with fangs, and his close-set eyes looked hellishly intense and bloodshot.

Another cry of pain shrieked from the doorway, accompanied now by growls. The prince saw one of the attackers there stagger into the room, a huge hound biting his neck in a deadly vice. He caught a glimpse of a flashing scimitar, driving a third bowman against the the wall. Daryth!

The loyal houndmaster, skilled at combat and stealth, must have heard the disturbance. With his blade helping, Tristan thought, the fighting odds looked more favorable.

Daryth leaped into the room, past the great dog that was just raising his head from the gored body. Abruptly, Daryth froze, his darkly handsome features gaping in shock.

"Razfallow!" he finally said, his voice tight.

Tristan's foe had also paused at the sight of the houndmaster. "So, Calishite, this is where you have run to," he snarled. You did not expect to hide from me forever, did you?"

"I don't need to hide anymore," muttered Daryth, advancing slowly in a crouch. "Especially from a killer of children!"

The monster chuckled, and then, before Tristan could react, he flicked one of his daggers straight at Daryth's heart. The silver scimitar moved very slightly, however, to knock the weapon harmlessly to the ground.

Razfallow obviously sensed that the battle was lost. Before Tristan could react he sprang to the window, thirty feet above the courtyard. He turned once to stare at the prince, hate spilling almost palpably from those crimson eyes, and then he leaped into the darkness.

"Guards!" shouted the prince, racing to the window. "Intruder in the courtyard! Take him alive!"

Already the black figure had disappeared into the night, but the cry of alarm was taken up throughout the castle. Turning, Tristan saw Daryth gently cradling the king's head. The great moorhound Canthus stood next to him, gently nuzzling the still form. The only wound upon Tristan's father was the little pinprick, barely bleeding, in his shoulder. Nevertheless, the houndmaster looked at the prince with deep pain and shock in his eyes.

"The King of Corwell is dead."

* * * * *

Like all of the gods, Bhaal communicated his will to his worshippers via his clerics—priests, priestesses, holy (or unholy) people. These clerics drew their strength from their gods, and many were capable of feats of magic rivaling those of the mightiest wizards.

As a powerful god, Bhaal numbered a great many clerics among his faithful. It so happened that one of the most powerful of these was on the Moonshaes. This one would serve his purpose now.

Bhaal decided, slowly, upon a scheme. It would entertain him, and it could enhance his status among all of the gods of the Forgotten Realms. It was a complex plan, but he had numerous willing hands to aid him.

To start, he would send the cleric of the Moonshaes a dream. He could regard it as a prophecy, or a command—in any event, it would be the will of Bhaal.

The cleric, Bhaal knew, would obey.

❧ 2 ❧

The Council of Corwell

Lengthening shadows extended the towers of Caer Callidyrr into needlelike spires that reached ominously across the city of Callidyrr, and beyond, to the waters of Whitefish Bay. Evening brought an end to the bustle and barter of vigorous trade that characterized this, the largest city among the lands of the Ffolk. Night came with its own forms of barter—sale of the ginyak weed imported freely from Calimshan, or even in the darkest of alleys, the trading of young slaves from Amn or Tethyr.

The wizard moved among these alleys, intimately familiar with them. Eventually, after night had fallen completely, he stepped down a stairway into a low cellar, ignoring a slumbering old man who reeked of cheap wine. He pushed through a curtain that masked one wall of the cellar, and entered a wide, round room. The chamber was illuminated by great pots of hot coals that gave the place a hellishly red glow and keept it uncomfortably warm.

A huge skull sat upon an altar in the center of the room. Carved from white marble, it was perhaps four times the size of a human head. Red streaks, which could only have been fresh blood, ran from the eyes of the skull across its cheekbones in a garish caricature of tears.

A man stood before this skull, his back to the wizard. The thick robes and cowled hood of the cleric could not conceal his immense size. Slowly, the man turned.

"Praises to Bhaal," he chanted.

"Hail the lord of death," replied the wizard in a smooth, incongruously pleasant voice.

"Have you acted upon my prophecy yet?" inquired the

huge man, stepping away from the altar with a reverent bow to the skull.

"Indeed, Hobarth," replied the wizard. "I am certain that Razfallow and his team will eliminate them shortly."

"There is more to be done. The woman will not be found at Caer Corwell."

"No matter—I will send Razfallow to the farthest corner of the Realms if need be."

"No!" Hobarth's voice was strong, and he stepped aggressively toward the wizard. "I must get her myself. Bhaal desires her blood to feed his altar."

"Where is she?"

"Bhaal has shown me, and only me, where she can be found. I will go after her."

"And why should the god desire this woman's blood to flow from his sockets?"

"Perhaps Bhaal desires the victim to be a druid. There are none closer than Gwynneth, anymore—thanks to you and your council."

Cyndre chuckled wryly. "As I recall, you and your god had a hand in the elimination of the druids from Alaron. Now, the Ffolk of Callidyrr lack any central spiritual guidance—they are ripe to your persuasive efforts."

"Indeed," agreed Hobarth, with a bow to the altar.

"I wish you success. The earthpower of these druids can be vexing—though no match for your own might."

"Mine is but the strength of Bhaal," said the cleric.

"Of course . . . how thoughtless of me." The wizard turned away so that his companion could not see the thin smile of amusement curling his lips. Clerics and their idiotic faith!

"I shall leave tomorrow . . . this druid will not see the rising of the next full moon."

* * * * *

"It's like they became invisible!" reported Randolph, the young captain of the castle guard company. The bearded warrior, not yet thirty, could not keep his voice from choking with frustration. "They disappeared into thin air!"

"We killed five," said Tristan. "How many could have escaped?"

"There must have been at least two more," insisted the guard, angrily clenching the hilt of his sword. "I found three of my men dead in the courtyard or on the wall. One had his throat cut; the other two were stabbed in the back."

"Quite a proficient band," Tristan muttered bitterly. "But what did they want? Why? My father never . . ." His voice choked, and he did not continue.

The guard said nothing. He and the prince stood quietly in the shambles of the king's study. Together they looked out the broken window into the courtyard, watching dawn's slow arrival.

In the next room, the king's body lay upon his bed, respectfully placed there by Friair Nolan, the cleric of Corwell Town. King Kendrick would be given a funeral befitting a leader of the Ffolk before being laid to rest in the royal barrow.

With growing grief, Tristan tried to accept his father's death. The knowledge did not seem to remain with him. For a time the truth would recede, and then, unexpectedly, would stab at Tristan with greater and greater force. Sometimes the pain was nearly unbearable.

"Where's Daryth?" he finally asked, trying hard to pull himself together.

"He was leading the search," replied Randolph.

Tristan turned to look at the door to his father's room. The captain of the guard started wearily toward the door.

Tristan heard the door shut, and then he looked outside again. A whirlwind of thoughts assaulted him. He struggled with guilt and uncertainty. Why had his last moments with his father been angry ones? And what would happen to him, to the kingdom? Now that his father was gone, Tristan began to realize how much he had depended on him. A brooding sense of loneliness threatened to overwhelm him, and he thought wistfully of Robyn, so far away. He longed for her presence more desperately than ever. Impatiently he paced the floor, wishing Daryth would return. Finally, he flopped into a chair and stared into the long-dead coals in the fireplace.

Practical thoughts pushed through his emotional storm. Messengers had already been dispatched to the cantrev lords of Corwell. These lords would arrive posthaste, and a council to determine the future of Corwell would convene. A new king would be selected.

The thought of the pudgy Lord Koart or the greedy Lord Pontswain sitting in his father's place revolted Tristan. Of all the petty leaders of the lands of Corwell, the prince could think of none worthy to sit upon the royal throne—to be his lord. It's my father's place, he thought, just my father's. Or maybe, now—maybe my own. . . .

Angrily he sprang to his feet, stalking to the window as he realized how dramatically his own feelings had changed in the last few hours.

Looking into the orange dawn, Tristan faced the truth that, hours earlier, he had argued vehemently against: he wanted, very much, to be the next king of Corwell.

* * * * *

Robyn gasped as she knelt beside the frail figure. An unfocused fear prevented her from touching him.

As she finally reached forward to turn the man onto his back, his eyes squinted against the sky. He gibbered something that was not even vaguely speech, and she saw that his tongue was swollen and cracked. She quickly grabbed the nearby water flask, pouring a few drops between the man's chapped lips.

"Don't touch him!" Newt warned. "He looks dangerous! I don't trust him!" For the first time, Robyn noticed that the little dragon had dived for cover under a pile of leaves when the stranger arrived. Buried up to the eyeballs, he stared watchfully at the pair of humans.

"Oh, hush," she chastised, pouring more water into the man's gaping mouth.

He coughed and choked spasmodically, but eagerly licked the droplets from his lips, straining to raise his head for more. Robyn gently moved his head back to the grass, offering him another splash of water.

Slowly the tension seemed to drain from his body, and he closed his eyes. His breathing slowed from frantic panting to a steadier rhythm. After a moment, it seemed that he had fallen asleep. She wished she knew how to aid him—he seemed so frail and weak. At the same time something about him frightened her.

"Who are you?" she whispered, examining the man.

His skin was cracked and dry, as if it had been exposed to extended periods of savage weather. His hair and beard were thin, but long. Branches and thorns had tangled them into mats. His fingernails were filthy and worn all the way to the skin. Did he find food by scratching at the ground for roots and grubs? Robyn wondered.

His only garment was a leather cloak that barely covered his nakedness. A crude fur belt stretched around his waist to hold the cloak. His thin brown hair and beard were long and matted with burrs.

But it was his eyes that drew her attention and frightened her. They stared fiercely one moment, then darted frantically about like a madman's—driven by some mysterious combination of fear and pain.

Robyn noticed that the man sprawled at an odd angle, with his hips raised slightly off the ground, as if he lay upon a sharp rock. She tried, gently, to move him, and she discovered that he had a small pouch tied to his belt, concealed by his buttocks beneath the ragged cloak. It was a filthy object, barely worthy of notice. Yet she found her eyes drawn to it—compelled to look at the pouch, and frightened by that compulsion at the same time.

Carefully, she reached for it, trying to pull the pouch from beneath the man. Her strong fingers felt a hard object, like a fist-size stone. As soon as she touched it, however, the man sat up, opening his eyes wide. Never had the woman seen such stark panic before.

The man screamed, and his voice shocked her ears. It was a piercing, monstrous sound, reminding her of some hulking reptile, ready to strike. But then he scuttled away from her like a crab, clutching the pouch to his breast. Robyn jumped up at the same time, stunned at the man's reaction, but then she held her hands up and gestured that she would not touch the stranger's possession. But what could this man be carrying that was of such incredible value?

"Come with me," she said quietly. "I'll take you to a place where you can rest and eat."

Slowly, Robyn reached for the man's arm, helping him stagger to his feet. He was very weak, swaying drunkenly. He certainly would have fallen if not for Robyn's supporting arms. He weighed little, however, and she had no difficulty holding him upright. Newt crept out of the leaves and buzzed warily behind.

Carefully she led him through the grove among the broad oak boles. They approached a vast tangle of brush beside the ring of stone arches that marked the Moonwell.

As Robyn approached the clump its thickly intertwined branches parted silently, creating a rounded arch that was slightly higher than her head—and revealing the tangle as a ring of brush, not a solid clump. Within the ring, she could see the tiny building that was the Great Druid's cottage. With its thatched roof and vine-covered walls, it looked like it had sprouted from the ground itself.

Robyn stopped abruptly, remembering that her teacher was taking a well-deserved nap. She decided to tell Genna about the stranger after she awakened. For now, she could tend to the man herself.

"Come this way," she said, changing course. "Through these trees." She led him between sheltering aspens, into a shaded area of lush grasses and soft flowers. "You can rest in the bower."

She helped the man into the meadow, leaning against a sturdy aspen to rest. A sudden growl erupted behind her, and she whirled—nearly dropping the stranger—to see a small mountain of brown fur rise from the grass. A huge creature snarled and bared its white fangs in annoyance.

The man cried out in fright and shrank against the tree trunk. His eyes nearly popped from his head at the sight of the huge bear.

"Grunt, stop it!" Robyn scolded, waving a hand at the animal. "Shame on you!"

The bear growled again but settled to all four feet and shambled across the meadow, disappearing into the aspens on the other side.

"I'm sorry," she explained, laying a hand upon the man's trembling arm. "He's very grumpy when he's awakened suddenly. Just ignore him—he wouldn't hurt you. Besides, the animals are forbidden to attack other creatures within the grove. You're safe here!"

She doubted that the stranger understood her, but he seemed soothed by her tone, for he clung tightly to her arm and allowed her to lead him further into the bower.

The bower was actually a grassy meadow, surrounded and covered by a converging tangle of trees. It was small, for they kept no animals and only used it for those periods when some injured creature of the wild needed the grove as a haven while recovering from wounds.

She helped the man, who seemed to grow weaker with every step, to a bed of lush grasses. Lowering him gently to the ground, she offered him more water.

Gradually his trembling subsided, and finally he slept. Even in unconsciousness, however, he clutched the tattered pouch and its rocklike contents tightly to his chest.

She rose silently when his breathing became deep and even, slipping through the curtain of aspens to leave him to his rest. There she found Newt perched suspiciously upon a low branch, waiting for her.

"Now, can we go swimming?" he asked.

* * * * *

"They were Calishites," reported Daryth. "At least, they learned their trade in Calimshan—at the Academy of Stealth." The Calishite's brown face was taut with anger, and his black eyes blazed.

"How can you be sure?" asked the prince. He shook his head, trying to clear away the grogginess of his short sleep. Suddenly, he remembered his father's body in the next room, but he clenched his jaw to stifle any display of emotion. Inwardly, he wanted to shout his grief at the heavens, to cry aloud for vengeance. Daryth had awakened him after what seemed like scant moments of sleep, although he could now see the sun outside the window.

"Their garments, for one thing," Daryth continued. The prince knew that his friend had studied at the Academy of Stealth, but Daryth rarely spoke of those experiences. It was not, Tristan sensed, something the houndmaster was proud of. "The assassins of the Pasha's school always wear the finest weave of Amnish silk—this silk." He held up a piece of cloth torn from one of the slain attackers.

"And these little crossbows are a favored weapon of the Pasha's elite. Smeared with poison, they are absolutely deadly within fifty feet." Daryth paused. "I'm sorry. It's a miracle that they didn't get you as well."

"Then there was Razfallow." The Calishite paused for a moment. "I studied under him when I was at the Academy. That was when I was young—but strong and quick. The skills taught at the Academy, I thought, would see me to a life of luxury and ease. But those skills—stealthy murder, theft, betrayal—they come with their own cost.

"And Razfallow made those costs clear to me. He is one of the deadliest assassins in the Realms. Eventually, I made him angry. The most convenient solution was for me to leave Calimshan, and so I did."

"Obviously, he remembers," remarked the prince.

"I gave him good cause to," muttered Daryth, but despite Tristan's curious look he would not elaborate.

"What is he?"

"A half-orc. His mother was a full blooded orc—it's a sore spot with him."

"As if a person might not notice," muttered the prince.

"Finally, we found two guards atop the palisade slain from a single stab wound—here." Daryth bent his head forward, gesturing with a finger at the base of his neck. "I know of no other assassins in the world who use such a tactic for surreptitious slaying."

"The Pasha of Calimshan sent assassins to Corwell?" asked the prince. Perhaps he could find a focus for his anger.

"Probably not. Although they were trained in Calimshan, they were paid with these." Daryth held out a pair of gold coins, stamped with the outline of a crenelated castle on one side. The prince reached for the coins and flipped them over. On the back was a familiar silhouette.

"Caer Callidyrr? They were paid with the coin of the High King?"

"So it would seem," Daryth nodded soberly. "It was careless of one of them to carry his coin with him—perhaps he did not trust his fellows. Now he has no use for the coin, and its presence on his body tells us much.

"What is the relationship of the High King to the rulers of the Ffolk, such as your father?"

"The title High King is more an honorific than anything else. Not since Cymrych Hugh has there truly been a king that united the Ffolk under one leader. Now, he wears the Crown of the Isles to signify his authority—that was the gold crown forged for Cymrych Hugh himself—but has little real authority, except over the Kingdom of Callidyrr. In Moray, Snowdown—and here in Corwell—we pay little attention."

"But what does that honorific mean?"

"In name, he is the lord of the kings of Corwell, Moray, and Snowdown. The High King is in fact the King of Callidyrr—the largest kingdom of the Ffolk. Though the other kings, including my father, owe fealty to him, there is no power behind the title. The current king, Carrathal, has brought much trade to Callidyrr from the nations on the Sword Coast. He has even hired a council of mages from Waterdeep and beyond to advise him. Still, he has been no more dynamic than any of the others in providing strong leadership—or bringing the nations of the Ffolk together."

Tristan paused. He and his father had discussed this more than once. Because the Ffolk had no single, strong leader, the Northmen had been able to conquer many of their lands—one by one. We cannot bring ourselves to unite against them, Tristan reflected—even when they bring all of their nations together against one kingdom. But he still could not follow Daryth's argument.

"Perhaps he knew that your father had no ambitions," conceded Daryth. "But perhaps your father was not the target of this assassin. It may be that he was simply an unfortunate victim—the real target could be one that the High King does not know to be a loyal vassal—the one most responsible for the great victory of last year."

"Me?" Tristan was shocked.

"Of course, that is just a guess," admitted Daryth. "But your father was no threat to the High King. Maybe you were."

"But what could be gained by slaying me? The king has enemies by virtue of his position. Who knows how many petty cantrev lords will be arriving here to fight for my father's position? One of them could have done this."

"I think that is unlikely," argued the houndmaster. "For one thing, the graduates of the Academy of Stealth do not work cheaply—I doubt whether one of the cantrev lords could have afforded them."

"Perhaps they were hired by the High King, or at least by some wealthy individual of Callidyrr," Tristan said. "I cannot accept the idea that I was the target." Still, he recalled his father pushing over his chair and the dart that followed.

"Very well," Daryth shrugged. "But have a care for your back nonetheless."

"I shall. The coming council of lords gives me enough cause for nervousness, in any event. The major lords of Corwell will ride here upon hearing of the news of my father's death. After the funeral feast they will select a new king."

"What do you plan?" asked the houndmaster.

"I plan to be the one selected."

* * * * *

The sliver of a moon cast little light over the vast wilderness of Myrloch Vale. It did not penetrate the thick canopy of aspen leaves, and thus the confines of the bower remained pitch black.

The shriveled figure there twisted and sat up, breathing heavily. He had slept all afternoon and now felt strong enough to move.

With exaggerated stealth, he reached a clawlike hand into his tattered pouch, pulling forth a black rock. It was curved, with smooth surfaces. Like a stone sculpture of a heart. Some of its facets were pure, deep black, and others seemed even darker. It absorbed light and radiated a faint heat. Deep within its center, it throbbed with a deep, evil cadence that few could hear—but those that heard it heard it most profoundly. Nervously peering into the woods surrounding him, he hunched over and clasped the object to his breast.

Rabbits and squirrels shifted uneasily throughout the woods as some nameless disturbance penetrated their rest. The flowers in the garden closed their petals. In the pond, the lilies shivered and shifted away from the sinister presences, until all of the blossoms had gathered against the far shore like a nervous flock of sheep.

Suddenly, a cackle of glee passed the man's lips, and he jumped in fright. Panicked, he jerked his head about, straining to hear if he had been detected. Carefully, he wrapped the object in its filthy pouch and lay down again upon the bed of grasses.

Within the cottage, two hundred feet away, Genna thrashed in her sleep, apparently caught in the throes of a nightmare.

And Robyn sat up suddenly, drenched with sweat—for she had just awakened from a numbing nightmare of her own. She had dreamed of the king, her step-father, laid upon his funeral bier. Surrounding him, descending slowly, was an unspeakably menacing black mist.

She could not return to sleep for the rest of the night.

* * * * *

"To Good King Kendrick. May the goddess reward him!" Lord Pontswain raised his mug, allowing foam to spill onto the broad tabletop.

The council of lords was meeting in Caer Corwell's great hall, for the royal study was not large enough to accommodate the gathered throng. The lords represented the villages and towns of the small kingdom, from tiny highland communities to thriving fishing cantrevs. They sat drinking dark ale in toast to their deceased sovereign.

All thirty-one of Corwell's cantrev lords had gathered at the castle to decide upon the future ruler of the kingdom. Tristan, as host, sat at the head of the table. Daryth sat to his right, while Randolph, in his role as captain of the castle guard, stood at the nearby door. Opposite Tristan, twoscore feet away, sat Friar Nolan, the cleric of the new gods who had won over some of the Ffolk of Corwell. Most of the Ffolk still held the Earthmother goddess to be the supreme deity, but as a rule her representatives, the druids, shunned human politics, and thus none were present.

Lord Galric lurched to his feet, splashing half the contents of his mug into the lap of the scowling Lord Koart, who sat beside him. As usual, Galric was drunk, and Tristan suppressed a smile—at least one of his rivals was ill-prepared to debate him.

"King Ken'rick," shouted Galric. "A splennid ruler 'n a fine figger of a man!"

"Hear! Hear!" The chorus of agreements was followed by more slurping swallows around the table.

Tristan examined the other lords, trying to determine who was most likely to offer him a challenge. Nearby sat Lord Koart and Lord Dynnatt. Neither had acquitted himself well during the war, and Tristan hoped this fact would be enough to mark them as unfit to rule. He knew them both to be ambitious, however, and the two lords were close friends—he had to beware of a potential coalition.

Farther down the table, Lord Galric's head was already dropping onto his chest. Galric ruled over a highland cantrev that had amassed considerable wealth from the mining of copper, iron, and silver. In any event, the lord was now too drunk to make a case for himself.

Beyond Lord Galric sat Lord Pontswain. He was a smooth, handsome man, with curling brown hair that flowed past his shoulders, and a firm, crackling voice that commanded attention. He had a sharp wit, and the cutting edge of his voice often left one wondering whether he had been complimented or insulted. The prince noticed that Pontswain's mug remained full. The lord spent more time sizing up the others at the table than he did in joining the toasting.

Pontswain ruled a large and wealthy cantrev to the southwest of Corwell. Tristan knew him to be very ambitious and judged him the most significant rival at the table.

The others, such as Lord Fergus of Kingsbay and Lord Macshea of Cantrev Macsheehan, ruled small fiefdoms which were still recovering from the war. Tristan judged these lords, as council members, to be honest and reasonable men, open to persuasion by the best candidate.

For a moment the prince thought again of the meeting's purpose. His father had been buried the night before, and he was about to make a case for himself to succeed the king. He could feel his palms beginning to sweat. His mug, like Pontswain's, sat before him, barely touched.

"My lords," he began, so softly that the group was forced

to quiet in order to hear him, "I thank you all for attending this most significant council. Your presence at the funeral last night, as well, is appreciated.

"My father served as king for twenty-seven years. With one notable exception, these were years of peace and prosperity. Trading vessels call regularly here and at Kingsbay. Taxes have remained low—practically nonexistent for those with little means to pay. I think you will all agree that he allowed you to rule your fiefdoms with little interference.

"When our neighbors in Moray suffered the misfortune of an invasion of Northmen, King Kendrick and the forces of Corwell were decisive in defeating the invasion.

"And last summer, when our own kingdom felt the brunt of such an invasion, he rallied the cantrevs to ultimate victory." Tristan didn't want to overstate his father's role in that conflict, for he knew that his own contribution gave him his best claim to the throne.

"In that campaign, where the stalwart Lords Koart and Dynnatt fought beside my own company, the Ffolk of Corwell drove off not only an army of Northmen, but supernatural horsemen. We triumphed with the aid of this potent sword—" he gestured to the Sword of Cymrych Hugh, "— over the Beast that the Northmen called their master!"

The prince paused, willing each of the lords to recall the Darkwalker War. "Many are the wounds that remain with us to this day, suffered in that struggle. Galric, whose cantrev was ravaged by the hungry wolfpack. . . . Fergus, and Macshea—their homes burned by the invading Northmen. Corwell itself, held by the narrowest of margins.

"While others of us, such as Ponstwain, were more fortunate. Not only were they spared the destruction of their homes, but they did not suffer the deaths of their people in combat." He paused again, allowing the facts to sink in.

Before Tristan could continue, however, Lord Pontswain rose smoothly to his feet, smiling politely around the table before nodding quickly at the prince.

"My . . . prince," he began. The pause was long enough that none could miss its significance. "Your gracious hospitality and entertainment is greatly appreciated. It is time, however, that we arrived at the true purpose of this council.

"Leave us, please, to attend to the man's task of selecting the next king of Corwell." Pontswain turned back to the lords, his gesture emphasizing the prince's dismissal.

Tristan had been prepared for a maneuver of some kind, but the bluntness of it took him by surprise. He found his voice a second later.

"My . . . lord." He mimicked Pontswain's pause perfectly. "I have earned the right to attend this council, as much as any other man here—perhaps more than some, if such earning is measured in blood shed for the kingdom." He saw the lords who had suffered during the war nodding in mute agreement, as attention turned back to Ponstwain.

"Now, now, lad . . ." Pontswain's patronizing tone gave Tristan his opening.

"Where do you earn the right to condescend?" he growled. "The laws of the Ffolk provide that my fitness to rule will be judged alongside of yours, old man—and it may be that it will be judged superior to yours!"

In a brief minute, the field of candidates for the kingship had been narrowed to two. Both men understood this and sized each other up for a moment before proceeding.

"None would deny," began Pontswain, "that, under the guidance of your father, you made some remarkable contributions to the realm. But your father is gone now—"

"Which is why we are here. . . ." Tristan interrupted flatly. "I stood without my father upon Freeman's Down, where my troops stopped an army of Northmen numbering four times our own! I found the Sword of Cymrych Hugh without my father, returning that weapon to the Ffolk after it had been lost for centuries! My father lay wounded within these walls when I faced the Beast in the courtyard and drove it from this castle. And it was also without my father that I pursued and slayed the Beast in mortal combat!"

"And since that time you have wasted your time drinking and carousing, and not done a single thing to better yourself!" accused Pontswain. Several of the lords turned to regard the prince somewhat critically, and he paused. It had not occurred to Tristan that his reputation would have reached these men.

"Perhaps I have enjoyed myself," Tristan finally conceded.

"But it was at my own expense. I have not been collecting and hoarding a fortune by overtaxing the peasants of Corwell!" Now several lords regarded Pontswain accusingly, for it was well known that Lord Pontswain was a harsh taxer and miserly with his expenses.

"My experience as the administrator of a cantrev has given me an opportunity to prepare for the kingship. My cantrev has been prosperous far beyond the norm—"

"Because you stood behind your stone walls while war ravaged the cantrevs of your neighbors and countrymen!"

"That accusation is not true," Pontswain returned, "and I'm glad you've given me the opportunity to respond.

"During the Darkwalker War, my troops diligently patrolled the southern shore of Corwell Firth. I myself rode at their head as we combed the moors, looking for Northmen or wolves or any kind of enemy!" Pontswain's voice quavered with outrage. "Am I to be blamed because the invaders did not challenge my lands?"

Several of the lords looked convinced, while others, such as Fergus and Dynnatt, scowled in obvious disgust.

"In any event," concluded Lord Pontswain, "your immaturity leaves little option for this council. Our king must be a man of steadiness, intelligence, and responsibility. I am clearly your better in those respects."

"Perhaps," said Friar Nolan, speaking for the first time. "And perhaps not." The cleric stood, and all of the lords waited patiently for him to speak. Though most of them did not actively worship the new gods of the devout cleric, Friar Nolan was regarded by them all with respect and a little awe. After all, his potent healing magic had benefitted more than one of them.

"It seems to me that you are all in too much of a hurry to make a decision. You have a ruler above yourselves, above even your king. Turn to him for guidance in this most critical decision. Allow the High King to determine which of these men shall become your king!"

"I cannot object strongly enough," growled Pontswain.

Fergus leaped to his feet, a smile lifting his broad mustache. "I, for one, like the friar's suggestion. Let the High King choose between them."

"Indeed!" chorused Koart. "Let the High King decide!"

A chorus of assents rumbled from the lords, and Tristan and Pontswain exchanged a sudden, challenging look. The prince looked back to the lords, unable to read the emotion in Pontswain's dark, confident gaze.

"I shall journey to Caer Callidyrr to petition the king for the throne of Corwell," Tristan said calmly.

"And I shall accompany you—and win that approval!" boasted the lord.

"Decided!" mumbled Galric, lurching drunkenly to his feet and raising his mug. "Let the High King choose!"

*　*　*　*　*

Once again the Council of Seven sat around their U-shaped table. Seven candles illuminated the large circular chamber. Its bleak stone walls were covered in several places by plush tapestries—abstract designs with crimson streaks of color flowing like blood across the velvet.

Cyndre sat at the base of the U. His voice, pleasant and conversational as always, floated through the chamber. He spoke to the wizard sitting at his right hand.

"Alexei? I sense reluctance as you hear our plans."

"We could be mistaken in using the assassin so readily. I fear he is not to be trusted—that fat cleric could be using us to further his own ends!" the one called Alexei answered.

"How dare you challenge the decision of our master!" interrupted the wizard seated to Cyndre's left. His sharp voice emerged from a black robe. He looked identical to all of the others present, except that he allowed himself the conceit of a small diamond brooch upon his shoulder. His fingers, nervously drumming the tabletop, glittered with a sparkling array of diamond rings.

"Now, Kryphon," countered Cyndre. "Please keep the discussion on a genteel level." The master of the Seven smiled benignly. Of course, none present could see the smile within the folds of Cyndre's robe, but they all felt it.

"Very well," replied Kryphon calmly. "I ask my colleague if the threat to our liege, the High King, should be ignored."

"Of course not," Alexei explained. "But our only evidence of threat comes from the prophecies of this cleric of Bhaal!"

"A very powerful cleric, of a very powerful god," added Doric. The woman sat to Kryphon's left. Her face, like the others, was hidden within her hood, but her voice was filled with cool arrogance. Her unnaturally long fingers tapped nervously upon the tabletop.

"True. But I feel that we should, through our own methods, determine the veracity of his claims."

"Do you think that I am a fool?" Cyndre asked. "Of course I have checked, using far more accurate means than that wretch of a cleric can hope to employ! For now, that cleric—and yes, even his 'awesome' deity—serve our purposes!"

If Cyndre noticed the shudders of nervousness that passed among the members of his council he gave no indication. The master of the mages continued, as if talking to recalcitrant children.

"The significant kings and lords of the Ffolk have been eliminated or neutralized. The way grows clear for our liege to rule all of the Moonshaes."

"Yes, master," said Alexei quietly. "I am—"

"Silence." Cyndre's single word came like music to their ears, but bound their lips like the ironclad order that it was.

The master gestured, and the Seven knew that the door to their chamber had been opened. Soon they heard the whisper of soft leather boots moving down the black corridor, and then three men entered the room, standing awkwardly at the open end of the table.

Actually, only two of them were men—the third was manlike, but stood taller than his companions. His arms were long and his face grotesque. Nervously licking his lips, he revealed wicked fangs.

"Well, Razfallow? What is the word from Corwell?" Cyndre's question was a formality, and no doubt the assassin knew it. The wizard's powerful scrying mirror had shown him the results of the mission as it had happened.

"We failed, master. The king sacrificed himself to save the prince. Then the prince's bodyguard—a graduate of the Academy and former student of mine—intervened. I lost five of my finest—"

"This is what I think of your finest." Cyndre's voice carried no trace of threat, but his left and right forefingers gestured at the men standing to either side of Razfallow. Spellbound, each instantly grabbed his throat and gasped. Choking, they staggered to their knees and then flopped to the floor. Twisting in agony, their faces growing slowly black, they died over a period of several minutes.

Razfallow watched the executions impassively. Finally, the assassin turned toward Cyndre.

"You only live because I have further need of you," explained the wizard. "Serve me well, and you may be granted the right to live out your miserable life. . . ."

* * * * *

"What is it, teacher? Why did you call?" Robyn clasped a hand to her mouth as she saw Genna's haggard face staring at her from the depths of her bed.

"Pain!" gasped Genna Moonsinger, collapsing into her soft quilt. Her eyes darted past Robyn, as if she feared that some apparition might appear in the doorway.

"Can I help you? Tell me what you need!"

"Leave me, girl! Go, now!" Genna's voice was sharp—more harsh than Robyn had ever heard before.

Confused and frightened, she stumbled from the cottage and banged the door shut. She saw the man—the 'stranger' she still called him—watering the roses as she had requested. Robyn quickly turned away from him and went around the cottage. She felt a need to be alone.

She heard a loud snuffle as she passed through the hedge that magically parted before her, and Grunt rose to his four feet. Absently, she scratched his broad head while she wondered about her teacher's strange malady. Genna had been taciturn and unpleasant recently, and her health seemed to grow worse every day.

Grunt suddenly rubbed against her, anxious for more attention, and knocked her to the ground.

"Dammit, you clumsy oaf!" she shouted, and then winced as she saw the deep hurt in his eyes. "I'm sorry. It's not you— I shouldn't treat you so." Mollified, the bear nuzzled in for more scratching, and she absently complied.

Her mind drifted to Tristan. She had been thinking of him a lot lately. Often she daydreamed about his sudden arrival at the grove. She pictured him galloping from the woods on his great stallion Avalon. She liked to imagine his joy upon seeing her—and the crushing kiss he'd greet her with.

She felt certain that something was terribly wrong—she feared that the king was indeed dead. She would have gone, except for the demands of Genna's illness, for the Great Druid desperately needed her help now.

Half-hoping, she turned to the forest beyond the grove, as if she expected to see the approach of the white charger and its handsome rider.

But there were only green leaves, swaying easily in the breeze.

* * * * *

The goddess, Earthmother, was a deity unlike Bhaal in every respect. While his interests spanned planes and universes, hers were focused only upon the Moonshae Islands. While he thrived upon death, she prospered from growth and life. Bhaal relished chaos and disorder, while the Earthmother desired only the proper balance of all things.

The islands had been her body, her life, since time began. But the power of the goddess was waning, for only through her druids could her body survive and prosper. The coming of the Northmen, in centuries past, had driven the druids from many parts of the isles.

And a challenge from another source, upon the large island of Alaron, had gradually removed that land from her. She did not know what had happened to the druids of Alaron—only that their lives had been snuffed out, one by one, as if some ravaging cancer had spread across the land.

Her islands of Snowdown and Moray, small and lightly populated, still held to the tenets of her ancient faith. Their druids were devout but simple people, the demands of their lands slight and easily met.

Only upon Gwynneth were her druids still truly strong. She sensed, in some godlike way, that she would need all of that strength if she was going to survive.

❧ 3 ❧

Black Wizard

The vast underground passage reverberated with soft echoes, as hundreds of dark, small bodies moved stealthily through the cavern. No light broke the inky blackness, but the figures moved quickly and easily, avoiding each upthrusting stalagmite, and carefully bypassing each sheer precipice that led to depths of the earth thousands of feet, even many miles, below them.

"Are your troops in position? My time is precious," remarked Cyndre smoothly. The black wizard was concealed as usual beneath his robe, but his posture and tone conveyed boredom.

"You will receive your payment!" barked one of the little figures, standing irritably beside the mage. He came only to the man's waist. His dark and swarthy face scowled at the passing file of similar creatures. "If your magic is as mighty as you claim . . ."

Dai-Dak, king of the dark dwarves—the duergar—glared a challenge at the mage. He was not used to hearing complaints. Cyndre waved a figure, whispering a soft word.

Dai-Dak, the cave salamander, froze in panic. His reptilian eyes bulged up at the wizard. Cyndre gestured again, and the dark dwarf stood once again beside him, looking considerably chastened.

"See that you do not question my magic again," said the sorcerer very softly.

Dai-Dak nodded quickly. "As we agreed, my army will guard the underworld approaches to Caer Callidyrr. We will let nothing in or out. And when you call us, we will be there to serve you!"

"Very good." The wizard smiled from the depths of his robe. "Now let us see to this attack."

"My troops are almost in position," pleaded the dwarf. "A few moments more, please!"

Cyndre looked with disinterest at the short, stocky column of fighters. Each was dark-skinned and bristled with hair and beard. Their bowed legs carried them roughly but steadily. Finely crafted armor of metal or leather protected their chests, and their arms were banded in steel.

The deep gnomes—svirfneblin—were the blood enemies of the duergar. The vast, underground community below them contained valuable gold and iron deposits, prime fungus-growing caverns, and good water supplies. It would be a fine addition to the duergar holdings. And too, the slaying of the svirfneblin would be grand sport for the malicious, merciless duergar.

Cyndre enjoyed the prospect of the coming fight, for his magic would insure the victory—and the duergar would then join the forces waiting to move on the sorcerer's command. The Scarlet Guard, and the duergar, had potent armies—and one more force, now waiting quietly under the sea, would soon join those legions.

"We are ready," said Dai-Dak. "Follow me."

The dark dwarf king led Cyndre through a narrow cave mouth onto a high promontory, still underground. They looked over a vast network of caverns—the realm of the svirfneblin. Huge stone pillars connected the floor to the ceiling, some five hundred feet overhead. Many gems studded these pillars, casting a soft, yellow light over the scene.

Below them, the round-roofed stone huts of the deep gnomes clustered against the cavern walls. The gnomes bustled about their community, busy as always. Potters, jewelers, bakers, farmers, smiths, all plied their trades— bartering constantly, for such is the way of the gnomes. They were a slight, wiry people, smaller than the duergar, and much less malicious. Beyond the village stretched the vast fungus-forests where the gnomes grew their food. A placid stream wound through the huge fungi, bridged in several places by neat, stone spans. The scene, throughout the caverns, was one of peace.

But that peace was ending.

"Seeriax, punjyss withsath—nere!" Cyndre whispered the words to his first spell, holding his fingers before him. A soft hissing surrounded him, and a long tendril of yellow gas flowed from each of his fingertips. The gas expanded into a huge yellow mass of air, sinking from the promontory toward the bustling village below.

The gas seeped through the doors and windows, slinking around the deep gnomes as they sat, or slept, or worked. And where it struck, it killed.

A hundred gnomefolk were startled by the yellow, silent death, and died before they could cry a warning. The gas flowed onward, seeping through the streets, flowing from the dead to the living. One old gnome, tottering up the street, his gray beard reaching nearly to the ground, saw the horror and cried a single word: "Flee!" Then the gas crept around him, and he died upon the tiny street.

With the alarm, gnomes poured from the buildings that had yet to be struck by the killing cloud. Hundreds of the creatures fled to the fields, through the vast fungus plants, to the bridges over the placid stream. And as they crossed the bridges, males, females, and young, they were met by the poised weapons of Dai-Dak's duergar.

Cyndre saw a group of gnomes—perhaps a hundred— break away from the rest, and flee toward a narrow cavern beyond the fungi. The sorcerer whispered a word and immediately disappeared from the promontory. In the same instant, he arrived at the mouth of the cavern—certain to be a secret escape route. He cast another spell some distance into the cavern and watched as the gnomes raced into the passage. Suddenly, they stopped, their escape blocked by a solid wall of iron that extended from the top to the bottom of the secret tunnel, and from wall to wall.

The turned as a mass to race for the entrance again, but the black wizard now stood there, waiting implacably for the gnomes' moments of maximum terror.

"Blitzyth, Dorax zooth!"

Cyndre's next spell sent crackling bolts of lightning siz-zling into the walls and ceiling of the narrow cave. Great chunks of rock broke free, crushing the trapped gnomes.

More and more stone fell, in a thunderous cloud of dust and debris, sending a cloud of dust drifting into the vast caverns where the massacre was now complete.

Cyndre smiled slightly, satisfied that his task was done. The dark dwarves had gained their food and water sources and their mining tunnels. Their senseless bloodlust had been satisfied. Indeed, the dark dwarves had gained all that they currently desired.

And the black wizard had gained the duergar themselves.

* * * * *

The feasting had ended and the lords had gone, except for Fergus and Pontswain. Tristan met with them, along with Daryth and Randolph, after the council. Fires burned low in the hearths, and a chorus of snores arose from various corners of the hall.

They had finalized the details of their journey—Daryth would accompany the prince and Lord Pontswain to Caer Callidyrr. There, they would each meet with the High King and plead their case for the kingship of Corwell. They agreed to abide by the king's decision.

"Very well," said Ponstwain. "How do we get there?"

"I was hoping to accompany Lord Fergus to Kingsbay, riding the length of Corwell Road." Tristan looked at the other lord, who watched the discussion impassively. "Can you furnish us with a boat to carry us across the Strait of Alaron?"

Fergus nodded, his handlebar mustache bouncing. "It shall be my pleasure."

"Very well." Tristan stood, followed by the others. "We shall leave for Kingsbay at first light."

Daryth and Tristan went to their quarters and gathered their belongings for the journey. Daryth carried his scimitar at his waist and concealed a pair of long knives in the sleeves of his cloak. Tristan wore the Sword of Cymrych Hugh and carried a bow and quiver of arrows slung over his saddle.

They slept little that night, but dawn quickly called them from their restless beds. They went immediately to the stables, where Daryth selected his mount, a chestnut gelding, and Tristan saddled Avalon, the mighty stallion that had served him so nobly during the Darkwalker War.

Lord Fergus and his son were already prepared, and even Pontswain arrived soon afterward. The young lord was dressed in a shining suit of plate mail and rode a proud charger of midnight black. In addition to his sword, Pontswain carried a long wooden lance.

The only other member of the party was Tristan's prized moorhound, Canthus. The great dog stood half as high as his master and weighed every bit as much. He was a keen hunter and steadfast companion who had received his training from Daryth.

Fergus waited astride a great dappled mare, standing in the courtyard at first light. His son, Sean, rode a small stallion of the same colors. The young horse skittered nervously away from Avalon as Tristan, Daryth, and Canthus emerged from the stables.

The great warhorse ignored the other stallion, moving into an easy trot as Tristan preceded the others from the castle gate. Canthus loped beside him as he gave the stallion his head. They cantered down the winding approach to the castle and turned toward the west upon Corwell Road. They would follow this, the kingdom's one highway, across Corwell to the eastern port of Kingsbay.

For most of the first morning they rode in easy silence, slowing their mounts to a walk after a short stretch. Fergus traveled beside the prince, trailing the rest of the party. Eventually the genial lord cleared his throat awkwardly.

"You know, prince, I am reminded of tales I've heard of the early days of the Ffolk upon Gwynneth and the other Moonshae Islands. Gwynneth, as you and I well know, was the grandest of the isles back then—in the days before Callidyrr, I mean." Fergus cast a glance at Tristan to be sure that he was listening. Satisfied, he continued, his great mustache bobbing up and down with each word.

"I was not actually present at Freeman's Down last summer. I did arrive at the castle in time to witness the siege and the rout of the Northmen.

"Those were the grandest sights I've ever beheld! It made me proud to be a lord of the Ffolk! And I cannot help thinkin' that it was you who brought those victories about." Lord Fergus turned to meet Tristan's gaze squarely.

"What I'm trying to say is that perhaps we're seeing a bit of that old glory return to Gwynneth now. You will be our king, and your reign will be good for Gwynneth, and for all the Ffolk. And I'll be the prouder for havin' served you," Fergus concluded. He cleared his throat again and looked awkwardly across the moor, away from Tristan.

For a moment Tristan said nothing, but his face burned with excitement and joy. He felt as though he had truly been born to be king of the Ffolk. Silently, he vowed to bring about a return to the days of Gwynneth's glory.

"Your words are heartening, my lord. It will be a comfort to know that I leave the kingdom in the hands of men and women such as yourself."

They passed through several cantrevs, but most of the land was devoted to sparse, stony pastures or small tilled fields. Small farms dotted the landscape every mile or two, but the road was empty of other travelers.

They talked little for the rest of the day. Tristan looked occasionally at Pontswain, riding beside Sean before them. The lord spoke constantly, gesturing broadly. The thought of his boasting made Tristan sick with disgust. But unwilling to let Pontswain dampen his excitement, he forced his mind to brighter thoughts.

Robyn. Where was she now? What was she doing? Did she think of him often? The familiar sense of longing returned—he missed her so! He felt guilty that he had not gone to tell her of his father's death. After all, King Kendrick had been her stepfather, the only parent she had ever known.

But, he reminded himself, it probably would have taken weeks to find the grove of the Great Druid, if he could have found it at all. Previously that difficulty had piqued his sense of adventure. Now, his mission prevented him from taking the time for such a search. Selfishly, futilely, he wished that she had somehow sensed his anguish and come to join him.

The journey to Kingsbay was normally a four or five day ride, but a sense of urgency pushed the little party over the distance in three.

"I would provide you with accommodations in my own

lodge," explained Fergus as they rode into the fishing cantrev, "but you will find the rooms at the Silver Salmon much more comfortable. There, also, we should find Rodger."

"Rodger?" Daryth inquired.

"He's the fisherman I'll send to Alaron with you. Very reliable fellow, and he can keep his mouth shut. With luck, you'll be crossing the strait by tomorrow morning."

* * * * *

The cleric hated the sea. He hated the thick, fishy stench of the salty air. He hated the sound of water sloshing along the hull and splashing constantly against the planks. He even hated the monotonous sight of the sea, stretching away to infinity in all directions, featureless yet full of inscrutable detail.

But most of all he hated the motion of the sea, the sickening swaying, rising and falling cadence that churned his stomach into jelly and threatened to tear his mind to pieces.

For the hundredth time he cursed the calling that had compelled him to serve upon these islands, where the only expeditious means of travel involved sailing. Not that he questioned the wishes of Bhaal, the cleric hastily reminded himself—and whoever else happened to be listening to his thoughts. If Bhaal wanted Hobarth to journey to Gwynneth and return with the fresh blood of this young druid, then the cleric would do so without hesitation.

And besides, he consoled himself, the journey was practically over. Even as he looked over the low gunwale for the thousandth time, he saw the sun setting over Corwell's easternmost port, Kingsbay.

Finally! Hobarth thought. I will get a decent bed below me—one that does not move with every breath of wind. Perhaps, he mused further, I might even be able to charm some young barmaid into making a decent bed still nicer.

The huge cleric stroked the fleshy folds of his neck, pleasantly intrigued by the thought. His tiny eyes gleamed from between low, sinister brows and bloated cheeks. Several large warts—punishments from Bhaal for a moment when the cleric had been less than devout—marred his nose. His appearance was altogether grotesque, but this was no obstacle when it came to wooing the young ladies. A simply cast minor spell would blind the lasses to his appearance and smell, creating admiration and eagerness where previously had existed fear and revulsion.

Finally, the boat reached the dock. Hitching up his only possession, the small pouch at his belt, he stalked from the craft without a word to the simple fisherman who had carried him from Alaron. Hobarth was certain that the wretch had enjoyed watching his agony.

Kingsbay was a smaller town than most communities of Callidyrr. The many cottages were roofed with round domes of straw instead of the wooden shingles that were common across the strait. The town was well-lighted by lamps and torches, however, and numerous inns beckoned the traveler with cheerful music and the aromas of succulent roasts.

Hobarth selected one called the Silver Salmon. He planned to drink and eat before he sought a maid, but his plans vanished as he walked through the door.

Sitting by the fire, leaning casually back in his chair and talking to a pair of men, was an image he had only seen in the vision sent from Bhaal. The prophecy had been so vivid that he could not mistake the identity of the man across the room. It was the Prince of Corwell. His presence here could only mean that Cyndre's assassins had failed.

The inn was not very crowded, so Hobarth had no difficulty finding a table near the prince. He sat with his back to Tristan and quietly ordered a mug of ale from a passing barmaid. Nursing the dark, foamy drink, the cleric strained to hear the conversation occurring five feet away.

"It's settled then," said one man. "We'll sail with the dawn."

"Aye," grunted another, an older man. "If the weather of the past days holds, we'll—" The rest of the phrase was drowned out by laughter from the bar as the barmaid slapped an adventurous patron to the uproarious amusement of the man's companions.

"No need for that," he heard the old man saying when the laughter had died down. "The *Lucky Duckling's* a small boat, and it won't take but a minute to store your gear. You can't miss her, she's berthed at the nearest quay."

"Fergus, can you see to our horses until we return?"

"It will be my pleasure."

"Very well," said the first speaker. "I'm going to catch what sleep I can. See you in the morning."

"Myself, as well," said a third man. Hobarth saw from the corner of his eye that this speaker was swarthy, perhaps a Calishite. He also noticed a great dog climb to its feet and follow the two men up the stairs. Hobarth shuddered, for next to the sea, he hated dogs above all else.

He had been considering following the men to their room and finishing the task of the assassins, but the presence of the dog changed that plan. His magic would probably kill the prince before the flea-bitten creature could react, but the thought of those long fangs lusting for his flesh sent shivers up and down Hobarth's spine.

But a new plan occurred to him even as he discarded the old one. Quickly, Hobarth drained his mug and walked from the inn, back toward the harbor. The *Lucky Duckling* was easy to find.

"I fear your luck has run out, *Duckling*," he murmured, chuckling at his private joke. After checking to see that no one was near, he sat upon the edge of the pier and began casting a spell of decay. Within a minute, he was finished, though the boat showed no outward signs of damage.

Still, Hobarth knew as he pushed himself to his feet, the *Lucky Duckling* would never make it to the neighboring island of Alaron. He would assure the little boat's doom with an additional spell in the morning.

For now, he lumbered back to the inn. He tried to remember what the barmaid had looked like.

* * * * *

"I shape," grunted the man, shuffling forward to reach for the thick hedge. Robyn looked up in surprise, as this was the first intelligible statement the fellow had made in the last four days.

Grateful, she stepped backward. "Help yourself," she offered, leaning against a tree to catch her breath.

"Keep an eye he doesn't take your job," warned Newt. The dragon, blue today instead of orange, was perched on the branches atop the hedge. He watched the humans dourly.

The day had been strenuous, as strenuous as all of the days since the stranger had arrived at the grove. They stood at one of the great curving walls of mistletoe that marked the far limits of Genna's grove, perhaps five hundred yards from the cottage and the Moonwell. The hedges served as bastions against unwarranted intrusion, for their tightly woven branches bristled with sharp thorns. Mistletoe itself was a plant potent in druidic magic, and thus served doubly to protect the domain of its mistress.

But the hedges required constant care during periods of rain, and this had been a wet summer. If not tended by someone, they would choke off all access and egress to the grove. Robyn's hands, beneath her leather gloves, were scratched and torn. Her arms were leaden with weariness, for she had been swinging a sickle all morning in an effort to drive the hedges back into their proper dimensions.

The stranger took the sickle from her, holding it as if he had used the tool all his life. Slowly but smoothly he began to slice at the overgrowth, striking it back with clean cuts.

Robyn was surprised by his apparent skill. For the first time she noticed that he was improving under her care. His bony frame had filled out slightly, and he could stand and walk without shaking. Now, he was even working.

For a minute she thought about running to tell Genna of her success, but quickly decided not to. The Great Druid had been cantankerous for the last few days, complaining of a stiffness in her bones and throbbing headaches. She had spent most of her time in bed, complaining to Robyn whenever the young druid was around.

Consequently, Robyn avoided the cottage as much as possible. This was not difficult, because the tasks she had to do would remain doubled as long as Genna was.

"His work's not too bad—for a mushroom-head," commented Newt in a stage whisper. He had taken to calling the stranger unflattering names, out of jealousy, Robyn suspected, for now she no longer attended entirely to the little dragon.

"Stop it," she chided. "He seems to be growing much stronger. All he needed was a little shelter and decent food!"

"Maybe he's strong enough to walk away from here," grumbled Newt. "And it'll be none too soon, I might add!"

"Why don't you go take a bath in the Fens if you can't be a little more polite?"

The stranger paused and turned to see if Robyn was watching. When he met her gaze, his face split into a wide grin, and he nodded enthusiastically before turning back to the task. For several minutes he chopped and trimmed, until the druid noticed that his strike was less sure.

"I'll take over again," she offered, reaching for the sickle. The stranger suddenly whirled, his face twisting into a beastly snarl as his eyes darted wildly about. He appeared to stare right through her. But then he relaxed and smiled, meeting her gaze boldly. He handed the tool over and then stood near as she continued the job.

"Stand back," she warned. "I don't want to hit you."

Obediently, he stepped away, but he still stared at her like an affectionate puppy. She could feel his unwavering gaze following her every motion, and found the sensation distinctly uncomfortable.

"Good! Good!" He cackled cheerfully, watching the hedge take shape.

"Who are you, anyway?" Robyn stopped working and stared at the stranger. She had not troubled about his identity when he was not talking, but now that he spoke, she wanted a name to call him by.

"I . . ." The man's voice was puzzled and unsure. Suddenly, his eyes widened in fear and he scuttled away from her. He crouched, his body wired with tension, as if he were about to flee.

. . . Or attack? For a moment she felt very frightened of this stranger. And very vulnerable. With an angry shrug, she tried to ignore the feeling.

Inside, though, she was deeply disturbed by his fear. What could lie in his background that made him so frightened of companionship, of revealing his identity?

He stared at her again as she went back to work. But now his eyes followed her body less like a puppy and more like a hungry wolf. Robyn shivered involuntarily, and she clutched the sickle tightly as she turned to the mistletoe.

* * * * *

Hobarth, cleric of Bhaal, stood upon a low hill just outside of Cantrev Kingsbay. He had a clear view of the bay itself and of the wide gray sea stretching to the east. Somewhere out there, he knew, the sun had risen, but a low-lying bank of clouds concealed the dawn from those on shore.

A half-dozen fishing vessels dotted the waters of the bay, moving toward deep water. There, salmon dashed in great numbers between the islands of Gwynneth and Alaron, and these fishermen made a fair living.

But one boat, Hobarth knew, had put to sea not to catch fish, but to deliver Tristan Kendrick dangerously close to Hobarth's and Cyndre's domain. Or at least attempt to deliver, the cleric gloated.

He meditated for a long time, sitting perfectly still with his eyes closed and his body upright. Gradually, he felt the presence of his deity, and Bhaal answered the summons of his faithful follower.

The spell he needed to cast was one of his most potent. It called for the direct might of his god, Bhaal, and allowed the cleric to control the very substances of the world around him. Bhaal eagerly powered the spell, for in fact he watched Hobarth's mission with more than slight interest. Magic flowed through the cleric's body and into the air.

Slowly but mightily he marshalled clouds heavy with water vapor, coaxing them from the highlands and forcing them out to sea. The force of his magic pushed and prodded the air, and gradually a breeze flowed from the shore. The breeze would become a wind and then a storm, if the cleric could maintain his spell.

And Hobarth knew that he could.

* * * * *

Canthus settled comfortably into the bow of the *Lucky Duckling*, while Daryth helped Rodger trim the lone sail. Ponstwain relaxed easily against the gunwale, staring at the water. He had removed his armor, wrapping it with their weapons in oilskins and storing the package in the hull.

"Fine offshore breeze," Rodger commented. "If it holds,

we'll cross the strait in two days."

Tristan had been skeptical of the old seaman's abilities when they had first met, for Rodger must have seen at least six decades. His build was slight, and his permanently stooped shoulders enhanced his look of frailty. His face was leathery, creased by hundreds of lines, and he did not have a tooth left in his mouth. After seeing the easy confidence with which he guided the *Lucky Duckling*, however, the prince felt considerably reassured.

They soon passed the mouth of Kingsbay and entered the Strait of Alaron. For a moment he looked over his shoulder at Gwynneth. As the island of his birth fell away behind them, he felt that he should feel excitement and anticipation. But instead, he wrestled with the feeling that he might never see his homeland again.

I won't think of that, he told himself. Or of Robyn. Or of Father. He peered resolutely over the bow. It was time to look before him again.

He watched the keen, albeit weathered, bow of the *Duckling* slice through the brine and enjoyed the sight of the wake foaming out to either side. He turned to see it spreading apart like a feathery trail behind the boat and saw that Gwynneth was practically out of sight. Daryth was relaxing in the bottom of the hull, his eyes closed and his head pillowed on a coil of rope.

"I hope the old fool can keep us on a straight course," said Pontswain, coming over to join him.

"Of course he can!" Tristan retorted, annoyed.

"It must be nice to have such faith in people," said the lord, with a sidelong glance at the prince. Shaking his head in amusement, Pontswain settled into the hull to sleep.

Tristan continued to watch the rolling waves, but gradually the experience became less pleasant. He began to feel his stomach heave upward every time the boat climbed a wave, and then threaten to lurch into his throat as they sliced down the other side. He began to dread the crest of each wave, his discomfort growing more acute. His footing grew shaky, and the strength seemed to drain from his arms as he tried to brace himself.

"First time at sea?" Rodger cackled the question from the

back of the boat.

Tristan could only manage a mute nod, for his jaws were tightly clenched.

"This is nothing," laughed the fisherman. "It'll get lots worse in the middle of the strait."

This remark pushed the prince over the brink of self control, and he hung his head over the side, sending the remains of his breakfast to the fish. At least Pontswain and Daryth are still asleep, he thought, nauseated. He clung to the side of the boat as the constant motion of the waves seemed to grow more pronounced.

The long day seemed endless, and his condition worsened as the wind picked up. The *Lucky Duckling* seemed to fly from one wavetop to the next, and the prince noticed that the waves themselves were growing considerably higher than they had been at the start of the journey.

"Best trim the sail," grunted Rodger to Daryth as the latter arose to look around. "Sea's getting higher'n I expected."

Daryth loosened a line, pulling the boom higher up the mast so that the amount of sail exposed to the wind was reduced dramatically. Tristan felt the boat slow beneath him and could sense more control returning to the fisherman. The wind still tugged fiercely at the exposed canvas, but Rodger was able to guide the little vessel carefully over the huge swells. In spite of his nausea, Tristan could not keep his eyes from the sea as it swirled around him. The waves were climbing higher than the sides of the boat. He swallowed hard, certain that soon one would smash into the hull, flood the craft, and end the journey for all of them.

But Rodger was a skilled pilot, and the *Lucky Duckling* rode the waters like a carriage along a hilly path. She lurched occasionally but never faltered.

Somehow Pontswain had managed to sleep through the growing storm. Now he awoke suddenly and stumbled to his feet to look, aghast, at the rising sea. "What kind of a sailor are you?" he shouted at Rodger. "Can't you read a simple change in the weather?"

Tristan wanted to object, but feared that if he unclenched his jaw he would again be overwhelmed by nausea. Daryth climbed to his feet and stepped to the lord's side.

"Let the man sail, you pompous fool," he growled.

"How dare you insult—" Pontswain's hand reached for the sword hilt that would normally be at his belt, forgetting that he was unarmed. Daryth stepped in closer.

"There is something unnatural about this storm, and if you weren't so eager to blame someone, you'd recognize it yourself!"

Pontswain seemed to pale slightly as the black eyes of the Calishite bored into his own. Finally, he turned with a shrug and looked back at the sea. Daryth settled back to rest, and Rodger sailed on as though nothing had happened.

By late afternoon, however, Tristan sensed that even the seasoned fisherman was worried. The swells had continued to grow, and they had trimmed the sail until it was no larger than a baby's blanket.

"'Tain't natural," groused the old man. "The weather failing like this. It'll be a long night if'n it don't settle down some."

For a few minutes toward dusk, it seemed that the *Lucky Duckling* would live up to her name. The wind faded and the seas grew marginally calmer. But as the surrounding seas turned from a dull gray to a deep black with the onset of nightfall, the gusts of wind swept forward again, carrying the little fishing boat with them. Now the seas rolled six feet high and continued to grow.

Canthus paced anxiously beside the prince as he darted from side to side of the boat, looking into the water for he knew not what. When the moorhound began to whimper, Tristan stopped to scratch the dog's broad head.

Rodger grasped the tiller firmly while Daryth raised the sail almost entirely. He left just enough for the sailor to retain steerage of the boat, but even so the little craft whipped forward recklessly.

A huge wall of black water rolled up to the stern of the ship and thundered past, sending a torrent of spray over the transom and leaving the *Duckling* awash, holding more than a foot of water.

"Bail!" cried Rodger, indicating a large bucket with a nod of his head. Tristan saw that the surging tiller nearly lifted the sailor off the hull with the force of the storm.

Desperately he knelt, noticing absently that he no longer

felt sick. Pontswain knelt beside him, heaving full buckets over the side. Tristan had to admit, grudgingly, that the lord worked diligently and with great strength. Of course, he no doubt realized that his own life was at stake.

Pitching bucketfuls of water over the side, they bailed frantically, but water seemed to pour over the gunwales faster than they could scoop it out.

Tristan filled another bucket, but suddenly gagged as a surprising stench assailed his nostrils. Gasping, he dropped the bucket and staggered backward. Maggots spilled from the container to slither about the hull.

He struggled to voice his shock but no sound emerged. More maggots seethed from the hull of the boat, and he felt the wood grow spongy beneath his feet. The sickly white creatures, creeping from the *Duckling*'s very planks, seemed to fill the boat. The horrible smell of rotting flesh rose from the hull with the maggots.

"Sorcery!" cried the prince, finding his voice.

"What black magic is this?" growled Ponstwain. The lord was not so much terrified as enraged. "You have brought this upon us!" he finished, shaking his fist at Tristan.

The prince shook his head dumbly and then watched as Rodger screamed, staring in horror at the death of his boat. The hull creaked as the center of the boat rose while the bow and stern dipped below the rolling waves. A black wall of water crushed the transom, covering Rodger as he screamed. As the water receded, Tristan saw the tiller banging loosely.

There was no sign of the sailor.

Daryth scrambled past him, and Tristan saw his companion lunging to grasp an oilskin bundle. The prince vaguely remembered that the package contained their weapons . . . the Sword of Cyrmrych Hugh!

The hull lurched apart, and the bundle of weaponry slipped into the black water and sank. Daryth dove after it, disappearing into the storm.

Abruptly, Tristan's muscles broke free from the paralysis that gripped him, and he ducked to the side to avoid the falling mast. He scrambled into the stern of the boat, which remained just underneath the surface. He tried to see Daryth, and heard Canthus bark, somewhere close, but the Calishite and the dog were invisible in the darkness.

Daryth suddenly popped to the surface in the wave trough, and Tristan could see that his hands were empty. Then the crest of the wave smashed against the wreck, and the remaining piece of the *Lucky Duckling* disintegrated. The young prince struggled for air, thrashing desperately against the press of the thundering sea.

All he could find was an infinity of black, choking water.

* * * * *

"Kralax Heeroz Zuthar."

Short, dextrous fingers stroked the surface of a mirror. A soft luminescence seemed to flow from the glass. The wizard spoke quietly as if, by his tone, he wished to soothe a nervous cat.

But the words were the dire commands of magic.

The luminescence grew cloudy, and gradually the outline of a room appeared in the mirror. Cyndre walked slowly around the council chamber, his concentration focused entirely upon the tall mirror. One of the blood-red tapestries had been pulled back to reveal the glass. Its gold frame seemed to catch and amplify the light from within.

The wizard stared into the mirror and saw the Great Hall of Caer Corwell, as he had seen for many days in a row. The hall was vacant, save an old cook gathering dirty platters from the large tables.

"Zuthax Eli."

The picture moved, as if the viewer had passed from the hall and begun to climb the stairs inside the castle. For several minutes the image meandered from room to room, passing freely through closed doors. Caer Corwell seemed quiet, almost abandoned.

Cyndre felt a flash of annoyance, but he blinked it away. Self control, he reminded himself, was all important.

He thought of the cleric Hobarth with smug satisfaction. Blindly faithful to his violent god, that fat buffoon would sacrifice his own life if his awful master demanded it. And how pitiful were his clerical powers, mused Cyndre, when compared to the awesome might of wizardry. Such reliance upon gods, Cyndre believed without question, was the way of fools and weaklings.

The image moved from the keep to the outer wall, and here he found a pair of guards standing listlessly at their posts. One, a young man, asked the other a question. The wizard smiled slightly as he heard the words. His smile broadened as he heard the other guard reply.

He now knew all that he required: The Prince of Corwell was on his way to Callidyrr.

* * * * *

With growing interest, Bhaal watched the drama unfold upon the Moonshaes. As his will focused upon the islands, he found the Heart of Kazgoroth, still clutched faithfully by its servant.

It was time, decided Bhaal, that the heart be given to one who could make better use of it. That one drew closer to it with each passing hour, and this closeness brought the god's desire to a fever pitch.

Hobarth would take the heart, would use it for the tasks it was capable of, in the hands of a powerful cleric. Hobarth would gain his tool, and Bhaal would recover the very soul of his lost minion. This thought was immensely pleasing to him.

And so Bhaal set in motion the things that would send the heart from the one who carried it to the one who would wield it. All he needed to do was take a man, already driven mad by the close throbbing of the heart, and make him irrevocably insane.

The throbbing grew louder and deeper.

♣ 4 ♣

Caer Allisynn

His Highness, High King Reginald Carrathal, sovereign of Callidyrr and monarch of all the lands of the Ffolk, had a most annoying problem. To wit, a large pimple gleamed insolently from his cheek, resisting the king's most arduous attempts to remove it.

Pouting, His Majesty turned from the mirror, his long curls flouncing, and marched across the bedchamber. The plush carpeting sank underfoot, thwarting his attempts to stomp noisily.

He stepped around a huge canopied bed, stalking alongside a wall that was hung in a fortune of silk curtains. In annoyance, he realized that he now stood before an even larger mirror—the one that hung above his dressing table.

"Blast it all!" he cried, picking up a small vial of rare Calishite cologne. He hurtled the container at the mirror, smashing both, before turning to stalk across the room again.

"Is there a problem, Your Majesty?" The smooth voice came from the wizard.

"How dare you enter my chamber without knocking?" the king huffed, squinting angrily at Cyndre.

"I was about to knock when I heard a disturbance. Fearing for His Majesty's safety, I hastened to your side . . ."

The wizard's voice, as always, soothed and comforted the king. He felt his annoyance vanish as Cyndre stepped forward. The mage's dark robe was open, revealing a soft cotton gown embroidered with gold. His hood lay back upon his shoulders, and his blond, curly hair framed a cherubic smile in a wide, almost childlike face. His hand reached forward to pat the royal shoulder.

"Well?" the king said. "What did you want to see me about?"

"I fear, Your Highness, that I bring grave news. It is with reluctance that—"

"Tell me, you fiend! Do not play games with bad news!" The king nearly hopped up and down in his anxiety. He licked his lips nervously.

Cyndre sighed, his reluctance obvious. "It seems that the usurper is on his way to Caer Callidyrr."

"What?" the High King squeaked. "But you promised me—"

"You need not fear him," said Cyndre, looking straight into the king's eyes. He did not add "yet," though it was on his mind. Slowly, the monarch calmed down.

"Our first attempt to punish him for his treachery met with small success," explained the wizard, pursing his lips. The gesture was a very strong one for Cyndre. "Nevertheless, I feel certain that we can still deal with him easily."

"But what should I do? You must tell me!" The king's words tumbled out, and the wizard could tell that he was losing what little control was left him.

"My . . . sources tell me that he is on his way even as we speak. He must land soon at one of the ports of Alaron. It would be a simple matter to arrest him as he steps ashore. All you need to do, sire, is declare him an outlaw."

"Yes, of course. That I shall do! Why, he is an outlaw, isn't he? He seeks to pretend a claim to my throne. I shall have him hanged!"

"Very good, Your Majesty. We can put a detachment in every port. He will be arrested the moment he steps ashore."

King Carrathal turned, a frown of worry creasing his brow. "But how do I know that my orders will be carried out? This prince is a popular hero. Can I trust the loyalty of my own men to arrest him?"

"Is it not for just this reason that you retain the services of your brigades—troops that answer to you alone?"

The king paled slightly but appeared to consider the idea. "Yes . . . I could use the guard. I pay them too much as it is—perhaps it's time I gave them a task." He slowly warmed to the idea. "But how do I know they're trustworthy?"

"The Scarlet Guard will follow your orders," said Cyndre reassuringly. "I brought them to you expressly so that you would have soldiers you could trust implicitly."

"But the people won't like it," replied the king. "Those ogres, especially, make everyone so nervous."

In truth, the ogres made the king himself very nervous, which was why he had not used them yet, though he had been paying them for more than two years. At least the Northmen had not bothered Callidyrr in the interim.

But now he considered using them against one of his own subjects, and this did not seem right. He knew that his people resented his employment of mercenary troops when the fighters of the Ffolk were perfectly capable warriors. Why had he let the wizard convince him to hire them?

"The people are your subjects!" argued Cyndre. His voice took on a hardened edge. "Will you let them rule the kingdom? I tell you, the guards are your best troops!"

"So you claimed," said the king, "when you persuaded me to hire them."

Cyndre lowered his head modestly. The monarch could not see the gloating light in his eyes.

"And the lords grow restless," whined the king. "They all owe fealty to me, but they don't act like it! I don't trust any of them—they would turn against me at the drop of a hat. Like that bandit O'Roarke in Dernall Forest. That rebel could serve as an example for other traitorous scum!"

"You hold his sister in your dungeon. Why do you not use her as an example? Show what will happen to those who resist your will?"

King Carrathal turned away. He did not like to be reminded of the way he had usurped Lord Roarke's land—nor was he completely comfortable with the idea of using the young woman as a lever to obtain his ends. "If only O'Roarke knew me," he whined. "He and his outlaws would see that I have only the best interests of the kingdom at heart!"

"Do not underestimate the extent of the problem," said Cyndre calmly. "But come, Your Highness, what of this prince? Will you do as I suggest?"

"Very well," sighed King Carrathal. "I shall declare the prince of Corwell an outlaw. The Scarlet Guard will meet him as he lands. They will arrest the usurper and bring him to me in chains."

*   *   *   *   *

Water pounded and crashed about Tristan, choking him and pressing him down. He kicked and flailed but could not find the surface. He felt his consciousness slipping away, though he struggled even more desperately to swim. He barely felt the vicelike jaws close over his arm, jerking him roughly through the sea. For a second his face broke free from the black water, and he gulped a great lungful of air. Then he became conscious of the teeth that were sinking through his flesh.

Thrashing upward, struggling for more air, the prince felt the grip on his arm slacken. But then he was grabbed by the collar and pulled backward helplessly. Miraculously, his face remained out of the water.

He felt a solid object strike him in the back, and he twisted around to catch a long section of planking. The *Lucky Duckling*, he thought. As he did so, the grip on his collar broke free, and he turned to find himself face-to-face with his panting moorhound. Canthus thrashed beside him, finally forcing his forelegs over the plank.

"Thanks, old dog," he choked, wrapping an arm around the broad neck. "You almost ripped my arm off, didn't you, buddy?" The presence of the hound warmed his heart, but did little for his hopes. "I fear you have only postponed the inevitable," he added, after he had recovered his breath.

"Daryth!" he shouted suddenly. Where was the hound-master? The bleak, despairing realization crept over him: his friend had drowned, along with Rodger and Pontswain. But he couldn't bring himself to believe that the man's cocky self-assurance, his casual energy, had been snuffed out. "By the goddess, no!" he cried aloud.

The feeling that he was doomed would not go away, and he had to grit his teeth and shake his head to dissuade himself from releasing the plank and sinking into oblivion.

Through the remainder of the long night, the young man and his dog bobbed, barely alive, across the heaving surface of the strait. Tristan lost consciousness once, only to awaken as Canthus dragged him back to the plank. Frightened and shivering, he nevertheless remained alert after that.

He groped to understand the death of the *Lucky Duckling*. Black sorcery had killed her, he felt certain, but how? And by whose hand? Over and over again he vowed vengeance against the force that had sought to destroy him. Gradually his anger began to sustain him. I'm not going to die, he told himself. I'm too mad to die.

Gradually he noticed that the waves grew smaller, and the wind died away almost completely. The swells lessened. Though the crests of the waves still loomed six or eight feet higher than the troughs, they seemed to carry him up and down with an easy and unthreatening rhythm. No longer did they curl over at the top, thundering down to crush anything below them.

The horizon lightened to a dull gray, and he peered around for any sight of land or sail or even debris. Visibility was still very poor, and he could make out no features beyond the rolling swells.

"Tristan!" He heard the voice as if from a great distance away, and he was certain that he imagined it.

"Tristan!" it repeated. "Over here!"

Now he squinted intently across the gray surface, wondering if he was losing his mind. There! He saw a flash of brightness over the crest of a wave.

"Daryth!" He croaked. He finally saw his friend, and Pontswain too, bobbing across the rolling summit of a wave. The Calishite was soon kicking toward him, buoyed by an air-filled wineskin and a loose bundle of wood, and dragging a sodden Ponstwain behind him.

"Are you injured?" asked Daryth.

"I don't think so. How about you?"

"Just wet and cold." The Calishite somehow found the strength to grin. Pontswain's formerly graceful locks hung like a wet blanket across his face. He looked barely alive, and he did not acknowledge the prince's presence.

"Aye," grunted Tristan. "And I've lost the Sword of Cymrych Hugh. The goddess alone knows how far it is to land from here, or what such land would be."

"Still, the seas are calming, and it'll be daylight soon. We may even sight a sail." But Daryth didn't look as cheerful as he sounded.

Pontswain coughed weakly and struggled to raise himself. His efforts sent the makeshift raft rolling, and everyone scrambled to regain their handholds.

"Be careful!" snapped the prince as the lord gave him a baleful glare.

"This is your fault! If you hadn't let that old fool take us in his rot-ridden craft, this would not have happened!"

"That man gave his life for us! Doesn't that mean anything to you?"

"He met the fate he deserved for his incompetence. He failed, and that's all that matters," said Pontswain.

But as twilight gave way to dawn and the clouds broke apart, the men saw no sign of anything except the rolling sea. They could tell which direction was east, for there the sun became a rosy glow against the horizon, finally breaking free from the sea to begin its climb into the sky. But that knowledge did them little good, for they had no idea which direction to look for land.

"What's that?" Daryth asked suddenly.

Everyone fell silent because they all heard it: A faint rumble seemed to arise from the sea itself. The sound was almost inaudible, but was so deep and powerful that they felt it as much as a vibration in their bones as a sound in their ears. The sound grew in volume and strength, until they heard a noise like crashing thunder, rolling constantly. The water itself seemed to shake.

Suddenly the surface of the sea turned to foam a scarce hundred yards away from them. Water frothed upward and then rolled away, creating a steady wave that forced them backward. A crenelated parapet, like the top of a tower, burst through the surface and sent spray and waves crashing away from it. Another, and then a third, exploded from the sea, thrusting skyward like gigantic lances.

And then the foaming water spilled away to reveal a vast surface of smooth stone. A glowing rosy hue shone from a wall as the thing caught the rays of the morning sun. More walls, and a gate, and more towers continued to rise for a minute until the vast object came to rest, seeming to sit upon the surface of the sea.

Tristan, Daryth and Pontswain, bobbing in the water and gaping in awe, stared at the most magnificent castle that they had ever seen.

It stood motionless, vast and imposing, like a monument to some forgotten era of grandness. Water spilled down its vast sides, thinning into a soft mist that floated around them. Tendrils of seaweed hung from the crenelated parapet, draping across the sides.

The whole structure was oddly silent, as if mere sound could not convey the grandness of its arrival nor the majesty of its appearance. And too, there was warmth flowing from the edifice—not a physical warmth, but a spiritual sense of power and majesty. Each of them felt this magical emanation as both welcoming and forboding.

The castle remained, and they knew they had no choice but to enter.

* * * * *

"Here, lady. Wood!"

Smiling broadly, the man dumped a huge pile of twigs and dried wood at Robyn's feet.

"Thank you, Acorn," she replied, warily meeting his gaze. She had taken to calling the man after the seed of the oak tree, for he could not remember any name of his own. The name seemed to suit him—his nature was childlike, but Robyn sensed that he harbored a deep inner strength. She wanted to nurture that strength, to see him grow. At the same time, she was still a little afraid of him.

"You did very well," she added, embarrassed by the way he beamed at the praise. "Now, if you will fetch some water so I can rinse these linens, we can take a rest."

Eagerly, Acorn scrambled toward the silver ribbon of bubbling water that ran through Genna's grove, only to pause and return sheepishly.

"Forgot buckets!" he explained, chuckling over and over as if it were some great joke.

As the days had passed, the scraggly stranger had grown more lucid and helpful. He was stronger than an average man and had skills that were useful in tending the grove.

All of which were very helpful, Robyn thought with a twinge of worry, for Genna's illness had grown suddenly worse. She had spent the last few days in bed, tossing deliriously in the depths of a fever, barely rational.

Newt had not spent much time in the grove, either. He had taken long excursions throughout the Vale, even visiting the Fens occasionally. Today, he had gone off to seek Grunt's company, almost certainly to annoy the old bear. Grunt had a notoriously short temper, and Newt delighted in driving the animal into a rage with his sudden spells of invisibility.

Robyn thought again about Acorn. He was friendly and almost pathetically grateful for any praise she gave him, but more and more the man raised shudders of uneasiness within her. One minute he seemed harmless, and the next minute she was afraid of him. But she did not know why.

"Here, lady. Here water!"

Proudly, Acorn returned with two sloshing buckets. He set them down at Robyn's feet as she thanked him, bobbing his head up and down eagerly. She quickly rinsed the light blankets and hung them to dry—well practiced motions, as Genna's sweaty fever necessitated frequent linen changes. She tried to ignore the feeling that Acorn's eyes were boring into her back as she stretched to reach the clothesline.

"Come along, now," she said as he followed at her heels. "Why don't we go and sit by the pond? I have some carrots and apples that we can have for lunch."

They walked across Genna's garden, a lush field of wildflowers and herbs. In the center of the garden was a broad pond with a grassy island at its heart. In places, the sandy bottom of the pond was smooth—perfect for swimming. Elsewhere, lily pads spread across the surface, home to myriad frogs and turtles. Great white swans swam regally among them. Robyn thought again, as she beheld the scene, that it must be the most beautiful place in the world.

As they approached the pond, the water swirled momentarily, and then the smooth bridge of sand rose to the surface. She took no notice of the phenomenon, so accustomed to the ways of the grove was she, but Acorn hesitated.

"Come on," she encouraged, stepping onto the firm bridge. Reluctantly, he followed her to the island while she selected a smooth place for their lunch.

She sat comfortably on the soft bank, stretching her legs over the water and kicking her feet to relieve her taut muscles. Acorn settled slowly, almost reverently, beside her. She noticed, uneasily, that the look on his face was no longer one of innocence. Instead, he looked as though he struggled to conceal some secret thought.

"Here," she said to cover her nervousness. "Have an apple."

Acorn took the fruit and chomped greedily into it, ignoring the pieces that scattered in his beard or sprayed into the air. In seconds he had finished and reached forward to snatch another from the basket on Robyn's lap.

She thought wistfully of picnics she had shared with Tristan. They certainly weren't like this! What he was doing at that moment, she wondered. Did he think of her? Did he miss her? A terrible sense of depression seized her, and for a moment she toyed with the idea of renouncing her studies and racing home to Corwell to see him. But in the next moment she discarded the thought, knowing she could not forsake the calling of the goddess. But why did she have to be so lonely?

She ate absently, suddenly aware of Acorn's closeness. She felt uncomfortable, but didn't want to offend him by moving away. Turning to look at him, she was startled to see him staring intently at her face. His eyes were clear, but they seemed to burn with a frightening intensity.

"Lady . . . you like me? My friend?" Still that burning gaze.

"Yes, Acorn . . . of course I like you. Haven't I—"

"I mean, you—" he cut her off awkwardly. "Lady, you are my lady!" Suddenly his hand reached out to clasp her thigh. He leaned quickly forward to force her backward onto the ground, his mouth seeking hers.

"No! Get off me!" she screamed, pushing against him and rolling to the side.

"Mine!" he cried, scrambling forward on all fours to lunge at her before she could stand.

She punched him in the face, but he still tackled her, his eyes gleaming madly. He pinned her to the ground and grasped a handful of her gown.

Terror galvanized Robyn and once again she twisted free,

but this time he ripped half her garment away. He paused, staring stupidly, and in that split second she recalled a piece of her training: a fast, simple spell.

"Stop!"

The command was a physical attack, slamming into the crazed man and holding him in place, poised to leap. Slowly, the light of madness died in his eyes.

She stared at him in hatred and anger. She wanted to strike him or kick him—to somehow cause him pain. But something, perhaps it was pity for his degraded state, stayed her hand. She was shaking with fright and tension and rage, and she didn't even want to look at him again.

Gasping, she gathered her gown about her and stumbled toward the cottage, leaving him bound by the spell.

* * * * *

"Come on!"

Tristan was propelling himself toward the castle even before Daryth spoke, too surprised to wonder if the grand structure was illusion or reality. Canthus and Pontswain swam beside them, their weariness forgotten. Soon the men and the dog reached the foot of the massive, smoothly hewn wall. The shining pink surface rose straight into the air above them and seemed to continue underwater as far as they could see.

"Rosy quartz," muttered the Calishite. "There'll be no climbing it here."

"Where—?" began the prince, dismayed at the thought of succor so close at hand yet possibly unreachable.

"Let's try the gate," suggested Daryth, swimming easily along the base of the wall. Pontswain followed, while Tristan and Canthus sputtered and splashed in the rear.

The Calishite reached the gate first. The prince watched him rise slowly from the water, pulling himself gradually up the wall. With a supple swing, the Calishite carried himself over the gate and out of Tristan's sight.

Tristan heard nothing for a few seconds, but then the portal began to drop with a steady creaking. In a moment, he could see his friend operating the smooth iron winch that patiently fed chain to the lowering gate. In another moment, Tristan, Pontswain, and Canthus had pulled themselves onto the flattened entryway and squirmed quickly into the castle proper.

"Is it real?" asked the lord.

"I don't know," replied the prince, unconsciously whispering. A sense of awe possessed him. The rosy stonework of the castle was bathed in a pale mist, shot through by slanting rays of early morning sunlight. The place was mystical yet somehow welcoming.

"This place is amazing!" commented Daryth, looking around at the high balconies, ornate columns, and sweeping stairways that surrounded the small courtyard before them. "What is it?"

"I remember a legend I heard once. I was just a child, so I can't vouch for the details," Pontswain said slowly, his voice unusually subdued. "It was about a young queen, bride of Cymrych Hugh. I think her name was Allisynn.

"The king erected a mighty castle, full of wondrous towers and lofty balconies, for her as his wedding gift. But she died soon after they were married. This was why Cymrych Hugh did not leave an heir.

"The king was so distraught by her death," Pontswain continued, "that he ordered the castle to become her tomb. It stood upon a tiny island between Gwynneth and Alaron, and, with the aid of the Great Druids of all the isles, he commanded the castle to sink below the waves, forever hiding and preserving the resting place of his beloved."

"The very stone feels sacred," said Daryth. "Like a shrine."

"Legends tell of fishermen and sailors occasionally sighting a castle here in the strait, but none have been verified. I don't recall hearing about it happening during my lifetime." Pontswain still spoke with quiet reverence.

"How do you know so much about this?" asked the prince, surprised at Ponstwain's knowledge.

"I listen to the bards," said the lord simply.

"That's fascinating. I've only heard vague stories about a castle in the sea—never the details."

"What good will it do us?" snapped Pontswain. "If the legends are true, the castle will stay here for a few hours and then sink. We'll be right back in the water."

"Let's find something to float on, then," suggested Daryth, pragmatically turning to look around them.

Shallow pools of water covered most of the surface, and strands of seaweed lay everywhere. Here and there a fish lay still, gills widespread, or flopped out its last strength on the hard stones. Across the courtyard, a mist-enshrouded stairway rose toward a balcony or entryway. The fog parted enough to give them a look at a pair of huge doors.

"Let's check inside," suggested the Calishite. "We might find something we can use as a raft."

"Or a weapon."

They reached the balcony and saw a pair of huge doors made of solid oak, strapped with gleaming bronze, and uncorroded by their immersion in the brine.

"We might as well try these first," muttered the Calishite, looking pessimistically at the massive portals.

A whirling blur of green was Tristan's first warning of attack. A savage shape slashed outward from the shadow of one of the columns.

"Look out!" cried the prince, bounding backward.

Daryth dove forward and somersaulted out of the creature's path. Tristan saw that the attacker was a humanlike creature covered with green scales. Wide gills gaped like wounds in its neck, and on the top of its head, trailing in a line down its backbone, was an array of barbed spikes. Wide, white eyes hung open like some ghastly blinding affliction, but the creature leaped after Daryth as if it could see very well. Its wide mouth gaped, displaying row after row of needlelike teeth. Webbed hands, studded with long, curving claws, sought the flesh of the Calishite, while similar feet slapped across the wet stone.

It wore only an oiled belt, and several silver bracelets lined its arms. Carrying a spearlike weapon, it moved haltingly, as if unaccustomed to movement outside of the sea.

A second monster moved forward on the heels of its companion, but Canthus lunged at this one and carried it to the floor. Clawed, webbed hands sank into the moorhound's flanks, but Canthus's white fangs drove toward the throat of the thing.

The first attacker whirled around, turning suddenly to

strike at Tristan with a long trident. The three-pronged fork nearly cut the prince's chest, but at the last moment Pontswain darted forward. The trident caught the lord on the temple, and Pontswain crashed like a stone to the ground. Tristan stared into the monster's face, the least human aspect of its appearance. It was a fish-face; the blank eyes and gaping maw belonged upon no other animal.

Canthus yelped as his opponent succeeded in pushing the dog to the side, but then the moorhound growled and lunged into the attack. The pair rolled several times across the wet stones, neither gaining a clear advantage. The monster attacking the two men darted forward aggressively, flicking its trident first at one, then the other. His weariness forgotten, the prince crouched to face the monster. "We'll do it same as we got the Northmen!" he panted to Daryth.

The Calishite remembered that battle well. "Ready!" he answered quickly.

Tristan darted to the side, and the trident followed him. At the same time Daryth dove and rolled. The creature swung his weapon back, but it passed cleanly over the Calishite, who came out of his roll to smash his head into the creature's midriff.

Tristan dashed at the monster, and now both of its opponents were closer than the dangerous end of the weapon. The prince seized the wooden haft and wrested the trident from the creature's grip as Daryth tackled it.

Daryth lay across the monster's abdomen, as its claws dug into his back. Tristan dropped his knees upon the thing's chest and then brought the heft of the trident down heavily upon its neck. He heard the cracking of bone. The monster's eyes bulged briefly outward before it stiffened and died.

The prince leaped to his feet, ready to run to the aid of his dog, but Canthus arose from the body of the other fish-man and shook himself. His wounds did not look too deep.

"Pontswain?" Tristan asked, kneeling beside the motionless lord. He saw that the man was breathing, but his eyes were closed. A deep purple bruise spread across his temple and cheek.

"What happened?" Daryth asked, joining Tristan.

"He saved my life—at least, he took a blow intended for

me. Perhaps I underestimated him."

"More likely he didn't think it through before he acted," suggested the Calishite.

"What were those things?" Tristan asked, after determining that Daryth was not hurt seriously either.

"I've never seen them before, but I've heard about creatures like them called sahuagin. They're supposed to live underwater. Sometimes they come out to raid ships or land. They're very bloodthirsty."

"You won't get any argument out of me." Though the fight had drained him physically, Tristan began to feel more confident than he had since they had taken to the water.

"At least we're armed now," mused Daryth, picking up the trident of the second sahuagin. They gently moved Pontswain into a small alcove in the wall of the keep, out of sight from the main courtyard. They could do no more for him at the moment.

"The keep, then," the prince suggested.

They stepped forward and each grasped one of the huge bronze rings hanging from the doors. To their amazement, each of the heavy portals swung smoothly open. Before them they saw a long hall with scattered pools of water on the stone floor and several pairs of doors along either wall.

Then they fell.

With the first shock, Tristan thought that the castle had begun to sink again, but he quickly saw that only he, Daryth, and Canthus were falling—not the entire castle. They plummeted down a wide shaft, a trap that had been triggered when they opened the doors to the keep, Tristan realized.

Abruptly, they smashed into a pool of cold water, hitting the surface with stunning force. Tristan felt the trident slip from his hands as he struggled to reach the surface. Daryth and Canthus quickly surfaced beside him, Daryth still holding his trident. Gasping and choking, it was all Tristan could do to simply stay afloat.

"That was stupid," coughed the Calishite. "I should have seen that from a mile away. Damn my carelessness!"

"Let's find a way out of here," said the prince. "And don't blame yourself—I didn't notice anything either."

They were in a small cavern, about thirty feet across. The smooth walls were far too steep to climb, and offered no doors or other passages.

"I'd say we've been caught," growled the Calishite.

* * * * *

Far from Gehenna, there existed a region of peace and healing, a land where the god grows mightier from acts of virtue and kindness, not murder. This deity, like Bhaal, had worshippers throughout the Forgotten Realms and all the other planes of the universe as well. Her name was Chauntea, goddess of agriculture and growth. She was the patron of all things whole and healthy.

Chauntea had great concentrations of power in many lands, places where her clerics preached the doctrine of her faith to all. These lands, without exception, benefited from her benign nature. And in other places, where Chauntea was not all-powerful or even universally known, she sent her missionaries to bring the words and acts of her faith.

One of these places was the Moonshaes.

❧ 5 ❧

The dead queen

The black water seemed to penetrate Tristan's flesh with freezing numbness. His arms grew leaden from the constant motion of treading water. He knew that he would die in this castle, for there seemed to be no way out of the trap.

Dim rays of sunlight filtered down the long shaft, which opened into the ceiling of the chamber. The ceiling was a dome made of rough-hewn stone all the way to the water, where it surrounded the prisoners.

For the twentieth time, Daryth took a breath and dove. The prince watched his companion's feet drive him down, and Tristan floated anxiously, counting the seconds. Surely no man could hold his breath for that long.

But the Calishite eventually returned to the surface with an explosive splash, floating on his back for a moment as he recovered his breath. A feeble shake of his head answered Tristan's question.

"Nothing," he finally gasped. "It's solid rock all the way around and deeper than I can dive."

"Save your strength," said the prince, acutely aware of the ebbing of his own endurance. The great dog, Canthus, swam in circles, and Tristan knew that the moorhound could not remain afloat for long.

"Get over to the side," suggested Daryth, propelling himself to the stone wall with easy strokes. "If you can find something to hold onto, you won't get quite so tired."

Numbly, Tristan did as he was told, finding a few rough niches in the rock wall that were sufficient to give him fingertip holds. At least he could keep his head out of the water without exerting himself.

"We can't die here!" Daryth suddenly swore.

"We won't," said Tristan. Suddenly, his foot slipped into a hole in the wall, and he felt a tug of current clamp around it. Forcefully, he pushed himself away, breaking free to gasp several lungfuls of air.

"There's a hole in the wall," he finally managed to choke out. "I felt a current pulling my foot in."

The Calishite shot past Tristan, swimming like a seal, and instantly dove to investigate the spot. He remained submerged for a full minute before slipping to the surface.

"It's an outlet!" he said, grinning weakly. "I've widened it some. In a few more minutes we'll have a way out."

Daryth rested against the wall for a moment, while Canthus swam between them, seeming to sense their hope.

"Where does the outlet go?" Tristan asked. "It could be way under the surface."

"No. The water flows from this room into that area, so the water level in there must be lower than it is in here."

"What if it's a water-filled pipe?" challenged Tristan.

"Then we'll all drown, and no one will ever know what happened to us," said the Calishite simply.

Daryth dove once again, and this time Tristan counted the seconds, stopping only after he reached one hundred. Still his companion didn't surface. The prince moved closer, certain that the Calishite was in serious trouble.

Finally, Daryth splashed to the surface, drawing in large gulps of air. "It's ready," he said. "I couldn't see any light on the far side, but I could hear splashing. That probably means there's an airspace. Should we try it?"

"Naturally," Tristan said. "I'll go first."

"Good," said the Calishite. "I'll send Canthus through after you. Try to keep track of him if you can."

"See you on the other side," said the prince. Wishing he had spent more time learning to swim, he dove toward the hole, surprised at how large it had grown. The water-saturated stone must have been considerably eroded, for Daryth had kicked a large amount of it away.

The current swept Tristan through, and only his hands, held out before him, deflected his head from a solid stone wall. The current swept him down through a narrow bottleneck and into a chute that was full of foaming water.

He slid downward, but the sides of the chute were gentle, and he quickly scrambled out of the water, coming to a stop upon a sloping slab of rock. The water rushed by a few feet down the slope. The prince barely had time to notice the dim illumination in this tunnel—it seemed to come from above him—before he saw Canthus bobbing madly.

"Here, dog!" he cried, slipping into the water to seize the panicked moorhound by his broad neck. Twisting desperately against the force of the current, he wrestled the dog onto shore a dozen feet farther down the chute from his original stopping place.

Daryth soon burst from the tight underground passage and crawled nimbly from the water to sit beside them. Somehow he had managed to carry the trident with him through the twisting tunnel.

"Not bad," he remarked. "Now where to from here?"

"Up," said the prince. He pointed to the shaft he had examined in the last few minutes. It was the source of the light that seeped into the tunnel, and sloped upward at a relatively shallow angle. "I'll bet that leads to the keep."

"Indeed," nodded the Calishite. "And the water from our trap is not the whole source of this stream. See how the water flows from farther into the castle?" Daryth gestured beyond the passageway they had emerged from, and Tristan saw the underground stream merging far into the subterranean darkness.

"Hsst!" Daryth whispered, quickly gesturing up the slope of the chute.

They stared downstream, and gradually Tristan saw movement against the water. A column of creatures was slowly moving upstream. The band drew closer, and Tristan recognized the sahuagin. They moved menacingly upstream in the shallow chute, arcing through the water like salmon returning to the spawning pools.

Several of the sea creatures stood before the rest, keenly peering about the tunnel while the others swam past. Then another group would take up the guard, farther upstream, while the last dove into the water and splashed ahead.

The creatures—Tristan counted at least two dozen—slid

past them about forty feet away. The light from the tunnel was at its most intense against the water nearest them, so they hoped that the sahuagin lookouts would be blinded to their presence in the shadows.

One of the leering fish-men took up the watch at the very foot of the slope where they hid. Its bulbous eyes seemed to see into every niche and cranny as it slowly pivoted its broad head. Its gaze passed the trio and then swung back. For a long moment, they peered into the darkness around them. Then the eyes passed to the front of the column, and the sahuagin leaped in with its fellows. Soon the band of monsters had moved out of sight.

"Let's go," the prince finally whispered, and they crawled from their hiding hole. Crouching, they moved along the slope toward the mouth of the shaft leading upward.

"I'll go first," whispered Tristan. Daryth was by far the better climber, and the Calishite, at the rear, would have a better chance of catching the prince or the hound if either should slip.

Tristan leaned forward into the shaft, which was about four feet in diameter and seemed to climb at an angle halfway between horizontal and vertical. The rock inside was slick but rough, and he was able to pull himself along using awkward handholds. Bracing his knees, he forced his torso upward and found higher handholds.

He neared the top after several minutes, his knees bruised and his fingernails cracked. Suddenly, his hand slipped from a wet knob of rock, and he started to slide back down the pipe. He arched his back instinctively and wedged himself to a stop with his back against the top of the shaft and his hands and knees against the bottom. The rough rocks slashed his skin, and salt stung his wounds, but he did not lose much of his hard-earned height. Pausing a moment to regain his breath, he inched his way upward again and finally crawled out the top of the shaft.

Tristan lay perfectly still upon the floor of a corridor. Solid iron doors lined one wall, and the surfaces of the walls were rough-hewn. The corridor was well-lighted, for high above him were several narrow windows.

In another minute Canthus lunged from the shaft, closely

followed by Daryth. They all rested briefly, while the two men looked for possible avenues of escape.

"That way?" suggested the Calishite, looking to the right.

"It seems to go up," agreed Tristan.

They got to their feet and slowly moved up the corridor. The iron doors stood in the left wall, spaced about thirty feet apart. No sound came from any of the rooms. Draped in seaweed, the first door was pocked with rust.

"Let me test that," suggested the prince. He stepped forward and selected a pair of bars that seemed the most corroded. Gripping one in each hand, he flexed the muscles of his broad shoulders, clenching his teeth with the effort. Slowly, the two bars spread apart until one of them broke off at its base. The resulting opening was just wide enough for them to squeeze through.

"Nice work," Daryth whispered. With his trident extended before him, he stepped over to the door to the outside and looked through one of the cracks. He blinked in pain as the bright light assaulted his eyes, but soon he could make out enough detail to see where they were.

"That's the courtyard," he said softly. "We're not far from the doors we were trying to open when we fell into the trap. That door—" he pointed to the other exit from the guard-room, "seems to lead into the rest of the keep."

The Calishite led the way again, this time with Canthus at his side, and they squeezed through the narrow entrance without pushing the door farther open. "It'll squeak for sure," he explained.

They entered a chamber that was illuminated by sunlight streaming in through narrow windows set high in the wall. Tall columns lined the vast room, supporting heavy wooden beams that seemed, somehow, to have escaped the corrosive effects of their long submergence. A wide hallway opened into the far side of the room, leading into the depths of the castle, while a smaller opening branched to the left.

"This must have been a grand ballroom or receiving hall," said Tristan, unconsciously whispering. Never in his life had he seen such an awesome sight.

"Should we check on Pontswain?" asked Daryth, suddenly remembering their unconscious companion.

Tristan shrugged. "He's as safe as we are."

Suddenly, the floor rumbled slightly beneath them, and the prince's heart leaped. Was the castle about to sink? But the rumbling ceased, and the castle did not seem to be moving.

"We've got to get out of here soon!" said Tristan.

"I haven't seen anything we could use as a boat—or even a raft," said Daryth.

"There's a lot more to this castle, it seems. Maybe we can find something in here."

Tristan started across the vast hall, peering around the heavy columns that lined two of the walls. Canthus accompanied him while Daryth checked the other side, toward the wide hallway. The prince approached the narrow corridor to the left.

"There's a stairway over here," called Daryth—his loud whisper carrying easily through the hall. "See anything?"

"Not yet." Tristan paused before the narrow corridor. He could hardly keep himself from entering it immediately. He was vaguely aware of Daryth, investigating the stairway.

And then Tristan was in the hallway, walking away from the great hall. He had not consciously decided to do so, yet he knew that he was going the right direction. Daryth was suddenly forgotten as he picked up his pace, hurrying toward his unknown but beckoning destination.

He stepped under a narrow stone arch and walked down another short corridor. Canthus followed, silently vigilant. Before him stood a similar arch, and beyond that was a well-illuminated room. The light seemed softer than the sunlight that streamed into the windows of the castle, however.

Intrigued, Tristan passed under the second arch to find himself in a round room. Its ceiling was a dome inlaid with gold, and its walls bore carvings of startling complexity depicting woodland scenes and pastoral farmlands. The detailed etchings had remained clean and sharp, even after centuries underwater.

But the dominant feature of the room was in its center, where a long glass case rested upon a solid, almost altarlike base. Cool white light emerged from the top of the case. Its sides were masked by plush purple curtains that hung inside the glass.

Tristan moved forward, all danger forgotten. Stumbling slightly at the nearly hypnotic sight, he reached the side of the case and looked in . . .

. . . and almost cried out in sadness.

The case itself seemed to glow with a soft, unearthly radiance. Tristan saw a young, frail woman. Her delicate face was impossibly beautiful, and long golden tresses spread from her head, cushioning her. She was dressed in a plain gown, embroidered very faintly with gold thread.

Her skin was so light as to be translucent. Her eyes were closed, and she lay perfectly still, as she must have lain for centuries. So beautiful, thought Tristan, and so long dead.

Then she moved.

*　*　*　*　*

Daryth sprang up a long flight of stairs. A feeling of urgency gripped him, but nowhere did he see anything that would serve them as a raft. He knew Tristan still searched the great hall, but he didn't dare risk calling to his friend.

The stairs ended in a long balcony, with hallways running into the distance to either side. He saw several open doorways that led to the balcony, and he looked quickly into each room as he jogged toward the righthand hallway. This upper floor was well illuminated by narrow windows, though the interiors of the rooms were rather dark.

Still, he saw nothing but wreckage in each chamber. The doors had apparently long since rotted away, and likewise any furniture that they had contained was now nothing but damp rot.

He heard a sound in one room as he ran past, and he thought that he might have seen a flash of movement. Daryth immediately flattened himself against the wall outside of that room, holding his trident poised to strike.

His alertness was rewarded as another of the sahuagin bounded through the doorway, its dead fish-eyes blinking warily down the corridor. Before it could react, Daryth thrust his weapon savagely at the monster's throat.

The sahuagin's gills flared in rage, but the middle point of the weapon caught it squarely in the neck. The Calishite pressed it remorselessly across the hall as the monster's webbed hands grasped at the shaft of the trident. It started to twist away, but then the wall opposite the doorway stopped its retreat. Daryth felt the tip of the weapon puncture the thing's scaly skin.

Red, oily fish blood spurted from its neck as the monster slowly slumped to the ground. It flopped reflexively several times, and then lay still. Daryth looked cautiously around, but saw no other signs of movement. Quickly he turned and continued his rapid journey down the corridor. For a minute he jogged past rooms like those he had seen earlier, but then he stopped.

His instincts had apparently been correct, for he now stood before a solid, varnished door of heavy oak. A silver keyplate, untarnished by the sea, seemed to beckon his tools.

With another look around, Daryth knelt before the door and pulled a thin probe from his belt. Placing his ear next to the silver plate, he carefully pushed and poked with the stiff wire. One minute later, he was rewarded by a sharp "click."

He pushed on the door and it swung smoothly open. The room within was dry. And it contained more treasure than he had ever seen in his life.

Crystal lanterns lit the room in a silky white glow. Golden and silver plates were stacked on the floor, and jeweled candelabra awaited their waxen charges, scintillating in the magical illumination. Several crowns lay on the floor—each studded with more gems than the Calishite had ever seen. A scattering of gold coins lay like a carpet across the floor, and bits of leather, crystal, and shining metal suggested even more treasures buried in the coins.

His eyes were drawn to a weapon, and his jaw dropped as he recognized his own scimitar! It can't be, he told himself, but the weapon was unmistakable. He noticed a sword next to it and picked it up, fairly certain that it was Pontswain's weapon. Though he looked for the Sword of Cymrych Hugh, there was no sign of Tristan's blade in the room.

He casually kicked aside some of the coins and discovered a pair of soft gloves that looked like they were the right size. On impulse, the Calishite put down the sword and pulled on the gloves. They immediately lightened in color until they exactly matched the hue of his skin. Each fingertip even had an artificial fingernail. Someone would have had to look very closely to see that he wore anything upon his hands. They were smooth and warm and quite comfortable.

Then he noticed another piece of leather, nearly buried by the coins, and he pulled free a smooth and tightly sewn sack. He saw another just like it and picked that one up, too. With luck, their flotation problem would be solved by these.

Gathering his belongings, he left the room. The door locked behind him.

*   *   *   *   *

With a sense of profound wonder, Tristan watched the woman rise. She sat up slowly, and for the first time the prince realized that the glass case had no top. She opened her eyes, and though her skin was pale as death, her eyes were deep brown, rich and loving.

Then she smiled, and Tristan's knees buckled from the beauty of her face. Unwittingly, he knelt before her, forced to drop his eyes in wonder.

"My lady," he gasped.

She studied him curiously, extending her hand and then speaking quietly. "My husband, have you come for me?"

But then her voice trailed off, and she stared at the prince for a full minute. When she spoke again, her voice was more confident.

"Rise, my prince, and step forward." Her voice was even more lovely than her smile. Dumbly, Tristan rose and moved hesitantly to the side of the case.

"This shall be yours again, until you find its true bearer." She held forth an object that had been by her side.

Tristan's senses returned as he saw the object that she extended toward him, hilt first.

She offered him the Sword of Cymrych Hugh—the sword that had been lost when his boat sank! How she came to hold the weapon, the prince did not try to guess, but he took it reverently and kneeled of his own will.

"You are Queen Allisynn," he guessed. "I do not know why you have performed for me this great miracle. But my sword shall be yours to command for the rest of my days!"

For a moment, her exquisite face looked sad. "Alas, but I am far beyond the need for swords. This . . . tomb is all the protection I will ever need." She sighed and Tristan's heart nearly broke.

"But you shall have need of that sword, and very soon," she continued. "Which is why, of course, I returned it to you. You did lose it, didn't you?"

"Yes. Forever, I thought."

"Do not say that. You cannot have any idea how long forever is." The rebuke was in words only, for her tone was still gentle.

"You are here for a reason, prince, and I shall tell you what that reason is so you may leave. You haven't much time, you know." As Tristan nodded, she continued.

"You have a destiny laid upon you, Prince Tristan Kendrick of Corwell. And it is mine to tell you what that destiny is. That is why, of course, your sword was returned."

Her voice grew solemn and serious. "The realms of the Ffolk are to be united again, as they were by my husband, Cymrych Hugh. They are to be united in your time, and in your presence. Now, this is the destiny I shall lay upon you:

"You are to find the next High King of the Ffolk—the one who will rule our people into a new age. You are to find him, and your sword shall become his."

Tristan's heart pounded at her words. To see the Ffolk united again under a strong High King! To find the one who would be that High King! He proudly gripped the Sword of Cymrych Hugh and raised his head to meet the eyes of the dead queen, though he still knelt before her.

"This I shall do, my lady, for the rest of my life, if need be. But tell me, how shall I know this king?"

"You shall know him with your heart. But you may better find him by knowing these things:

"His name shall be Cymrych, and he will bear that sword.
      His destiny will carry him many places.
            He shall fly above the earth,
            Even as he delves its depths.
            Wind and fire, earth and sea
            All shall fight for him,
      When it is time for him to claim his throne."

She finished speaking and appeared to grow very tired. Tristan sprang to his feet only to see her lie again in the case, her body reposed in the eternal stillness of death.

* * * * *

The mustering of the Scarlet Guard was a thing spectacular in sound and sight, fearful to behold. The citizens of Callidyrr scurried into the nearest buildings as the king's mercenaries assembled in the heart of the town.

Each of the four brigades of the guard gathered in its own quarter of the city and then marched toward the great, open square that stood below the towering majesty of Caer Callidyrr. All the towers of the castle streamed with pennants proclaiming the proud emblem of each of the dozen companies in the force.

First, three brigades of human mercenaries, battle-hardened soldiers, marched in tight formation into the square, standing at attention around three of the four sides.

Each member of these brigades, composed of three companies each, wore a cloak of blazing scarlet and a tall helmet plumed with crimson feathers. Their weapons were clean and gleamed in the midday sun.

Fierce, implacable warriors, these human mercenaries were feared along the length of the Sword Coast. No crime was too heinous, no murderous or rapine task too hateful, for the Scarlet Guard to take on.

But none of these three brigades could match, in might or in terror, the reputation of the fourth brigade.

King Carrathal stood upon the rampart of Caer Callidyrr with his close adviser, the wizard Cyndre, beside him. His pulse raced at the spectacle before him.

"Oh, I say! This is simply splendid! They look so . . ." His Majesty groped for the right word ". . . so military!"

"Indeed, sire," nodded the sorcerer. Cyndre was pleased at the sight as well, but did not reveal his emotions quite as openly as did his master.

"Hmmm, isn't there supposed to be one more?" King Carrathal was busy recounting the troops before them.

"I believe the ogre brigade is arriving soon, Your Majesty." The ground shook underfoot as the tromp of heavy footsteps pounded the street. There was no sign of any citizen of Callidyrr now, as there was no mistaking the source of that mighty cadence.

The ogre brigade marched as a long column into the square, thumping steadily to the place of honor before the castle.

The ogres stood at attention, but it was obvious that they were not particularly skilled at this, though they excelled at shuffling, spitting, grunting, and nose-picking. Each of the great brutes stood at least eight feet tall, with crooked, trunklike legs and a stocky, stooping body.

Their faces were bestial, with long foreheads that sloped down to beady, glaring eyes. Broad noses flared upward, revealing wide nostrils and even wider mouths. Wicked tusks extended from the corners of those mouths.

These brutal monsters came from every corner of the Realms, gathered and disciplined—barely—by the good pay of their human commanders. And in truth, ogres were well-suited to the needs of the guard. Huge, fearless fighters, they could crush any band of humans that dared to stand before them—and would as easily spit a child upon a spear as an opposing swordsman. The ogres relished the tasks of the guard, for killing and mayhem were their most basic desires. The missions of the brigade gave them an opportunity to do both.

"Somehow, I never realized that there were quite so many of them," said the king hesitantly. "They really make up quite a force, don't they?"

"Indeed, Your Majesty. They are an army mightier than any upon the Moonshaes, and they will do your bidding alone." The wizard smirked a little as he said it.

"We had better send them off, hadn't we?" blurted the king. "You do think they'll catch him, don't you?"

"I'm certain they will, Sire. The Prince of Corwell shall have a very short visit to Alaron. A very short visit indeed."

* * * * *

"Teacher, I'm frightened."

Robyn spoke quietly, not certain that Genna was awake. The Great Druid lay muffled in a down quilt, though the day was warm. Her steady breathing was her only sign of life.

"It's Acorn," Robyn continued, pulling her shawl more tightly across her shoulders at the vivid memories. As far as she knew, the stranger was still spellbound, standing stupidly beside the pond. Nevertheless, she had latched the door of the cottage when she entered, for she knew that the spell would eventually lose its potency.

Genna's eyes flickered open, and she turned to gaze intently at her pupil. Her gray hair, pulled back from her face, emphasized her severe expression. She struggled to sit up, and Robyn helped her, placing pillows behind her back.

"Evil!" she hissed. She stared at Robyn, but it seemed to her that the Great Druid actually looked right through her. "He is evil!" she said again. It was the most articulate statement she had made in many days.

"Acorn?" Robyn said. "But, I thought . . . Oh Genna, what should I do? Help me!"

This time the older woman looked at her niece with an intensity that made Robyn squirm. Genna coughed once, a dry, rasping sound, before she spoke again.

"You must kill him!"

* * * * *

Bhaal watched the Heart of Kazgoroth carefully, feeling its thrumming power. The shred of the Beast had begun its work. Soon, now, the task would be complete.

He took note of the feeble earthmagic of the druid and sneered. Her strength, and the might of her dying goddess, could not hope to stand against him, as he had demonstrated upon Alaron.

There, he had commanded his cleric to destroy the druids. Hobarth had used the ambitious wizard to help, even convincing Cyndre that the plan was the sorcerer's own idea. One by one, the druids of Alaron had died, drawn out by Hobarth's power, slain by magic or the cold steel of the assassin's blade. Their mutilated bodies had been used to pollute and defile the Moonwells from which they drew so much of their power.

That power was now broken forever. The next to fall would be the druids of Gwynneth, the keepers of Myrloch Vale.

❧ 6 ❧

Alaron

The sound of Canthus barking savagely brought Tristan back to his senses. Immediately he felt the tremors in the floor below him. He staggered forward, turning to run like a drunk from Queen Allisynn's tomb as the marble surface heaved and rocked. He charged down the short corridor and into the great hall beyond.

Canthus bounded before him, racing for a great double door leading to the courtyard. Daryth had just reached the door. Tristan saw that he now carried a sword.

"All I could find," he gasped as Tristan ran to his side, helping to pull open the huge portal. His eyes widened at the sight of the Sword of Cymrych Hugh, girded again at the prince's side, but the Calishite said nothing. The castle shook once more, sending them stumbling.

The door creaked open stubbornly. Tristan was about to run through the door when Daryth's voice halted him.

"Wait!" The Calishite probed the flagstones before them with his trident. The iron barbs clunked against the surface several times, and Tristan was startled by a sudden "click."

Two sections of floor gave way, swinging freely inward to reveal a long, dark shaft. Uneasily, the prince stepped back.

"Same kind of trap," the Calishite smiled ruefully. He stepped nimbly along the side of the pit. The prince jumped after him and made it through the door with no difficulty.

They found Pontswain where they had left him. The lord was sitting up, rubbing the bruised side of his face. "Where did you go?" he demanded. "Leaving me to—"

"Shut up!" barked the prince, then looked a bit sheepish. "Uh, thanks . . . you know, for helping me out in there."

The lord looked surprised but offered no argument. Instead he climbed unsteadily to his feet.

The castle was beginning to sink. Already water was pouring through the gate. They had left the outer portal down after entering, and the seawater now rushed into the courtyard through the wide opening. They stood upon the balcony outside the keep, five steps up from the courtyard itself, and watched the water slowly climb the stairs.

"There's no way we can fight the current through the gate," said Daryth. "We might as well wait until it comes over the walls and hope that we can float out. Here, fill this with air," said Daryth, handing each of them a leather sack. "This is how we'll float."

Skeptically, Tristan took the bag and blew a lungful of air into it. The bag barely puffed out. Again and again, he breathed enough air to fill the bag several times over.

"It has a leak," he said, looking quickly at the rising water.

Daryth blew into his bag. "That's what I thought at first. But they're holding all the air we've blown into them."

"How?" said Tristan, looking at the limp sack.

"These are magical bags. I found them in the castle treasure room. They will hold a lot more than their size would indicate. Now, keep blowing!"

Still doubtful, they nonetheless continued trying to inflate the bags. Slowly, Tristan's began to grow, and finally it was reasonably firm. Daryth took a length of twine from his beltpouch and lashed the three sacks together, tightening the line about the mouths of the bags.

In another minute the water had reached the level of the balcony. Soon they stood waist-deep in water.

The bags rose beside them as the water lifted them off the ground, and Tristan was surprised at how bouyant they were. Soon the men were carried from their feet, but they floated easily into the courtyard. They were even able to support Canthus with their makeshift floats.

The water inside the courtyard was within six feet of the top of the wall when seawater poured over the ramparts. Crushing waves now roiled around them, threatening to tear the bags from their grip. Desperately holding on, Tristan tried to see if Canthus was still with them, but he lost sight of everything but the bag under his hands and the water. As more of the sea poured into the courtyard, the surface slowly calmed, and Tristan was relieved to see that Canthus, Daryth, and Pontswain were still hanging on. In no time, they were floating easily again.

"Still no sign of a sail," said Daryth. "I guess this puts us about where we were this morning."

"Not exactly," said Tristan. "I've got the Sword of Cymrych Hugh again!"

He debated telling them of the prophecy of the dead queen. But a look at Pontswain's suspicious face told him he should not. Perhaps later he would tell Daryth.

* * * * *

"Master, we must discuss a problem."

"Must we discuss it now, Kryphon? I am very tired. His Majesty was most petulant today."

Cyndre turned from the mirror to regard Kryphon. The master of the council had been gazing at an undersea setting. Kryphon watched the greenish image of a pale, luminescent city slowly fade from sight. He saw several fishlike figures, carrying weapons, drift lazily past the mirror before the picture disappeared.

"It could have the gravest consequences for us all, master." Kryphon spoke in a rush. "Alexei has been disloyal."

"You would condemn a brother wizard, Kryphon? I am surprised at you."

"The charge is justified! He tried to convince Doric that you have been manipulated by the cleric. Fortunately, she spoke to me immediately after the discussion. I wasted no time in seeking you!"

"Are you certain of this? Is Doric telling the truth?"

Kryphon nodded vigorously. "I placed her under a charm spell as she spoke, and she told me the truth. She would have babbled all night if I hadn't finally put her to sleep."

Cyndre tapped his chin in thought. "You have done well," he said at last. "I fear our comrade Alexei is lost to us. We can but see that his loss causes us no damage."

"Is Razfallow the solution?"

"No, Kryphon. I have other plans for the assassin. But we

can afford to be patient in the matter of Alexei. We shall wait. He will do nothing for some time. Alexei is not a man of action. But our time will come. When the cleric returns from his mission to Gwynneth, he will find Alexei waiting for him, ready to offer his blood as the tears of Bhaal."

*   *   *   *   *

Robyn walked hesitantly toward the pond. She had replaced her torn gown with a leather jerkin. "I can't kill him!" she repeated to herself. For once, her teacher had asked her to do something that she could not reconcile with her faith. Or was this some kind of test? Did Genna seek to examine her devotion to the goddess, her obedience? "I don't care!" she told herself angrily. "I can't kill him!"

But neither could she allow Acorn to remain in the grove. No other possibility even entered her mind. The man's look of stark madness—his clutching, greedy hands—stuck vividly in her memory and sent a shiver down her spine. Fortunately, her druid spell had been able to stop him.

She made up her mind to expel him from the grove, sending him away with a command never to return. It was not what her teacher had commanded her to do, but she could not bring herself to slay him. Evil, Genna had called him—and he was. Still, Robyn felt that he was not entirely responsible for his actions.

She crossed the garden and moved among the great oaks, nearing the pond. As she passed the place where she had been tearing up the vines weeks earlier, she noticed that the stout stick she had used to pry the vines now lay beside the sturdy trunk. Feeling vaguely uneasy, she picked it up.

She wished for Tristan's presence with a sudden, surprising intensity. The prince, she knew, would have had no difficulty enforcing Gennas' order.

She emerged from the oaks, expecting to see Acorn still frozen upon the riverbank. But the stranger was gone.

Her uneasiness grew into worry as she stepped from between the huge trees. She moved carefully along the grassy bank, looking at the ground for signs of his departure. The riverbank here was a narrow strip of field, bordered by the river on one side and thick undergrowth on the other. The river was about forty feet wide and three feet deep. Its crystalline waters, racing over colorful stones, formed the southern border of the Great Druid's grove.

Suddenly she heard movement in the undergrowth and whirled to see Acorn lunging toward her with a crazed gleam in his eyes. He cackled unintelligibly as he moved far faster than his feeble appearance suggested possible.

She lifted the stick and chanted the single word again. "Stop!"

Acorn did stop, but not from any effect of her spell. Instead, the madman stomped his feet and howled with laughter. Then he became very quiet, peering at Robyn with intense concentration.

His look was the most frightening thing she had ever seen.

When he began to mumble words that sounded like spell-casting, her fright turned to sheer terror. Her mouth fell open. But Acorn couldn't cast spells—or could he? What did his words mean?

And then she understood that he commanded druidic magic, as upon Acorn's final word, a buzzing swarm of insects hummed from his hand to cluster about her on the riverbank. Robyn felt a fiery stinger lash into her cheek as more of the creatures landed upon her, seeking every patch of exposed skin. The sound of the swarm was a droning so loud that it seemed certain to drive her mad.

She suppressed an urge to scream—she dared not open her mouth. Instead she turned to run awkwardly to the stream. Her eyes were tightly shut as she flung herself headlong into the cool water. She forced herself to stay underwater, swimming downstream for as long as she could hold her breath. When she finally burst to the surface, she saw that the mass of insects was gradually swarming across the river, out of the Great Druid's grove. The pain from her stings slowly subsided, but her skin still burned.

A small portion of the swarm broke toward her as she emerged from the water, but she cast a simple spell of protection, making a rapid gesture about herself. The wasps stormed forward angrily, but then buzzed in a circle around her, unable to close through the magical barrier she had raised against them.

Acorn was already looking for her, giggling and staggering along the riverbank. Robyn splashed toward shore, hoping to get out of the water before he reached her.

The feeble-minded wildman paused again, and again Robyn felt that intense concentration that could only mean he was preparing to cast a spell. Crawling onto the riverbank, soaking wet and gasping, she felt very vulnerable.

She grabbed a root to pull herself up, and suddenly it squirmed in her grasp. The end of the root lashed upward, growing eyes and long fangs. She jerked back just before the undoubtedly venomous spell-cast snake struck. The snake's fangs embedded themselves in the soft loam as she snatched her hand away.

More snakes slithered toward her from a tangle that had, before Acorn's spell, contained only dry sticks. She sensed the serpents closing in from all sides. She paused, pulling a tiny sprig of mistletoe from her belt, and chanted a few words very softly as she crushed the plant to dust. She felt the aura surround her, and she knew that she had become completely invisible to the snakes and to all other animals of the natural world. The creatures writhed past, and her stomach knotted as she saw several forked tongues flick forth to seek her.

The madman still saw the young druid before him, but he also saw that the snakes could not find her. His carefully marshalled discipline—that self control that had allowed him to recall powers he had long kept buried—began to crumble under the frustration of the thwarted attacks.

Abruptly, he howled in rage and charged toward Robyn, his fingers outstretched, clutching for her throat. His howl gave way to an equally inarticulate cackle as he reached her.

Robyn saw the man charge, and she seized a stout stick with both hands. Raising it high, she swung it like an axe at the madman. She had never hit anything so hard in her life!

She felt the shock of his broken neck travel through the stick to her wrists and arms. He dropped without a sound, his head drooping grotesquely over his right shoulder.

Robyn's whole body shook. She staggered backward and sat down heavily, feeling sick. Acorn's eyes stared at her from his unnaturally bent head, and she watched them slowly grow dull.

But the power of the goddess had flowed through her, and from her, and her own strength had not been expended. Her shaking stopped, and she walked over to the body.

Acorn was unquestionably dead. His skin was already pale, and his head lay at that absurd angle. Still she knelt and listened for breathing, felt for a pulse. He was dead.

Then she noticed his pouch.

She had forgotten about the tattered wrap and its treasured contents in the time Acorn had been with her. But now she vividly recalled his fear when she had reached for it. Robyn reached for the ragged sack again and pulled the drawstring free. She hefted the thing, which seemed to contain a fist-size rock. Turning it upside down, she shook it.

A black rock fell beside her knee. It was rounded and smooth, oddly shaped. It looked like a carving of a vaguely human heart that some craftsman had rendered from a piece of hard coal. It lay several inches from her, but she felt its warmth even through her leather breeches. The rock was surprisingly large for its weight. Its density was more like soft pine than stone.

She tried to look away from the stone and found that she could not. Reluctantly, yet at the same time feeling a tingling excitement, she reached for it. Her fingers finally reached the smooth ebony surface . . .

. . . and her world exploded into black.

*   *   *   *   *

Newt meandered through the pines, thoroughly bored. He buzzed around looking for something, anything, to catch his interest. The air in the woods was thick and heavy, and lethargy contributed to his boredom.

His path took him back to the grove, but he was in no particular hurry. Without an urgent reason, the faerie dragon could not possibly travel in a straight line, and so his arrival could be anywhere from hours to days away.

He reached the shore of a broad pond, hovering silently with a steady fluttering of his gossamer wings. Slowly he settled onto a wide pine bough, looking around the shore. Such watering places, the dragon had discovered, were likely to yield his quarry.

Indeed, he soon saw a tiny fawn, staring into the clear water on the other side of the pond. Instantly, Newt crouched, his tail arrowing straight behind him. When he was quite certain of achieving surprise, he acted.

He cast a simple illusion spell upon the reflection of the young deer. The unfortunate creature found itself looking at a purple-furred, fang-toothed horror that appeared to lunge out of the water, gaping maw extended. With a sharp squeal of terror, the fawn tumbled backward in a rolling bundle of gangly legs.

"Hee hee hee!" Newt squealed as the little creature finally stumbled to its feet and sprinted awkwardly into the woods. "I can't stand it!" he shrieked. He nearly lost his grip as he slipped to hang below the branch, supporting himself with his two left legs. Tears clouded his vision as he scrambled back atop the bough.

"Oh, but that was marvelous!" he boasted to the forest at large. "Nothing like a good joke to move a day along!"

He decided that he must share this wonderful story with Robyn. She would cluck disapprovingly at his prank—she always did when a cute and helpless animal was involved— but Newt suspected that, deep down, she would be amused. And he simply had to tell somebody!

Springing into the air, the faerie dragon beat his wings so hard that they hummed. He zipped like an arrow across the pond and darted into the forest on the far side. Weaving among the tree tops, he raced toward Genna's grove.

But when he reached the stream at the southern edge of the grove, he slowed. Something did not look right.

Newt gasped when he saw the bodies on the ground and quickly buzzed down to light upon Robyn's back. With relief, he felt her breathing beneath him, albeit slowly. The man, he saw with little surprise and no regret, was dead.

"Oh, Robyn, wake up!" he pleaded, leaping to the ground and gently nudging her shoulder. "Please! It's me, Newt! What should I do?"

He shook his tiny head frantically, looking around for some answer to his question, when he spied the black rock at Robyn's side. Something about the stone seemed unnatural, repulsive. His nimble brain quickly connected the rock to his friend's unconsciousness.

Grasping the offending stone in both his forepaws, he leaped into the air. With the most strenuous thrumming of his wings, he climbed, feeling like a lumbering condor. Slowly he flew across the stream, away from the grove of the Great Druid. After he had gone a mile or so, he dropped the stone in the woods and raced back to Robyn's side.

With relief, he saw that she had already begun to stir.

* * * * *

"A sail! Tristan, a sail!"

The prince jerked from his slumber. He raised his head from the air bladder and shook it to clear the cobwebs. Blinking the saltwater from his eyes, he followed Daryth's pointing finger.

"I see it! It's coming right toward us!"

"Things are starting to look up," grinned the Calishite.

"Call them," croaked Pontswain, hope lighting his eyes.

"Too far," said Daryth. "But they're coming right at us."

The little vessel indeed skipped closer. It had a single mast with a sail colored in a broad rainbow pattern. The prow was high, so they could not see the interior of the craft. As it neared them, however, they heard strains of a song sung in a clear, female voice.

"I knew a merry widow, to her neighbors quite demure,
But all the lads that saw her said,
The lady's far from pure.
Now I can't say the lads are right
(but I can't say they're wrong)
And I know that merry widow couldn't—

"And what's this?" The song was abruptly interrupted as a beaming, weatherbeaten face peered suddenly over the bow at them. "Three drowned rats—and some flotsam!"

Tristan's greeting died in his mouth, so astonished was he by the question and answer. The speaker was a stout woman, perhaps forty years of age. Her round face was split by a smile as wide as the sea. A garish hat, festooned with grapes and apples and huge flowers, sat astride her head, sagging nearly to her shoulders.

"Well, come aboard before I sail on by!" she cried, suddenly ducking out of sight.

But then a rope snaked into the air, splashing into the water between them, and each of them grabbed it as the boat passed only a few feet away. Tristan saw that it was a craft about twenty-five feet long, low of beam, but with sleek lines and an eager, seaworthy look.

They hauled on the rope as the boat's lone occupant hoisted the sail and the slim craft drifted slowly to a stop. The woman had a lute strung across her back, and an assortment of canvas bags had been thrown into the hull.

She reached down with a large red hand and pulled Tristan from the water. The prince no sooner flopped into the bottom of the boat than Canthus, Pontswain, and then Daryth, fell in beside him.

"The name's Tavish!" said their hostess, standing with her hands upon her hips as she scrutinized her passengers. She was shorter than Tristan, though she certainly weighed as much. Her face was pretty in a solid, farmwife sort of way. It was impossible not to be cheered while in the range of that beaming smile.

Her face grew thoughtful as she took in the sword at Tristan's side. Self-consciously, he looked at the plain leather hilt, the worn scabbard that had rotted away to reveal some of the glistening silver blade and its ancient runes. Tavish looked back to his face.

"And, judging by your weapon," she said, "I'm guessin' that you'll be the Prince of Corwell!"

*   *   *   *   *

Hobarth moved at a steady plod through the meadows and forests of Myrloch Vale. He was impervious to the beauty around him, interested only in drawing closer to the grove of the Great Druid. There, his god had told him, he would find the young druid. And Bhaal was never wrong.

It never occurred to the huge cleric that he would have any difficulty removing Robyn from the care of her teacher. Hobarth had used his powers against druids before, and their feeble nature magic had proven to be no match for the aroused might of Bhaal. Indeed, when allied with the Council of Seven, the power of Bhaal had been sufficient to drive the druids from Alaron.

True, these woods seemed more eternal than the forests that still remained upon Alaron. But he shrugged off the notion that druid magic was a force to be reckoned with.

He began to sense the nearness of his destination, and with it a powerful, arcane calling. Something was in the woods to his side. It radiated a sense of cool evil that the cleric found very pleasant, even exhilarating. He stopped for a moment, looking curiously into the brush. Whatever it was, the source of the calling struck a highly responsive chord in the cleric's breast. He was unable to ignore it.

Hobarth thrashed his way into the clump of bushes, pushing brambles and briars aside. He could tell that he neared the source of the calling, but that only made his desire to reach it stronger.

Suddenly he saw it, lying at the foot of a dead oak tree. A glistening black rock lay upon the ground. It attracted him strangely. Hobarth stepped forward and picked up the object. It felt very warm and smooth in his hand, as if it belonged there. Amused, the cleric hefted the object, tossing it from one hand to the other and back. Smiling, he turned back toward the grove and continued his march.

Hobarth was not attuned to nature and took no notice of the fact that all of the plant life within fifteen feet of the stone was withered and dead.

In another hour he arrived at the bank of a small stream. Somehow, he knew that this was the border to the Great Druid's grove. As he stepped into the stream, intending to wade across it, a sudden blow smashed his body and knocked him back to the shore. Springing to his feet, the cleric peered around, seeking his assailant.

But he saw nothing. More slowly, he reached forward and touched the invisible barrier he had struck. It seemed to run along the shore of the stream and was solid as iron. Cursing, he considered this evidence of druidic might. He watched a small bird dart across the stream and saw that it was unaffected by the barrier. But when Hobarth reached forward, the invisible wall stopped him cold.

He chanted a short phrase, and magic suffused his body. He rose slowly from the ground and floated twenty feet up in the air, to discover that the curtain of protection extended up at least that high. He did not want to go higher, for that would have carried him above the treetops and he did not wish to be observed.

Frustrated, Hobarth lowered himself to the ground and stalked along the shore of the stream. He was not used to being thwarted, and rage built within him. This crude druidic protection was certainly a nuisance! He wondered if a truly stunning display of Bhaal's power might blow it away, but he decided to postpone experimentation. Such a spell would surely call attention to himself.

He heard voices before him. Quickly, he dropped into the underbrush and carefully moved forward, using the shadows of the woods to advance around a bend in the stream. There before him he saw his quarry.

The druid he sought knelt beside the stream, splashing water into her face. One of the pesky little dragons common to the Moonshaes was with her, hovering about like a worried nursemaid. Elated, Hobarth considered his options, and as he did his elation faded.

How was he to get her out of the grove when he could not enter it? He considered and discarded several simple options. He could not expect to charm the woman from the grove with magic. The druid, he sensed, would be very resistant to his spells upon the sacred ground of her teacher's grove. And he, or rather, Bhaal, wanted her alive; her blood must come fresh to the altar of his god. Thus, he could not use a baneful spell to kill her and another to lift her body out. No, he would need to use a more subtle tactic.

Hobarth absently stroked the black rock in his hand. His beady eyes gleamed from within their deep pouches of fat as he looked around for a suggestion.

Then he saw the body behind the druid, and an idea slowly formed in his brain. Yes, he smiled to himself. That body will do quite nicely. Praying reverently to his god, Hobarth concentrated on the corpse in the field. The young druid's back was to the body, as she once again knelt to splash her face. And then the sinister might of Bhaal—or was it the potent evil of the black rock?—flowed from the cleric, unnoticed by Robyn, to the still form.

She was still kneeling as the body began to move.

* * * * *

"So you want to see the big city?" said Tavish, chuckling.

"Yes," explained Tristan, sticking to the story he had developed. "I've never even seen the island of Alaron. They say it's rather unlike Gwynneth—has more farms and people. And the city of Callidyrr, and Caer Callidyrr itself—I want to see the most splendid palace of the Ffolk."

For a moment Tavish almost looked sad. "They are splendid works, indeed, but there is a way of looking at the splendor of your own kingdom—the untamed forests, the rocky highlands—that makes the wonders of Callidyrr pale by comparison. I prefer the earthiness of Corwell, myself."

"Do you travel the Isles much?" asked Daryth.

"Why, yes. Didn't I tell you I'm a bard?"

"No, you didn't," replied the prince. He was not surprised.

"Indeed I am. Not that I've visited Corwell recently—it's been a decade or more, I should say. I've spent a lot of time on Moray recently. Now there's a sad story. . . ."

"What do you mean by that?" asked the prince.

"The king and several of his loyal lords have all been murdered in the past year. No one seems to know who's behind it; there's no lord trying to step into the vacancy. And who would want to?"

"Indeed," said Pontswain. "Moray has always seemed a bleak and barren land. Nothing but sheep and tundra." But the lord sneaked a sideways glance of alarm at Tristan. The prince felt a cold knife snake into his bowels at the news.

"There's a lot more to it than that," said the bard firmly. "But now the land is without a leader, and the mystery is without an answer. It makes for lots of suspicions and arguments."

Tavish paused, looking them over. "The tales out of Snowdown are no better," she continued. "The king disappeared on a hunting trip and has not been heard from since. No one's in charge—the whole kingdom's in an uproar!"

Tristan digested the information with heightened interest. Moray was another of the lands of the Ffolk, nominally under the rule of the High King. And there, as on Corwell, the king had been slain by mysterious assassins, while the last king of the Ffolk—save the High King himself—was missing from Snowdown.

"I'm on my way back home to Alaron," continued Tavish. "Though the prospect doesn't bring the joy it once did."

"Why not?"

Tavish sighed. "There, too, are troubles. The High King seems to fret about a thousand imagined challenges to his throne. Who would imagine that such a worrier would come to wear the crown of the Isles? More than one good and true lord has been locked in the royal dungeon, his lands confiscated simply because the king imagined some cause to fear him."

The bard steered silently for a while as the companions ate and rested. Tristan felt strength seeping back into his weary muscles, but his mind remained agitated. Tavish's information, coupled with the prophecy, created strong doubts in his mind about the High King. When they reached Caer Callidyrr itself, what could they say to a man who feared treachery from every quarter?

"Land!" cried Daryth, spotting a stretch of green on the eastern horizon.

"Take a look at Alaron, fellows!" laughed Tavish. "We'll be lashed to the dock by nightfall!"

The prince's mood of foreboding vanished. "It can't be too soon for me," he remarked with a true sigh of relief.

"I recommend The Diving Dolphin—fine food, good drink, and wonderful music—I'll be there myself, you know."

The men laughed and promised to see the bard at the inn. By this time they were passing the breakwater, and Tristan stood in the prow, eager to get his first look at the island of Alaron. The land was green and pastoral, dotted with white farms and neat stone fences.

The town of Llewellyn was the biggest community Tristan had ever seen. His first impression was of all-encompassing whiteness. Stone walls, plastered buildings, wooden houses—all were painted white. Tavish told him that the town was home to nearly five thousand people.

The sense of wonder remained with him as they glided up to a smooth stone quay. Tavish sprang to the shore, pulling the vessel tightly against the stout wooden bumpers. The passengers climbed out and looked around. Trying hard not to stare, Tristan was embarrassed by his lack of traveling experience. Everything seemed so new!

The dockside at Llewellyn consisted of a large, parklike area of grass, surrounded by a multitude of shops. Cool alehouses quickly awakened Tristan's thirst. He saw vendors of apples, cherries, and more exotic fruits hawking their wares. Hot meat sizzled on a small grill in one place. He saw beads and baubles, crystal goblets, and steel weapons on display in a variety of small, glass-fronted shops. Narrow streets lined with two-story buildings led to the south, north, and east. Several dozen pedestrians, a few horses, and a half-dozen two-wheeled carts were in motion.

"The Dolphin is that way," said Tavish, pointing up the street that led away from the sea. "Go on and settle in. I'll be there before long."

So saying, the bard turned back to her boat. She uttered a single word—Tristan couldn't quite hear what she said—and for a moment it looked as though she had destroyed the vessel. The keel of the boat bent double, as the bow and stern rose to meet each other. The craft, thus raised, did not sink, but instead the raised fore and aft sections folded downward again to halve the boat once more in size. Tavish now pulled the thing— it looked like a wide board, about eight feet long—from the water. It continued to fold up on the shore until it had reduced itself to a box that would have strained to hold a pair of heavy boots.

"See you in a little while!" she called, striding purposefully toward the northern avenue.

"There's more to the lady than meets the eye," mused Daryth, staring after the bard. "I'm glad we'll see her again."

"Let's find that inn and get something to drink, then," said the prince. "I'm thirsty!"

"I shouldn't doubt it," said Pontswain sarcastically. "Although a hot meal would do me good."

The streets of Llewellyn were crowded, at least by Corwellian standards, but the Ffolk they passed seemed unusually quiet. There was none of the friendly banter that the prince was used to.

The Diving Dolphin stood a short distance from the park. The whitewashed facade was weatherbeaten and faded, and the wide steps leading up to the front door showed signs of many repairs.

"No dogs," grunted a huge, black-bearded man as Tristan started through the door. The fellow stood in the shadows but moved forward quickly to block the entrance.

The prince stopped, annoyed. Daryth spoke before Tristan had a chance to rebuke the man, however.

"He'll wait out here for us. Down, Canthus!" The houndmaster pointed to a corner of the wide porch, and Canthus walked to it, flopping heavily onto his belly. He lay his head upon his forepaws and did not move.

The man stepped aside, and Daryth prodded the prince through the door. Tristan turned upon his friend as soon as they had entered the huge inn.

"What did you do that for? He had no right—"

"Actually, it's the custom in most places," said the Calishite. "Corwell is the only place I've lived where dogs are treated as well as people."

Tristan felt sick. His naiveté had almost caused him to make a fool of himself! Some future king he was!

"Don't worry about it," laughed Daryth. "You've got me along to look after you! Now, let's get something to eat."

* * * * *

The Seven sat about their wide table again. Six black hoods rose in fascination, absorbing the words that came from the seventh—the wizard in the center of the group.

"The assassin will be here shortly. We shall give him his task, and the last of the heroes among the Ffolk shall presently be eliminated. Then we shall be able to direct our energies to more productive tasks, such as bending the other lands to the will of our liege." The last word, thick with irony, lay heavily in the air after he spoke.

Alexei, seated to Cyndre's right, sat quietly. He watched his master through narrowed eyes, thinking deeply.

How much he hated Cyndre! How he craved the power

that the master selfishly kept for himself by doling out small tastes of it to those mages who pleased him.

He looked beyond, to Kryphon, and his hatred grew, threatening to choke him. The worm! He was certain that Kryphon tried to manipulate the master in an effort to unseat Alexei himself from his place at Cyndre's right hand. Alexei daydreamed of a time when he would watch them both squirm, rot, and die.

But Doric. The slender woman just beyond Kryphon would be his again—as she had once been and as she was meant to be. The thought of Kryphon's pleasure as he gratified his lust upon the woman that was Alexei's by right of conquest fueled the flames of jealousy into a white heat.

The other three—Talraw, Wertam, and Karianow—were the weaklings of the council. Alexei was certain that the three mages, barely beyond their apprenticeship, would follow the strongest leader. His heart pounded at the thought of his revenge, of the pain and humiliation he would inflict upon his former master.

"Alexei?" The soft voice called him back to reality.

"Master?" The word almost caught in his throat.

Cyndre turned his head slightly, fixing his assistant with a gaze of cool interest. "Alexei, you have raised many questions—about the cleric, about my judgement. Why? Do you doubt my abilities?"

The blood drained slowly from Alexei's face, and a knot of panic built in his stomach. No! It was too soon—he was not ready yet! He looked into Cyndre's eyes—pools of pale blue, as harsh as the arctic sky—and he could not answer. He struggled to speak, but no words came forth.

"Can you give me some reassurances, Alexei? Some proof of your trustworthiness?"

He knows. The knowledge burned Alexei's face, and he could speak no reply. The truth would doom him, and he could summon no lie to his lips.

"Very well," said Cyndre, his voice dripping with regret.

The wizard gestured, and streams of colored lights rushed from his fingertips to swirl about the recalcitrant lieutenant. Alexei's hood flew back, his stark features outlined in terror. The mage was tall and thin, but the eerie shadows from the spell gave his face a gaunt, emaciated look. His mouth opened in a soundless scream—or perhaps the noise he made was masked from the council by the filtering curtain of lights.

Alexei's long, thin hands clasped the arms of his chair, but already his image grew blurry. In moments he had faded from view, banished, the other wizards knew, to a lonely imprisonment in a place known only to the master.

* * * * *

A few hours later, the assassin and his band dashed through the courtyards of Caer Callidyrr on galloping black steeds. Racing through the night, they thundered along the streets of the town and soon disappeared along the King's Road. They rode to the south.

* * * * *

Chauntea heard Bhaal's challenge and saw the game of the evil god. She briefly pondered her response. The Moonshaes were a small realm, unimportant in the vast scale of her domains. Were they worth the trouble of a conflict?

Yet the isles had shown some promise. The people there, the Ffolk, were a good people—strong and devout in their own way. It saddened her to think of them falling under the thrall of Bhaal's evil.

And too, the acts of the evil god needed a counter, or they would grow too powerful and arrogant for the safety of all the planes. Since Bhaal had chosen the Moonshaes for his game, and Chauntea, alone among the gods of good, had power there, should she not resist him?

Chauntea, like Bhaal, had clerics among the Ffolk. Though perhaps not as powerful—and certainly not as deadly—as the minions of Bhaal, her clerics had skills of their own: healing, beneficial powers.

Perhaps one of them could aid the players in this game. She selected several of her worshippers, not certain what the future would hold. Perhaps one of them might have the chance to do her bidding.

Chauntea made her wishes known to these clerics in the guise of a dream.

❦ 7 ❦

The Scarlet Guard

Robyn took a deep breath and felt her body relax as she exhaled. She felt weak but immeasurably better than she had upon first awakening. Whatever the nature of Acorn's black rock, it had been far mightier than her ability to protect herself. Her fingers were blistered and hot, though the damage did not look permanent. She splashed one more handful of cool water against her face.

She stood up and stretched slowly, trying to shake off a sense of guilt over Acorn's death. She had had no choice! Angrily, she wondered about the sudden transformation. Certainly, he had made her nervous before, but what had driven him to attack? Why, when she would have spared him, had he been driven by such bloodlust? And a deeper, even more frightening question arose within her: How had he come to learn druid magic?

"What did you do with that thing—that rock?" she asked Newt, who buzzed worriedly at her shoulder.

"Oh, that awful stone! I hated it, and I took it away from here. It was no good for you! I hope you're not mad at me—I only wanted to help!" The little dragon shivered at the memory of the rock, peering hopefully at Robyn.

"No, you did the right thing," she said reassuringly. "Poor Newt. You worry too much, like an old nursemaid."

"Well, I just wanted to see you awake again! And I must say, getting rid of that nasty fellow doesn't bother me at all. Maybe it should, but it doesn't. I think we're all better off with him lying dead over—ack!" Newt squealed in terror and zipped past Robyn, hovering over the stream and pointing speechlessly over her shoulder.

Robyn spun around and thought immediately that her senses had deserted her. The stranger was dead—she knew this, for she had checked carefully. So what was this thing lurching toward her?

The body was only ten feet away, shuffling forward with an awkward gait. The neck was still broken, for the head hung grotesquely over its shoulder. A swollen black tongue extended from its gaping mouth, and the two eyes were dull and glazed, though still open.

But the hands clutched for her eagerly, each finger like a living snake, thirsting for her blood. The thing took another step forward, and another, as she stood transfixed, too shocked even to scream.

"Run!" Newt cried. Somehow, the little dragon's warning restored her self-control and she turned and sprinted down the riverbank.

Gasping and shaking with fear, she turned to look. It came ahead slowly, shuffling awkwardly but steadily toward her. She wanted to cry out her fear, but she bit her tongue and used her mind. How could she fight this thing that was already dead?

"Run, Robyn!" cried Newt, buzzing in a tight circle around her. He darted forward to hover in the air between her and the animated corpse, wringing his forepaws in agitation.

"No, Newt!" she shouted, seeing by his concentration that he was preparing to cast a spell.

Newt's magic, although unpredictable, had saved her from bloodthirsty enemies before, but she feared it would be of little use against this nightmare.

Multicolored flames exploded from the ground in front of the shambling figure, quickly surrounding it in a ring of fire that covered the spectrum from bright red to deep purple. The corpse hesitated, but only for a moment, and Robyn knew that it would not be daunted by Newt's illusion.

The body lurched through the curtain of fire, its fingers still twitching eagerly. Robyn stumbled backward, desperately trying to think of something—anything—to stop the unnatural attack. She looked around for a stick or a rock, but the field mocked her with wildflowers.

Sprinting again, she dashed away from the thing, stopping to gasp for breath at the edge of the forest. Tireless, it marched forward.

Trying to slow her breathing, Robyn marshalled her faith in her goddess. She felt the body of the goddess under her feet. Carefully, she pulled a leaf of mistletoe from her waist. She let the leaf spiral lazily into the breeze as she chanted one of her most powerful spells.

Plants erupted from the ground around Acorn's body. Shoots of grass and thick-leafed weeds curled upward, clasping toward the undead thing.

But the plants withered and curled away as they made contact with the creature, falling to either side and opening an unobstructed path to Robyn. Once again, she turned to flee, darting underneath the low limbs of a tree behind her. In her haste, she did not duck low enough, and pain flashed through her skull as she cracked it against the heavy bough.

Dazed, she staggered against the tree, squinting through blurry eyes at the monster only ten feet away. She watched as Newt swooped into the thing's face, and she saw the dead man's hand slash through the air with stunning speed. With a low squeak, the faerie dragon flopped to the ground.

Robyn tried to run, but the encircling branches of the tree cornered her. The monster moved in, and she crouched like a cat, determined to fight to the last with her bare hands.

Suddenly a shape moved behind the creature, and Robyn heard a loud growl. The body lurched to the side, half turning, and now she saw a brown form, great teeth bared, swat the creature's outstretched arm. The limb snapped loudly and dropped to the monster's side.

Robyn watched Grunt smash the monster to its knees with a blow to the hip and then stretch it upon the ground with a vicious cut to the already broken neck. She watched as the bear seized the corpse in his powerful jaws, shaking the thing like a rag doll before tossing the body casually to the ground and tearing at it again with his long, curved claws. The corpse stopped moving, but Grunt savaged it further, tearing pieces away and tossing them aside until the corpse was unrecognizable as a human body.

Limply, Robyn stumbled to the bear and leaned against his broad flank, trying to draw strength from him. Her shock gradually gave way to uncomprehending terror. Finally, for the first time in many years, she sobbed uncontrollably.

* * * * *

Hobarth crouched among the branches of a thick bush, ignoring the thorns that pricked him. He dared not move for fear of alerting the druid across the stream.

He had watched her battle the zombie. Although disappointed with the outcome, he had other plans. He squeezed the black rock in excitement, his eyes never leaving the woman. The stone, like the heart of evil that it was, seemed to answer his pressure with a warm caress of its own. He watched Robyn stumble weakly from the clearing, leaning against the bear, until she disappeared from his sight.

The cleric remembered his surprise as he had cast the spell to animate the corpse. Such a spell normally called for the discipline of Hobarth's faith, coupled with the might of Bhaal. Once cast, the spell would vanish from Hobarth's memory until a suitable period of praying to his deity would restore it to him.

But somehow the black heart had changed that. The power to raise the corpse had arisen from the stone, not from Hobarth. The memory of the spell remained with him. He felt that he could immediately recruit another corpse from the dead—in fact, as many bodies as he could find.

Hobarth squirmed from his position in the bush, his mind alight with possibilities. Bodies—hundreds of them, raised into an army of undead! He needed bodies! The cleric was unaware of Bhaal feeding him these images. He knew only that he wanted such an army under his control.

Common sense told Hobarth to look for bodies at the site of a battlefield. He was not a historian, but he knew a little local history. A year earlier a battle had been fought not many day's march from here.

Quickly, eagerly, the great cleric turned his steps back toward the south. He would call upon the wisdom of his god to show him the exact route, but he knew that this was the general direction to Freeman's Down.

* * * * *

Genna opened her eyes and studied Robyn with a look of great tenderness and understanding that the pupil had not seen for many weeks. She rose to her feet, and the young woman saw again the sturdy muscle of the stout druid's body. Trying to banish her lingering sense of horror, she embraced Genna in relief. The cottage door was securely bolted behind her, and Grunt sat just outside. But even the cozy fire in the stove and the lace curtains filtering the afternoon sunlight could not entirely soothe her.

"What could it have been?" she asked Genna.

"A creature animated from death—a zombie," Genna explained. "But how it came to be here I cannot imagine."

"I felt so helpless," Robyn said. "My magic was useless!"

"The powers of the druid are the powers of life and growth. We have no power over death or death's creatures."

Genna looked warily across the grove, probing the waters of the pond and the flowers of the garden with her eyes. "Whatever the source of this abomination," she said, "we must take great care that it does not happen again. The results could be disastrous."

* * * * *

"And it's genuine crystal from the famed glasskilns of Thay. Note the detail, the colors, and the shapes!"

The old sailor leaned in, burping discreetly, to examine the shining object. The diminutive salesman pressed his pitch. "This one has come thousands of miles by galley across the Sea of Fallen Stars, by camel across Anauroch, the Great Desert. It's passed through the hands of pirates and bandits and traders. Why, it's certain to be the only one in the Moonshaes—perhaps along the whole Sword Coast!"

"Crystal of Thay, huh?" mumbled the sailor, intrigued in spite of himself. He looked through bleary eyes at the little fellow who held the glass ball in his hand. A halfling, he was, one of the little folk, half the size of man.

"Why'd you bring it to Llewellyn?" he asked suspiciously.

"A shrewd fellow you are, to be sure," said the halfling with a conspiratorial wink. "To tell you the truth, I had no intention of stopping in Llewellyn, much less selling the crystal. I've become quite attached to it, you know." The halfling, his large brown eyes sliding furtively around the room, leaned in close.

"I had a little trouble up in Callidyrr. I have to get off the island in a hurry. The money'll make that possible."

"Who are you? Where is your home?"

"The name is Pawldo, of Lowhill," said the halfling easily. "I hail from Corwell. Oh, it's nothing serious that has me in a hurry to leave. It involves, if you must know, a young lady."

The sailor chortled knowingly and went back to examining the bright crystal sphere.

"Five gold, eh?" the old sailor mumbled, turning the fascinating sphere in all directions, watching it catch the light from a nearby lantern, diffusing it into a million colors and patterns. He had just been paid, and though the price represented half a season's salary, the object was like nothing he had ever seen before. "I'll take it!"

"A fine deal. I'm grieved to part with it, but the crystal's yours," said the halfling in a voice that almost dripped with regret. The sailor fumbled across the coins and lurched unsteadily to his feet. He clutched the sphere covetously to his breast and staggered out into the street, looking to show off the object to his mates.

Pawldo counted the money, biting a slightly tarnished coin to satisfy himself that it was indeed gold, and smiled to himself. He hoisted the duffel bag he had placed under the table, careful not to jostle its contents. It contained several dozen more of the crystals, each of which he would sell as the only one of its type. He worked his way through a crowd and climbed to a stool, carefully placing a silver piece upon the bar. He would not pay with gold—the little folk had long ago learned to conceal their wealth around humans, particularly drunk and disreputable ones.

This tavern was filled with both types. The Old Sailor was an ancient establishment in one of the most run-down sections of Llewellyn. Fights and theft were common. But the halfling knew that his trail could easily be buried here, and in case two of his customers should chance to meet up after a sale, Pawldo needed quick anonymity.

He sipped at a mug of ale and looked around at the other patrons.

A pair of Northmen were engaged in an arm-wrestling contest in the center of the room, and most of the patrons had gathered around to place bets and cheer on their favorites. Pawldo could see little of the match. The hulking forms of the humans formed an effective barrier for one of his stature. Instead, he saw the door open and a heavyset woman enter. She had a broad face and round cheeks, but she was very attractive in a large sort of way. She stepped confidently up to the group around the wrestlers, and the halfling saw that she carried a lute upon her back.

Interested now, Pawldo watched her join the onlookers. She obviously knew them, judging from the familiar tweak she gave one man. She talked for a moment and then left.

Halflings are nothing if not curious (except about magic), and Pawldo was compelled to see what the bard-lady had said. He hopped to the floor, hoisted his bag, and strolled over to the sailor she had tweaked.

"Any idea where I could find some music?" he asked.

"Huh? Oh, sure, there's a party at The Diving Dolphin tonight. Seems the Prince of Corwell's in town, and . . . damn!"

The sailor's attention jerked back to the wrestlers. One had just crushed the other's brawny arm to the table. Muttering a stronger curse, he counted out three silver pieces and passed them to a sailor to his left before turning back. He was surprised to see no one there.

"Now where'd that little fellow go?"

* * * * *

"To Rodger!" Tristan solemnly raised his mug.

"Rodger!" echoed Daryth.

Pontswain ignored them, seizing another massive boar's rib and biting greedily into the succulent meat. Red juices ran into his beard, but his hair, brushed again, had regained its elegant curl.

Moments later they slammed down the empty stoneware next to the empty pitchers. Tristan felt vaguely guilty. This was the first time he had thought of the fisherman who had given his life to carry them to Alaron. "I didn't even find out if he had a family," he said.

"He was a widower, his children grown," replied Daryth. "He told us that in Kingsbay."

Tristan felt another twinge of guilt. He had drunk so much beer that night that he barely recalled the conversation. "I'll see that they're provided for," he said, raising his head. The thought made him feel slightly better.

He looked around The Diving Dolphin. The inn was pleasantly crowded, with a steady buzz of conversation. Pretty maids bustled about replenishing pitchers, mugs, and platters. Heavy beams of dark wood crisscrossed the ceiling, and bright lanterns showed the place to be clean and well-maintained. The huge skin of a cave bear served as a rug before the vast fireplace, and the head of a leering sea monster was mounted above the hearth.

Daryth showed his companions the gloves he had found in the castle and told them how he had found their weapons in the treasure room.

"Where did you find your sword?" he asked Tristan.

The prince smiled. The rush of alcohol made his secret seem even more pleasant. He felt better than he had in days. He leaned back in his chair and lifted a booted foot to the table. "Magic," he said smugly.

They found the beer to be a bit watery to their palates, but that hadn't stopped them from finishing four pitchers. Actually, Tristan had had most of it. Daryth had filled his mug a few times, but Pontswain was still on his first.

"Another, gentlemen?" said a freckled barmaid. A great spray of red hair fell across her shoulders. She had a pretty face, though Tristan was barely aware of it. He was more consumed with the ample shape of her figure straining against the tightly laced stays of her bodice.

Even in his fog, though, Tristan caught Pontswain's warning glance; the lord obviously disapproved of his consumption. That alone was enough to make him want to order more, and he was about to signal the lovely maid to bring it.

"Not for now!" announced a voice. Tavish marched up to the table, bearing a pitcher in each hand. She ignored the barmaid, smiling at Daryth as he rose to offer her a seat.

"So, how do you like this place?" she asked as Tristan watched the barmaid flounce away. He thought wistfully of

Robyn and turned back to his companions.

"It was rather empty earlier, but it seems to be filling up," observed the prince.

"Oh, it gets pretty crowded," said Tavish with a secretive little smile. "Especially on nights like this!"

"What's so special about tonight?" asked Daryth.

"Music, for one thing." She smiled, but would say no more.

A screeching sound drew their attention to the hearth, where several pipers were tuning their instruments.

"I love the airpipes!" shouted Tavish over the noise. "The audience is always ready for something different when they stop!"

Tristan observed the pipers through a thin fog as they played a fast jig, drawing several dancers, including Daryth and Tavish, to their feet. A few more songs followed, and after each Tristan noticed more and more of the patrons looking over at his table. Finally, one of them shouted "Tavish!" In moments, the room vibrated as everyone called for the bard.

"Hometown girl," Tavish smiled at her companions' looks of surprise. Grinning easily, she took her lute and stepped to the makeshift stage vacated by the pipers. Twanging a few soft chords, she assured herself that the instrument was tuned. With the first chord, Tristan recognized the song.

> My tale's of far Corwell, on Gwynneth so wild,
> Of heroes, and demons, and druids, and war.

> And the Beast that rose darkly, from waters deep black,
> And stalks all of Corwell, in times old and new. . . .

Tavish's clear voice carried the Song of Keren to heights Tristan had never before heard. She sang almost without accompaniment, using the lute only to establish an occasional harmonic chord.

The song took him back to the war, and with it as background he remembered the summer of battle in a dramatic, almost poetic light. He saw but one image: Robyn, her black hair flying in the breeze, standing alone atop the high tower of Caer Corwell, using the staff of her mother to call upon the powers of nature itself, bringing lightning crackling into the ranks of the Bloodriders that would otherwise have slain them all.

> Thick sky spit forth death's fire, the Rider's fell—black,
> While the white steeds' charge rumbled—

"Hold!"

The sharp command cracked through the room like a thunderclap. All eyes turned to the doorway.

A tall man stood there, arrogantly looking about the room. He was dressed in a heavy red cloak, with gold braid decorating his shoulders. His head was protected by a steel helmet that did not cover his face. In his upraised hand he clenched a shining steel longsword.

"I arrest the Prince of Corwell in the name of the king!" he announced. "He is charged with treason against the crown!"

* * * * *

Pawldo raced down the street, almost forgetting to cushion his bag. Tristan! he thought to himself. In Llewellyn! How they would celebrate, the two old friends. Of course, the prince had probably brought that Calishite along—but even Pawldo had grown to trust Daryth, so that was all right. A long year of traveling was coming to an end, and the halfling was eager to think about home and old companions.

He found The Diving Dolphin and dashed up the steps, only to bump into a massive figure. He recoiled quickly as he looked into the tusked face. An ogre!

"Closed," muttered the monster, giving the halfling a casual shove that knocked him across the entryway. Stunned, Pawldo looked around to see a dozen ogres, all clutching weapons and standing ready to charge through the door. His gaze rested upon a familiar shape in the corner.

"Canthus?" he whispered, and the great moorhound thumped his tail in greeting. He did not raise his head from his paws, however, instead shifting his brown eyes to stare mournfully at the door to the inn.

* * * * *

The cleric of Chauntea slept soundly, secure in the warm embrace of his goddess. His breathing was deep and slow as the night reached its deepest hour. Finally, the goddess sensed that he was ready for her dream.

The cleric dreamed that he awakened to find a sword on the steps of his chapel. Though unskilled in weaponry, he recognized the blade as a wondrous piece of work.

But the weapon had been damaged. Its silvery blade was tarnished, chipped, and bent. The tip had been broken off. Its smooth, leathery hilt was worn away by rot and decay.

The cleric took the weapon into his chapel, which had suddenly become a forge. Though he knew nothing of smithing, he took a hammer and fired the forge. The handle of the hammer was smooth and comfortable in his hand. He stroked the weapon across the anvil, caressing it with gentle taps of the hammer. Slowly it regained some of its former shape. The metal was straightened, and the tip gradually sharpened into a point. The hilt healed itself; the rot fell away, and the leather grew once again sturdy and thick.

And then the blade was done, and it was a glorious thing to behold. The cleric held it up to the sun, and the light of it nearly blinded him.

Patriarch Trevor awakened suddenly and sat up in bed. His breathing was ragged, and his heart pounded. Elated, he sprang to the floor and knelt in reverence before a statue of his goddess. He had received a vision! He did not know what the dream meant, but he had no doubts about its nature. And so he would wait.

* * * * *

Tristan saw anger in the faces around him. Not anger directed at him, the alleged traitor, but toward the officer who stood at the door. Grumbles of displeasure came from many throats, and he saw men fingering their weapons.

"Mercenary scum!" cried one huge man, lunging to his feet. "How dare you speak for a king of the Ffolk?"

The captain made a slight nod to his left, and a window exploded inward. Shocked patrons turned to see a leering ogre's face, its yellow tusks gleaming over a huge crossbow. A huge bolt punched through the chest of the standing man, knocking him over two tables as it killed him. More of the ugly ogres crowded in the door behind the officer, while others broke into the room from the kitchen. The rest of the windows crashed inward, and at least a half-dozen of the massive crossbows were sighted on the crowd.

For a quick moment, he looked up into the heavy rafters and the shadows beyond. Escape! He pictured a quick leap, a grab of the beam, and they would be off into the darkness beyond. But then he stumbled drunkenly backward, and only Pontswain's strong arm held him from falling to the floor. The look of utter disgust on the lord's face burned its way into Tristan's bowels, and he jerked away.

More of the Ffolk were rising to their feet now, and a startlingly clear vision burst through the fog in Tristan's brain: He saw a massacre of these brave but outmatched Ffolk—a massacre for which he, at least indirectly, would be responsible. Shaking off Pontswain's supporting arm, he forced himself to stand up straight.

"The charge is untrue!" he announced, somehow managing to keep his words from slurring. He addressed the soldier. "I will accompany you and refute it before the High King himself."

For a moment, he thought that the patrons of the bar would still fight, but gradually the tension eased. The three visitors walked over to the sneering man. The captain's black eyes glittered at them above his sharp, hawklike nose and neatly trimmed mustache and beard.

"I must have your weapons," he announced, holding out his hand expectantly.

Tristan momentarily regretted his decision, but he saw again the brutal crossbows leveled at the innocent bystanders. Reluctantly, he ungirded his belt and handed it over. The Prince of Corwell would hold the Sword of Cymrych Hugh again, Tristan vowed.

* * * * *

The heart of Kazgoroth provided all of the strength and endurance that Hobarth needed. His path carried him up a rocky pass and through winding gorges, yet he never wavered in his course toward a place he had never seen.

Some of this confidence came from his faith in Bhaal, for the god showed him visions of his destination. But another part of it came from the black heart, as if that stone wanted him to find the battlefield for its own reasons.

After several days without food or drink but also without pause, he came down the center of a broad, forested valley. Before him lay a wide field with a rounded hill upon the far side. That hill, he knew, was Freeman's Down, and it had given its name to the battle fought here the previous year. The huge cleric made his way to the top of the burial mound, fondling the black rock as he approached.

He held the heart to the ground and remembered the spell that allowed him to animate the dead. As before, the knowledge of the enchantment came from his mind, but the power to enact it came from the black rock. It was a far greater power than any one cleric could hope to generate.

Hobarth suppressed a shiver of delight as he felt the ground tremble beneath his feet. The earth was rent by great cracks that ripped across the grass. The scent of moist dirt arose but was quickly extinguished by a stronger smell: the stench of dead, decayed flesh.

In the bottom of one of the fissures, Hobarth saw movement. Skulls gaped upward at him, and bony hands clawed at the dirt, pulling whole skeletons jerkily from the earth. Bones clicked together as the creatures crawled from the soil like a swarm of insects emerging from a narrow hole. They crawled over each other, mindless of those that were dragged down or reburied. More and more of the things emerged as the fissures deepened. The skeletons lurched away from the graves to collect in loose ranks of dirty bone.

Next came the zombies.

The flesh on these bodies had not entirely rotted away, but hung loose in great flapping folds of carrion. Clutching the lip of the fissure with sinewy, skinless fingers, the zombies dragged themselves from their graves in answer to Hobarth's command. Empty eye sockets gaped dully from swollen, misshapen faces. Black tongues thrust from lipless mouths, hanging stupidly from torn and rotted jaws. Like the skeletons, the zombies formed careless lines, moving off the desecrated burial mound and spreading across the field.

And still Hobarth's army rose from the earth.

❦ 8 ❦

The Crystals of Thay

Wide-eyed, Pawldo watched from the shadows as Tristan, Daryth, and another prisoner were prodded through the door of The Diving Dolphin. He kept one hand on the neck of the moorhound. One of the brutes cuffed the prince roughly, and Canthus growled, deep within his cavernous chest. Pawldo pressed reassuringly against the bristling neck and whispered soothing sounds into the dog's ear.

In another moment the prisoners had been shoved down the stairway, and their escort moved them quickly up the street. Soon the captives disappeared into the night.

Another dozen ogres remained around the inn, staring belligerently through the doors and windows. They poked curiously at anyone who attempted to enter or leave. Finally the ogres grew bored and moved on, but the halfling remained still for several minutes. As the customers began filtering out of the inn, he stood up and dusted himself off.

Pawldo had some things to do. He found some old rags and quickly repacked his duffel, burying each of the Crystals of Thay in several layers of cushioning cloth. Next he pulled out a sturdy leather tunic that fit snugly over his shoulders. Lastly he took a slim blade and girded it to his waist. That blade, no more than a long dagger to a man, had sipped the lifeblood of more than one foe.

Finally he turned again to the moorhound, who had lain motionless while he completed his preparations. "Tristan?" said Pawldo, inclining his head to the street.

The huge dog instantly sprang to his feet and bounded from the entryway, pausing only to give the dirt road a cursory sniff. He trotted in the direction the ogres had taken, and Pawldo had to jog in order to keep up.

Canthus, for his part, loped as quietly as a shadow through the streets of Llewellyn. The dog's path carried them to the fringes of the town. He circled anxiously for several minutes at an intersection, allowing Pawldo to catch his breath while the dog sought his master's spoor. Finally he picked up the trail again, turning to the left and bounding up a gradual hill. Pawldo followed him, still puffing.

Suddenly the dog darted toward a gatehouse in a high wall that ran several feet back from the street. A huge ogre stood carelessly within the gatehouse.

"No!" Pawldo hissed, pulling the huge dog aside just a moment before he would have reached the circle of light created by the ogre's torch. "This way," he whispered, sprinting away from the gatehouse and cutting sharply into a lane that ran along the property. Here he found a large oak tree. No gardener had removed the lower branches. The halfling found a nearby clump of bushes and ordered Canthus to lie there, hidden from casual view. Pawldo then had no difficulty scampering up the knotty bole until he reached a point where he could see over the wall.

He saw a huge manor house within the yard, surrounded by formal gardens and placid pools. Several ogres wandered around, patrolling the area.

Somewhere in there was the Prince of Corwell.

* * * * *

"It's about time you woke up!" Pontswain's biting tone blasted through Tristan's weariness.

The prince sat up awkwardly, trying to ignore the heavy manacles that bound his hands and restricted his movement. His head pounded. Daryth, similarly restrained, looked at him morosely.

"What happened?" groaned the prince.

"You don't remember?" Pontswain stalked from the barred window to stand before the prince. Tristan sat on a hard bunk and looked up at the lord in anger and chagrin.

"Of course I remember what happened!" he snapped. "I mean, how did the guards know we were there? Were they waiting for us to come ashore? We hadn't been here for more than a few hours."

"Just long enough to get drunk."

"All right!" Tristan growled, standing up to face the lord. The chain binding his wrists clanked noisily. "I made a mistake. For what it's worth, I'm sorry. Now drop it, or by the goddess I'll force your teeth down your throat!"

He expected Pontswain to strike at him—in fact, he would have welcomed the physical release. He wanted to hit something, and the arrogant lord seemed like a good target. To his surprise, Pontswain shrugged and walked away.

"I'm beginning to understand," said Daryth quietly.

"Will you explain it to me, then?" asked the prince.

The Calishite stood and paced across their small cell in frustration, joining Pontswain at the lone window. Finally, Tristan joined them. They looked across the well-tended gardens of a large manorhouse.

"Don't you see? Our arrest, maybe even the sabotage of the *Lucky Duckling*. It's all been an attempt to stop you from seeing the High King!"

"So you think the High King is afraid of me?" countered Tristan. "Why?"

"The other rulers—Moray, Snowdown—all killed or vanished, as your father was killed. You are the only one left!"

"What threat does a country prince offer to the High King?" asked Tristan.

"Certainly, with your victory in the Darkwalker War you could seem like a threat—especially to a weak-willed ruler," Daryth said. "The soldiers here were waiting for you. Not just any outlaw lord or king. And somehow, they knew you were coming. . . ." All fell deadly silent as each realized the implications of the Calishite's words.

Tristan nodded his agreement. He wondered as he did so if the walls were listening . . . or watching.

*　*　*　*　*

"These feathers steady and steer her in flight. The muscles in the wings are strong enough to allow her to lift a large rabbit from the ground."

The young eagle sat calmly in Genna's lap as the Great Druid stretched out its long wing. Robyn watched attentively as her teacher lifted the graceful bird.

"Of course, this one is still small," added Genna. "She must grow before she can attempt anything so ambitious."

They sat upon a bench in the garden, amid red and purple flowers and the stately boles of a few ancient oaks. Fat bees buzzed lazily from blossom to blossom, sipping nectar.

"She has the keenest eyes of any of our creatures," continued Genna. "And speed! Her form is one of the most useful when one must travel from one place to another in hurry."

"I would love to try that!" exclaimed Robyn, imagining the joys of flight. "To see the whole valley—the whole world!"

"Soon, child," said Genna, surprising her. "Your lessons have progressed very well despite my recent . . . lethargy. You are almost ready to learn the secrets of the animals, to assume their forms when the need is upon you."

"Teacher . . ." Robyn asked, hesitantly voicing a question that had been concerning her. "Your lethargy—had it to do with the stranger's presence in the grove?"

Genna paused a long time before answering. For a while, Robyn wondered if she had heard the question.

"My ailment cannot be blamed upon the stranger—at least, not entirely," explained Genna at last. "You see, I am getting old—quite a bit older than I look, if the truth be told! The infirmities of age sometimes weigh heavily upon me. At first, I thought that was all that was wrong with me.

"After the stranger's coming, however, I felt something much more sinister—the presence of an ancient and powerful enemy—one whom I had hoped I was done with, at least in this life. That presence brought a kind of madness upon me." She raised a hand at Robyn's look of surprise.

"No, not the stranger himself. I know him now; he was a powerful druid in Myrloch Vale. Trahern of Oakvale was his name. I thought that he was killed during the war.

"No, it was not Trahern that caused my ailment. It was a presence that came along with him—something that wore me down and frightened me. Perhaps it had inhabited his body, or maybe it was something that he carried."

"Why didn't you tell me?"

"I couldn't," explained the Great Druid. "The madness that infected me kept me silent. I dreaded that presence, but I could not articulate the words to warn you. It's gone now, or at least lessened greatly in strength."

"The black rock!" Robyn exclaimed.

"What? What black rock? Why didn't you tell me about this?" Genna demanded.

"I didn't know about it—at least, not until he died. The first time he died, I mean." She proceeded to explain about the ragged bundle Acorn had carried, and described the rock that fell out of it after his death.

"Where is it now?" asked Genna.

"Newt took it away after I was stunned. I don't know exactly where he put it. Newt?"

The little dragon blinked into sight a dozen feet away. He had been buzzing about the garden, invisible, shaking the stems of flowers as bees attempted to land upon the petals.

"Is it lunchtime already?" he cried, eagerly zipping over to the bench. "It's been a long and hot morning. You two are being very, very boring, today, you know. What's for lunch? Hey, where's the food? I don't see any food!"

"Wait," cried Robyn, holding up her hand. "We'll eat soon. First, I need you to tell me where you took that black rock."

Newt shuddered nervously, twisting his agile neck to look in all directions, as if he expected savage enemies to burst from the woods at any moment. "I hid it!" he explained in a stage whisper. "I took it into the forest and dropped it!"

"But where?" persisted the young druid.

"Over there, somewhere," replied the faerie dragon with an irritated gesture to the south. "Now, can we eat?"

Robyn couldn't help but laugh and agree. She turned to go to the cottage to gather some bread, cheese, and fruit.

Only then did she notice Genna's eyes, squinting warily into the woods in the same direction as Newt's gesture.

* * * * *

Pawldo was about to jump from the tree back into the narrow lane. The sound that froze him was little more than a faint scuffing, indistinguishable from wind in the grass or a dozen other common noises. But the halfling strained his ears, cursing the clouds that blocked the moon. There it was again! He was not alone in the lane.

A crease between clouds dropped a slow wash of illumination, and the halfling saw dark shapes moving toward him. Men on horseback, he suddenly realized, but why could he not hear the horses?

The riders pulled up at the base of the very tree concealing Pawldo, and he counted six men, shrouded in black. Each rode a midnight-black horse whose hooves were shrouded in thick leather bags.

Pawldo did not like these characters—not that he knew who they were, or what they wanted. His dislike was compounded by fright, as he saw the riders dismounting below. As quietly as possible, the halfling moved upward, certain that the pounding of his heart would give him away.

Pawldo could only watch as the men leaped into his tree and started to climb upward. One stayed behind holding the horses, but the other five swung into the middle of the tree.

Pawldo lay headlong upon a wide limb no more than ten feet above the sinister figures. Shaking with fright, he squeezed the branch as tightly as he could, hoping to blend with the darkness.

"He'll be in one of the tower rooms," hissed a man.

"How do you know?" questioned another.

"Ogres," answered the first speaker. "They always store treasure and prisoners up high if they can."

The men wormed their way outward along a pair of stout limbs, looking over the manor. Pawldo felt certain that they were talking about Tristan.

"Rasper, you take this," said the first speaker, apparently the leader of the band. Pawldo couldn't see the object that changed hands, but he heard more. "Drink that before we cross the wall—you'll be the lead man, but invisible. Let's stay out of the paths of those ogres, but if we run into trouble, the four of us'll keep 'em busy. Fallow, you know what to do then."

"Don't worry," said Rasper. "The prince is a dead man!"

Assassins! In his fright, Pawldo squeezed a piece of bark from the tree. The flake of wood broke with the tiniest of cracks, but the conversation below him ceased immediately.

Pawldo discerned slight movement and realized that some of the men had moved to the bole of the tree, while several more remained below him. In utmost silence, the assassins spread out to close the net.

Clenching his teeth so he wouldn't cry out in fear, Pawldo wormed his way farther out on the limb. The tree's branches thinned above him—he would gain nothing by climbing. The men were below him, and between him and the trunk, so it seemed that out was the only way to go.

The branch narrowed as he moved and began to bend under his weight. Now he heard whispered commands in the depths of the tree. He swung his feet into space, tightly clasping the end of the bough, and felt it swing down under his weight. His feet touched a lower branch and he let go, trusting his sense of balance. Tumbling free, he barely grabbed the lower branch, but this one also sagged.

Suddenly he saw movement in the lane below him and remembered the sixth assassin, who had remained below with the horses. He saw a shadowy figure moving to meet him as he landed.

"Canthus!" he cried, dropping to the ground and sprawling headlong. The assassin loomed over him and then suddenly lurched to the side. Pawldo saw the form of the giant moorhound bearing the man to the ground. Canthus's long white fangs were buried in his shoulder.

"Let's go!" cried the halfling, jumping to his feet and running to the horses. The dog followed, leaving his victim moaning softly in a spreading pool of blood.

Pawldo darted among the nervously shuffling horses. "Hee-yah!" he shouted, slapping one of the steeds in the rump. He grabbed the stirrups of two more and yanked them sharply. Spooked, all six horses galloped down the lane and raced into the street, the halfling swinging wildly from one stirrup. Canthus raced behind, urging any stragglers ahead with sharp barks.

* * * * *

"Any more ideas?" asked Pontswain. For once, his voice was not laden with sarcasm. Tristan had tried to bend the bars on the window.

"I can't do anything about the lock without my tools," announced Daryth, turning from the door. "They took my picks and probes before they tossed us in here."

Tristan paced back and forth while the other two flopped onto the mattresses. The prince truly hated confinement—a thing he had never experienced before. The room seemed to grow smaller with every passing minute, and tension threatened to consume him. He felt that he might soon be driven to beat his brains out against the iron door in a quest for freedom. Forcefully, he suppressed the primitive urge. Faint starlight was visible through the window, and the tiny specks of light seemed to mock his plight.

"Do you think the High King is eager to hear your petition?" asked Pontswain. "He certainly has taken great pains to see that you waste no time getting to him."

Tristan whirled on the lord, but then halted. He didn't know if the man was baiting him or asking an honest question. Judging by the curious, slightly amused look on the man's face, Pontswain didn't know either.

"That's not too likely," said Daryth quietly.

"Why?" asked the prince.

"After an assassination attempt—two, if you count the sinking of our boat—they're not likely to haul you all the way to Callidyrr."

"If they want me dead, why didn't they kill me already?"

"Perhaps because they didn't dare do it in a public place," interjected Pontswain. "Remember the mood at the inn?"

Daryth nodded and stood, nearly tripping on the chain linking his manacles. Cursing, he pulled his hands apart—and stared in shock as one of the iron rings slipped over his hand to clink to the floor.

"How did you do that?" asked Tristan.

"I don't know." Daryth was obviously mystified. He tugged on the other hand, and it, too, slipped through the tight and rusty bond. He looked at Tristan as he threw the manacles to the bed. Suddenly he laughed.

"These gloves are from the sea castle!" he cried, holding up his hands. "I knew there was something special about them—they're magical!" He pulled one of the gloves off and looked at it.

"Let's see," said the prince, wondering if the gloves would work on his hands. He tried to pull one of them on, but it was too tight. "But what's this?" he asked as he examined the glove and noticed a tiny pouch inside.

"What's what?" asked the Calishite, taking the glove. He looked inside and pulled out a thin piece of stiff wire from the hidden pocket. "A picklock!" he announced. "I'll have you out in no time!"

Daryth knelt beside the prince and pushed the thin probe into the keyhole of Tristan's right manacle. After a minute of delicate probing, the lock snapped open. In another moment, both of the prince's hands were free.

"That's great!" said Tristan, jumping to his feet. "Now we—"

"Shhh!" Daryth hissed suddenly, holding up a hand. The faint scraping sound of metal against metal reached his ears. He looked anxiously toward the door. Nodding in agreement, Daryth pantomimed a probing gesture.

Someone was picking the lock to their cell.

* * * * *

Pawldo crouched next to the gatehouse, telling himself he was crazy. His wild plan didn't have a prayer of success. To the contrary, it virtually assured that he would be killed, no doubt squashed like a bug beneath some ogre's boot.

The prince of Corwell was a decent friend, but nowhere was it stated that friendship meant senselessly sacrificing one's life for a comrade who was probably already dead. And Tristan's no-good friend Daryth deserved whatever he got! At least, these were the arguments raging through the halfling's brain.

But it was no use. Pawldo decided that he had no choice but to go through with it. It would be the last thing he ever went through, but do it he would. He would try his plan.

He tentatively hoisted one of the Crystals of Thay, tossing the sphere up and down a few times until he had captured the right degree of jauntiness. He tried to whistle cheerily, but only after licking his lips repeatedly could he call forth a few faint notes.

Finally he was ready. He emerged from the shadows and sauntered into the street, whistling a little jig and tossing the crystal into the air as if he hadn't a care in the world. Canthus followed at his heels.

He smoothly approached the ogre standing at the gatehouse, blocking entrance to the manor grounds. The monster regarded him in surprise, blinking its wide, dull eyes. The yellowed tusks, jutting upward from its lower jaw, looked very deadly. Pawldo hoped that the look held more curiosity than belligerence. He stopped whistling as he reached the ogre.

"Hi there!" he beamed. "How'd you like to buy a crystal? It's the only one of its kind in the Moonshaes!"

* * * * *

The army of undead crawled like a living organism across the land. Needing neither food nor drink, completely tireless and insensitive to pain, the creatures trampled beds of flowers and thickets of thorns with equal impunity.

But the plants suffered from more than just the shuffling footsteps. As each of the undead stumbled forward, each blade of grass, weed, and flower stalk that lay in its path simply turned brown and shriveled. It died before the monster even reached it. The bushes and trees that the army walked past gradually dropped their leaves. Slender branches drooped lifelessly.

The zombies moved in the vanguard of the army. The dirt had been washed from them by a sudden downpour, and their rotting flesh hung in great folds of gore. Some of them carried rusty weapons. Others had no weapons except their bare hands, but even these were formidable, for most of the skin and flesh on the fingers had rotted away, leaving twisted claws of bone extended. The eyes had rotted from the sockets of most, but the lack seemed to make no difference. All of them moved with the same shuffling gait, tripping and stumbling often, but climbing to their feet to march forward. Often, they left a piece of rancid flesh clinging to a thorny branch or sharp rock.

Curiously, the zombies' hair remained in full, except for patches where the flesh had torn away. Thus, some of the males had tufts of beard, and many women retained long tresses that hung in careless disarray.

The skeletons were gradually cleaned, as a succession of rainstorms washed the dirt from their white bones. Like the zombies, some of the bare skeletons carried weapons or wore tattered bits of rusty armor. But they had no flesh to be scraped away by thorns. Empty eye sockets stared ahead as the unearthly force stumbled forward.

The army moved without rest, for the undead suffered no fatigue, nor did they feel the need to sleep. And in Hobarth's case, the Heart of Kazgoroth had become his sustenance.

The army marched, and the ground beneath it blackened and died. It left a swath of death running up the valley from Freeman's Down, across the high pass, and finally streaking down the mountain slopes, into Myrloch Vale.

The vanguard of the army, twoscore ghastly figures that had once been Northmen, shuffled into a shallow pond. Flies buzzed around the zombies, landing and feeding greedily, but the creatures took no note. Some lumbered forward, their faces so covered with flies that they appeared to grow black, buzzing beards.

As the undead feet slurped into the mud of the pond, the water grew stagnant and black. Thin wisps of pungent steam rose into the air with each footstep, and fish floated, belly up, to the surface. These first zombies crossed the waist-deep water and trudged through the muddy shore on the far side. They moved into a field, bright with flowers, and the petals fell like snowflakes. As more of the army crossed the field, more of it died; the force left a muddy wasteland of death in its wake.

One zombie, who had nearly lost her leg to a Northman battle-ax, suddenly collapsed as that leg gave way beneath it. Those behind, the bodies of friends and foes alike, trudged mindlessly over the twitching corpse, trampling it into the mud until only a clasping, clenching hand could be seen above the ground.

The animals of the vale sensed the approaching horror and fled upon hoof, paw, or wing. The army marched through a lifeless forest.

Soon, now, Hobarth dreamed, the girl would be his.

* * * * *

Tristan and Daryth stood to either side of the door. Pontswain, still manacled, sat upon a mattress facing the door. He nodded at the other two and they understood; he would try to distract whoever it was that tried to enter their cell. The faint sounds of the picklock indicated a thief of considerable skill—there was no wasted motion or clumsy probing. Or an assassin, trained at the Academy of Stealth, thought Tristan. In a moment the lock released.

The men held their breath, tension rising as they waited to see who was breaking into their cell. With a low creak, the door began to slide open. Daryth moved like a striking snake, reaching through the widening crack to grasp at the shirt of whoever stood outside.

But his hand closed upon air. Stunned, he pulled the door open to reveal the intruder, but they saw no one standing in the hallway—until they looked down.

"Pawldo!" cried the prince, reaching down to clasp his friend warmly. "How did you get here?"

"You'd never believe it if I told you," replied the halfling in a tense whisper. He threw an anxious look over his shoulder. "Come on, now, we've gotta move!"

"Just a minute!" said Daryth, passing Pawldo to look cautiously into the hall. He darted back to Pontswain and slipped the wire probe into one manacle. After a moment's hesitation, Pawldo joined him and worked on the other.

"Thanks," the lord said, briskly rubbing his wrists.

"Let's go!" hissed Pawldo, turning to the door.

Tristan sensed a note of panic in Pawldo's voice. "What do you mean? What do you know?"

"Assassins!" Pawldo whispered. "They're here to kill you! In this building—maybe coming up the stairs right now!"

"Wait!" cried Tristan. "I've got to find the Sword of Cymrych Hugh. I can't leave without it!"

Pawldo looked like he wanted to argue, but he finally turned with a sigh of exasperation. "All right, I've got an idea where they might be keeping it. They've got an ogre on guard outside one of the rooms downstairs."

"Damn!" cursed Tristan. "How are we going to get past it?"

"That's the least of our problems," said Pawldo. He took the lead, his little shortsword drawn as they slipped quietly down the spiraling stairway. They circled three times to reach the ground level, where a door led to an alcove off the great hall of the manor. As Pawldo reached for the door-knob, they heard the unmistakable snort of an ogre coming from the other side of the door.

"How are we going to fight that thing?" whispered Daryth in exasperation. "With nothing but that little pigsticker between the three of us!"

"This little blade has stuck some pretty big pigs!" declared Pawldo. "Now, shut up and follow me!"

Before the men could react, the halfling pushed open the door and stepped past the hulking ogre who stood outside. Tristan and Daryth were about to lunge after their friend. At the very least they could not let him die alone.

But the ogre didn't move. Pawldo turned after a few steps, gesturing them forward, and kept on moving. Stunned, Tristan watched the ogre for a reaction.

The monster clutched a glass ball in his huge and hairy palms, staring intently at the object as he turned it this way and that. He did not look up as the unbelieving trio tiptoed stealthily past. Tristan looked back to see the ogre still in the thrall of the shiny sphere.

Pawldo, meanwhile, had pushed aside the curtain screening the alcove and stepped boldly into the great hall. Here, too, were ogres—three of them. Each of the monsters sat upon the floor, legs outstretched to either side, and each stared intently at a glass bauble that seemed to be a match for the one in the alcove.

Amazed at their good fortune, the men followed Pawldo across the hall to a wooden door. Although the halfling boldly stepped over the outstretched leg of one of the ogres, the men could not bring themselves to test the limits of their good fortune further. Instead, they slipped quietly along the walls until they reached Pawldo. The halfling had already removed a wire probe from a slim leather case. He handed his sword to Daryth and knelt, carefully concentrating, as he began to pick the lock of the huge oaken door.

"This one was guarded," he whispered. "I'll bet it's where they've put your sword." In a second the lock clicked free, and Daryth raised his eyebrows in admiration.

Pawldo shrugged, unsuccessfully trying to conceal a smile of pride. With a cavalier gesture, he pushed it open.

"You miserable oaf! I ordered you to knock—" The hawk-nosed captain shrieked as he rose. But the tirade halted as abruptly as it began when the speaker realized that the intruders were not clumsy ogres. The officer's hand went to the hilt of his sword, but not before Daryth could act.

The Calishite sprang over Pawldo and through the door, landing in a catlike crouch halfway to the man's desk. Pawldo's blade quivered overhead as Daryth held the tip in his fingers, poised for throwing.

"Stay where you are or die," he snarled, his voice low.

The captain appeared to consider drawing his sword, but his eyes flicked to the slim dagger. He lifted his hand from the hilt of his sword.

Tristan ran to his side and drew the sword himself, turning it against its owner. "Where are our weapons?"

The officer nodded to a cabinet against the wall of the room, and Pawldo hurried over to open it. He pulled out both swords and the scimitar and was about to close it when something else caught his eye. He lifted out a leather sack, hoisting it a few times to hear a satisfactory clink, before closing the cabinet and handing the Sword of Cymrych Hugh to Tristan.

"Here," said the halfling, handing the other swords over to Pontswain and Daryth. "Of course," he told the Calishite, "it won't do for throwing, but it'll give you a better reach."

Daryth laughed. "I couldn't have thrown this clunky thing either. I just had to make him *think* I could." He smiled at the captain as he handed the weapon back to Pawldo.

"Check the hall," said Pontswain, walking to the desk. The captain stood behind it, hatred burning in his eyes. The lord met his gaze squarely, stopping before the man. In a lightning-quick gesture, he drew his sword and thrust it through the man's chest, squarely into his heart.

The officer fell instantly, blood spurting from the mortal wound. Pontswain turned and stalked toward the door.

"What did you do that for?" demanded Tristan, enraged. "He wasn't going to stop us!"

"Not until we were gone. But as soon as we were out of his sight, he would have had every ogre in this town on our tails. Now, we'll have a few minutes head start."

"You took a man's life to buy us a few minutes?" The prince was still incredulous. He had killed in battle before, but his companion's action had seemed so . . . ruthless.

"I did!" Pontswain snapped. "And it will be worth it if we use that time to escape instead of argue!"

"He's right!" said Daryth, opening the door. "Follow me!"

The ogres still sat, bemused, as the halfling trotted into the entry hall adjacent to the great hall. Here a pair of huge doors stood shut.

"Do you have a plan?" the prince asked the halfling.

"Plan?" Pawldo snorted in amusement. "I was sure I'd be dead by now. Why would I need a plan? I did, however, take the precaution of securing and hiding six fast horses around the corner. This is the way I came in," explained the halfling, lifting the latch and pushing open one of the doors. They walked across a wide stone veranda, thankful that the moon remained hidden by clouds. An ogre sat upon the front steps, staring in rapture at his crystal. They descended and started on a path that wound through the huge formal garden, moving stealthily among tall hedges.

"There—I left Canthus at the gatehouse," said Pawldo, pointing at the large structure looming before them.

They didn't see the movement until it was too late. One moment the pathway to the gatehouse lay open before them, and the next, four black figures had materialized from the bushes to block their way. Silken cloth of darkest black covered their bodies, but Tristan nonetheless recognized the hulking form that stepped ahead of the others.

"The Prince of Corwell, and Daryth of Calimshan!" said Razfallow in a soft, cultured voice. "Rarely, perhaps never, have two deaths given me more pleasure than yours shall!"

The leader pulled his silken mask aside as the moon broke from the clouds, washing the garden in milky light. The half-orc's beastly features leered at them, but his voice continued smoothly. "And that little fellow who spied upon us— what a delightful surprise! See how nicely he waits for us, Rasper? Didn't I tell you we'd find them here?"

One of the assassins nodded agreement. The little cross-bow in his hand did not waver from them, however. The weapon was identical to the one that had killed Tristan's father. Tristan saw another of the crossbows held by a second assassin. Those bows could kill two of them before they could move.

"So, Razfallow," said Daryth pleasantly. "Still whoring for the highest bidder, I see."

"Indeed," replied the half-orc. "And you could have joined me and lived to a ripe old age. You were good, back then. I would have made you my lieutenant instead of my victim."

"Working for the likes of you is no choice," Daryth stated simply. Razfallow shrugged, uninterested. He turned to the assassin with the bow.

"Now, Rasper, who should we kill first?"

* * * * *

The strength of the goddess was centered in Myrloch Vale. Nowhere else was her power so concentrated. Nowhere else were her druids so strong and the forces of disruption so weak.

Yet even that strength was not sufficient to withstand the plague of death that marched into her most sacred realm. Each unnatural footstep—and there were thousands every minute— brought fiery pain to the soul of the goddess. Each of the undead creatures was a blasphemy against life itself, a chaotic disruption of the balance of all things.

She recoiled and suffered, for she had no power over the army of death. She withered and flinched beneath the footfalls, fearing the approach of the cleric and his evil god.

The goddess was not without allies. Her children were her staunchest defenders, to be called in time of direst need. But the oldest of her children, the Leviathin, had been slain by the Beast. The vast wolfpack she was capable of summoning might have been some help against the army, but the pack was spent, dispersed to a hundred dens across the Isles.

There remained only one of her children—one who had suffered grievously in the war with the Beast. Yet that one she could not afford to leave to his rest.

And so the goddess, once again, summoned Kamerynn the unicorn.

❧ 9 ❧

Fugitives

The assassins raised their crossbows, and Tristan could almost physically feel the dart focus on his chest. He was about to make a desperate dive to the side—almost certain to get himself killed—when Daryth surprised him with a long, low whistle.

"I've just gotten you figured out, Razfallow," said the Calishite smoothly. He repeated the whistle again.

The silver dart in the crossbow shifted slightly to point straight at Daryth. Razfallow, the half-orc, spoke. "You have been amusing, Calishite." He snorted a soft chuckle and actually seemed reluctant to give the order to kill. "In fact, I shall have you killed last to show my gratitude."

Tristan had been puzzled by his friend's whistle, but he suddenly remembered something Pawldo had said. Instantly, he understood Daryth's plan. Time! They needed to stall the assassins for a few more seconds.

"I'm a dead man, anyway," said the prince, devoutly hoping he was wrong. "Tell me, then, why are you doing this? Where do your orders come from?"

Razfallow laughed, a sound like a crackling fire. "You are indeed a dead man, and I do not waste my breath talking to dead men." The half-orc nodded to his men, and the pair raised their silver crossbows.

"I grow tired of this game," said the assassin. "Larrell, you kill the one with the curly locks." He sneered at Pontswain. "Rasper, you put your bolt into the prince. Aim low."

Tristan saw a flash of movement in the moonlight behind the assassins. Daryth slowly raised his hand as if in supplication, but the prince saw that his companion's finger was pointed directly at the archer. Again he saw the motion in the road, closer now.

"Canthus, kill!"

Daryth's sharp command was timed exactly with the great dog's leap. The well-trained moorhound attacked silently and savagely. Rasper stumbled forward from the brutal impact, and though he tried to shoot the deadly dart into Tristan, the hound's attack had thrown off his aim. The missile flew harmlessly into the night as the man turned in desperation to grapple with the mighty jaws that eagerly sought his throat.

The one called Larrell turned slightly in surprise. Pontswain dropped to his stomach in the path as the assassin released his dart. The prince could not see if it struck home.

At the same moment Tristan, Daryth, and Pawldo leaped forward, drawing their blades. The three assassins crouched to meet them, Larrell dropping his bow and drawing a slim shortsword.

The assassins backed slowly away as Rasper screamed in pain. He twisted and struggled as the moorhound's teeth tore at his face. Locked in mortal combat, they rolled from the path, leaving the two trios faced off, a dozen feet apart.

Daryth looked sharply to his side at Tristan—behind the prince, actually. Tristan cast a quick glance behind him and saw only Pontswain in the bright moonlight. The lord stumbled to his feet, dazed but uninjured, and the prince and the Calishite turned back to the assassins.

"Look out!" cried the Calishite, suddenly whirling toward the prince again. Tristan twisted in surprise and then shouted in pain as he felt a sharp blade slicing through his back. But there was no one there! The prince lurched forward and crashed to the ground in agony. He coughed and choked with fright as he spit up blood.

Daryth leaped at the source of the attack. Through a thickening haze, Tristan saw him strike at . . . air! Daryth's blade snaked forward, and then the tip disappeared. He saw it again as the Calishite pulled back, and now it dripped with blood. He heard a groan as something heavy but invisible fell across his legs.

Tristan clenched his teeth to keep from crying out, and he struggled to remain conscious. The invisible sword had stricken deep into his back. It would almost certainly have killed him had not Daryth's warning caused him to turn at the last minute. Dimly, he realized that one magically invisible assassin had crept up behind them.

Pawldo rushed forward to keep the three assassins at bay. Now the Calishite leaped forward to stand at the halfling's side, as Pawldo stumbled rapidly back before three slashing attackers. Pontswain climbed to his feet and charged forward, waving his longsword before him.

Daryth sliced savagely at Razfallow's face, but the assassin ducked the blow easily and almost took off the Calishite's ear with the counterthrust. One of the others tried to follow up his master's advantage with a lunging stab, but this one overstepped his reach. Daryth's downward cut lopped off his arm at the elbow, and the man stumbled to his knees, holding the bleeding stump in shock.

Pawldo attacked aggressively. The Calishite crouched and jabbed at Razfallow, but neither of them could gain an advantage. Ponswain ducked about the edge of the melee, looking for an opening. Suddenly, the halfling shouted in alarm—his attacker had just knocked the blade from his hand. Pawldo ducked as the assassin took a wild swing at his neck. The attack was the man's last mistake, as Pontswain leaped into the fray and stabbed the man in the throat with a single lightning thrust.

Razfallow slashed immediately after Daryth, but the Calishite parried smoothly. The two blades clashed again and again as the fighters hurtled themselves at each other.

Pawldo scrambled to regain his sword, and rage twisted Razfallow's face into a hideous mask of hatred. He spit in Daryth's face and sprang backward, snarling.

"I will see you again, Calishite!" His voice was a rasping, inhuman growl as he turned and raced into the darkness.

"I'll get that baboon-faced—" growled the halfling, at last finding his sword. He lunged after the half-orc but Daryth caught him by the collar and pulled him back.

"I admire your courage," he said sincerely. "But he would kill you—or me! The darkness is his element—he wants us to come after him! Besides, our companion needs our help."

Tristan saw his friends coming toward him, and then nothing more.

*   *   *   *   *

"Come here, little fellow. You know I won't hurt you."

To most listeners, Genna's voice would have sounded like an assortment of chirps, squeaks, and clicks. Robyn, however, had no difficulty understanding her teacher's speech.

Neither did the small red squirrel, obviously, for the little creature bounded to the end of a long limb, and then hopped lightly onto the great druid's outstretched hand. The creature jumped to her shoulder and sniffed curiously at her ear as Genna smiled at Robyn.

"I really think the mammals are the most fun of them all," she said. "They're the most like us, of course. And I think they can be friendliest of all our creatures, when they want to be."

"Food?" the squirrel chirped.

"Oh, you little beggar," sighed Genna in resignation, nevertheless reaching into a pocket of her loose gown to draw forth an acorn.

Robyn looked up suddenly as the limb next to Genna sagged slightly. "Don't you dare, Newt!"

Scowling, the dragon became visible. Perched over the squirrel, he had been about to squeeze the animal's tail—a prank that certainly would have sent it shrieking in terror to the highest branches of the tree.

"You should be ashamed of yourself!" rebuked Genna.

"I can't help it," whined the dragon, his wings and tail drooping pathetically. "I'm so bored! You two never have time for anything fun anymore! It's always lesson this and teach that and learn the other thing!

"And you're always yelling at me, too," he pointed out defensively. " 'Newt, where are you?' or 'Don't do that, Newt!' or 'Stop eating that, Newt!' or something else."

"We have been working hard," said Genna with a look at Robyn. "I suppose I have been trying to make up for lost time. Why don't we have lunch at the pond? We can share a bottle of wine and have a quiet afternoon."

"Yesyesyesyes!" shrieked Newt, blinking into invisibility in his excitement. A second later he was back, buzzing happily.

"I was going to introduce you to the bats today," said Genna as they started toward the cottage. "But that can wait till later. They're more talkative at night, anyway."

Robyn walked thoughtfully back to the cottage. She felt at peace for the first time since the stranger had come. When Newt had removed the heartlike rock from the grove, it seemed as though a whole world of trouble had vanished. But another thing bothered her, and now she felt she could talk about it.

"Teacher, I'm troubled by a dream I have had several times in the past weeks. I'm certain it is a vision from the goddess."

Genna looked at her quizzically.

"It's about my . . . father, the king. And Tristan, too. I'm afraid something terrible has happened! They need me!"

"You wish to cease your studies?" Genna asked softly.

"No! But I must learn what has happened, I must go to them! Can you forgive me if I leave you for a while?"

Genna smiled sadly. "There would be nothing to forgive. You are a capable and accomplished student, able to make your own decisions. If you must leave, for a time, so be it. I only hope you will return."

"Genna, I will!" Robyn pledged. "And thank you!" She felt a giddy sense of relief and anticipation. She would travel to Corwell as swiftly as possible!

The women had almost reached the cottage when they heard a pathetic bleating in the distance. They paused and heard it again. The sound originated to the south, near the edge of the grove, and seemed to be coming closer.

"That sounds very bad," frowned Genna, turning to run toward the cries. Robyn joined her and quickly outdistanced her teacher. She raced through the garden and into the oaks where she almost ran headlong into a terrified doe.

She grasped the trembling creature around the neck and stopped its flight, muttering soothing sounds. Kneeling beside it, she felt the animal's shaking subside, although it did not cease entirely. In moments Genna joined them.

"What's the matter, brown-eyed one?" she whispered in a

voice so soft that Robyn could barely hear.

The deer bleated again, a sound that Robyn could not understand specifically, but she easily recognized the deer's sheer terror. Burrs matted the animal's sides and belly, and its legs were covered with many small scratches.

Genna looked at her student, and the lines of concern around her eyes deepened. She stroked the deer a few times, and gradually it settled down. She did not rise until the creature began to graze contentedly on the sweet grasses of the druid's grove.

"I do not understand what frightened her," she explained. "But never have I seen such lasting terror. She has obviously run many miles."

"What should we do?" asked Robyn. The deer's panic aroused deep feelings of anger within her. She wanted to punish whatever had tormented the creature so.

"I must go and have a look," said the druid.

"Let me come with you!" pleaded Robyn.

"No, you cannot yet. I will call upon powers you have yet to learn, though your abilities grow daily." Her teacher smiled at her and patted her shoulder reassuringly. "While I am gone, I want you to remain in the grove. We may have other creatures coming here to seek our help."

As she finished speaking, a huge flock of blackbirds squawked into sight. Thousands of feathered figures raced through the sky until they were all safely within the confines of the grove. There they settled, still agitated, into the highest branches of the towering oaks.

Robyn and Genna both noticed that they, too, had fled from the south.

* * * * *

Death reached out with cold fingers to seek the Prince of Corwell. Tristan only vaguely felt the chill presence beside him, for all of his feelings were blanketed in a gray fog.

The pounding cadence of the galloping horse penetrated his consciousness only barely, and he did not sense Daryth's arms around him, holding him in the saddle. The pain of his wound had long since vanished. His only discomfort now came from straining for air in his wounded lung.

For a time, the prince was ready to yield to the dark figure that rode beside him. The struggle to breathe was too exhausting to continue. The blessed relief promised by the one who held those arms outspread seemed the most pleasant recourse.

"Tristan. Look to me, my prince!"

For a second, he didn't react to the distant voice. When he did, it was as if his body was mired in thick mud; he couldn't open his eyes or turn without expending great effort. But finally, he saw.

An ocean of mist spread around him, muffling the sounds of the horse's hooves. The jolting gait became smooth, even comfortable. He could see that they were racing across this plain of fog, and then the mist parted to reveal a wide, smooth lake. It seemed to him that they were galloping along the shore, though he couldn't see any ground below him. In truth, he did not look down.

"Tristan."

The voice again reached seductively for his mind, and he struggled to see who was speaking. Then he saw the white figure, standing serenely on the waters of the lake. Her arms were spread wide, beckoning. Queen Allisynn stood some vague distance away. It seemed that she was very far, yet he could see tears welling in the corners of her eyes. He could hear her voice, though she spoke in the softest of whispers.

How beautiful she was! Her blond hair billowed like a flag in a gentle breeze, while her snowy gown seemed more like water than cloth as it flowed across her body. She looked very sad, and the prince wanted to hold her, to comfort her.

And then he understood her sadness.

His quest had failed! He had disappointed her. A black sense of despair grasped him, and once again he saw the specter of death seated beside him.

Desperately, he struggled to reach the queen, but his body would not move fast enough. A sob forced itself from his throat, and already her image grew dim.

"My queen!" he croaked. He struggled to hold out a hand to her so that she could pull him to her side.

"Stay there!" she cried, her voice growing stern. "Do not

come to me. You must not come to me!"

He made no reply, but his throat choked with sorrow, and tears flooded his eyes. The agony of watching her slip away was more than he could bear. Yet somehow, though his ghostly horse raced like the wind and the queen stood still upon the water, she remained beside him.

"You must go on, my prince." Again he heard her. She began to fade from view, but her voice was stronger than ever. "Go to Caer Callidyrr. Only from the High King himself will you learn the secret of your destiny. And prince, beware his wizard. Beware Cyndre!" She had almost disappeared from his sight, and despair threatened to drown the prince in his well of self-pity.

"My lady . . ." he moaned softly.

"No," she said, and suddenly her image was clear again. "Your lady is another—a woman who needs you, and who can help you! Call to your lady, my prince, do not call to me!"

And then she was gone, and in her place stood a green-eyed druid with flowing black hair. Her beauty brought a lump to his throat. By the goddess, how he needed Robyn! He must see her again! He must live!

"Robyn," he croaked, quietly, and the sound became a sob.

But then his companions slowed the pace of their flight, as the black horses grew winded. The pain returned, lancing through his chest and throat in fiery agony. The taste of blood was bitter in his mouth.

But with the pain came awareness, an understanding that he did want to live, that he had a mission to perform. With this understanding he banished the specter of death from his side. The prince was unconscious to his surroundings; he did not feel his companions lift him from the saddle nor see them enter the battered door of a frail country chapel. But he was aware of his life.

And he was determined to keep it.

* * * * *

The courtier timidly approached the great throne, his powdered wig trembling as he walked.

"Your Majesty," the man began, his voice cracking. "The . . . um . . . the wizard cannot be found."

"Imbecile!" barked the king. "Out of my sight! Fool! Do not return until you have found him!"

The king rose and stalked down the stairway leading to his throne. He reached the bottom of the staircase and turned to the side in agitation, wrapping the robe about his legs and almost tripping himself.

"Out!" he screamed. "All of you! Go away!"

The courtiers, jesters, and ladies-in-waiting in the huge chamber all turned and fled for the doors. In seconds the vast room was empty except for the king.

And one other.

Cyndre stood beside the throne, his black robe billowing and swelling around him. The king turned back, pacing, and suddenly saw him. He gasped and clapped a hand to his mouth, but quickly straightened to march purposefully up the steps.

"Where have you been? I have had every messenger in the palace searching for you! Why can't you be where you're supposed to be?"

"I came as soon as I could, sire. I was in the midst of some arcane meditation. To interrupt it would have been extremely dangerous." The wizard made a slight, almost imperceptible gesture. The king's shoulders sagged as he turned to flop wearily into his throne.

"I have been so worried!" he whined. "Has there been any word of that upstart from Corwell?"

"We have had word of his arrival at Llewellyn. A strong garrison of the Scarlet Guard is posted there. I am certain that we will hear of his capture very soon." The wizard's voice was soothing, and the king began to relax.

"I'm sorry I shouted at you, Cyndre. My nerves are not what they used to be." The wizard did not reply, and his thin smile of amusement was masked by his robe.

"When he is captured," continued King Carrathal, "I want him brought to me immediately. I am curious about this prince. I wish to learn why he pretends to my throne."

"At the earliest opportunity, sire, I will have him delivered to you," replied Cyndre, silently adding, "his corpse will not tell you much."

"You will protect me from him, won't you?"

"Of course, sire. You know that you have nothing to worry about. Perhaps you need something to take your mind off this little distraction—an execution, perhaps. Is there a prisoner you would like put to death? Perhaps that sister of the outlaw, O'Roarke?"

"No, not yet!" The king spoke firmly. "I still hope to make him see reason. I will never be able to do that if she is dead."

The wizard gestured subtly and whispered to the king.

"Very well," sighed Carrathal. "Have her put to death in the morning." For a moment, a look of stark horror flashed across the king's face. Once again, he saw the ghosts arrayed against him and sensed their number growing. But then he yawned listlessly. "Thank you, Cyndre. Sometimes I wonder what I would do without . . ."

The king could not finish his sentence, for he had already fallen asleep.

* * * * *

"I shan't be gone for more than a day," explained the Great Druid. Her manner was solemn. "Try to keep them from fighting. Talk to the leaders—they will help you."

Robyn nodded, trying to conceal her doubts. The grove of the Great Druid had, overnight, filled with terrified animals. Many deer, rabbits, wild pigs, squirrels, mice, and other little mammals were overrunning the place, nervously trying to avoid the few wolves, foxes, badgers, and weasels that had also come here for protection.

But protection from what? They still knew very little about whatever menaced the grove, save that it had caused an unprecedented fear among the wild creatures.

"If you have to, ask Grunt for help," said Genna. "He will complain a lot, but he could be your best ally."

"I will," said Robyn. Indeed, the old brown bear was a cantankerous and surly fellow, but she knew him to be an unusually steady and reliable animal.

"I will hurry," added the druid. "Take care, my child."

Genna turned toward the south and her short body shifted and blurred before Robyn's eyes. She grew smaller, and her brown robe slowly became a coat of golden feathers. Her arms became wings, and her nose became a beak. The smooth head, no longer even vaguely human, turned to look at Robyn, and the young druid saw the blessing glittering from the small, black eyes. Then the wings struck boldly downward, and the great eagle that was Genna Moonsinger sprang into the air and climbed steadily skyward. She rose without faltering, circling over the grove until she was no more than a speck in the southern sky.

A heavy sense of menace began to bear down on Robyn as the day progressed, removing any joy from her daily tasks. At first she thought that the feeling was produced by the threat to the Vale, and indeed, that must have been a part of it. Yet more and more she found her mind drifting to thoughts of Tristan.

Instead of the usual ripples of pleasure that his memory ordinarily gave her, her thoughts of the prince actually increased her anxiety. This feeling grew every time she thought of him, which was nearly every minute. She could not escape the feeling that he was in terrible danger.

She wrestled with a strong temptation to flee the grove, abandoning everything in a headlong dash to reach him. Yet even if she had known where he was—and she felt certain that he was far from Corwell—she could not have brought herself to renounce her trust with the goddess. And so once again she turned herself to her many chores.

But the work had a hollow, meaningless quality today. She was certain that it did not come from within herself.

Then she felt a strange peace fall over the grove. The squeaks and squawks of the animals quieted as she looked up. Something had already entered the grove. It was a presence mighty yet serene. Robyn walked quickly through the oaks, finally breaking into a run. She suspected the visitor's identity even before he stepped from between the oaks to regard her. She thought she saw a benign smile upon his face as she shouted with joy and ran to clasp her arms around his neck.

The smile was in her imagination, of course, for although he, too, felt great joy, Kamerynn the unicorn could not be expected to smile.

* * * * *

A cool, strong breeze flowed steadily northward, lashing the waters of the strait into rolling gray swells. Tavish fought the wind, tacking back and forth, but she still made only slow headway toward Corwell.

For the hundredth time she wondered if she was doing the right thing. After all, she reminded herself, what could she have done to rescue the prince? Painfully, but pragmatically, she knew that she was no fighter—a daring escape from the heart of the enemy stronghold was something she could never hope to accomplish.

The only place that seemed to offer the chance of help was the prince's homeland. She didn't know what kind of help the lords of Corwell could offer, but she had nowhere else to turn.

And still the wind blew and the gray waves rolled.

* * * * *

"Put him in here," said the short cleric, pushing aside a wool tapestry to reveal a small room. The only furnishing was a narrow bed, but Daryth and Pawldo were grateful for the chance to lay Tristan upon even that tiny platform. Pontswain remained outside, sword held at the ready, looking up and down the long ribbon of darkened, empty road.

The cleric ran back to the doors of his chapel and saw that the road was empty. The deepest hours of night were just beginning to yield to morning.

"Cowan!" he called. "Come here!"

Moments later a lad of about fifteen emerged from a small alcove, rubbing his eyes and yawning. He blinked curiously at the visitors, and his eyes widened as he saw the bloodstained prince stretched, pale and deathlike, on the bed.

"See to their horses, lad!" barked the cleric. Cowan hurried from the chapel as the man turned back to them. "I am Patriarch Trevor, a cleric of Chauntea," he said, moving quickly to Tristan's side. The man moved with a smooth and easy grace. He took the prince's hand in one of his while pressing the other to Tristan's forehead.

"He is very near death. A few more miles on horseback, I'm certain, would have killed him." The patriarch closed his eyes, still touching the prince's wrist and face. He whispered softly, a ritual sound that lasted nearly a minute.

A warm glow seemed to surround the prince, visible as a faint light to the watchers. Daryth had a feeling of deep reverence, and wanted to drop to his knees. He stubbornly resisted the urge, instead staring, spellbound, as the cleric worked his healing magic.

"Chauntea," said the cleric reverently. Tristan winced and thrashed on the narrow mattress. A sudden, shocking spurt of red blood burst from his mouth to spatter the cleric, but the patriarch ignored it. Daryth's hand leaped to his sword; he feared for the prince, but the cleric held a steadying hand up, and the Calishite relaxed.

The prince groaned and twisted on the bed. His eyes opened, but the pupils rolled so far back in his head that only the whites were visible. The cleric whispered again, and the soft glow brightened and then slowly faded away.

As the cleric finally opened his eyes, Tristan's chest began to rise and fall with deep, regular breathing. Slowly, color began to creep into his face.

"He sleeps," explained the cleric. "Now, let us talk."

Daryth and Pawldo followed him into another small room. Here Trevor pulled a bottle of wine from a wooden chest and gestured them to sit at the small table.

"You are fugitives," he said finally. "But from what?"

Pawldo and Daryth exchanged quick looks, obviously surprised by the blunt question. Finally, the halfling spoke.

"The High King's ogres took the pri—uh, my friend on false charges. We helped him get away, but he was wounded during the escape."

"Ogres of the Scarlet Guard!" growled the patriarch with surprising venom. "The mercenary scum!" Seeing their startled looks, he explained.

"The guard is just another example of the blight that seems to have fallen across our land. We watched them march through Grady—that's this little town—some days past. The sight of the people huddled in their homes, shivering in terror, broke my heart. Remember, these are the troops of their own king! I ask you, what kind of king would bring such terror to his own subjects?"

"Those kings are more common than you'd like to believe,"

said Daryth. "Though this is the first I've heard of such a ruler in the Moonshaes. In my experience, the Ffolk have been ruled with freedoms that far exceed the norm."

"True," agreed Pontswain, coming through the door. "The road is quiet. How is the prince?"

"He will live," said the patriarch.

The lord did not respond as he moved to sit in the only vacant chair. Daryth wondered whether Pontswain considered the news good or bad.

"Why haven't the lords of Callidyrr stood up to the king?" asked the lord. "I can't imagine that we, in Corwell, would stand for such behavior."

"They have tried. Several have disappeared, others have gone to the dungeon. Those that disappear have had their lands confiscated and their holdings assigned to allies of the king. One, the former Lord Roarke, has become an outlaw in the forest, railing bitterly against his fate, but helpless to do anything about it."

"Why hasn't there been a rebellion?" pressed Pontswain.

"I don't know," shrugged the cleric. "Perhaps because they lack a strong leader. Or, more likely, because the Ffolk are frightened." The patriarch seemed to consider his statement, and his situation. He was silent for a moment.

"I am glad that I could help you, but you have powerful enemies. I can hide you here until nightfall, but then you will have to be on your way. It is not for myself that I fear, but this entire village would doubtless be destroyed were you discovered here."

"We understand," said Daryth. "And thank you for what you have done."

"But you must decide where you will go from here," the cleric reminded them. "Or do you already know?"

"To Caer Callidyrr to see the High King."

The voice drew their attention to the doorway, and they turned to see the Prince of Corwell standing there, watching them grimly.

"Tristan!" Pawldo jumped to his feet as the men looked in astonishment at the prince. He leaned against the door, his face drawn with pain. But the color had returned to his skin, and his eyes glowed with determination and anger.

"You should be asleep," said Trevor, rising to offer the prince his chair.

"I shall be soon. But we need to plan first."

"Are you certain you want to go to Caer Callidyrr?" asked the patriarch.

"Yes."

"Very well. The King's Road, the highway you took from Llewellyn, is certain to be patrolled in strength. It would mean almost certain capture for you to travel there. But there are other roads, trails really, that lead to the west of here, and then north, through Dernall Forest. The soldiers of the king do not venture into the forest much, but the forest has its own challenges. For one thing, the trails are few and difficult to follow."

"We have some woodcraft," said the prince. "We'll travel the forest roads."

"I can give you a map and some directions. You will have to trust to your good sense for the rest of your guidance." The cleric proceeded to sketch a spiderweb of winding trails onto a sheet of parchment. "You will be very weak for several days," he warned Tristan. "That wound would have killed most men, I'm certain. So have a care for yourself, and rest when you need to."

"Thank you, friar. We shall," said the prince. "I have but one question: Why have you done all of this for us?"

"The ways of my goddess are not for mortals to understand, not even her clerics. I but do her bidding. Remember this, if you think of nothing else: Chauntea is your ally. She hopes for the success of your mission, and she will aid you as much as lies in her power.

"Now that you are here, I understand. Your mission to Caer Callidyrr—no, don't tell me any more about it. But I understand that a king who hires monsters to protect himself from his own people cannot work for the good of those people or their land. This king is offensive to my goddess, and therefore her blessing falls upon your mission.

"May you ride like the wind and be as difficult to catch," concluded Patriarch Trevor.

The cleric's words seemed to have a pleasant effect. Tristan felt warmth spread through his body, and a feeling of benign goodwill descended upon him. "Thank you for everything," he said, clasping the patriarch's hand firmly. "You have given our mission new hope!"

"As you have done for mine, also," said the cleric quietly.

Then they slept, and when darkness fell the men mounted their black horses and slipped into the night, the great moorhound trotting watchfully ahead.

* * * * *

Bhaal wallowed in the fire pits of Gehenna, luxuriating in the sensual feel of lava fueled with fresh blood.

The god of death, lover of all murderous acts, was in fine fettle. His devotees, and even those opposed to him, were acting in concert to provide entertainment. But even more than entertainment, each act of killing strengthened Bhaal, increasing his influence among the gods and enhancing his ability to interfere in the affairs of men.

And so Bhaal watched the events unfolding before him. He thrilled at the sight of the dead army that was defiling Myrloch Vale. They would be his mightiest achievement when he was done, creating a legion of death that would bring the entire land beneath his baneful rule. Bhaal drooled at the thought of the young druid's blood warming his belly as Hobarth performed the ritual sacrifice.

He watched the events upon Alaron with less interest, but took mild note of the occasional body left in the wake of the fleeing prince. More than once he had thought that the death of the prince himself was imminent, but each time the mortals had managed to fend it off—just barely.

But Bhaal was patient.

❧ 10 ❧

Shapeshifter

The unicorn nuzzled Robyn's shoulder affectionately. The druid said nothing, but the weight of responsibility she had borne this day seemed to grow lighter.

She leaned back and looked at the great creature, child of the goddess herself. Kamerynn's white beard hung in a thick tuft from his jaw, and his ivory horn jutted proudly before him, more than four feet long.

His large eyes were bright and clear, and Robyn whispered a soft prayer of thanks for this miracle. Only a year earlier, the great unicorn had been blinded, his skin and eyes scalded by the power of the Beast. But his healing seemed complete, and his broad nostrils snorted as if to belittle the hurts he had suffered.

"Kamerynn, you big horse!" Newt shouted with joy as he buzzed into the oak grove and saw his old friend. He darted like an arrow to the unicorn, perching proudly on Kamerynn's long horn.

"Thank the goddess you're here!" he chattered. "Robyn has been having an awful time with the animals. Oh, she tries you know, but she's still so young. Now that you're here, I'm sure we can get all of these—"

Kamerynn turned his broad head to the rear, interrupting Newt's explanation, and the dragon was forced to grasp the moving horn tightly to retain his perch. The bushes behind him parted very slightly, and a tiny face looked timidly at Robyn. The unicorn gestured with his horn, and the little creature stepped forward.

Robyn saw that it looked like a small man, about two feet tall, except that it had gossamer wings sprouting from each shoulder and long pointed ears. As the little creature bowed, she noticed two long things, almost like the antennae of a bug, growing from the fellow's forehead. She knew then that this was a wood sprite. He was dressed in a green tunic and cap, and he carried a small bow and quiver in his hands and a dagger at his belt.

"Welcome to the grove," she said, extending her hands.

"Yazilliclik!" cried Newt, diving from the horn to hover before the sprite. "You're here too! We should have a party!" He turned to Robyn, hovering up to her eye level. "Can we have a party, Robyn? Can we have a party, please?"

"No! Can't you tell there's something serious going on, Newt?" She felt genuinely angry at the dragon. He had been no help at all as she had struggled to control the animals.

Newt looked piqued for a second before zooming back to Kamerynn's horn to watch the proceedings with interest.

"I . . . I must tell you of the danger," said the sprite in a high and musical voice that sounded an odd contrast to the seriousness of the missive. Robyn understood his nervousness. Sprites were among the shyest of the creatures in the Vale. Though there were many of them in the surrounding woods, she had never seen one. She knew that it must have taken great courage to bring Yazilliclick here.

"There is terrible—t-terrible—danger abroad! We have seen the army that defiles the vale," said the sprite. "It is coming here!"

"An army!" gasped Robyn.

"That is not the worst of it—not the worst!" added Yazilliclick. "It is not an army of men, or llewyrr, or even firbolgs. It is an army of corpses!"

"Corpses? But how . . . ?" Robyn was too stunned to think. Certainly the little sprite could not be telling the truth!

Yazilliclick nodded his head, his tiny antennae bouncing. He looked like he was about to start crying. "I d-don't—don't—know!" he wailed. "But they come this way—this way! And they are evil! Evil!"

None of them saw the great eagle dropping silently from the twilight skies until it settled to the ground beside them. The eagle's shape shifted and suddenly Genna Moonsinger stood beside them. Even in the dim light, Robyn saw that she was pale. She started to speak, and her voice was strained, as if she struggled to control it. She had obviously heard the sprite's last remark.

"They draw nearer with every minute—they will be upon us in two days at the most.

"I have sent the sparrows to summon the other druids of the Vale. We will gather here as quickly as possible. Perhaps together our might will daunt this force somehow." The druids of the Vale, several dozen in number, each tended their own sacred groves, scattered across the face of Gwynneth. Here, at the grove of the Great Druid, they gathered occasionally for councils, but for the most they were solitary men and women, seeking little human companionship.

Genna turned to look at Yazilliclick, and her eyes softened. "Thank you, little one, for coming here. I know how hard it was for you."

"I'll s-stay, to help," blurted the faerie, looking immediately as if he regretted the offer.

Next, the Great Druid raised her chin and looked her pupil squarely in the eyes. "Robyn, you must remain here awhile. I know of your concern for the king and for your prince, but you are needed here."

Robyn sensed the command in her teacher's words, but that command was not necessary. She knew where her duty lay, and she nodded in response. There was nothing else that she could do.

* * * * *

The patriarch's map proved invaluable as the black horses carried the riders through the night. They alternated mounts frequently, allowing two of the steeds to run free while the others carried Tristan, Daryth, Pontswain, and Pawldo. Keeping the mounts fresh, they made excellent time.

The hours in the saddle wore heavily on Tristan, however, as the pain of his wound grew into a throbbing ache across his entire back. He said nothing, fearing that his companions would slow their pace, but he was nonetheless relieved as dawn approached and they began to look for a place to hide during the day.

There were few likely spots along the winding country lanes. Alaron—at least, this portion of it—seemed devoid of wilderness, or even of large tracts of forested land. They eventually left the road, riding across several fields and crossing numerous stone fences before finding a little clump of woods in a secluded hollow. Here they dismounted, ate some of the bread and fruit that the cleric had sent with them, and prepared to rest.

Pawldo left the three men to fill his watersack in a nearby stream, and they sat quietly for a time.

"I suppose you've realized that our original mission no longer has much relevance," said Pontswain, lounging.

Tristan looked at him suspiciously. He could not help but suspect the lord's motives, but he nodded now. "Indeed, there's not much point in petitioning approval from a man who has ordered me arrested and killed."

"Then let's go back to Corwell and leave this madhouse to its inmates!" said the lord. "What can you hope to accomplish here?"

"I can gain a measure of vengeance for my father's death! I can force the king to admit his crimes against the Ffolk— perhaps even to make some of them right again!"

"You're mad! He's tried to have you killed already! Now you want to travel to his very stronghold and tell him you don't like what he's done? You don't have a chance!"

"On the contrary, I think I have a good chance. We have avoided his pitfalls thus far. And besides, I have to try something! I cannot let my father's death go unavenged!"

"Your foolish vengeance will get us all killed!"

"You are free to return to Corwell whenever you want. We can go on without you," Tristan challenged. Pontswain slumped silently, scowling.

Pawldo returned with a dripping goatskin of water and passed the bag around. Silently, they drank, as the halfling flopped to the ground beside them.

"How do you propose to gain entrance into the castle?" asked Daryth as they settled into their makeshift beds.

"I don't know," admitted the prince. "But if there's always a way to escape from a place, as you've told me, then it follows that there's always a way to get in."

"The opposite of escape is capture," announced Pawldo.

"We have to get there before we worry about getting in," observed the Calishite. "And from the looks of this country that's far from guaranteed, especially if there are troops out looking for us."

"On the other hand, the troops of the High King seem to be none too popular in this part of the country, if the Ffolk in The Diving Dolphin or the cleric Trevor are any indication," said Tristan.

"Still, let's try and stay hidden," warned the halfling. "I don't want to have to rescue you again!"

"I've been meaning to ask you about that," said the prince. "How did you pull that off—distracting the ogres?"

Pawldo chuckled, not a little proud. He told the story of the assassins in the tree and his entry into the manor house. For once, he embellished the details only slightly.

"It was our good fortune to have a friend like you lurking in the shadows," laughed the prince. Pawldo grinned, enjoying the praise.

"Now tell me," asked the halfling. "What did you scoundrels do to get in trouble with the law? Were you stealing milk from a baby? Or perhaps you got enthusiastic about the young daughter of some local lord?"

"Nothing so straightforward," said Tristan. He explained about the assassination of King Kendrick and their mission to Alaron. After a long hesitation, he described the castle of Queen Allisynn and the prophecy he had received there.

"I'm sorry to hear about your father," Pawldo said.

Tristan felt a moment of sorrow. It came suddenly and then passed. He realized, with a twinge of guilt, that it had been many days since he had thought of his father. But now he could feel some sense of atonement. "We did more than a little avenging in Llewellyn," he said. "I'm certain that the men with Razfallow were the same who accompanied him to Corwell."

"I wish that bloodthirsty devil hadn't gotten away," said Daryth bitterly. "But we've certainly trimmed down the numbers of his band."

"It's too bad we couldn't have put an end to his killing," said the prince. "But we'll have another chance, I'm certain."

"Especially with your subtle plan," snapped Pontswain. He had been listening to their conversation, using a saddle to keep his head off the ground. But now he sat up.

"I didn't ask you to come along!" retorted the prince, his anger kindled.

"No, that was my decision. And now that I'm here, I'm wondering what kind of madness you're planning next!"

"My lord Pontswain, this is my fight—and it has become a personal matter. I neither seek nor welcome your involvement in it! If you have concerns that can be better addressed elsewhere . . ."

"Indeed I do, prince. I want our kingdom to prosper—to see some of the glory it had ages ago. If I am king, I think it will. Perhaps the same thing can happen under your rulership. But I haven't seen any proof of that yet!"

Tristan flushed, instinctively reaching for his sword. Anger blazed from his eyes as he met Pontswain's level gaze. The lord's face was curiously unemotional.

"Oh, you wield your blade well—certainly better than I do," continued Pontswain. "But I wonder how well you can wield your mind!"

Tristan forced down his rage, but the remark cut him deeply. In a dark corner of his mind, he realized that Pontswain was too close to the truth. What ideas did he have to offer? What kind of a plan had he assembled?

"Perhaps under the tutelage of your wisdom I'll learn!" he snapped, trying to turn Pontswain's sarcasm back at him. But the challenge sounded hollow, even to himself.

"On that cheerful thought, I'm going to get some rest," said Daryth. The others, too, rolled into their blankets. Tristan was still livid. His mind coughed up numerous sharp remarks that he regretted he had not thought of at the time. But as his anger cooled, a strange thought struck him. For the first time he saw Pontswain not just as a rival for the throne, but as a man who truly cared for the kingdom. The knowledge was disturbing, and he took it with him to sleep.

That night they rode again, gradually turning north. They found themselves entering wilder country now, though still tame in comparison to Corwell. The prince's wound still hurt, but did not seem to have gotten worse during the last day. This time they found it easy to find a secluded place to spend the day, and on the following night they rode into Dernall Forest itself.

"At least we're a bit more secure here," remarked the prince as they trotted down a dark forest lane. Canthus, as usual, loped along before them. "We should have no trouble finding a place to hide during the day."

All of them felt more relaxed among the thick, sheltering branches. Though the moon was half full, the canopy of leaves made the road almost black.

That changed very suddenly. Their only warning was a low growl as Canthus froze, staring into the darkness. Harsh words in a strange language barked from the night.

"Magic!" cried Pawldo in alarm, and even as he spoke the ground itself suddenly glowed with cool, bright light.

The little party halted, clearly outlined by the bright spell, and blinded from seeing anything beyond their circle.

"Do not move, strangers," said a voice from the darkness. The voice was strong, filled with the authority of command.

Tristan's eyes finally adjusted to the brightness enough that he could make out forms moving toward them from all sides. He saw men, armed with the largest longbows he had ever seen, in a circle around them. He counted several dozen with his first glance, and he saw that each member of his party was in the sights of a weapon.

The prince hauled back on his reins, searching for escape, but the ring of archers was solid—and very menacing. There was something frightening in the lack of emotion he detected among them, as if this was simply in a day's work.

Yes, he realized now, they were captives once again.

* * * * *

"The Black Rock is gone," said Newt miserably. Yazilliclick nodded in agreement. "Somebody must have taken it! This is all my fault!" The faerie dragon was on the verge of tears. His wings drooped miserably when he landed on the bench, returning from the mission Genna had given him.

"You helped us very much by removing it from the grove," said Genna. "You are not to blame for the evil that has befallen us."

Robyn stroked Newt's head and long neck, surprised at his contrition. She had never seen the faerie dragon expressing anything approaching remorse before.

"Now," continued Genna, addressing the creatures that had gathered before her cottage. "You must all listen very carefully." Around her were arrayed Kamerynn the unicorn, the great brown bear Grunt, and a hundred or more of the animals—the strongest and wisest from among the teeming throngs.

The Great Druid sought to calm the fears and soothe the tensions of the gathered wild creatures. She needed them to remain peaceful throughout the night, for she and Robyn would not be able to watch them. Finally she finished, and the animals drifted away to rejoin their kind.

"Now Newt, Yazilliclick," said the Great Druid. "I must ask you to care for the grove while we're gone. The other druids should be arriving soon; you must tell them where we have gone. Will you do this?"

The sprite nodded.

"Can't I come along?" pleaded Newt. "You will get into—"

"We need you here," soothed Robyn. "You must help us."

"I will," said the faerie dragon with a resigned sigh. He darted to Kamerynn's horn and looked away from them.

"Now, my dear, it is time," Genna said quietly, turning to Robyn. The two druids entered the cottage. There, Genna opened several clay jars and removed pieces of holly and mistletoe. Robyn picked up her long staff—the legacy of her mother. She handled the smooth ashwood staff reverently, grateful for the potent magic it contained. It alone provided her a weapon that might slow the unnatural army approaching through the Vale.

"Come along." Her teacher walked outside again, with Robyn following. They crossed the now-silent grove to its heart—a sacred place where even the animals did not go. Here the Moonwell illuminated the surrounding ring of stone columns with a soft, milky glow. Here the power of the goddess was most accessible to her druids.

"Woman, you must concentrate like you never have before. You must realize that your youth and lack of experience make this even more dangerous than it must be."

"I understand, teacher," said Robyn solemnly.

"I would not even allow you to consider this action, were it not for our dire emergency. And I admit, the fact that you have displayed an inherent talent gives me some reassurance that you are capable of this feat.

"Now, hold your staff, and listen to me."

Robyn planted the staff at her side, grasping it firmly in her right hand. She heard Genna whisper something—private words to the goddess.

"Remember your lessons," intoned the Great Druid, her voice taking on the cadence of a chant. "Remember the bright eyes. Remember the long, light bones—and the feathers. Think of the beak and the claws, so hard. Concentrate!"

Robyn remembered well. She pictured the powerful bird upon her teacher's lap, and she saw every detail of its graceful body. She didn't feel the magic of the Earthmother wash over her or even notice the sudden change in her body, so intently was she focused within her mind.

She only noticed as she stretched to keep from falling. Driving powerful wings downward, she felt her feet lift from the ground. She looked around, and her eyes saw the Moonwell in minute detail, falling away below. Again and again she extended her wings, aware of Genna soaring beside her, but only slowly did she understand.

She was an eagle. She was flying!

* * * * *

Alexei endured days and nights of black silence, chained to the wall of a stone cell. Madness came closer daily, and the mage had few weapons with which to fight for sanity.

Only hours after Alexei's imprisonment, Cyndre and a cruel painmaster had paid a visit to the cell. The painmaster was an expert from Calimshan who had gleefully broken Alexei's hands, taking care to shatter every bone.

For a time the agonizing pain of those wounds had served to give him focus. But gradually the bones healed, freezing the appendages into twisted claws, useless for the delicate spell-casting gestures required by Alexei's craft. And as they healed, the pain lessened, and Alexei had only the darkness and solitude to comfort him.

Now that the pain was gone completely, he had only his hate to keep him going. And so he nurtured that hatred, caressing it in his mind, building it and storing it for the moment it could be released. He hated the king and Kryphon; he was certain that they had betrayed him. And he hated the painmaster who had broken his hands.

But most of all he hated Cyndre. The mage thought over and over of ways to destroy his former master. He relished thoughts of the sorcerer's death, a lingering death, utilizing a variety of methods, most of them magical.

But even had he been able to use his hands, he could not have cast a spell, for Cyndre had encased his cell within a cone of silence. Neither a chip of stone falling to the floor nor a hoarse scream from a terrified throat made any noise in that awful stillness.

For a time, the mage wondered why Cyndre had kept him alive instead of slaying him outright, but then he remembered the lurid god of the cleric Hobarth and his bloodthirsty altar. Blood of high magic flowed through Alexei's veins, and when Hobarth returned from his mission, the altar of Bhaal would welcome Alexei to its eternal night.

* * * * *

"Welcome, travelers!"

A tall man jumped smoothly from a tree limb into the pool of magical light. He was dressed in brown trousers and a long green shirt, and his face, through his flowing red beard, was aloof though not openly hostile. He spoke again.

"You really should take more care, you know. Traveling the ways of Dernall Forest on a night so dark!"

Tristan looked at the ring of archers surrounding them. None had moved a muscle. "Perhaps you would be good enough to provide us with an escort?" he asked.

"Ha ha!" The man gestured broadly, as if inviting his men to join the laughter, but they remained poised to shoot. "An audacious one—I like that in a man. Perhaps you'll be allowed to hang onto a coin or two!"

Tristan felt a small measure of relief. These were bandits, and this encounter would certainly cost them money. But they were not soldiers and thus were not likely to turn them over to the king's mercenaries. Still, this was no ragged band. The discipline shown by the bowmen was worthy of a veteran company of warriors, and they were supported by one or more magic-users, as evidenced by the light spell. These men could be very dangerous, he was certain.

"Now, gentlemen, if you'll be good enough to hand over your purses, we can conclude this little interview. Don't be stingy, now!"

Tristan saw Pawldo scowling to his right, and he realized that the halfling was probably carrying a heavy pouch of coins. Neither the prince nor Daryth had much to lose by paying the bandits, but the halfling had no doubt assembled a tidy profit from his year-long endeavor. Then, too, Tristan remembered, he had lifted a pouch from the officer of the Scarlet Guard.

"May I inquire, sir, whose coffers are being fattened by these ill-gotten gains?" asked the prince.

"Ill-gotten?" The bandit chief looked distressed. "Sir, you wound me! Consider it a toll, if you will. . . . A toll for keeping these paths free of the king's scum! Your contributions will go to the coffers of Hugh O'Roarke—that is, myself!"

The name meant nothing to Tristan.

"We are no friends of the king ourselves. We ride these forest paths expressly to avoid the scum you refer to."

"Could it be that you are fugitives?" O'Roarke's expression was mildly curious.

"It could. In fact, we have a small pouch of the king's own gold that we would happily contribute to your cause in exchange for passage through your domain and perhaps information that may aid us in our mission."

"Hey!" Pawldo hissed. "That's mine! You can't—"

"Be still," growled the prince out of the side of his mouth.

"Travelers with a mission, eh? Let us have a look at this pouch, and perhaps we can talk."

"My squire has it in his pack. Pawldo, pay the man."

Muttering curses, Pawldo drew forth the sack he had lifted from the officer's cabinet and tossed it to O'Roarke. As he did so, Tristan realized that they had never checked to see that the pouch contained gold. But the gilded metal was clearly visible in the bright light, and even some of the archers wavered their attention as the bandit ran a glittering stream into his hand.

"Very well," he said, smiling broadly through his red beard. "You will enjoy our protection for a time." He looked at their weapons and apparently liked what he saw. "It may be that there is a place for you among our band of cutthroats."

His last remark worried Tristan more than anything else the bandit had said. The prince wondered if they would ever get the chance to leave.

* * * * *

The wizard turned from the mirror and stalked angrily across the council chamber. His cool detachment had vanished the moment he had learned of the events in Llewellyn. The prince had escaped!

Forcefully, Cyndre brought his emotions under control. The sorcerer knew that only through calm reflection could he hope to devise an effective plan for dealing with the young upstart. Not until the prince was out of the way would Cyndre have any opportunity to expand his own power. Already, Callidyrr seemed too small—and Corwell was the logical next step in the wizard's dream of conquest. For a second, he wondered if the prophecy of Bhaal, warning of the danger inherent in the Prince of Corwell, had meant more than he suspected. Could it be that the prince was destined to defeat all of the council's plans?

Of course not! Cyndre knew that the young man had been very lucky several times. And that the assassin Razfallow had failed him for the last time. The half-orc was marked for death, though this task must take a lower priority than the slaying of the prince. There would be time enough to deal with the assassin.

"Kryphon." The wizard's command was spoken softly, and its target was sleeping soundly in a distant part of the castle. Nevertheless, within seconds Kryphon had materialized beside his master. Kyrphon's black eyebrows were raised inquiringly, and his tight, narrow face betrayed a look of interest as he waited for his master to explain the summons. The thin black beard encircling his jaw twitched nervously,

and he licked his thin, almost nonexistent, lips.

"Kryphon, our friend Razfallow has failed us again. We shall have to take matters into our own hands."

"Yes, master," the young mage said. He tried, unsuccessfully, to conceal a thin smile of anticipation. Absently, he stroked one of the bright diamond brooches he was prone to wearing on his robe.

"The prince escaped from the Scarlet Guard in Llewellyn, so you should start there. I shall continue to seek him in the mirror. When I find him, I will let you know where he is."

"I should like to take Doric with me. Her powers can be a great asset in a task like this." Kryphon said.

"Indeed," agreed Cyndre, although he looked carefully at his subordinate. "I sense it is more than her fire-magic that you want. Very well, Doric shall accompany you.

"But Kryphon," Cyndre added. His voice was very quiet.

"Master?" The wizard met Cyndre's gaze evenly, but his heart chilled at the look in those pale blue eyes.

"Take care that you do not fail me, as well."

❦ 11 ❦

Doncastle

The exhilaration of flight lasted all too briefly. Robyn quickly gained control of her avian body, soaring and gliding on currents of wind. She observed that while Genna climbed with little effort, she herself was forced to flap her wings steadily in order to gain altitude. Gradually, she saw how the Great Druid took advantage of every rising eddy of air, and she was able to copy the movements of her teacher. She delighted in the sensation of flight.

But then she looked down.

They had flown miles in the few moments since taking wing, or so it seemed to the young druid. And now they saw before them, trailing off into the hazy distance, a brown pathway of blight and decay. Dead trees stood barren, their leaves gone. The grass across a wide belt had withered to brown. Even the air grew heavy with the foul stink of rot.

The route of the army was easy to see, for they had murdered the land as they moved. The swath crept northward, and Robyn could see that its path took it directly toward the Great Druid's grove—and the Moonwell.

Directly below them, hundreds of tiny figures crawled methodically forward. Even from this height, she could see the inhuman nature of the creatures. The skeletons gleamed a ghastly white against the withered ground. All the undead moved with a lurching, shambling gait that reminded her vividly of the zombie that had attacked her in the grove. The spirit of the forest itself seemed to cry out in agony as the undead advanced, stretching the boundaries of the wasteland, moving ever northward.

Robyn watched hundreds of remarkably humanlike figures plod purposefully northward. Her keen eyes saw several huge forms among them, and she bristled at the sight of the firbolg bodies. The army entered a grove of quaking aspens, their white trunks and silvery leaves glistening brightly in the sunlight. Horrified, she saw the leaves turn brown and fall like a blizzard of dead snow. The white bark turned brown and curled away from the trees; the grove seemed to sigh sadly as it died.

Thick fumes rose into the air, threatening to gag Robyn. The stink of the bodies, the stink of death that arose from the land itself, made the air both heavy and poisonous. She swirled through the foul stuff, seeking a breath of freshness, but there was none to be had. As the army moved on, it left the grove barren and defiled.

Robyn saw Genna tuck her wings and plummet toward the earth. In another moment she did the same, falling with dizzying rapidity. She spread her wings desperately as the ground rushed toward her, surprising herself by gliding quickly forward. She had to circle to land beside the Great Druid, a half mile from the army of the undead and directly in its path.

The rocky knoll Genna had chosen came up fast, and Robyn twisted desperately to avoid a thrusting boulder that threatened to end her flight abruptly. The air slipped from beneath her wings and she crashed heavily to the ground, feeling a sharp pain in her left wing.

Slowing her breathing, she willed her body to become her own again. She was certain that her arm was broken. But as she stretched and grew, the pain in her limb vanished and she felt a smooth transition back to her human form. She once again held her staff in her hand and slowly climbed to her feet. Genna, too, had changed to human form and now stood looking to the south.

Robyn saw that the Great Druid had selected a rounded, rocky hilltop, almost barren of trees. The undead would be slowed by the rugged ground, and the spells of the druids would be unlikely to do serious harm to the forest here.

"Remember," said Genna. "Do not use your staff unless it becomes absolutely essential. Its powers are best held for our final defense. Our goal tonight is to delay and harass."

"And when we have delayed them?"

"Then we escape. You are to change upon my signal. When you have done so, I will follow. We must then return to the grove with all possible haste!"

Genna turned to the south, and Robyn followed her teacher's gaze. Gradually, through the widely spaced trunks of the oaks that spread away from the base of the hill, they began to see the vanguard of the horrible force. A few zombies, shuffling mindlessly forward, appeared among the trees.

"Why?" Robyn whispered. "Why are they doing this?"

For once, her teacher had no answer.

Robyn's horror gradually turned to anger. She wanted to destroy the unnatural creatures, wiping them from the face of Gwynneth. She clenched her staff and gritted her teeth as they drew closer.

"Protect yourself, dear," said Genna quietly. The great druid cast a simple spell upon herself, and Robyn did the same. The minor spell, called barkskin, toughened their natural skin without changing its appearance or flexibility. They hoped it would be unnecessary, for they did not intend to get close enough to the enemy for the claws of the zombies to strike them, but it seemed a wise precaution.

"Here," added the teacher, handing acorns to Robyn. "I have enchanted these—you have but to throw them."

The acorns felt warm in Robyn's hand, and the knowledge that she held a potent weapon steadied her nerves.

The monsters had now reached the base of the hill and started to creep among the boulders, shuffling up the slope. Genna stared at them, and for a moment Robyn saw vehemence flashing in the Great Druid's eyes. The woman blinked slowly, and her face became a mask of concentration.

Several dozen zombies now moved up the hill, clumsily tripping and climbing to their feet. The creatures' smell preceded them, and Genna reached into a pocket to draw forth some crushed herbs. She rubbed some of the fragrant mixture upon her nose and upper lip and handed the rest to Robyn. The young druid did the same and realized that the odor became unnoticeable.

She was shocked at the visible difference between these

zombies—dead for a year—and the sight of Acorn's undead body. She had thought nothing could be more horrible than the man's broken neck and limply hanging head. But now she saw the gruesome colors—black, gray, even green—on the flesh of the attackers. Occasional patches of bone showed through gaps in rotten flesh—a forehead here, or jawbone there. Most were missing their eyes and ears, and many had lost limbs to the battle that had killed them, if not the decay that had followed their deaths.

A number of bodies followed, but these had no flesh whatsoever; they were simply walking skeletons. From a distance Robyn thought the skeletons looked even more unnatural than the animated corpses.

She realized that these humans had been dead for a long time, and suddenly she knew where they came from. She could see the long blond hair and coarse beards of Northmen, and thought she knew the stockier bodies of her own Ffolk. Memories of the Darkwalker War assailed her, especially the part she had played in the battle at Freeman's Down. And from that field, she knew, came this army, tragic warriors doomed to fight yet another battle, this time on the side of the enemy.

The monsters must have sensed the druids on the hilltop, for they quickened their pace, closing on the rounded summit instead of continuing their straight northward march. She wondered whether they had been commanded or if they simply sought, by instinct, to attack the humans that stood in their path.

Robyn wanted to shake Genna or scream at her, anything to force the Great Druid into action. But she dared not disturb her teacher's concentration.

The nearest zombie was no more than twenty feet away when Genna finally barked a single, sharp command. The ground itself seemed to shudder from the order, and Robyn saw huge boulders twist and roll from their places.

Dozens, then hundreds, of the great rocks sprang with a life of their own from the dry earth, erupting with explosive power to bound and thump down the hill into the midst of the undead horde. She saw one rock, as big as a horse, smash a zombie to a pulp and then crash through a bunch of skeletons, crunching bones like dry sticks.

The zombie nearest to them tried to dodge a boulder, but the creature was far too slow. The great rock smashed into its body, crushing both legs and half of its chest. Still, as the rock rolled on, the arms of the thing twitched and clutched toward the druids, dragging the crushed pulp of its body behind. The sight made Robyn gag.

Every rock on that hilltop sprang free under the prodding of the Great Druid's spell. The animated boulders leaped and rolled with a life of their own, even turning from their paths to strike down undead to the sides. The air was filled with rumbling and crashing sounds, made all the more eerie by the lack of sound from the attackers.

But at last the spell had run its course. Many dozen of the zombies and skeletons lay crushed and scores more struggled to move, but they had been too badly damaged to do so.

But hundreds more of them still emerged from the trees, picking their way through the rubble of rock and bodies at the base of the hill, and shambling relentlessly up the pitted slope. Robyn heard a scuffling sound to her left and almost screamed as she saw a zombie lurch through a hole where a rock had been. His rotted face showed patches of skull, and his eagerly clutching hands looked like animal claws.

She lobbed one of the acorns Genna had given her. The missile struck the thing in the chest and immediately erupted into flames. The zombie paused, dumbly, as the fire devoured its chest. Its mouth dropped open, and in another moment it fell apart, collapsing into a heap of smoldering arms and legs.

Another zombie lurched close, with a dozen skeletons some distance behind. Robyn threw another of the acorns. This one struck the ground at the creature's feet, swiftly consuming it in flames. The body stumbled and flailed aimlessly, finally falling to the ground and stiffening into a grotesque charcoal sculpture.

Robyn noticed that Genna was chanting another spell. The young druid suddenly covered her eyes as a wall of bright flames exploded from the ground before her. The earthpower of the goddess had answered her druid's call, sending the blaze directly from the earth. Tongues of orange fire snaked upward twenty feet or more, forming a ring around the two druids. The approaching skeletons were caught in the eruption, and many burned to ashes.

Strangely, Robyn could feel no heat from the flames, though they surrounded her and were only thirty feet away. But the fire was undeniably hot; the brush on the hillside sprang into flame, and still more skeletons were disintegrated as they stumbled mindlessly through.

"Come," chanted Genna.

Robyn was surprised to see the Great Druid start resolutely from the hilltop, marching toward the heart of the undead army. She followed, clutching her staff to her breast, but lifting her head proudly as she joined her teacher. The flames moved with them.

The ring of fire kept Genna at its center as the two druids moved carefully but steadily over the torn ground. Genna stumbled once, and the flames suddenly diminished, but Robyn caught her arm and steadied her. Once again the fire burned bright.

In a few minutes, they reached the ring of boulders at the bottom of the hill. Already several undead had been unable to avoid the advancing inferno. Robyn helped Genna step among the rocks, and still the fire burned around them.

Then, as they walked away from the rocks into the center of the army, the fire went out, snuffed as quickly as it had erupted. Genna gasped and clapped a hand to her mouth.

"What is it?" asked Robyn, suddenly very frightened.

"I don't know! Something interrupted my—"

The Great Druid's eyes widened as she saw something, screened by the undead. Robyn looked and saw a large body among the zombies, moving toward them strangely. It did not have the same lurching gait as the others. . . .

"We must flee!" hissed Genna. "Change, girl! Now!"

Robyn gasped as she saw the figure more clearly. It was a man! A living man among this army of death!

"Quickly!" urged Genna, stepping in front of Robyn. The young woman saw the man striding arrogantly toward them. He clutched some object before him with an unnatural intensity. It was a small thing, like a stone.

The sight of the man sent waves of terror through Robyn,

and she stood mutely, staring at his approach. Now she could see his face—he was grinning with demonic glee.

She shook her head suddenly and remembered Genna's command. Inhaling deeply, she forced herself to be calm. And she thought of the new body, the one she would change into. She felt herself fall forward, landing lightly on strong forepaws. A snarl—an instinctive mixture of fear and anger—curled her lip. The sleek body of the gray wolf felt fast and powerful.

Genna looked back and saw that Robyn had changed. The great druid closed her eyes quickly in concentration, but then she staggered under the impact of a zombie attack. The creature slashed at her again, and she fell to the ground.

Robyn was horrified to see the zombie lunging at Genna. Several others were moving in with stilted eagerness.

The body of the gray wolf crouched, and a deep growl rumbled from its chest. The Great Druid kicked at the zombie but turned her head toward her student.

"Flee, Robyn! While you still can!"

But Robyn sprang instead, and the force of her leap knocked the zombie to its side. Burning with canine rage, Robyn felt no revulsion as her teeth sank into the creature's arm. With a savage bite, she pulled the limb off and tossed it to the side.

Other zombies closed in, but Robyn heard a growl behind her, and she knew that Genna had changed. Whirling, Robyn raced to the side of another wolf, larger and more grizzled, but still very swift.

Like two gray ghosts, they darted among the clumsy creatures until they had passed from the ranks of the army. But even as the enemy fell far behind, the two wolves kept racing to the north toward the grove.

* * * * *

"Kralax withyss, torral."

Space shimmered suddenly under the combined influence of Kryphon's and Cyndre's spells. And then the younger man, with Doric, was instantly transported from the chamber in Caer Callidyrr to a place many miles to the south. Kryphon transported himself, but Cyndre's spell had been necessary to move Doric, for she did not have the power of teleportation yet.

The pair arrived in a small stable. Their appearance startled the assassin into wakefulness. Razfallow's hand darted to his dagger, but Kryphon was ready.

"Dothax, mylax heeroz, he said softly, gesturing swiftly at the assassin. Razfallow relaxed and stood.

"It is good to see you again, my friend," he said.

"And you," Kryphon replied. He smiled thinly, not from any pleasure at the greeting, but from this evidence that his spell had worked.

"Now, go back to sleep," Kryphon ordered. "I will tell you what I need later."

He turned to Doric, who stood silently at his side. The master was gone. Alexei had been dealt with. Finally, he had the woman all to himself. He reached out and threw back her hood, his thin smile growing into a crooked leer.

Doric smiled back at him. Her black hair framed her thin face, and her green eyes glittered with excitement. She was nearly as tall as Kryphon, and very thin. Most men would have described her as gaunt, but the wizard thought that she was the most desirable thing in the world—at least, for the moment.

"My pretty one, you shall serve me now—and only me. I will see that untold power is yours."

Doric narrowed her eyes and gazed coolly at him. He sensed, with disappointment, that the charm spell he had used to beguile her earlier had worn off. Still, she did not look unhappy.

"You don't have that power to offer, yet," she said, with a trace of a sneer. "But perhaps my desires are not so different from yours." She came easily into his arms, and the heat of her body was like a furnace.

Their mission could wait.

* * * * *

"It's not the grandest place on the isles, but we like it here," said Hugh O'Roarke modestly, gesturing into the deep valley before them.

"I don't understand," said Tristan. "Where's Doncastle?"

"Right there," grinned the bandit, pointing to the center of the valley. Tristan saw an expanse of green treetops, covering the entire valley floor except for the course of a bright and winding riverway that meandered through the forest.

O'Roarke had claimed that his town was large—and that it lay in the heart of this deep, forested valley. Yet there was no sign of anything but energetic nature.

"In fact, many of our houses are in the treetops," boasted the bandit chief.

"I've never heard of dwellings in the trees before. Isn't it a little inconvenient?" asked the prince.

"Perhaps inconvenient when staggering home from a night at the tavern, yes, but we find it very convenient when the troops of the king come to attack."

"You have stood against the army of the High King?" asked Pontswain, surprised.

"Certainly! His legions swarmed from the woods, but we were ready. The battle was a slaughter—for the king's troops! He has never bothered us again!"

Something about the bandit's bravado sounded empty, and the prince doubted he was telling the whole truth—at least, the unexaggerated truth. He wondered if the bandits had fought more than a small detachment.

"Legions, eh?" said Pontswain, echoing Tristan's doubts.

Hugh scowled, but then shrugged. He didn't say anything else, and Tristan didn't want to risk antagonizing their host any further. Instead, he surveyed the countryside as they neared the outskirts of Doncastle.

They rode along an open path that wound through a green-domed forest of towering oaks. All of the undergrowth between the trees had been cleared, creating a woods of quiet beauty and easy travel. Only when he looked closely did the prince see that a hundred yards off the path on either side the underbrush not only had not been removed, but it had been encouraged to grow into a high tangle of impenetrable branches. Anyone approaching the city would be nearly compelled to do so through the wide corridor.

"The Swanmay River," said the bandit, pointing to the placid waterway as they rode along its bank for a short distance. Expanding circles of ripples marked the surface where trout rose to strike at careless flies. The path twisted away from the river, back into the forest. "And this is Druid's Gate."

Tristan suddenly noticed that there were dwellings among the trees here. He saw a plank wall and several vine-covered roofs. Smoke emerged from several stumps, and he realized that these were cleverly disguised chimneys. Now he saw numerous round houses, roofed over with grassy sod. He also saw buildings of wood, built against the trunks of the oaks. So cleverly were they shaped that, at a distance, they looked like part of the tree itself.

Before he knew it they were in the town, yet the place still felt like a wilderness. Tristan saw people moving about on the ground, dressed in leather or simple woolen garments. Some of them looked at the travelers, nodding to Hugh without speaking. He saw few women and children, though somewhere he heard a baby crying. It felt as though he had entered any normal, if slightly impoverished, community of the Ffolk.

When he looked up he saw large shapes in the trees and long limbs extending throughout the canopy. He realized that these were bridges and that they connected many of the trees to each other.

Hugh led them to a clump of white aspens. The silvery leaves shimmered in a light breeze, and the trunks grew so close together that a small man would have had difficulty moving through the wood.

"The stables," announced Hugh, turning to the prince.

Several of the aspen trunks suddenly moved to the side, startling them. They saw that the trunks were actually lashed together to form a gate, though they looked like living, rooted trees. Beyond, the companions could see into the cleverly disguised corral. A man, dressed as the other bandits in brown and green leather, held the gate while Hugh's horse and the six steeds of the companions were herded inside.

"We must remain ever alert," proclaimed O'Roarke. "We never know when an attack will come again."

"Why does the king attack you?" asked the prince.

"You mean, of course, why am I a bandit here in the forest?" Hugh snapped. Tristan shrugged.

"I was not always. Once, I was a lord—a loyal lord—of Callidyrr. My holdings were not great but prosperous enough. But the king decided my lands could be better administrated by one of his lackeys, a fellow his wizard had brought to him, I believe. He took my lands, my family—everything. It was only good fortune that I was out hunting at the time and did not fall into his net.

"I returned to find the king's troops in my house, and to learn that he had declared me an outlaw. My sister had been taken to Caer Callidyrr—I do not know even now if she is still alive—and I had no one else to care for but myself.

"If the king would brand me an outlaw, I decided that an outlaw I would be. So here I am."

"How many lords has the king forced from their lands?" asked Tristan.

"Who knows?" shrugged Hugh. "Some have just disappeared; others have been murdered in the night. It is said that his assassins range across all the lands of the Ffolk, not just on Callidyrr."

"I have heard . . . about that too," said the prince. Then he decided to say more. Perhaps O'Roarke, in his apparent desire for vengeance, would help them.

"That is what brings us to Callidyrr. We seek to challenge the king and demand an explanation for what he has done!"

"You'll never get it," said Hugh. "The assassins are not the worst of the king's defenses."

"What do you mean?" said Pawldo, alarmed.

"Seven wizards have sworn loyalty to him. The mightiest of them, Cyndre, is a sorcerer with awesome powers."

"Nevertheless, we intend to try," said the prince.

O'Roarke looked at him with a strange intensity. Tristan could not read the emotions in the man's inscrutable face.

"Well," said Hugh O'Roarke, sounding vaguely amused. "We shall see about that, won't we?"

* * * * *

The gray wolves loped steadily through the long night. At last, panting and limping, they reached the stream that marked the border of the Great Druid's grove. Wearily, they flopped to the grassy bank. First Genna, then Robyn, changed shape.

The young druid lay on her back, enjoying the cushion of the soft grass. She felt better; her weariness, and the pain in her paws and haunches, had vanished with the canine body.

"Come, girl, there is much to be done," said Genna, quickly climbing to her feet. She stopped suddenly and turned to the younger woman.

"Thank you," she said quietly. "That was very brave of you. And you made the change more smoothly than any initiate I have ever taught. You have the capacity to do great work for the goddess—and I fear we shall need all of your strength now, and mine as well. Even then, I don't know if we can prevail."

Genna stepped into the stream and Robyn followed. She had to hurry to match her teacher's purposeful stride.

"That man," Robyn began. "Who, or what, was he? Why was he with the dead?"

"I don't know who he is. He must be a cleric of some powerful and very evil god, judging by his might."

"You mean that is *his* army?" Robyn suppressed a shudder.

"I think so. It was certainly his magic that dispelled my ring of fire. And he did that very easily."

"What can we do?" asked Robyn. She felt panic rising within her.

"Do? Why, my dear, we can fight!"

They emerged from the stream but did not waste time drying themselves off as they started into the grove. Robyn gasped in surprise as she saw a human figure standing beside one of the trees, but she relaxed when she realized it was another druid.

"Isolde, thank you," said Genna, clasping her friend in a firm hug. "I need your help, very badly."

"Of course, I came as soon as I got the message." Isolde was a powerful druid who tended Winterglen, a grove at the northern fringe of the Vale. She was tall and stern, with bright red hair that would not stay confined within her hood. "What is the emergency?"

"Come, I shall tell you as soon as we reach the Moonwell.

How many of the others are here?"

"Perhaps eight or ten. I have been here for several hours, awaiting your return, so I am not certain. The wood sprite told me that you had gone to the south."

A small sparrow darted between them and settled to the ground. It quickly grew into a man wearing a plain brown robe like Isolde's.

"Waine, come with us please," said the Great Druid, not even pausing as the man fell into step beside them.

Robyn held back, slightly awestruck at the gathering of these mighty druids. The youngest of her order, she had never attended a druidic council before.

Genna led them between the vast stone arches that ringed the Moonwell, and here they found ten more of the druids, waiting patiently for their leader. Genna strode to the edge of the pool. There the milky glow from the sacred water illuminated her, even in the brightness of the morning sun. Each druid turned to the well and bowed, whispering a soft prayer to the goddess.

Robyn expected to see a ritual, a dramatic affirmation of their faith, and a stirring evocation by Genna of the danger facing them. She was disappointed when her teacher, very hurriedly, told the druids of the army that marched upon them, emphasizing the imminence of the danger. With a final word of hope, she sent them off to the fringes of the grove to work on whatever preparations they could make before the attack.

Robyn used her power to raise tall hedges of thorns across the clearings and to entangle the branches of the trees and bushes wherever they grew close together. Newt and Yazilliclick kept a guard out for the approaching horror.

Finally the grove was surrounded, and Robyn returned to find that Genna had sent most of the animals away to the north. Only the wolves, foxes, badgers, weasels—the creatures with sharp teeth—remained, as well as several sturdy bucks and grizzled boars, and of course, Grunt.

Legions of hawks, owls, and blackbirds swarmed through the sky, flying to the south and circling loudly over the enemy force. Other druids arrived, soberly joining ranks with their leader. By the end of the day, all of the druids of

Myrloch Vale—nearly three dozen strong—had arrived.

And as the day waned into evening, the circling flock of birds could be seen close to the south. Their cawing and squawking was clearly audible in the grove.

The army would be upon them that night.

* * * * *

Bhaal arose from his steaming lava bath, where he had been watching the drama unfold in Myrloch Vale. The god was pleased to see that Hobarth now carried the Heart of Kazgoroth.

Acidic drool hissed to the ground as the god contemplated the young druid surrounded by death. When Hobarth brought her to the Altar of Bhaal, her blood would provide sweet sustenance.

And, too, it would be another milestone in the effort to rid the Isles of the druids. As the power of the new gods gradually dominated the faith of the Ffolk, there would be great struggles for primacy. In effect, a new pantheon of gods would be created.

And Bhaal would sit at its head.

❧ 12 ❧

Desecration

"Here they c-come—they come!" Yazilliclik clutched his tiny bow, stringing one of his slender arrows nervously. "N-Newt, wake up!" He prodded the little dragon's flank.

"Hello! Is it time to eat?" Newt lifted his head, blinking.

"N-no! We must tell Genna—tell Genna! They c-come!"

"Wait!" Newt peered with interest into the pre-dawn darkness. The sprite's keen eyes had seen the approaching figures clearly, but the faerie dragon had to squint and stare. Finally, he saw several shambling figures clumping steadily through the forest. A continuous rustling of brush told him that many more followed.

"I have an idea!" he said. "Follow me. It'll be great fun!" Blinking into invisibility, Newt bounced from their high limb and darted toward the undead army.

"N-no! Wait! Stop!" Yazilliclick whispered, but the dragon was out of earshot. The sprite's tiny, pointed ears twitched in agitation. His two antennae wriggled miserably. But then he, too, blinked out of sight. He could see Newt's outline ahead, and he frantically buzzed behind his reckless friend. The dragon came to rest on a broad bough. Yazilliclick, trembling in fear, landed beside him.

"N-Newt—let's go! We have to tell—to tell Genna!"

"Look!" whispered the dragon.

A huge man loomed out of the darkness. Yazilliclick thought all humans were gross, ugly creatures, but even by those standards this man was exceptionally repulsive. Rolls of fat sagged around his neck, and several huge warts sprouted from his bulbous nose.

"Watch this!" said Newt, again bouncing into the air. This

time he floated to the ground—right before the human!

Yazilliclick moaned softly and once again clutched his bow and arrows. He saw the man's eyes blink, as if his trance had been broken. His gaze swept across the ground and suddenly focused upon Newt. The dragon was invisible, but somehow this man could see him.

"Now, spell!" cried the faerie dragon, willing his illusion onto the ground.

The sod ripped away, and blue flames flicked deep within the pit that was suddenly exposed. A ghostly hand reached upward to grab the man's foot as he stepped forward off the edge of the pit.

But the foot landed upon solid ground, and the image of the pit quickly dimmed. Without slowing his pace, the huge figure marched right through the illusion. Unheeded, the magic waned.

Now the man pointed a finger at the annoyed fairie dragon. He chanted a word softly—the command to a spell that was definitely not a mere illusion.

But just as the magic flash exploded outward, the man cursed and twisted, plucking a tiny arrow from his shoulder. He snapped the missile like a matchstick, but the distraction had been sufficient. His bolt of magic sizzled into the darkness beyond Newt, striking one of the skeletons instead. The fairie dragon zoomed quickly upward as the skeleton exploded into a heap of crumpled bone.

"Did you see that?" Newt complained. "He ignored it! He didn't even slow down! Well, this time I'll give him a spell that he can't—ulp! Urf urf!"

Newt struggled to speak, but Yazilliclick's grip upon his snout was too strong. The tiny faerie pulled the dragon behind him as he darted high into the sky, beating his wings frantically to carry them both away from this place.

Of course, Newt complained all the way back to the grove.

* * * * *

Thick hedges of thorns stood in high tangles around the edge of the grove. The druids had worked through the day, and most of the night, raising what barriers they could.

But now the dragon and the sprite had brought them

word, and the time for preparations was past. In minutes, it would be time for battle.

"You all know, of course, to seek the cleric," Genna said. "It will not be easy. I expect that he will hold back and allow his creatures to do his fighting. But if we can strike at him, we strike at the army's head. Therein, I think, lies our only chance to stop them.

"Join me for a moment of prayer. The goddess shall be with us. May her strength carry us through this fight."

"And give us victory," thought Robyn.

The druids stood with Genna near the stream. Each of them had been given a portion of the grove to defend. Genna and Isolde, together with Grunt, would stand in the center. Others stood near, men like Ryder Greenleaf, who tended a grove on the western shore of Gwynneth, and Gadric Deepglen, an old druid who still managed to watch over a region of canyons and cliffs at the northern fringe of Myrloch Vale, near the domain of the Northmen.

A young female druid, Eileen of Aspenheight, stood directly behind the Great Druid, ready to carry messages or otherwise come to the aid of her mistress. The rest of the druids, men and women nearly three dozen strong, stood to either side in a long line. Each of the druids would be aided by some of the larger animals—the wolves, boars, and stags that would give their lives for the cause of the goddess.

Robyn would fight beside Kamerynn, Newt, and Yazilli-click. Genna had assigned her to a post far from the center, where the fighting was not as likely to be furious, but she had begged her teacher to reconsider. Her mother's staff, Robyn pointed out, gave her the capability to cast powerful spells—spells that might mean the difference between victory and defeat. Reluctantly, the Great Druid had acquiesced.

And so they waited. They would fight the undead army with earthmagic. When that was expended they would use sturdy clubs, sharp sickles, and even their bare hands. All of the druids were compelled by a single thought.

They must keep the desecrators from the Moonwell.

* * * * *

In the end, it was the boy who told the tale.

The old cleric had proved too stubborn, even for one of Razfallow's skill. Finally, the man had died, but even as he did so his lips only opened to croak a prayer to his goddess.

The lad, however, proved much more susceptible to the assassin's persuasive blade—particularly since he had watched his master die a death of unspeakable agony minutes earlier. A few quick nicks of the knife against the lad's cheek, and he was eager to talk.

"And where did they go from here?" asked Kryphon.

"The forest!" gasped the lad, pointing to the north. "He gave them a map of Dernall Forest. They fled there!"

"Again!" Doric said breathlessly. She stood beside Kryphon, her eyes bright with excitement. "Again with the knife!" she urged.

Razfallow looked to Kryphon, a question in his eyes. The wizard shook his head slightly, regretting the need to disappoint Doric. Still, they needed their information.

"You have suffered enough, child. Tell us the truth, and you may go."

"I *am* telling the truth," he sobbed. "My master helped them—one of them was hurt. Then he gave them a map and sent them on the road to the forest."

"How long ago?"

"They were here not three nights previously. If you hurry, you can catch them!" The boy was still terrified, but a glimmer of hope crept into his voice.

"What paths did they take?"

"I don't know!" wailed the youth, terrified. His eyes widened as Razfallow inched the bloody blade closer to his skin. "My master didn't tell me!"

"Very well," said Kryphon, turning to look around the chapel.

"Now?" said Doric. The mage nodded and walked away, deep in thought. He did not hear the pitiful, weakening cries of the lad as Razfallow slowly killed him. Doric, he knew, would be highly excited by the spectacle, and that was reward enough for him.

By the time the youth was dead, Kryphon had determined a course of action. First, he would use a charm spell to keep

Razfallow out of the way. Then—Doric ran to him, tearing him from his thoughts. She clutched his arm tightly, her eyes still sparkling. Together they walked from the cleric's abode and place of worship. The pressure of the woman's body against him was maddening. The sight of blood had inflamed her in a way that Kryphon found delightful.

"Stand guard," he ordered the assassin, pulling Doric into the darkness. She willingly followed, throwing herself to the ground as soon as they were out of the assassin's sight. Their passion was brief but explosive. They used each other like animals in heat. Her fingernails raked his back, and his response was violent, swift, and satisfying, like an explosion of powerful magic.

"Now we must be on our way," he said brusquely, arranging his robe.

"Wait," said Doric, lazily rising to stretch. "Can I use my spell?" Her tone was supplicating, but with an undercurrent of tension that warned him against refusal.

"Very well," he agreed. "But quickly."

With a little squeal of delight, Doric turned and raised her finger, pointing at a chapel. Razfallow stood some distance away, never questioning the mage's delay. Good, thought Kryphon, my charm spell has beguiled him completely.

"Pyrax surrass Histar!" cried Doric, chanting the words to her most potent spell.

A small, bright ball floated lazily from the end of her finger and drifted slowly toward the building. Doric's eyes were wide and staring, and her lips were pulled back from her teeth in a ghastly grin. The pebble-size ball meandered through the chapel's open door.

"Byrassyll!" Doric's voice rose to a shriek.

The blackness of the night was overwhelmed by an orange glow that exploded within the tiny chapel. Kryphon imagined the building as a huge skull—its windows were glowing eye sockets, and the door, blown from its hinges, was a gaping, screaming mouth.

And then the waves of fire tore the roof away and devoured the walls. A billowing ball of flame rose into the air, blossoming into a huge globe of heat a hundred feet overhead. Heat assailed them, brightening Doric's eyes. Her face was stretched into a sickening mask of delight. The sight of her suddenly disgusted Kryphon, and he seized her roughly by the arm, twisting her away.

"Let's go," he snarled. She glared at him. He met her gaze, challenging her to confront him—but she pulled away from him and stalked into the night.

* * * * *

Robyn looked toward the ring of stone arches, invisible in the darkness and distance. She could vividly picture the milky white waters glowing with the benign presence of the goddess. The thought of the Moonwell's desecration filled her with dread.

The young druid's uneasiness grew as she looked toward the rushing stream to the south. The foaming surface of the water was visible in a few places, but all else was darkness. Heavy clouds screened the starlight.

The first warning came as an almost silent rustling of the hundreds of great birds who waited in the branches above. Hawks, eagles, falcons, and huge owls were shifting, stretching claws and wings as they prepared for flight. Robyn noticed, too, that the boars had grown unnaturally quiet.

She looked to her teacher and saw the color slowly drain from Genna's face. The Great Druid clutched her hand quickly to her breast, and Robyn's heart skipped a beat. Genna let her hand fall to her side. She closed her eyes, and her lips moved in whispered prayer.

Robyn felt the ground shift and knew that her teacher's magic was at work. She smelled the cool, earthy odor of fresh dirt, and heard a dull, tearing sound. She saw a hulking, vaguely human shape rise from the earth to stand before the Great Druid. Even in the darkness, Robyn could see the clumps of dirt that made up the thing's limbs, and the broken twigs and pieces of stone that added texture to its skin.

The thing stood like the statue of a giant, stoop-shouldered and stupid, but very powerful. Its limbs had the thickness of tree trunks, and Robyn could feel the ground itself shake as the creature slowly shifted its weight from one stumplike foot to the other.

"Turn!" barked Genna. She pointed to the south. "Attack!"

"An elemental," said Robyn softly, awestruck. She had seen one of the hulking things before—a being conjured by the might of druidic magic from the body of the Earthmother herself. It took great power to summon one of the creatures from its distant realm of earth and rock to their own world, though it was a mighty ally against any physical foe. Still, Robyn was surprised by the creature's sudden appearance and huge size. Though it was but twice the height of a tall man, it looked like a walking mountain as it shambled into the darkness.

"Now is the time to remember your staff, girl."

"Yes, of course." Robyn stepped silently through the brush, walking to the position her teacher had chosen for her. The cool wood of her staff brought her a feeling of strength, but still the forest seemed very dark.

*　*　*　*　*

Tristan and his three companions spent most of the day luxuriating in soft featherbeds under the sod roof of a cozy inn. Refreshed, they spent the evening touring the town, which O'Roarke had given them the freedom to roam. He had not said anything about leaving, however, and the prince had decided not to ask—at least, not immediately.

In many ways, Doncastle seemed like any other community of the Ffolk. There were several inns with good, simple food, and an occasional harpist or minstrel for entertainment. They saw one flourishing blacksmith shop with a pair of smiths laboring over blazing forges and solid anvils. Several huts held weavers, and the smells of dye and fresh wool were pleasantly familiar. A small stream flowed into the Swanmay River near the heart of town, and there a millpond provided water to turn a large wheel, though they saw no sign of grain. It was a month before harvest season, Tristan reminded them. But they wondered if Doncastle had any arable land in its environs.

"Perhaps they steal their grain, too," Pontswain said.

But the Ffolk that they saw appeared to work hard. They were friendly, smiling and greeting these strangers from

Gwynneth. The baker offered a fresh loaf of bread; the smith offered to sharpen a dulled weapon.

Most of the buildings were on the ground—only an occasional small cottage, and a single large inn, had actually been built in the trees. The other houses, shops, and inns were either cleverly concealed among the flora or were underground. The rolling grassy hummocks that rippled like tiny hills throughout the town were actually sod-roofed homes, much like the burrows favored by halflings.

A whole network of walkways connected the city above the ground, spanning from tree to tree with long suspension bridges. In some places, the buildings were close enough together to form actual blocks, but these were generally so well screened by thick foliage that an observer could stand before one building and not realize that it had close neighbors.

The four men did not see the bandit lord that night, nor the following day. They spent the daylight hours exploring the surroundings of the community.

"It's ideal for defense," remarked Daryth.

"And ambush," added Pawldo. "An attacker wouldn't even know you had a force here until your arrows gave him warning!"

"This whole city is unbelievable!" added Tristan. "So many people living here—so well concealed and defended. And they seem prosperous enough."

"True," agreed Pawldo. "Though they do without a few comforts that I'd miss." The men had seen remarkably few metal goods, and the fare of the inns they had visited was limited to a few brands of ale, with wild game constituting most of the menu.

"It's wrong that they should have to conceal themselves here!" exclaimed the prince, surprising himself with his fervor. "These are industrious and decent Ffolk. It can't be right that a king would condemn such people to exile."

"Or worse," muttered Daryth.

"I think we should tell O'Roarke about our mission. With a little luck, we could persuade him to help us," declared the prince.

"That's madness!" objected Pontswain. "The man is a bandit. He can't be trusted!"

"He is a bandit, true. But doesn't he want the same thing we do—an end to the reign of this king?"

"Pontswain has a point about O'Roarke," said Daryth. "The more he knows about us, the more dangerous he is!"

Tristan looked from his friend to his rival. Pawldo stood silent, watching the exchange. "What do you think?" the prince asked the halfling.

"I think it's worth a try. You can't just walk into Caer Callidyrr and tell the king you don't like the fact that he killed your father. And O'Roarke, much as we might not trust him, seems to be our best hope of getting help."

"You'll do what you want, anyway," Pontswain said with disgust. "Nevertheless, this is madness!"

"I hope you're wrong," said the prince. "I'll talk to O'Roarke as soon as I get a chance."

"Hey! You men!" A fresh-faced youth raced toward them along the rampart.

"I'm glad . . ." he began, pausing to gasp for breath, ". . . I finally found . . . you. Lord O'Roarke requests your company at dinner. I looked all over for you—I was afraid you had left town."

"And if we had?" asked the prince, eyebrows raised.

The lad looked confused. "Why, he'd have sent someone after you, of course."

"We'll be delighted to accept. When and where?"

The lad gave them directions, and they recognized the inn in the treetops they had seen while exploring the city. They were to be there at sunset—less than an hour away.

They took their time reaching the inn, crossing one last bridge that swung alarmingly in the dying breeze. They could see their host before they crossed, for the inn had no walls facing them. O'Roarke smiled and gestured them to his table.

Just before they reached him, a young woman emerged from the shadows and began to strum a harp. Tristan noticed with a sudden pang that the minstrel resembled Robyn, at least in her long black hair and serene demeanor. But Robyn was much more beautiful, he thought, suddenly growing lonely. He imagined her, doubtlessly relaxing in the pastoral confines of the Great Druid's grove. He missed her very much.

A sudden bolt of alarm shot through him. Was she relaxing? Or was she, too, beset by the danger that seemed to pervade the kingdoms of the Ffolk? He tried to convince himself that Myloch Vale was the safest place on the isles, the most secure from external depredations. But his worry clung to him like a looming vulture, bearing down heavily upon his shoulders. Distracted, he barely heard O'Roarke speak to them from across the room.

"Join me, please," called the red-bearded bandit.

Two other men were already seated with O'Roarke. He nodded at one, a clean-shaven muscular man with deeply tanned skin. "This is Annuwyn. You may not remember him, but he cast the spell that brightened your night so well the other evening!" Hugh chuckled at his joke while Tristan nodded to the magic-user. Annuwyn nodded back, a thin smile creasing his lips.

"And this is Vaughn Burne, our high cleric," said O'Roarke, and the other man rose and bowed. Vaughn Burne was a slight, pale man with a clean-shaven pate. He wore a plain robe, and his thin face betrayed little emotion—except for his eyes. They shined with interest and energy as he waited for the men to be seated.

"The reason I asked you here," O'Roarke said at last, "is to tell you that I would like you to stay with us in Doncastle."

Tristan's heart thumped in his chest, and he tried to display no emotion. Still, this was the worst thing the bandit could have said to start out their conversation.

"I need brave men," continued Hugh. "And such I know you are—most travelers flinch and wail when they are accosted by us. None of you betrayed any fear.

"I will offer you places within' my militia. It is not large, but my men are stalwart, and they fight well. You could earn positions of command—I can use men with battle experience.

"And you would be safe here. You are outlaws, fugitives from the king's troops. There is no place upon Alaron where you will be safer." O'Roarke's voice grew more strained as he saw that his guests were not eagerly jumping up to accept his offer.

"My Lord Roarke," began Tristan, carefully choosing his words. "I'm sure I speak for my companions in saying that we are honored by your offer—by the trust you have shown. But perhaps we could offer you a better way of honoring that trust—that we could perform an even greater service for you than leading a company of your men into combat."

Hugh O'Roarke sat impassively, waiting for the prince to continue. Only the slight lowering of his bushy eyebrows betrayed his emotions.

"We have embarked to Caer Callidyrr upon a mission—a mission that could aid not only ourselves, but all of the Ffolk," Tristan continued.

Hugh waved impatiently for him to go on.

"I am a prince of the Ffolk—Tristan Kendrick, of Corwell."

"You are the one who slayed the Darkwalker?" asked the lord. Tristan nodded and sensed the cleric across the table staring intently at him as he did so. Vaughn Burne then turned to his lord and gave an almost imperceptible nod.

"But how did you come to be an outlaw?"

"My father, King Kendrick, was slain by assassins. The Council of Lords ruled that the High King should choose either Lord Pontswain or myself as his successor. We began our journey to Callidyrr to petition the king for this decision, but we were attacked on the way and arrested by the king's troops as we landed at Llewellyn.

"Our mission changed, obviously, after this development. I still intend to gain an audience with the High King. He will give me a satisfactory explanation of these events—and I doubt that there is such an explanation—for he will die by my sword!"

O'Roarke's jaw dropped. "You're mad!" he hissed.

Tristan flushed. "I believe we can do it with your help. You know this kingdom! Help us get into Caer Callidyrr. We will do the rest. Think of the benefits. If the High King is pulled from his throne, your lands are yours again. No longer will you have to hide in the forest, waiting for the next attack!"

Hugh scowled darkly, but then startled them with a burst of laughter. "You truly are mad. I shall let you go on with your fool's mission, but you will get no support from me. In fact, I shall keep your horses as payment for my troubles!"

At that untimely moment, several kitchen maids emerged with platters of potatoes and stew. Hugh ignored his guests as he lifted forkful after forkful of food to his lips.

Tristan inwardly cursed the man, though he did not press the topic any longer. Pitchers of mead sat upon the table, and his tongue itched for the taste of the foamy stuff. He ignored the craving and drank only sparingly.

The meal passed slowly, and in silence. They had almost cleaned their platters when a young man entered the inn and gestured to Hugh O'Roarke. He was dressed in green leather and spattered with mud, as if he had just come from a long ride. The lord rose, carrying his full mug of ale, and went to the man. The fellow said something in a low whisper. Suddenly, the bandit leader whirled and threw his mug against the wall where it shattered with a crash.

"News?" asked Tristan quietly, raising his eyebrows. For a moment, he wondered if the bandit was about to attack him, so red was his face. O'Roarke's hands clenched at the air as he stalked back to the table.

"My sister has been executed by the High King!" he snarled. "She was a captive in his castle, and two days ago he had her put to death!"

A pall of silence descended over the room. O'Roarke's look challenged anyone to speak, to give him a target for his anger. Pontswain looked down, strangely subdued. Tristan felt a pang of sadness for the outlaw and renewed loathing for the High King.

"But why?" asked the prince.

"Why?" Hugh cried, his voice choking with agony. "Perhaps to draw me out of Doncastle, where the Scarlet Guard can meet me on its own terms."

Tristan began to see an opportunity in the tragedy, a chance to use the bandit lord's grief constructively—for himself, and perhaps even for Hugh O'Roarke.

"There's a better choice. You can help us get into Callidyrr, where I will confront this king!"

"And then what? Even supposing you made it that far, which you won't, what can you hope to accomplish?"

"We can avenge your sister. I can gain vengeance for my father's death. Think, man! We have to do something! We can't stay here in the woods, hiding in your pleasant little town! Help us!"

"Are you assassins, that you will sneak into his castle and stab him as he sleeps?"

"I am not an assassin," Tristan said. "I shall not kill him . . . in cold blood. The king will have a chance to defend himself against my charges. If he cannot, he will have a chance to defend himself against my blade!"

"I tell you, it is no use!" persisted O'Roarke, slumping into his chair. The energy drained from him—he looked dejected and defeated.

"We are not without skill," Daryth said quietly.

"No, you are not. But you were all four taken by my clumsy ambush. And you can be sure that the traps of the wizard, Cyndre, will be far more deadly!"

Tristan flushed, whether in anger or embarrassment he was not sure. Then he spoke.

"We have to try. You have lost a sister and your cantrev. I have lost my father—my king. How many more losses will it take to move you?"

Hugh was silent for a long time. Once again, his thick red eyebrows sank into a deep scowl.

"I will help you," he said finally. "But I have a condition: One of you must remain here, as proof against a betrayal. You will come to know my most valuable agent in Callidyrr. Should harm come to him, your man will die as well!"

"That is unaccep—" Tristan began to object, certain that he had the upper hand, when Pontswain cut him off.

"I shall remain here," said the lord.

Tristan looked at Pontswain in shock, wondering if the lord was afraid to face the High King. Or perhaps he hoped that the prince would be slain, leaving the path open for his own claim to the kingship. Still, it solved the problem. And Tristan knew that he wouldn't miss the man's company.

"Very well," he agreed.

"We can disguise you," offered O'Roarke, as if relieved to have reached a decision. "And slip you into Callidyrr on a fishing boat that is returning to harbor at the end of the day.

It will be risky, but it is still our best chance."

"Why a boat?" asked Daryth suspiciously.

"Because the walls are high, and the city gates are guarded around the clock. A boat returning to port with the same number of men aboard as left in the morning may escape inspection."

"And once we're in the city, what then?" asked the prince.

"I have people in the city," said the bandit lord. "They will do whatever they can for you. My agent, Devin, may get you into the castle. If there's a way, he'll know it!"

"When can we get started?" Tristan asked.

"Tomorrow. We'll take to horse at first light."

* * * * *

Cawing and crying in a harsh cacophony, the birds of prey took wing. The hawks and eagles and owls exploded from their perches together, arrowing toward the stream and the as yet unseen enemy.

The birds rushed from the darkness against the army of the undead, slashing with beak and claw against the zombie vanguard. Flesh was torn away from the dead faces, and limbs were rent from bodies—but still the dead moved forward. Birds fell, shrieking in pain, as the claws of the undead tore at their feathered breasts or crushed their powerful wings.

And when the birds fell, the skeletons came upon them, lifting the struggling creatures and tearing them to pieces. A few of the zombies dropped, badly torn. But the fate of the flyers was much worse. Soon, the flock was decimated.

The army marched into the stream. At the far shore, sprawling in the darkness, was the grove of the Great Druid. And at its heart was the sacred pool of the Moonwell.

* * * * *

The vast caverns of Dwarvenhome glowed with an eerie green radiance as light spilled from the green fungi that grew on the high walls. Clinging stalactites dropped like drooling fangs over the huge council chamber, where hundreds of the short folk had gathered around a high platform. Three dwarves, looking nearly identical behind bristling beards, stood above their fellows. They heard the acclaim of their community arise from many barrel-chested comrades. The voices were strong and deep, and the chant was always the same: "Finnnnnellllen! Finnnnnellllen!

One of the trio stepped forward, looking out at the vast sea of bearded faces. Her jaw jutted forward belligerently, but she apparently liked what she saw, for she nodded slowly, affirmatively.

"Dark dwarves in the Moonshaes? They'll be there about five more days, I reckon—about as long as it'll take my fighters to march there, or my name's not Finellen!"

The chant grew to a roar, and then the dwarves dispersed to gather their armor and weapons. In another hour they would assemble as an army to follow their heroic leader— the real champion of the Darkwalker war, as all the dwarves knew—through the vast caverns of the underdark. Their route would take them under land and sea; for the length of the march, they would never look upon the sun. And when they reached their destination, they would fall upon their hated enemies—the dark dwarves—with a vengeance.

The outcome would be bloody but glorious.

*　*　*　*　*

Slowly Robyn squeezed the wood of her staff, as always drawing strength and reassurance from her mother's gift. She held the ashwood shaft before her and listened. Moments later, she heard a squishing, sucking noise that told her the zombies had emerged from the stream. They approached her, crossing the little meadow.

Kamerynn paced beside her. She sensed that Newt was still perched upon the unicorn's horn, though she couldn't see the little dragon. Neither could she see Yazilliclik, but she knew that the sprite stood beside her, ready to launch a hail of tiny missiles from his little bow.

And then she saw the shapes emerging from the darkness, and her nostrils caught the scent of the zombie horde. Though the night was frightening, she thanked the goddess for sparing her the horror of seeing the undead in their gory detail.

Robyn offered a silent prayer to the goddess and felt the answer of the Earthmother flowing through the wood. There was power and peace in that answer—but there was also rage. Robyn channeled that power into a spell, aided by the staff, and released it as the skeletons stumbled toward her from the darkness.

And the rage of the goddess was fire that erupted from the ground, a wall of flame spreading across the clearing. Robyn saw Genna cast the same spell some distance away. Other walls of fire erupted before her as the druids ignited their first line of defense.

Zombies lurched into and through the flame, sizzling in the intense heat. The monsters stumbled forward and collapsed on the ground, writhing in silent torture as their flesh blackened. Before the fire died, their bodies shriveled into misshapen lumps, stiff as statues carved from charcoal.

The skeletons, too, suffered from the intense heat. Bones splintered as the orange tongues of fire licked them. Bodies broke apart, collapsing into heaps of unrecognizable ash.

The birds that had been harassing the monsters flew up and away as the fire erupted, but Robyn grieved to see that several moved too slowly. Tongues of flame greedily stroked the feathers of owls and hawks. The birds screeched and writhed in agony as the fire dragged them to earth and consumed them.

But some unspoken command was turning the mindless army away from the fire. The zombies slipped to the left, the skeletons to the right, and the undead came on. The walls of fire were limited, not long enough to encircle the grove, and the monsters now came around them.

In the lurid light, the young druid saw a moving mound of earth as the elemental answered Genna's command. It moved to block the skeletons. Huge, fistlike appendages swung from the thing's sides, and it used these like clubs, smashing a dozen of the undead in the first press of attack.

From where Robyn stood, the elemental looked like a rough-skinned giant. It fought quickly, remorselessly. For a moment, the press of the skeletons was shattered—though the undead knew no fear, the elemental was killing them faster than they could advance.

But then a whirling storm of silvery axes emerged from the darkness. The shining blades gleamed with an internal light. The hafts were long, the blades heavy, and they filled the air with a glittering array of razor-sharp attacks. Hundreds of the missiles swirled about the elemental, hacking off chunks of earth. For a second, Robyn wondered at the unnatural way they hung in the air. Magic! The elemental stumbled as one of its legs was severed, and then fell into rubble as the blades tore it to pieces.

Now the zombies had completely passed the wall of fire, and they lurched quickly toward Robyn. They were still being harassed by the birds, and now the wolves and boars raced into the attack. The animals were a pitiful few against the numbers of undead, however, and they were swiftly killed or driven back with grievous wounds.

As the wolves whined and ran, Robyn turned to flee as well, but her foot caught on a root. She sprawled headlong and heard the squishing footsteps of a zombie nearby. Terror seized her, but she managed to cling to her staff as she leaped to her feet and sprinted through the darkness.

She saw Genna and the other druids running with surprising stamina toward the center of the grove. Grunt loped along behind the Great Druid, turning to bellow his rage at the undead who pursued them.

Gasping in horror and fear, Robyn stumbled along behind, wondering how they could hope to stop this nightmare before it reached the Moonwell.

* * * * *

Cyndre stood before the vast mirror as the three mages at the table watched him closely. The master turned to look at them: tall, lean Talraw, the dark-skinned Wertam, and the short, ugly little woman called Kerianow.

The image in the mirror was a vast field of green. Leafy treetops waved slightly in the breeze. Only upon closer examination could the wizards see the buildings cleverly concealed among the foliage, the smoke rising from well-hidden chimneys.

"You have seen this prince outwit the finest assassin in the land," said Cyndre. "Now, our colleagues Kryphon and Doric

pursue him. We can only hope that they fare better."

"We know he is in Doncastle." Talraw spoke hesitantly. "Why don't we simply destroy that town and have done with him—and it?"

"Remember," said the wizard gently, but his undertone told them all that Talraw was a fool for asking such an obvious question. "It is not our power that will win over the Ffolk. We must appear to act only as the king's advisers. Only through him can we gain the power we truly deserve. When that power is ours we will be free to act as we wish.

"But that day draws near. Have patience and listen well: One of you must remain here always, watching the mirror. We have found the Prince of Corwell, and we will not lose him again."

"Yes, master," they chorused, awed at the responsibility he had laid upon them. In truth, they were not ready, but Alexei was lost to them, and Kryphon had a mission of his own.

"And it may be that you will see one looking back from the mirror," said the sorcerer, his voice dropping low in warning. He described the one he sought and watched as the three mages exchanged frightened glances. "Should you see this in the mirror, you are to interrupt me immediately.

"For I seek to talk to the sahuagin."

💮 13 💮

Callidyrr

One after another, the druids gathered at the Moonwell, stumbling in from the surrounding darkness to gasp weakly against the sturdy stone pillars. There, they quickly recovered their strength. The milky water glowed softly.

The circle of arches here in the center of the grove was illuminated faintly by the light from the Moonwell. Robyn felt rather than saw the other druids around her. And she knew that the army of death was very close.

Something white moved through the darkness to stand beside her, and she threw her arms about Kamerynn's broad neck. The presence of the mighty unicorn bolstered her own confidence.

"We haven't long to wait," said Genna. The Great Druid emerged from the darkness to stand beside her pupil.

"Did you see the . . . human?" Robyn asked, wondering if one who commanded such an army could actually possess humanity.

"No, but it was his spell that destroyed the elemental. He cast it from beyond the stream. Perhaps the barrier still prevents him from entering the grove."

"Barrier?" Robyn was surprised. "I've never seen a barrier at the edge of the grove."

"No one can see it. And only one such as he, a being consumed by evil, feels it. He cannot pass into the grove through it, though I fear that now his army may have damaged it enough so that he can."

Robyn saw Eileen of Aspenheight and the stalwart Gaddric step wearily toward them. Their brown robes were torn, and bloody scratches covered their bare arms and legs. Gadric's stout staff and Eileen's sickle were covered with ripe gore.

"How did the undead pass it, then?" Eileen asked.

"These poor, mindless creatures are not inherently evil. They are simply driven by his foul command. As such, the barrier had no effect upon them." Genna sighed sadly. "All they want is to return to death. The cruel truth is that the cleric has taken from them the only thing they had—the peace of eternal rest."

Robyn had not thought it possible to feel sympathy for the ghastly invaders, but she found herself suddenly pitying their unnatural plight—and hating the cleric who had done this to them.

"Now, to your posts—all of you," chided Genna, tenderly. "Remember, the arches must be held at all costs!"

She swept her arm in a great circle to indicate all twelve arches. These arches provided the only access to the Moonwell. Earlier, the druids had prepared their defenses by filling the spaces between the arches with an impenetrable tangle of thorn bushes. Now each arch was to be guarded by several druids and the remaining animal defenders.

Eileen clasped Robyn's hand and gave the Great Druid a quick embrace before turning back along the shore of the Moonwell. Gadric looked at them both sternly, nodding his gray, shaggy head gruffly as he hurried away.

"Wait, Robyn," said Genna softly. She looked at the young druid tenderly, hopefully, as Robyn turned back to her.

"Here," said the Great Druid, giving a handful of acorns to Robyn. The nuts felt warm against her skin. "You might find a use for these."

"Thank you."

"And this . . ." Genna paused and reached into a pocket of her robe. "I've been making it for you. It's not quite finished, but you may need it now."

The Great Druid held a straight stick, perhaps a foot and a half long. Intricate carvings covered it from end to end. Robyn took it slowly, and it, too, felt warm to her touch.

"A runestick?" she asked reverently. She took the druidic talisman and touched the carvings, each of which she knew Genna had inscribed with her tiny knife. The runestick was covered with pictures—a spiraling mural of the land around her.

Tears came into Robyn's eyes. There was no more significant nor caring thing that one druid could do than carve a runestick for another. "I will treasure it," she whispered.

"You will use it, I hope," said her teacher with a smile. "They're very near, now." Genna turned away and walked along the shore of the Moonwell. She joined Grunt at the south arch.

Robyn stood with Kamerynn, Newt, and Yazilliclick at the arch on the north side of the grove.

"We won't get to see anything over here," moped Newt, sitting on Kamerynn's proud horn.

"I'm fri-frightened," whimpered Yazilliclick, standing next to Robyn and unconsciously leaning against her leg.

"Let us tend to our duties," said Robyn as calmly as she could, "and remember, the goddess is with you."

With that, Kamerynn left them to stand before of the twelve arches circling the Moonwell. The spaces between the arches had been blocked off by their earlier efforts. Now thick walls of thorns and sturdy young tree trunks intertwined to channel the only approaches to the well. Grunt stood stolidly beneath one of the arches, Genna stood at the next, and then Kamerynn.

Robyn and Newt stood at the next arch. Spreading out to either side, the arches were guarded by little bands of pixies, armed with small but sturdy bows, and sprites, who would fight with their silvery swords. Most of the faeries were invisible. The few remaining wolves and boars guarded the arches across the circle, where the enemy army was least likely to strike.

Robyn remembered her teacher's blessing, and she felt certain that the goddess was standing with her. She was very calm, somehow detached from the madness around her. She also felt very strong. And as she stood guard to protect the most sacred place on the isles, her calmness slowly grew into a powerful, controlled rage.

"I'm frightened," whimpered Newt, landing on her shoulder and leaning against her.

"So am I, my friend," she reassured him, realizing that the

statement was a lie. She realized that she was *not* afraid.

Then she felt a slight disturbance, like a flutter, in the power of the goddess. The night seemed suddenly blacker and colder as an unseen menace closed in.

"*He* has entered the grove," she whispered, not certain how she knew this.

But the ground felt strong beneath her feet, and the feel of the smooth staff in her calloused hands reassured her.

* * * * *

"How could he have escaped?" shrieked King Carrathal. He removed the Crown of the Isles from his head, holding it loosely in his hand as he mopped at his sweating brow with a delicately embroidered handkerchief. His eyes were wide with terror.

"He is resourceful," said Cyndre with a shrug. "And far luckier than any man has a right to be."

The king turned away and paced across his throne room in agitation. Once he had been able to meet with Cyndre again, he had assumed that everything would be all right. Instead it seemed that his problem was growing larger every day.

"See how the usurper seeks shelter in Doncastle. I have urged you, sire, to wipe that nest of rebels off the map. Surely you can now see the necessity for that?"

"We must do *something*!" whined the king, turning back to the wizard.

"I have my most trusted assistant on his trail."

"When will your man catch him?" demanded the king.

"Very soon, I am sure. Now, why don't you take your mind off this? Do something to amuse yourself! Would you like another prisoner put to death?"

The king shook his head angrily. He would not admit it to the wizard, but the execution of Darcy O'Roarke had been troubling him for several days. He dreamed of her defiant laugh in the face of the headsman's axe. She had vowed that her brother would avenge her. In truth, the king feared the wrath of Lord Roarke and all of his outlaw clan nearly as much as he feared the relentless approach of the usurper from Corwell.

*   *   *   *   *

The zombies, as if sensing the proximity of their goal, hurried forward. Many tripped and fell, but the others reached forward mindlessly, groping for the sustenance that glowed before them. They made no sound except for the scrape of their footsteps along the ground.

Genna and Grunt stood in the archway. The glow of the well cast its encouraging light against their backs, while the nightmare emerged from the darkness before them.

A clawed hand reached forward. Rotted flesh exposed its tough muscle and tendon, and white bone extended sharply from the last knuckle, where the flesh was gone completely. The bone caught the light from the well, and then Grunt stood upon his rear legs, blocking out the light.

Grunt slashed at the thing, and his six-inch claws tore the top half of the body away. Its legs lurched sideways once and then collapsed. With a roar, the huge animal lunged forward and crushed another rotted corpse beneath his paws. His jaws snapped shut on the barren skull of a skeleton, crushing the bone to splinters. The monster staggered aimlessly until it fell, though it continued to twitch and jerk across the ground.

More zombies lurched over the bodies of their fellows, to be met by Genna and her long sickle. The Great Druid had expended the last of her magic, but her muscles were driven by the might of the goddess as she struck and cut. Genna did not try to destroy each zombie—that would have taken too much time, too many blows. Instead, she slashed at knees, calves, thighs, and hips, immobilizing the creatures.

The other druids, standing beside wolves, boars, or their own human comrades, were drawn into the fight as the attack spread along the ring of arches. Isolde of Winterglen saw the horror approach. She stood with five gray wolves, and they savagely pressed back the undead. Sickles and staffs and clubs fought bony claws, for now all of the druids had spent their magic.

And finally the creatures reached Robyn's arch—the last one. Skeletons and zombies emerged from the night, seeking her flesh and blood. The sight of the eyeless sockets, staring from gruesome skulls, no longer terrified her. She raised her hands and threw the first of the acorns—the fire seeds—at the first fight of the enemy. It sizzled into the leading zombie, burning it to ashes. Taking care to aim, she threw the others. Each one ignited at the feet of an attacker, burning it away.

Then she gripped her staff and brought it crashing down upon the skull of the nearest skeleton. The bony thing dropped to the ground, and she quickly smashed another.

Kamerynn bucked and kicked beside her, crushing a skeleton to bone fragments with his heavy forehooves, and then impaling a zombie on his horn. He tossed the limp body aside as he reared above more skeletons, crushing skulls to his right and left with savage kicks.

Newt buzzed forward, slashing with his claws and sharp teeth at the loose flesh of the zombies, pulling great hunks of skin and meat off the rotting corpses. Then the faerie dragon hovered, blinking rapidly, and focusing upon the ground. He pointed and chanted quickly.

A purple monster burst from the ground in the path of several zombies. Green, glowing claws reached for the rotted bodies, and black teeth bristled from a gaping maw as the illusion attacked the attackers.

But the illusion required fear to be effective, and the zombies knew no fear. They reached to attack the thing, and when it had no substance, they stumbled through to attack the next thing—which was Newt. The little dragon went back to tooth and claw, tearing away pieces from the arm of the leading zombie until the limb itself fell to the ground.

Yazilliclick, with his tiny dagger extended, stood beside Robyn. He shrieked with fear as a zombie approached, but then darted forward to hamstring it. Robyn cracked the thing with her staff as it twitched upon the ground.

Somehow the forces of the goddess held the army of death back from each of the arches. Robyn bled from half a dozen wounds where the claws of the undead had raked her, but still a pile of bodies grew steadily before her.

But then she saw the cleric, and she froze. His eyes glared from the darkness long before she could see the rest of him. Finally his face materialized as he stepped closer. She watched his tongue flick across his thick, drooping lips and was reminded of a snake. The look on his bloated face frightened her more than had all the ghastliness of his army.

He neared her, walking very deliberately. Robyn picked up her staff and held it crossed before her. She was terribly afraid. The cleric raised his hands and extended them, palms downward. He chanted one sharp word, a sound full of terror and violence.

The ground convulsed beneath her feet, rippling upward and throwing her to the side. Robyn's head cracked against the stone pillar, and she went down like a falling tree to stretch motionless upon the ground.

* * * * *

Kerianow observed the prince in the vast mirror. He slept soundly under the roof of the Doncastle inn. Why, she wondered, could she not do the same thing? She rapped her plump fingers on the table before her, cursing the fate that always seemed to give her an unfair shake.

Her body, for example. It was short, fat—wholly unattractive, even to herself. And, as the newest member of the Council of Seven, she was bullied by the others— particularly by Talraw and Wertam, the two other lesser mages. As they had arranged their watches, for example, she had been given the hours from midnight until dawn.

She struggled to stay awake, wishing there was something more interesting to watch in the mirror. But Cyndre's orders had been explicit. Now that they had found the prince again, they could not afford to lose him. And so she stared at the motionless picture in the mirror.

Kerianow thought of Cyndre. How powerful he was! She remembered the way he had discovered her during her apprenticeship in Waterdeep. He had brought her to Callidyrr and taken her into his council, teaching her many of his own spells. She was no longer an apprentice: she was a sorcerer, albeit not as powerful as her master, or even Kryphon or Doric.

The master had shown great patience in teaching her, helping her to reach her potential. He had taught her that mercy was a fool's creed; it was only through might and cruelty that one could become truly powerful.

As she often did, Kerianow found herself thinking about Cyndre the man. His cool confidence excited her. His mastery—of her, of the council—warmed her. Small shivers of pleasure rippled along her spine as, lost in her musings, she let her head drop softly onto the table. With a little sigh, she fell asleep.

She awakened with a start, to see the glimmerings of dawn shining through the high, narrow windows. The mirror was blank.

"Kraalax—Heeroz," she chanted quickly. The image returned. Again she saw Doncastle, the quiet inn. But a bolt of cold panic cut to her heart as she looked at the bed.

For the Prince of Corwell was gone.

*   *   *   *   *

Seeing the boat brought back all the memories of the *Lucky Duckling* and the prince's fateful journey over water. The little craft might even have been made by the same boatwright; it had the same open-hulled frame, though not quite as big. The *Swallow* was also older and more weatherbeaten than even the *Duckling* had been.

"She'll just run you along the coast," explained O'Roarke, as if sensing his uneasiness.

Following a day and a half of hard riding, they had reached the shore of this vast bay. Somehow, Hugh had arranged a rendezvous, for this little craft and her young captain were waiting for them here. Two men and a halfling had left the boat, to be replaced by Tristan, Daryth, and Pawldo. The fishermen had even brought a moorhound with them, and the dog left with the trio so that Canthus could enter the port with the companions.

"They keep track of the number of Ffolk sailing out in the morning. As long as the same number come back at night, the Scarlet Guard won't pay any attention," explained the youthful captain.

"We will return to Doncastle when our mission is completed," said Tristan, offering Hugh O'Roarke his hand.

The bandit appeared surprised, but took the prince's

hand. "I'm sure your friend, Pontswain, hopes so.".

Tristan nodded curtly. He had spent a lot of time wondering about Pontswain's motives. The only conclusion he could reach was that the lord hoped that he would be killed, leaving him with no rival for the throne. Tristan felt a sense of loathing, but also of betrayal. The notion bothered him more than he had thought it would.

They sailed swiftly northward along the coast of Alaron. The land, to the west, was green and rolling—more fertile than Gwynneth, and always more populous. The water below them was also green, and it stretched to the east far beyond the horizon. Tristan drew a strange thrill from the knowledge that the nearest land in that direction was the Sword Coast, many days' travel away. Pawldo and Daryth slept comfortably, for the ride had been exhausting, but Tristan stood eagerly in the bow, staring in awe at the land and sea around him. Canthus stood at his side, sensing his master's excitement.

In a few hours they rounded the wide point that marked the entrance to Whitefish Bay. Now their course swerved to the southwest, and Tristan stared intently forward. Very gradually, their destination appeared in the distance.

Finally, he could see the vast harbor, protected by a strong, druid-raised breakwater. Beyond it was the largest city of the Ffolk, teeming with activity, commerce, and life. A white stone wall surrounded it, snaking beside the buildings and streets as they climbed the hills beyond the shore. A pall of smoke hung over the city just above the waterfront, but the sun shone unimpeded over the rest of the city.

Tristan saw proud stone buildings, and manors with columns before them. He imagined the gardens and fountains that must lie between them. But his eyes swept up even higher, past the manor houses and beyond the rambling wall of the city.

For now the prince had eyes only for the structure high on the hilltop above the city.

A lifetime of description and imagining had not prepared him for the splendor of Caer Callidyrr. The fortress sprawled across three hilltops, in itself bigger than many a town. The high stone walls, accented by lofty towers, gleamed brightly in the afternoon sun. They seemed impossibly smooth, as if they had been polished only that morning. Crenelated battlements lined the top, and several tall gates provided access through the walls. Each of these was shielded by a drawbridge and guarded by a high gatehouse.

Colorful banners streamed from the highest towers, proclaiming the lineage of the High King, while lower flags denoted the lords who had pledged allegiance to the throne. Several blood-red banners fluttered in one corner of the castle.

As the boat approached the breakwater, Tristan noticed one tower that was made of darker stone than the rest of the castle. This one was long and slender, standing alone at the far end of the castle. Though the late afternoon sun cast brilliant rays along the entire length of the fortress, this tower seemed to linger under some kind of inherent shadow. Whether its walls were not as clean as the rest of the castle, or were made from a different color stone, Tristan had no clue.

They sailed past the breakwater to enter the huge harbor. Dozens of fishing boats were returning as the day drew to a close. Several huge trading galleons and a pair of longships were anchored in the port, and the prince saw a huge shipyard to one side, where a pair of sturdy ships appeared to be nearing completion.

The docks themselves were bustling with activity. Mechanical cranes, operated by pulley, block, and tackle dipped into the holds of the fishing boats and scooped out the catches, carrying them into numerous canneries that lined the waterfront. These fish houses took in fish by the netful, and the stench of their contents extended far into the harbor.

Even amidst all of the activity, the bright uniforms of the Scarlet Guard were plainly visible. Human officers with parchment sheets compared the names of the returning fishing craft and performed quick head counts as the boats approached the dock. Huge ogres scowled suspiciously at everyone, fingering their mighty swords.

Finally, the *Swallow* pulled alongside the dock, and the crane swiveled over to them. The captain and his crew, Tristan saw, had managed to fill the hold with a respectable catch before they had picked up the companions.

Canthus sprang onto the dock, and Tristan, Daryth, and Pawldo hurried behind him. The prince looked around—for what, he wasn't sure, but Hugh had promised they would be met at the dock. He suddenly realized that he and his companions stood a scant twenty feet from a leering ogre. The beast scowled and squinted at them, letting its fat, red tongue hang from between its drooping lips.

Canthus growled at the monster, and it took a step forward, its gross hand coming to rest on the hilt of its sword. Then a pretty maiden rushed up to the prince, embracing him and kissing him warmly on the lips. He flushed, but quickly returned the embrace.

"Oh, Geoff!" she said breathlessly. "I was so worried about you! I worry every day, but especially today. Mother has a hot stew on for you—oh, and I'm to tell you to bring your friends!"

The girl was perhaps sixteen years old. Her red hair framed a freckled face with bright, sparkling brown eyes. She was dressed in a red and white frock of poor but clean material.

She smiled warmly at Daryth and Pawldo, while giving the prince's arm a pleasant squeeze. He allowed himself to be pulled along the dock, his companions quickly following. He sensed the glower of the ogre burning into his back, but he dared not look around.

The maiden steered him past several fish houses, and then pulled him through the door into one of the factories. The smell of cod was everywhere. The place was dark, and the floor was slick with oil. "Quickly!" she urged, now leading them at a run.

They passed through the building and emerged from a rotted door to find themselves in a filth-strewn alley. The young woman said nothing further, but led them down the alley, around a corner, and through a narrow street. Finally, they arrived at a ramshackle house. Here, she looked to see that the street was empty of guards, and then bounded up the steps. Pushing open the door, she pulled the companions inside.

A fire crackled in a small fireplace, but the house was otherwise dark. The girl led the fugitives through the first room and into a narrow hallway. There, she pulled aside a rug and lifted a heavy trap door. "Down here," she pointed, indicating the steep stairway that was revealed. Canthus leaped through the secret passage, and the lass came last and pulled the door shut behind her.

They stood in a secret hideaway, hidden in the cellar of the house. The room was large, with several shadowy alcoves. Lanterns filled the air with thick smoke, and a roaring fire warmed the room.

A middle-aged man turned from a worktable as they descended. He wiped his hands on a leather apron and frowned.

"I am Devin. This is my daughter, Fiona," he said. His brown beard concealed his chin, and his pate was nearly bald. He gestured around him, and Tristan saw that they stood in some kind of blacksmith shop. Several narrow cots were visible in the corner.

"We only learned of your imminent arrival yesterday," Devin explained bluntly. "Hence, we cannot offer you better accommodations."

"What you have done for us already is more than sufficient," replied Tristan. "How can we repay you?"

"You cannot. You can simply do what you need to do, and then leave me and my daughter in peace." The man shrugged. "My lord Roarke has asked me to assist you in any way that I can. This I shall do."

"All right," he said. "We'll make our plans and be gone as quickly as we can."

The prince wondered about Devin's loyalty to the bandit lord and the risks he was taking for them. As if reading his mind, the fellow looked him in the eye and explained. "I was Lord Roarke's captain of the guard before the Scarlet Guard came to the cantrev. My men resisted and died to the last lad. My lord, myself, and a few others escaped—including Fiona here. The two of us came to Callidyrr, and now we serve our lord in whatever way we can. If it comes about that you can return his lands to him and remove the evil puppet that sits upon *our* throne, then my help comes willingly. But if you seek to betray or harm my lord in any way, rest assured that my vengeance will find you!"

Tristan was taken aback by the threat, but found his voice. "Rest assured that your lord's objectives and my own are the same. By helping us, you are helping him."

"Very well. Fiona, fetch us something to drink. Our guests will eat as soon as they have refreshed themselves. And, as for getting into the castle, there might be a way. . . ."

*　*　*　*　*

Robyn gasped for air, trying to see through a red haze. She willed her muscles to move, but they would not answer her mental commands. Wide-eyed, feeling like a fish cast upon the shore, she watched the huge cleric lumber toward her. Those fat lips opened into a grin of pleasure, and she looked into his mouth. It was like staring at the maw of a devouring dragon.

The ground convulsed again, tossing her to the side. Again the ground heaved, and she felt pain as the dirt smashed into her face. The heaving ground had forced the wind from her lungs. Wide-eyed, she saw the huge man stalk closer to her.

"Cease!"

Genna's command instantly stilled the quaking ground. Robyn tried to wriggle away from the advancing figure, but she moved at an agonizingly slow crawl. He was almost to the arch. In moments he would enter the circle!

"To the mother! Fall!"

Again, Genna's sharp voice carried through the night, and now Robyn felt a deep straining in the ground beneath her—a sympathetic effort, as the land strived to work the will of the goddess. The advancing cleric paused.

Robyn could see the broad crosspieces atop many of the druidic arches, and all of those in her field of vision began to wobble. Balanced upon sturdy pillars, the heavy stones had not budged during the convulsions of the earthquake, but now they twisted and rolled.

With a thunderous crash, one of the crosspieces fell to the ground nearby, crushing a score of skeletons that had begun to advance. Then another and another crashed to the earth, crushing all of the undead beneath them, and leaving a barrier before each of the arches.

The crosspiece of the arch in front of her struck the ground with enough force to throw Robyn several feet into the air. She saw the cleric's face twist into a snarl of frustration as he leaped backward to avoid being crushed. Flecks of spittle flew from his lips.

Newt buzzed to the ground before her, peering anxiously into her eyes.

"Robyn? Are you all right? That was awful! Did you see the look on his face? Genna showed him, though—when that rock fell, I thought he was going to be splattered all over! Are we winning yet? Get up, Robyn—we can fight some more!"

"Where is he?" she gasped, as her lungs finally filled with oxygen. She grabbed her staff from the ground beside her and stood shakily. She leaned against the block of stone for support and looked over the top into the darkness. There was no sign of the cleric.

But he was near, she knew. Her fear forgotten, she seized her staff. She would find him and kill him. "Come on!" she cried, jumping onto the block. "We've got to stop him!"

"Let's get him!" cried Newt, darting after her.

"W-wait!" stammered Yazilliclick, before he too sprang after her.

"No!" Robyn heard Genna's voice, but the words did not register, so intent was she on pursuing the hated intruder.

She darted across the wide block and leaped to the ground on the other side. But before she landed, she bumped into a solid *thing*—an object she could not see, but that blocked her path like a stone wall.

Her head snapped back from an unseen blow, and the staff flew from her fingers. She slumped toward the ground, but a mighty limb picked her up.

"What's the mat—" Newt's question was interrupted as an unseen attack clubbed him from the air with one blow.

"Ouch! Hey!" cried Newt. He flapped his wings and sprang from the ground, but buzzed erratically to the side before flopping down again. "Come back!" he squeaked, bounding like a squirrel after an invisible stalker.

"Newt!" cried Robyn, twisting desperately. She was powerless in the grasp of . . . what? The thing made no noise, but grasped her around the chest and waist so firmly she could barely breathe. It felt as though she was ensnared in the coils of some massive snake.

But no snake could move as fast as she was now borne across the ground. Her captor moved smoothly and swiftly, as if it were flying just inches above the land. She was borne away from the Moonwell at a breathtaking pace. Her hands were free, and she pounded and punched her attacker.

She felt a tough and leathery skin beneath her fists—but the thing was unnaturally smooth. It seemed to have no hair, or scales, or appendages. It gave off no smell, nor did it make any sound. As she pushed at the limb imprisoning her, she felt it bend away, but then another snaked around her waist, nearly crushing her abdomen. Wherever she attacked, her invisible captor melted away, only to instantaneously reconstruct in a new shape that held her like an iron clamp.

The alienness of the thing terrified her, and drove her to a frenzy of effort—but to no avail. And still it moved over the ground without any jolting or jerking, as if it had no feet. She kicked against the body with the tips of her toes, and, reaching upward, pounded its skin as high as she could reach. It seemed to have no end—it was certainly much larger than she was.

She struggled ferociously, scratching, kicking, even biting the thing, but nothing seemed to affect it. She twisted and pulled, groaning in desperation and anger. But the thing only squeezed tighter, until it felt as if her body was trapped in a vice.

* * * * *

"It's not fair!" protested Pawldo for the twentieth time. Daryth and Tristan ignored him, slipping into the bright red cloaks that Devin had brought them only a few minutes before. "You two can't do this without me. You're doomed for sure!"

"Sorry, but I don't imagine the Scarlet Guard has many officers' uniforms in halfling size," explained the prince. In truth, Devin had told them that all of the officers of the Guard, even those commanding the ogre brigade, were humans—despicable bullies, most of them, but human. "Besides, someone has to stay with Canthus, and help us escape!"

"Hurry!" urged Devin. "We must get to the gate by dawn! We'll just have time to get you to the east gate. That's where the officers congregate after a long night out on the town. They're allowed to enter when the guard changes, just before dawn."

"And we're to act as though we've been drinking all night?" checked Daryth.

"Yes. Security is very lax when it comes to the officers of the guard, at least at this hour."

"And you have the diagram?" Devin asked Tristan.

"Yes. I'm certain we'll get through the garrison area without running into those guardposts."

"Once you reach the royal quarters, you'll be on your own," said Devin. "None of my people have been able to get in there—I should say, get out of there—with a description. Two of my men risked their lives to gain these uniforms."

"We appreciate their sacrifice," said the prince. "You've already done more than we could have hoped."

"I'm ready," said Daryth, standing proudly. He looked like a typically arrogant young officer of the Scarlet Guard, thought Tristan. The high hat, with its crimson plume, accented his red cloak and dark trousers. The shiny black boots, higher than his knees, looked suitable for trampling roughshod over the lives of lesser folks.

"And I," said the prince, adjusting his tunic. The fit was almost perfect. The Sword of Cymrych Hugh swung loosely at his side.

"Be careful!" warned Pawldo, looking at them very seriously. "I'm not sure I'll be able to rescue you this time!"

"And good luck," said Fiona, kissing each on his cheek.

Devin scowled at his daughter and led them up the stairs and through the silent house. He stopped at the door and studied the street before waving them forward. They hurried down the steps and along the street, seeing no one.

"Around the next corner, you'll see the gate. There'll probably be a few officers waiting there. You don't want to arrive too early, or you'll have to talk to them. When the guard marches out, the gate will remain open for a few minutes, and you two should *walk* in with the other officers. Remember, act like you own the place!"

Tristan looked at Devin and wondered about the motivations of this apparently frightened but obviously brave man. Devin rubbed a hand through his thinning hair as he looked nervously back at the prince, eager to leave them.

"I know we've put you in danger," said Tristan. "And I'm sorry. Perhaps, if we are successful, you will be able to return to the cantrev you were driven out of. Thank you."

Devin met his gaze with a look that combined skepticism and hope. "Good luck to you," he finally said. "May the goddess grant that you are right!" Then he turned and darted back down the street, bolting from one stretch of shadow to another like a creature of the night.

The pair stepped into the street, supporting each other and stumbling along as if they had been drinking heavily. They turned the corner and saw a dozen or more officers in uniforms similar to theirs standing beside the road. A file of red-garbed soldiers was marching from the castle. After the column of soldiers had passed, another group, waiting on the other side of the street, marched into the castle. Then the waiting officers stepped into the street and followed the guard through the looming gate.

* * * * *

Genna stumbled backward as a pair of zombies crawled over the fallen crosspiece. She chopped with her sickle—once, twice, and two heads thumped onto the ground. The bodies twitched harmlessly off the stone, but four skeletons came scrambling up behind them.

Isolde stood at the next arch. Her wolves lay dead at her feet, and a circle of zombies closed around her. The druid's stout stick rose and fell, each time smashing an attacker to earth, but bony claws reached for her legs, her thighs, her waist. Still clubbing, she fell under a sea of death, disappearing below the rotted corpses and ghastly jaws of the zombies. A dozen of them clustered around her, pressing in for a chance to bite or claw at the druid. Finally Isolde's club fell from her bloody, lifeless hand.

Genna, still striking with the sickle, fell back from the arch. The other druids, too, were gradually driven from their posts. The light of the Moonwell felt warm upon the Great Druid's back, but even the power of the goddess, she knew, would not stop the relentless attack. There were less than a score of druids left.

The battle could have only one outcome.

Or could it? The Great Druid turned back to a zombie that advanced, seeing that half of the thing's face was already gone. The leering skull seemed to mock her plight, and rage powered her arms as she drove her sickle through the skull, the neck, and halfway into its chest.

No, they could not win this battle. "Goddess, our mother," said the druid, slowly and reverently—even as she raised her sickle to smash an encroaching skeleton. "Do not let them have us."

No longer could she see the waters of the Moonwell behind her. But she felt the milky surface begin to pulsate with earthpower, and she could see the bright light that suddenly washed through the grove. All of the druids had been driven to the water's edge, where they made their last stand, striving to keep the horror from the sacred water.

The waters of the Moonwell began to bubble, like a great rolling boil, and spray foamed into the air. The undead halted and then lurched away, for the first time showing fear. The waters foamed higher, and suddenly the middle of the well turned into a fountain of white water, exploding upward and outward to cascade over the druids.

As the glowing water spattered onto the undead, the monsters twisted and staggered, their mouths flapping in mute agony. But as it fell onto the druids, it had a different effect.

Genna had a last look at the cleric as he approached from the darkness and then halted fearfully at the display of the Earthmother's power. Then the water washed over her, and she felt no more.

Finally, the bubbling and boiling abated, and the waters flowed back into the well. The undead cowered around the arches, unable to approach. Only Hobarth dared to stride forward and witness what the goddess had wrought.

He saw the druids still standing, curiously immobile, around the waters. He approached cautiously but then more boldly, finally stopping before the Great Druid. The cleric raised his fist as if to strike her, but then he threw back his head and roared with laughter. His howling cries filled the grove and sent waves of terror rolling across Myrloch Vale. But Genna could not hear him, nor could any of the others.

For the druids of Myrloch Vale had become statues of smooth, white stone.

*　*　*　*　*

Tristan looked around as they passed through the gatehouse, not entirely believing they had actually entered Caer Callidyrr. The high walls towered all around them, and he felt like he was in a deep, rocky gorge, not a man-made citadel. The light of the growing dawn colored the alabaster stone a rosy hue along the tops of the towers and walls, though the courtyards and passages were still enshrouded in twilight. The column of guards who had escorted them into the castle marched across a wide courtyard to a group of long wooden buildings. Even without the map from Devin, Tristan would have identified the structures as barracks.

The returning officers, meanwhile, split into small groups and went a number of different directions. Tristan and Daryth waited until the others had moved on and then picked a direction none of the others had chosen.

They passed through a second high gate, though this one was open. Two guards snapped to attention as they passed, and Tristan felt a bit of relief to know that their disguises were good enough to fool the soldiers. He and Daryth found themselves walking down a high-ceilinged corridor, where they noted several portcullises partially lowered from the roof. The place would be easy to defend, even if a huge army managed to breach the outer wall.

"The stables are up here," said the prince, remembering the map Devin had given them.

"And beyond that, somewhere, are the royal quarters?"

The prince nodded.

Finally they emerged from the corridor into another courtyard. The stables were unmistakable—not only were the barnlike buildings obvious across the yard, but a slight breeze carried to them the distinctive scent of the equine inhabitants.

They hurried across the courtyard and around the stables, noting that boys had already begun to tend to the horses. Dawn had lightened the sky, but the sun had not yet risen as they approached a vast, high-walled keep beyond the stables. They were nearing the center of the castle.

"Hurry, now!"

The voice came from around the corner of a large building, startling them both. There was no place to hide, so Tristan and Daryth each instinctively relied upon their disguises, marching confidently forward.

A group of a half-dozen soldiers came around the corner. They wore uniforms similar to the companions', though they lacked the gold braid and high, plumed hats. Their officer, a young man with dark hair and a black beard, had no such deficiencies. His uniform was identical to theirs, though his hat had a black plume instead of a red one.

"Hey! You men! You can't come in here!" he snapped, eyeing them suspiciously. "Only the Royal—"

"Silence!" growled the prince, stepping up to the arrogant little gamecock. Tristan's heart had leaped into his throat when the man accosted them, but he now swiftly decided to take the offensive.

"Who are you to speak thus to the captain of the Royal Inspection Corps? Answer me, man!"

"What Royal Inspection—"

"Are you deaf? I want your name, sir, and quickly!"

"B-but," the officer struggled to recover his composure.

"Never mind, fool! But have a care who you insult in the future! We are here to inspect the king's kitchen. There have been some serious complaints lately. Where is it? Be quick, man!"

"There," exclaimed the officer, pointing through an archway into an adjacent courtyard. "Through the door on the left!" The fellow's sigh of relief was almost audible as he turned to march his company away.

Tristan and Daryth passed under the arch and found themselves in a small courtyard. The stench of garbage rose overpoweringly from a pile of fruit cores, bones, rinds, and other refuse. A cloud of fat black flies buzzed into the air. Daryth threw open the door, and they both strode into the building.

They found themselves in a large entryway with several hallways branching in different directions. Daryth started down one with the prince behind him. They soon reached an open door at one end of the corridor, and here the Calishite paused, leaning against the wall out of sight.

For several moments they heard sounds of movement within. Pans clanked against an iron stove, and something sizzled in a frying pan. Soon the aroma of succulent bacon drifted through the doorway.

"Let me try this time," whispered Daryth. Tristan nodded, and the Calishite led the way into the kitchen. All of the activity came to an abrupt halt as they marched imperiously through the door.

The kitchen was huge, with long counters and several large ovens. Several middle-aged men and women were bustling about the stove and counters, and a group of serving wenches were laying out china on trays in the far corner of the room.

"You!" said Daryth, pointing to a stout man with several pink chins. "Tell me—who is the miserable wretch who prepares breakfast for the king?"

"Th-there she is, sir!" said the man, relieved to divert the officer. He pointed an accusing finger at a sturdy matron near the griddle. The woman's face grew pale.

"Come here," said Daryth more softly.

"Yes, sir," she said, meekly stepping over to them. She stared at the floor, shifting nervously from foot to foot.

"Don't be afraid," continued the Calishite. "We are looking for one of the serving wenches. Tell us, which one took the king's breakfast to him yesterday?"

"Sheila!" screeched the woman, turning to point at a black-haired lass. It was now the unfortunate girl's turn to grow pale. "Come here, immediately!"

Sheila stumbled numbly over to the men, and Tristan regretted the need to cause such fear among these Ffolk. Her eyes were wide and slowly filling with tears. Nevertheless, the prince had to continue the charade.

"Come with us!" he ordered.

The young woman nodded dumbly and followed them from the kitchen. In the hall, they turned to her. She sank back against the wall and quivered like a terrified doe.

"We have uncovered a plot that could bring grave harm to the king!" Tristan said sternly. "Has anyone spoken to you about the food you have taken to him?"

"No, your lordship! No one!"

"Very well. It may be that the plotters are working through a different avenue. You may help us to discover who and where they are. Do you understand the importance of this?"

She nodded fearfully.

"You must retrace for us, exactly, the route you took in bringing the king his breakfast yesterday. Every step, every hallway, every door. Do you understand?"

"Yes," she said, squeaking like a frightened mouse. She led them from the kitchen into a vast hall. She paused before a wide stairway and bit her lips. Hesitantly, she pointed to a curtained alcove below the stairs. "I-I stepped in here, j-just for a moment," she whimpered. "Garrick, the tailor's son, met me. I was only there for a moment! He pulled me in. I fought him to get away. I really did!"

Tristan forced down an urge to smile, embarrassed that they had stumbled upon the wench's amorous little secret. "Very well," he said sternly. "And then?"

She turned to climb the stairs, her footsteps silenced by the deep pile of the red carpeting. At the top of the stairs, the lass turned down a long hallway.

The walls here were gleaming marble, and tall mirrors dotted them at frequent intervals. High windows at each end, screened with cut crystal panes, broke the morning light into a series of colorful patterns.

"And here I took the food," said the maid as she pointed to a door—the only one along the wall of the hallway.

"You have done well," said the prince. "Now, return to

your duties!" The wench scurried back to the stairs and raced out of their sight

Tristan reached for the latch, about to push it open, when he had second thoughts. Instead, he lifted his hand and knocked firmly against the smooth panel. The door was pulled immediately open, and he stood face to face with a very startled young soldier of the Scarlet Guard.

"You can't—" the guard began.

"Yes, we can," snarled Daryth, who had flicked the point of his sword against the man's throat in the blink of an eye.

"We have an audience with the king," announced Tristan, smoothly stepping through the door. Daryth prodded a bit with the sword, and the young guard's eyes bulged.

"Yes sir," he said, his voice squeaking.

The guard stood in a small room. Beyond him another gilded door led to the royal chambers. The guard stumbled across the chamber and pulled it open, while Tristan and Daryth strode calmly through.

The Prince of Corwell stopped in shock. Even his wildest imagination had not prepared him for the sight of the preposterous figure sitting before him. Could this man, concealed by a curled and powdered wig, his face heavily made up, actually be the High King of all the Ffolk?

* * * * *

The largest city among the Moonshae Islands was not Callidyrr, as the humans thought. Rather, it was a community known only to a few of the airbreathing peoples, a vast metropolis, more ancient than any town of the Ffolk. The city sprawled across miles. Its densest reaches filled the bottom of a deep, narrow canyon, but its most elegant structures clung precariously to the sides of the canyon. Vast gardens spread to either side of the gorge, on top of the fissure, and the hunters and warriors of the city ranged a hundred miles or more in search of plunder and prey. But no living man had ever been here.

For this was a city on the bottom of the sea.

It was a city of coral with lofty green towers and low, rounded buildings. Its colors were green and blue and red, and a myriad of other variations. The onion-shaped domes

of its towers often rose a thousand feet or more from the bottom of the sea, reaching from the bottom into the higher stretches of the canyon, still many thousands of feet under the surface.

Huge balconies hung from the sheer sides of the canyon. Tendrils of kelp draped from these, giving the place a jungle-like appearance. Sharks swam slowly among the kelp, for these fish were the watchers of the city; they protected its inhabitants and attacked its enemies.

The city's gardens were seaflowers and anemone. Its monuments were the broken hulls of sunken ships—and the dead who crewed them. The skeletal monuments surrounded the high domes, and decorated the vast balconies. The gold and silver plundered from these vessels ornamented the most elegant dwellings, or adorned the most prominent citizens. Throughout the city, the bones of dead sailors supported doorways and arches. Light curved stools were crafted from skeletons.

Kressilacc was its name, and it was a city of the sahuagin, the undersea race that ruled its domain with a harsh and merciless hand. The sahuagin had lived in Kressilacc since the birth of their race, and their city had grown in size and beauty as they had grown in might and numbers.

The sahuagin were ruled by their king, Sythissall, and his high priestess, Yssalla. Both of them, creatures of the greatest evil, had grown bored with their absolute mastery of the sea. They sought other realms to loot and conquer, other sights to amuse them.

Sythissall claimed as his residence the vast palace along the crest of the canyon's wall. Together with his hundred concubines, his huge octopi guards, and the skulls of his enemies, Sythissall sat in his vast throne room. The hugest of the sahuagin, the king neared giant proportions. His teeth and wide, flaring gills gave his head a broad, stubborn cast. He held a huge trident of whalebone. With it, he had once slain six prisoners, rival sahuagin, with a single blow.

The spines along the king's head, and down his back, were fully four feet long when Sythissall was aroused. He had ruled the sahuagin for centuries, and the fish-men were pleased with his leadership. They tortured and killed for him—under his direction, they had conquered or destroyed every other group of sahuagin for hundreds of miles. To celebrate their final victory, a decade earlier, Sythissal had ordered one thousand prisoners tortured slowly, and then fed to the sharks. That spectacle had been the grandest in sahuagin history.

Ysalla, the High Priestess, dwelled in her sprawling temple, across the canyon from the king's palace. As Keeper of the Eggs, Ysalla's influence among the sahuagin was nearly as great as the king's. As a female, she lacked the sharp spines along her head and backbone. Her scaled skin, and the skin of her priestesses, was a bright yellow—in contrast to the natural green of her kind. The yellow, a badge of pride and chastity, was proof that the priestesses did not breed. Tenders of the eggs, they would produce none of their own.

The priestesses of the sahuagin adorned themselves with golden bracelets, headbands, belts, and anklets. They swam among their kin with imperial arrogance, for none of the sahuagin dared harm, or insult, a priestess.

Like others of their order among the worlds of men, orcs, and ogres, these priestesses were clerics of Bhaal.

Sythissall kept the sahuagins' most precious relic in his throne room. The Deepglass was a mystical artifact, crafted by sahuagin at the dawn of their race from the ice of the farthest north, forged in the fire of the deepest undersea volcano. Sythissall kept, and controlled, the Deepglass.

But only Ysalla knew how to use it.

The High Priestess could unlock the power of the Deepglass, aided by the immense power of Bhaal. Through it, Ysalla and Sythissall could look at anything they chose, anywhere. They studied the world of sun, and air—and though they found the setting unpleasant with its warmth and horrid dryness, they saw many objects that they desired for their city and themselves.

And also through the Deepglass, they found the wizard, Cyndre. The sorcerer had been watching them and waiting, for he knew that the Deepglass would eventually lead the sahuagin to his mirror. Sythissall flew into a rage at the sight of the human staring back at him.

But Ysalla was more patient. She learned that the human could speak to them, that they could understand him and speak in return. The shrieks and clicks of their conversation echoed through the huge throne room with its coral pillars and tapestries of hanging kelp. Sythissall's rage cooled as he heard the words of the black wizard promising gold, and bone, and blood.

As they listened to Cyndre's plan, they were intrigued. Sythissall saw a way to extend his influence into those realms that had been hitherto untouchable. Yssalla saw a way to serve her god and further the aims of her followers. The soft hiss of Bhaal's voice came into her ear, telling her that the human would be a useful tool in the god's scheme.

And Bhaal watched, and listened, and smiled.

❧ 14 ❧

Dungeon

Kamerynn bucked and kicked, crushing zombies with his forehooves and then lashing out behind him to splinter a pair of skeletons into hundreds of bone fragments. The madness of combat was upon him, and the great unicorn killed for the joy of slaying the enemies of the goddess.

He had started the fight beside Robyn at the arch, but his bloodlust had carried him upon a rampaging gallop through the attackers. He was now some distance from the Moonwell, and he turned to gallop back to the defensive ring. But then his sensitive ears detected a worrisome noise.

He paused for a moment and shook his head, causing his white mane to float like a cloud about him, while he looked for other victims. He felt the unnatural vibration of the cleric's earthquake spell, though he easily held his stance upon the rocking ground. All around, he saw druids and undead stumbling and falling.

Then he watched as Genna called down the crosspieces of the stone arches, seeing the blocks tumble into the open spaces beneath the arches. He leaped the block that had fallen before him, and once again stood within the circle, looking for more of the enemy to slay.

Then he heard Robyn's voice, crying in pain. He saw the young druid as she was swept up by some invisible force and carried swiftly away. With a snort of rage, the unicorn leaped the granite block and landed at full gallop, pursuing his friend's captor. He barely noticed Newt and Yazilliclick, except to see that the dragon had been stunned and the little faerie now tended him.

He raced like a bolt of lightning through the grove, but the thing that carried Robyn moved even faster. Though Kamerynn had lost sight of his quarry, he thundered ahead, racing through the stream at the edge of the grove. His huge body threw curtains of spray into the air as he burst from the stream to stand, tensely, upon the south bank. His broad nostrils quivered as he sought the spoor of his quarry.

And a faint passing breeze brought to him that knowledge—Robyn's sweet scent came from the woods before him, a little to the left. With another snort, the unicorn was off again.

* * * * *

Robyn felt the arms of her invisible captor relax slightly, and she twisted desperately, only to feel the vice-like limbs clamp more tightly about her. Then the thing suddenly stopped, as if it had reached the destination it sought. She felt the broad body close around her, like a solid wall, holding her motionless in the middle of a small clearing.

Her heart slowed, though it still pounded in her breast, and she wondered about this *thing* that had captured her. She had heard of such invisible servants before: They would work for evil or good, as commanded by a cleric or sorcerer of might. She knew that this one worked for evil.

Then she heard the thunderous pounding of hooves and turned hopefully to see a white form racing from the woods. In the slowly growing light she could see the unicorn galloping toward her.

"Kammerynn!" she cried.

The unicorn whirled toward Robyn, his head low. His white mane swirled like a cape across his neck, while rockhard hooves pawed the earth. With a snort, the great creature sprang toward the invisible thing that still held the young druid immobile.

Kamerynn's body became a blur. Like a white arrow, his horn struck the body very close to Robyn's—the body she could not see. The unicorn had no such difficulty, as his horn drove unerringly into the invisible presence. Robyn felt the thing twist backward from the jolt of the impact— and suddenly she was free. Tumbling to the ground, she looked up in time to see the unicorn rear high into the air, flexing his broad shoulders to drive the horn, once again, deeply into his opponent. It was a strange attack, Robyn thought absently. Normally he would have used his hooves in such a close combat. Perhaps he sensed that only his horn would affect this obviously magical foe.

Again and again the unicorn drove that ivory shaft into the thing. The dying creature made no sound, but Robyn sensed its agony, somehow, and felt welcome relief.

Finally the unicorn ceased his pounding, settling to his four hooves to stand, breathing hard. He lowered his head and probed at the shapeless thing on the ground, meeting no resistance. Whatever it was had vanished into the air.

Robyn stood weakly and stumbled to the unicorn's side, drawing strength from the feel of his broad flank. She seized his neck and hugged him, mutely thanking him for her life. Kamerynn's white head turned and he gently nuzzled her shoulder as she sank, exhausted, to the ground.

* * * * *

"N-Newt? Are you all right?" Yazilliclick peered into the dragon's dilated pupils, gently nudging his scaly head.

"Yazikilill—Yazillikillikk—Yazilliclick?" blinked the dragon. "What happened? Where's Robyn?"

"You got thumped—got thumped!" said the sprite. "R-Robyn's gone." The faerie whimpered slightly as he thought of their friend being carried off by the invisible thing.

"Well, let's get her! I'll show that stupid thing how a dragon fights! I've got a spell that will put—"

The faerie dragon stopped, stunned by a sudden wash of pale light that spilled from the Moonwell into the darkness around them. The pair sat on the ground, just outside the ring of arches. As the light exploded, they both sprang to the slab of stone beside them, the stone that had, until recently, marked the top of one of the druidic arches.

They stared in awe. Even Newt was silent as the foaming waters of the Moonwell spurted from the pool to blanket the druids, boiling and hissing and then withdrawing to leave the druids as stone statues. The undead staggered away from the explosion, recoiling as drops of water struck their decayed skin or barren bones.

"What happened to Genna—to Genna?"

"I don't know," said Newt, mystified—and very curious. "Let's go see!"

The sprite looked sadly at the druids and shook his head. Suddenly, he had an idea—a way to get Newt away from this dangerous place, too.

"L-let's get Robyn. Let's find her!" Yazilliclik urged.

Newt was puzzled by the metamorphosis, but he couldn't think of anything he could do about it. "Okay. Which way did she go?" Yazilliclick pointed, and the two creatures of faerie darted into the dawn, seeking their friend.

* * * * *

Robyn awakened with a start. Frantically she looked around, taking in her surroundings. The great unicorn stood watchfully over her, and the sun was high in the sky. She saw that they were in a small, flowery meadow, near a clear pool of water that reflected the blue-green images of towering pine trees.

The young druid stood and stretched. Suddenly she remembered the battle—and the thing that had borne her away. "Kamerynn, we've got to get back to the grove!" She grasped a handful of the unicorn's mane and was about to swing onto his back when she heard an excited voice calling from the forest.

"Robyn! Here you are! We've been looking all over for you!" Newt, followed by Yazilliclick, buzzed toward her. The faerie dragon hovered to a landing on his favorite perch, Kamerynn's horn. "You should have seen it! The Moonwell got all white and foamy, and water sprayed all over Genna and the druids. And when it stopped, they were all statues!"

Robyn gasped. "You mean Genna—all of them— turned to stone?"

Yazilliclick settled to the ground. "St-stone, yes. All white and smooth. They didn't move—didn't move!"

With a groan, Robyn sat heavily on the ground again. The battle was lost! And her impetuousness had carried her away at the most crucial time!

"D-don't cry," said the faerie, his antennae bobbing slowly as he frowned at Robyn. "You couldn't have done anything—

anything to stop it! You're the one who got away. Now you can go back and fix it—fix it!"

Robyn felt as though she *was* about to cry. Never had she felt so lost, so alone. The undead were in possession of the Moonwell, and Genna and the other clerics were trapped within stone. She had no idea what she would do next.

A soft whispering of wind pulled her attention across the meadow, though she felt no breeze upon her. The water of the small pool was rippling as if caressed by a gentle breath of air. It swirled slowly, hypnotically, almost as if a whirlpool had opened beneath it.

Robyn's weariness and despair were forgotten as she saw a shape rising in the water. No ripple was disturbed as a silver helmet broke the surface. Robyn's breath caught in her throat as the image of a beautiful woman rose slowly from the center of the pool. Her hair was silky blond, flowing past her shoulders, and she wore a silver breastplate that showed dents from many blows. But her skin was clear, like ivory—untouched by age, or trouble, or hurt.

The woman finally seemed to stand on top of the water, though she was not wet. Her commanding gaze forced Robyn's eyes upward to meet her own. Robyn found herself wondering if this was some kind of trick, but she immediately discarded the notion. The sight of the woman brought a feeling of deep reverence to her heart. She did not feel that such an emotion could be caused by deceit.

"Who are you?" Robyn asked, climbing to her feet and stepping toward the pool. Kamerynn turned to watch the woman impassively, Newt still perched on his horn. Yazilliclick had blinked into invisibility at the first sign of her.

"I am one who cares for you, and your prince, and your land," said the woman, in a longing tone that brought an ache to the druid's heart. "I am the spirit of one long dead, who hopes that her life will gain meaning through your acts."

"But . . ."

"Druid of the Vale," said the woman. Her voice was serene yet commanding. "Your prince is in danger. He awaits his death upon Alaron, but you can help him."

"Tristan? Awaits his death? What do you mean?" Robyn

gasped, fear choking her throat.

"You must go to him. He needs you."

"Where? Where can I find him?"

"Seek him in Dernall Forest, in the living heart of that wood. Now fly, if you would reach him in time!" With these words, the woman slowly sank into the pond, disappearing from sight in a few moments.

"But how can I find him?" she cried.

Her only answer was the slow swirling of the water, and then the whirling died away and the pool was still and mirrorlike once again.

* * * * *

The vastness of Dernall Forest was a maze of trails and tracks, any of which could have been taken by their quarry. Yet Kryphon trusted to Razfallow's tracking skills for the most part, and his own intuition for the rest. He was fairly certain that the prince and his party would travel north, and he let this guide their path.

But even the prince should keep a step ahead of him. Kryphon understood the inherent value of his presence in Doncastle. The town had been a vexing problem for Cyndre and the High King. Their attacks, in the past, had been thwarted by the steady defenders, as well as magical aid from an unknown source.

The wizard and his companions traveled cautiously. Razfallow and Doric moved in the lead, seeking signs of the six horses and the large moorhound. Kryphon followed, several hundred yards behind, concealed by a spell of invisibility. Any ambush directed against his companions would almost certainly overlook him, leaving him in position to rescue, or avenge, as the case might be. In any event, Kryphon had insured that he, himself, would remain safe.

They pressed northward through the dark woods for two days, and gradually the sign of their quarry grew more and more faint. For most of the second day they moved by guesswork with no clue to indicate they were on the right track. Kryphon began to worry; he feared Cyndre's wrath should the prince escape them.

Then fate intervened, as eight men leaped from the

underbrush to surround Doric and Razfallow, brandishing swords and crossbows. Kryphon, invisible, watched the scene with interest as he quietly approached them. In a minute he had moved within earshot.

"Gold!" one of the strangers demanded. "Will ye hand it over, or shall we search ye for it?"

"You shall have what you require," she said slowly. With great deliberation, she began to fumble in the pockets of her robe. She was taking plenty of time, but the bandits seemed to be in no hurry. Their attention was riveted to her, as her robe swirled aside to reveal a long stretch of her leg.

Kryphon smiled to himself as he reached the confrontation, still secure in his mantle of invisibility. This was going to be very easy. He drew a pinch of sand from his robe, allowing the grains to pass slowly between his fingers while he concentrated on a simple spell.

"Sleep, children," he said mockingly. With the casting of his spell, several things happened: he became visible to all of those gathered on the forest path, and seven of the eight bandits staggered and then slumped to the ground, breathing deeply but sound asleep.

The eighth bandit—the one who had demanded the gold—whirled toward Kryphon in shock. His shortsword quivered as he staggered backward.

"Where . . . where did you. . . ?" His voice cracked and then faded.

Kryphon smiled. "Be at ease, friend," he said softly, his hands executing a series of gestures. "I mean you no harm."

The spell—the same one he had used to charm Razfallow—worked remarkably well. The bandit relaxed and lowered his sword, offering a tentative smile. "Sorry. It's just that, well, you surprised me."

"I understand," said the mage, benignly. "We are looking for some . . . friends. We think they might have passed this way." He described the prince's party, speaking without urgency, but his heart pounded with tension. Would this man know anything useful?

"A halfling, you say?" asked the bandit, as Kryphon described Pawldo. "Sure—they were in Doncastle just yesterday morning."

Kryphon forced his voice to remain calm. "Doncastle, eh? How can we find this place?"

The man beamed with pleasure, elated that he would be able to help his new friend. "Why, it's a few hours from here. I can take you there myself!"

Kryphon smiled, his mouth tightening into a thin line.

* * * * *

Tristan felt a strange mixture of emotions as he stood before the High King. His desire for vengeance flared within his breast, but was tempered by the knowledge that this man was his lawful liege. Yet the fellow's ridiculous appearance, and the stark fear that shone blatantly from his eyes overruled the tradition. At once, the Prince of Corwell decided that this man did not deserve his respect.

"Who . . . who are you?" the king demanded, his voice quivering slightly. He stared at the intruder, disbelieving.

"I am Tristan Kendrick, Prince of Corwell!" he declared.

"Why . . . er, what . . ."

"Did you have my father killed?" Tristan demanded. He did not draw, or even handle, his weapon, but the High King recoiled as if physically assaulted.

"No! I didn't!" His voice cracked and he pushed his chair backward, his uneaten breakfast tumbling to the floor.

"Why did I find your coin upon the killers?" Tristan took a step forward. He felt, rather than saw, Daryth's reassuring presence behind him, guarding the door.

"Don't kill me!" squealed the king. "The kingship is yours! Just let me live!"

"Kingship? Of Corwell?"

"No—the High Kingship!" For a moment the king looked puzzled. "That's what you want, isn't it?"

"Who told you that?" asked the prince.

"Why . . . I thought everybody knew that. That's why you came here, isn't it? To claim my throne?"

Tristan leaped around the king's table, too quickly for the monarch to evade him. He grabbed the pathetic little man by the throat and shook him. "I came here," he growled, "to punish the person responsible for my father's death." The king gasped and twisted, but could not escape.

"If that person was not you," Tristan snarled, "who was it?"

"Perhaps it is me you seek."

The voice, soft and sinuous, came from the far side of the huge dressing room. Tristan and Daryth turned in surprise to see a person, shrouded in a dark robe, standing before them. He had not been there a moment earlier.

"Who are you?" demanded the prince, retaining his grip on the king's throat.

The stranger didn't answer directly. Instead, he pulled a small gray pebble from a pocket of his robe with his left hand, while his right emerged from another pocket with a pinch of what looked like dust.

"Wissath Duthax, Hisst!" said the man, sprinkling the dust over the stone.

Tristan suddenly felt himself falling, head first. The room whirled around him as he released the king, struggling to raise his hands and protect his head before he landed. He crashed into a hard stone surface and felt the wind explode from his lungs. For a fraction of a second, he had the feeling that he, and the king beside him, were lying on the *ceiling* of the room. Then the force of gravity returned to normal. He had been on the ceiling. Now he crashed to the floor where he lay, stunned. A crash, somewhere behind him, told him that Daryth, too, must have been ensnared in the spell.

"Guards!" squealed the king, squirming away from Tristan. The prince found his muscles paralyzed, and his head pounded. He had nearly been knocked unconscious by the strange fall.

"Korass, Sithtu—" the wizard began, pulling more items from his robe.

"No!" cried the king, somehow scrambling to his feet and stepping in front of the wizard. "Do not kill him . . . yet."

Tristan could not see the wizard's face beneath his cowled hood, but the sudden tension in the mage's body signalled his annoyance with the king's order. Nonetheless, his movements relaxed.

"Very well," he said quietly. The smooth voice, Tristan thought, sounded incongruous coming from one of such arcane power.

The door burst open and a dozen guards flew into the

room. "Seize them!" ordered the king, and the groggy pair of trespassers were swiftly clasped by strong hands.

"I will interrogate them myself!" he barked. "Take them to the dungeon!"

* * * * *

The iron door slammed shut, leaving Tristan alone in the darkness of his cell. Daryth had been taken somewhere else—the vast dungeon seemed to have no shortage of suitable enclosures.

Angrily, the prince pulled against the chains that secured his wrists and ankles to the hard stone wall. They clanked taut with his movements, but gave no further. Reaching awkwardly behind him, he felt the mounts of each of the chains. They were solidly embedded in hard, dry mortar.

His eyes adjusted to the gloom of the small cell. As in Llewellyn, a feeling of terrible suffocation threatened to choke him. This time, the feeling was intensified by darkness, and the fact that he was chained to the wall, alone in a cell.

He shouted at the darkness. Furiously, he struggled with the chains, trying to tear them from the walls with brute strength. All he gained for his struggles were chafed wrists and strained muscles.

He thought of Robyn, wishing there were some way she could know of his plight. But then he imagined her young druidic powers facing the magic of the king's wizard—a man who had the power to reverse gravity itself! Robyn, he knew, would face the wizard, unflinching in her courage and her faith. And she would be doomed by his power to a horrible death.

Only the fortuitous intervention of the High King, he felt, had saved Daryth and him. Why had the king wanted him to remain alive, after dogging their trail with assassins and sorcery? Certainly whoever had sabotaged the *Lucky Duckling* had not wanted them to remain alive for questioning. Nor had the assassin Razfallow with his band of killers.

And what had the wizard said when he suddenly appeared in the king's dressing room? "Perhaps it is me you seek," or words to that effect. Was his quarrel indeed with the king's wizard, and not the High King himself?

"Tristan," came the soft, musical voice.

"Huh?" he grunted stupidly, opening his eyes and raising his throbbing head. A white figure stood before him, glowing with a brilliance that hurt his eyes. He blinked several times, and saw her blond hair spilling across a silver breastplate. His heart leaped as he recognized his visitor.

"My queen!" he croaked. "Thank the goddess you have come! Please, unfetter me!"

Queen Allisynn's eyes were brighter than he had ever seen them. She was *here* in the cell with him. He longed to reach out and touch her, but she came no closer. The light surrounded her body, and caused her hair to glow like fire. He looked full upon her face and felt the pain in his skull melt away under the healing warmth of her gaze.

"I cannot free you." Her voice heavy with sadness. "My power is useless against the cold iron that binds you."

Tristan moaned and dropped his head in defeat.

"Do not despair, my prince! You have learned what your enemy fears most, and that is valuable knowledge."

"Learned?" he said scornfully. "I learned that I'm a fool! I don't deserve to be a footman in Corwell's army, much less the king! I was taken prisoner like a chicken walking into a noose!" His anger threatened to consume him, and the Queen flinched under the onslaught of his rage.

"I have no right—I forgot where I was for a moment. Can you forgive me for my self-pity?"

"I fear you place undue weight upon my approval," she said. "There is a lass upon Gwynneth who would be sorely touched by your plight. Perhaps it is for her that you should fight."

Tristan bit his lip with guilt. In the glory of the queen's presence, he had forgotten about the woman that he loved—that he wanted to have share his life. "But, you . . ."

"I am . . . far too old for you." She smiled coolly. "Though your affection touches me deeply. It has been a long time since a man looked at me with such . . . love."

"I do love you, my queen!" he gasped. He suddenly felt deep humiliation for his imprisonment. "May the goddess grant me the power to prove that someday!"

"I think that she will. Think about what you have learned.

And now rest, my prince."

She slowly faded from his sight, but he could not call her back. He had already collapsed into sleep.

His awakening came as his cell door clanged loudly open. He jerked his head up to see a sudden wash of torchlight precede two figures into the dingy room.

The first was the bent and leering turnkey who had eagerly latched the chains to his wrists and ankles. And the other was the High King.

The turnkey stepped out of the way, holding the torch high. The monarch marched past the turnkey and stopped, just out of the prince's reach. He looked more self-confident than he had during their first encounter, though still not quite the picture of a High King that Tristan had always imagined.

He wore a long purple robe, trimmed with white. His wig of loose curls gave his head an unnaturally large appearance, though he was a broad hand shorter than the prince. A tiny mustache twitched below his long, pointed nose.

"You intrigue me, Prince of Corwell," said the king, staring intently at Tristan. The prince said nothing.

"You say that you come here for vengeance?"

"Yes, I do."

"You did not journey to Caer Callidyrr to claim the throne of the High Kings—*my* throne?"

"Of course not! I don't know where you got such an idea!"

"This is very interesting. Of course, I do not know whether or not to believe you. . . ."

"Your Majesty?" said a figure from the doorway. The king whirled around in surprise as a dark-robed shape entered the cell through the open door.

"Cyndre! We will talk later! Leave me now." The king's voice was authoritative but a trifle shaky.

"I am afraid this cannot wait, sire. I come to you with a matter of the greatest urgency!" In the flickering torchlight, Tristan saw the wizard's hands float through a delicate series of gestures. The king shuddered slightly and then sighed in quiet resignation.

"The usurper?" asked the wizard softly.

"He . . . he is . . ." The king seemed to have trouble collecting his thoughts.

"He is a threat, you mean," finished the wizard. Tristan was horrified by the way the sorcerer manipulated the ruler. For the first time the prince truly feared for his life.

"It is time that he died," concluded Cyndre, still speaking in that musically pleasant voice.

"Very well," replied the king quietly. He did not look at Tristan as he spoke.

* * * * *

The chains that held Daryth of Calimshan were no less stout, nor were their mountings in any way inferior to those binding the Prince of Corwell. But the Calishite had one advantage that the prince did not: He wore the gloves he had recovered from the treasure vault of Caer Allisynn. The guards, even after a thorough search, had not discerned the gloves, so perfectly did they match Daryth's brown skin.

Daryth waited for several minutes after the guards had left. He heard them escort Tristan deeper into the dungeon. Some time later, he heard the guards approach again. One stuck a torch through the small iron grate in the door, illuminating the room and apparently satisfying himself that the prisoner was secure. Then they moved on.

Carefully, Daryth pulled his right hand against the tight manacle. It slipped through the rusty ring smoothly. With a gentle tug, his left hand came free as well. He drew forth one of the long wire probes concealed in the gloves, and crouched to examine the clasps binding his ankles. His nimble fingers located the tiny keyhole, even through the supple leather of the gloves. It was the work of several minutes to release the mechanism securing his right foot. The left one popped loose after another thirty seconds.

Daryth waited for a few minutes, scarcely daring to breathe. The dungeon was silent. He crept carefully across the cell, taking care in the inky blackness that he did not bump into anything or make any sudden noise.

The door was easy to find, though the lock proved more challenging than the clasps that had secured his manacles. It took him nearly ten minutes to figure out the complicated mechanism, but it finally revealed its secrets to his persistent probing and clicked free.

He inched the door open and looked into the corridor. A torch flickered somewhere in the distance, but elsewhere all was dark. The cold stonework dripped with moisture, and the air smelled dank and heavy with mold. The Calishite slid carefully into the corridor, noting that there was no sound in either direction.

Daryth knew that Tristan had been taken to a cell farther down the corridor, to his left. The torch that flickered faintly was some distance to his right, while all was dark in the other direction. Realizing that he needed some light, he first glided silently the hundred feet to the torch, which sputtered in a rusty wall socket. He seized the flaming brand and turned back toward the depths of the dungeon.

But then he thought of their weapons—particularly the Sword of Cymrych Hugh. They had come too far with it to abandon it here, he decided. He held the torch before him and started up the corridor, determined to at least investigate the nearest guardroom.

He slipped carefully around a corner and recognized the stairs he had come down. The guardroom, where their weapons had been taken from them, was just at the top of the stairs. He sprang up the steps, three at a time, pausing below the top to observe. He cursed at the sight of an iron gate, closed across the passage. Beyond it, a guard sat dozing upon a chair—and beyond him, their weapons dangled from a hook in the wall!

Daryth carefully propped the torch against one of the steps, and removed the wire probe from his glove. Trying to work as quietly as possible, he gently prodded the mechanism. In moments, it freed with a loud click.

The man sat bolt upright in his chair, his eyes widening as Daryth flung open the gate and dove into the guardroom. The Calishite's fist caught the man's jaw just as he opened it. His shout of alarm died in his throat and he collapsed, unconscious, against the wall.

Daryth turned toward the weapons and swiftly pulled down his scimitar. He girded the weapon to his belt, took the rest of the weapons, and locked the gate behind him.

There were only occasional doors along the walls here, he

realized as he passed his own cell. As he passed each door, he held the torch to the iron grate that was set at eye level, illuminating the interior as he searched for his friend. The first four cells he examined were empty.

But the fifth held a man.

The figure was chained to the wall. His head hung low, so that Daryth could not see his face. The man did not look like Tristan—he seemed smaller than the prince—but the Calishite could not be sure in the dim light.

"Tristan!" he hissed. There was no answer, nor any sign of life from the figure.

Cursing to himself, Daryth set the torch down and began to pick the lock of this cell.

His familiarity with the lock paid off, and the door clicked open in several minutes. He crept into the room, but the man still made no move. Holding the torch before him, Daryth moved slowly forward.

Suddenly the man raised his head, and looked at the Calishite with an expression of hopeless longing. It was not Tristan—this man was older, smaller, and emaciated. His gaunt cheeks flexed as if he tried to speak, but no sound emerged. His hands, Daryth realized, were twisted claws—they had been horribly mangled.

The man blinked a few times, apparently realizing that Daryth was not a guard coming to torment him. He moved his mouth, soundlessly, again. In fact, everything about him was soundless. His chains made no noise as he rattled them. His gasps of breath were completely inaudible.

"Who are—" Daryth began, but he could hear no sound. Sorcery! The hair at the back of his neck prickled as he realized that the cell was blanketed by some kind of magical effect that eliminated all noise.

The man looked at him boldly now, and Daryth saw, behind the haggard look, a face of courage and dignity. He remembered tales of the good lords and loyal citizens that the High King had imprisoned.

Not understanding fully why he wasted his time thus, the Calishite stepped forward and began to pick the locks on the prisoner's manacles.

* * * * *

Hobarth spent the day alternating between bursts of delight and fits of frustration. The druids had been defeated! His army of death had won a grand victory! Bhaal's army of death, he reminded himself with a reverent nod of his head—Bhaal's army, but under his own command.

But they had been cheated of the pleasure of the kill. Sealed within their stony prisons, he was certain that the druids were watching, mocking him.

He examined each smooth and lifelike statue, satisfying himself that they all were solid stone. He hefted a heavy iron axe, taking the weapon from a standing zombie, and smashed it against one of the statues, trying to snap off a druid's upraised arm—but instead of the stone, the blade of his axe shattered. A stinging numbness throbbed in his hands as he dropped the useless weapon.

Yet the blow had given him a sense of satisfaction. He enjoyed striking the druid, even if she could not feel his blow.

A rumble of hunger disturbed his huge belly, and Hobarth, with almost childish glee, decided to hold a victory banquet. His table would be the stone slab that had fallen from one of the arches. His food would be the meat and wine of Bhaal himself. Dropping the axe handle, Hobarth turned to the stone and chanted a simple spell. Immediately, the surface of the slab was covered with succulent cuts of red meat, ripe fruits, and heavy bread. He threw his empty wineflask onto the slab, and uttered another incantation. Then he picked up the new flask and drank long and deep of the tart, strong liquid. A warm glow spread through his body as he tackled the feast—enough to feed four men—and finished it. Several times he created more wine, and his head buzzed pleasantly by the time he had consumed all the food.

Hobarth next looked around the scene of the battle. Bodies of his undead lay everywhere, shattered and broken so badly that they had died a second time. Those bodies were useless to him. Many hundreds had survived the fight, however, and these now stood or sat like statues of flesh and bone around the Moonwell and the broken arches, waiting for their master's next command.

Several of the druids had died during the fight, and he looked for these bodies with interest. He found one—a woman—who had been torn by the zombies. Her face and limbs were gashed to the bone, and her eyes were gaping, bloody sockets. The zombies had shown a penchant for gouging the eyes from their victims.

He lifted the Heart of Kazgoroth from its pouch and held it in his hand, staring at the body of the druid. Concentrating, he willed the might of Bhaal to enter the body. First, a leg twitched. Then the jaw stretched, flopping aimlessly. The cleric concentrated some more.

The body of Isolde of Winterglen sat up slowly and climbed unsteadily to its feet.

♣ 15 ♣

Alexei

Tristan looked from the king to the wizard to the turnkey. The High King could not meet his gaze, dropping his eyes to stare awkwardly at the floor. The grotesque turnkey leered eagerly, flecks of spittle dropping from his lips. The wizard threw back his hood and smiled coolly.

"The task is too important to leave to the headsman," said Cyndre. "Or even to magic. I will handle this myself."

He drew a black-hilted dagger from beneath his robe and took a step toward Tristan. The prince jerked frantically against his chains, but they were not about to give. The king turned away, while the turnkey raised his torch to shed more light on Cyndre's intended victim.

Then the torch clattered to the floor, and the turnkey's head—still leering—flew through the air while his body lurched and fell to the ground. Tristan saw a flash of silvery steel as Cyndre hissed in anger and turned in a catlike crouch. The light faded but did not disappear as the torch sputtered and sizzled on the wet flagstones.

A figure slashed into the room, and the prince saw the bright flash of a weapon again. The wizard screamed and fell backward as his dagger was knocked to the floor. Tristan saw that the mage clutched his right hand as blood spurted from his clenched fist.

The king shrieked in terror and darted from the door as Cyndre struggled to avoid the attacker. Tristan heard the monarch's cries for help fade into the distance as he raced up the dungeon corridor.

The wizard, meanwhile, moved with surprising agility as he scrambled away. The prince recognized Daryth, now, as the Calishite brandished his scimitar with liquid smoothness, trying to force Cyndre into a corner. The Calishite kicked and slashed with merciless persistence, constantly forcing Cyndre to duck and twist away.

Cyndre sprang to his feet and charged Daryth suddenly, crying out as Daryth's scimitar bit into his raised forearm. But the rush had thrown the Calishite off balance, and before Daryth could strike a lethal blow, the mage sprang through the door out of the cell. There he nearly knocked down another person—one whom Tristan had not noticed earlier.

Still hissing in rage, the wizard raced up the corridor following the path of the king.

"Quickly," the stranger urged Daryth. "We must free him and be gone—the guard will be upon us in minutes."

Daryth snatched the keys from the body of the headless turnkey and found the one that released Tristan's manacles.

"Why didn't he use his magic?" asked the prince.

"The wound," said the stranger, turning to look at him. Even in the dim light, Tristan thought that the man looked more dead than alive. The skin of his face had shrunk tightly, giving him the visage of a skull. His hands were twisted claws. Seeing his gaze, the man held up those hands and continued.

"A magic-user needs his hands to cast spells. The scimitar did enough damage to prevent Cyndre from casting—a fact to which we owe our lives. But as soon as he visits a cleric, the damage will be repaired, and he will be after us with a vengeance."

Tristan looked intently at the man as Daryth opened the last lock. "Your hands . . . Are you, too, a sorcerer?"

"I was, until my 'master' "—he spat the word— "decided that I threatened his base of power."

"You are one of the Council of Seven?" asked the prince, remembering the information O'Roarke had given him.

"*Was* one of the council," said the mage. "My name is Alexei, and I will do what I can to stop them now. They will come to regret leaving me alive."

"Let's go," Daryth hissed urgently. "We can talk later!"

Tristan flexed his muscles and found that he could still

move, albeit with some pain. "Where do we go?" he asked.

"Follow me!" said Alexei, hobbling from the cell. "The upper reaches of the castle are sure to be sealed off, but the wizards have secret ways through here. We might be able to slip into one of them before the guards discover us."

"Wonderful," muttered Daryth. "Where to?" The Calishite picked up the fading torch, which flared back into light as it was raised from the floor. He waited for Tristan to follow the wizard, and he brought up the rear.

Alexei led them away from the direction in which the king and the wizard had fled. The mage moved stiffly, and suddenly he stumbled and fell headlong.

"Come on," encouraged the prince, lifting him under the arms. The man was no heavier than a straw dummy.

Once they heard a sound behind them. Pausing momentarily, they heard the pounding of heavy boots and the clanking of weaponry somewhere in the distance. Pursuit had begun! Urging the mage to move faster, Tristan and Daryth pressed urgently along the slippery passage.

"Slow down," cautioned Alexei. The wizard examined the water-streaked walls of the corridor as they moved carefully along. He seemed to be searching for something, and at last he held up a clawlike hand.

"Here!" he said, pointing at a blackened stretch of stone that looked no different from any other part of the tunnel walls. He reached forward and tried to twist a small outcropping of rock, cursing as his broken hands could not grasp the small and slippery surface.

"Help," he mumbled in frustration.

Daryth stepped forward and twisted the knob of rock. Nothing happened. He tried again, maneuvering it this way and that, and suddenly they heard some kind of mechanism click within the walls.

With a slow creaking, the stone wall swung away, revealing a passage barely as high as a man, and no more than three or four feet wide. They could hear the heavy tramp of pursuing guards as they stepped through the opening and saw the secret door close behind them.

* * * * *

"We'll be in Doncastle soon. You'll be amazed, I promise you! Lord Roarke is quite ingenious—the defenses are his idea." The bandit, who had called himself Evan, chattered away under the influence of the charm spell.

"And all who live there are outlaws?" asked Kryphon. He was annoyed with the man's loquaciousness, but the information he provided was certainly valuable.

"All of us," boasted Evan, as if the term 'bandit' was a badge of honor. "The king and his wizards have tried, time and again, to conquer us—but we have always driven them off!"

"How do you face the magic of the king's army?"

"We have a magic-user and a cleric of our own. We used to have the support of the druids, until the king and his wizards drove them away—or killed them!"

Kryphon smiled privately, relishing that personal triumph. The battles with the druids had been savage, but wizardry had prevailed. "I would like to meet some of these . . . spellcasters. Perhaps you could introduce me when we reach the city?"

Before Evan could answer, Kryphon felt a familiar pull upon his arm, accompanied by the langorous press of Doric's body. They had been walking for several hours, and he knew that she was getting tired.

"Can't we stop for a while?" she whispered, plaintively. "You and I can take a little rest. We'll still get to this city before dark!"

"No!" he hissed, pulling his arm away. He realized that he was growing very tired of Doric. Her constant need for attention was becoming a burden. Sulking, she let go of his arm and walked ahead of him.

Kryphon was surprised and a little amused at how quickly his affection had cooled for the woman. He looked at her now, and he saw a gaunt scarecrow where before he had seen a desirably slender woman. In the past, he had vanquished her poutiness with physical release or by allowing her to exercize her incessant need for cruelty. Now he found her moods tiresome and annoying.

Perhaps, he mused, he could find a young woman more to his liking in Doncastle.

* * * * *

Alexei could scarcely believe his luck. Rescue! He chuckled inwardly at the irony of its source: the ones his former master had worked so diligently to destroy! His weariness and pain were forgotten as he shuffled along with Tristan and Daryth. His body grew numb to the efforts of their march.

But his mind whirled with possibilities.

The hatred that had sustained him in the darkness of his cell now blossomed into raging heat, fed by the fuel of opportunity. He would make Cyndre, the council, Hobarth—even the High King—pay!

And, for the time being, what better way than to aid the one whom Cyndre had branded their most dangerous foe? After a while, of course, Alexei would be capable of dealing his vengeance alone —but for now he needed allies, and fate had provided him with a ready pair.

First, Alexei decided, he would need tools to help him regain some of his lost powers. That was why he had directed the men to this secret passage and now urged them to hasten downward.

He knew where to find those tools.

* * * * *

The unicorn looked sad, thought Robyn, as she, Yazilliclick, and Newt made their farewells. "I wish you could come too, old friend, but without wings. . . ."

Kamerynn lowered his head as she stepped away. She held the runestick in her hand. It was now her only possession, since she had dropped her staff beside the arch. Yazilliclick had told her that the Moonwell was still surrounded by undead, so she dared not risk an attempt to regain it.

"Wait here for us, Kamerynn! We'll be back soon, won't we, Robyn? I'll find you something nice from Alaron. And Tristan will be with us. We'll *have* to have a party then!" Newt exclaimed, with a reproachful look at Robyn.

"Farewell again," said the druid, clasping the unicorn's neck. "Will you watch over Genna and the others until I return?" Stifling her tears, she turned to the two faeries.

The faerie dragon and wood sprite rose quickly into the air as Robyn held the runestick to her side and closed her eyes in concentration. Once again she felt her body shrink and tumble forward, and she instinctively spread her wings to break her fall.

But she noticed more subtle changes this time. She felt her heartbeat accelerate. She opened her eyes, and the keen vision of the eagle was more brilliant even than before.

And she took to the sky with the dragon and the sprite. The other two were dwarfed by her massive wingspan, but they darted easily around her in flight. They headed east, toward Alaron.

* * * * *

Daryth led the way through the narrow tunnel. It descended sharply, often as steep as a stairway. Rubble along the floor made footing very treacherous. In places, rivulets of water trickled along the floor and walls, making the surface as slippery as ice.

"This is a path of the sorcerers," explained Alexei. "Unknown to the guards of the castle—although it has challenges all its own!"

"Where do you come from?" asked the prince after several minutes. "You don't look like one of the Ffolk."

Alexei shook his head. "None of the wizards are from your islands. Cyndre recruited his council from throughout the Realms and brought us here to achieve his ambition."

"What ambition is that? What does he want—and what power does he hold over the High King?" asked Tristan.

"He desires to rule a large kingdom. The Realms of the Ffolk seemed to fit his needs, as best as I can guess—a weak ruler, divided peoples, but a large and rich land, ready for exploitation. The king fell prey to a simple charm spell long ago. Cyndre constantly tightens his hold on the pathetic worm, until it has reached the point where the king will not make a move without the wizard's approval."

"And your role . . . ?"

Alexei's eyes flashed anger. "I was his right hand, the first to be recruited from Thay, where Cyndre also passed his apprenticeship. I watched my master's back, while he practiced his evil. He is in league with a powerful cleric—thinks he controls the cleric, though I have my doubts. But together they make a potent force." Alexei did not add his knowledge of Hobarth's mission—the capture of the druid who loved this prince. It did not suit his purposes to distract Tristan from aiding his escape.

They made good time. The passage widened into a cave about thirty feet wide, still dropping steeply. After some time, Tristan guessed that they might have descended as much as a thousand feet underground. He wondered when they would begin going up.

"Here," said the mage, suddenly pointing to a narrower cave that branched to the left. "I recognize this place!"

They allowed him to lead the way into the passage. He hurried forward for about a hundred yards and then stopped as the narrow passage opened into a huge chamber. Stalactites hung from the ceiling, and several pools of water, so clear as to be almost invisible, dotted the floor. The torchlight flickered and flared, creating moving shadows that gave the place a menacing look.

But the strangest feature of the room was at its center: A table and a dozen stone chairs rested upon a flat space in the floor. The obviously manmade furnishings looked completely out of place in a locale of such natural splendor.

Alexei noticed his companions' looks of puzzlement. "This is a secret meeting place for the council," he explained. "For when Cyndre wished to avoid gathering in the castle. It is used very rarely; I doubt the younger wizards even know of its existence."

"Amazing," murmured the prince, looking in wonder at the beauty of the cave.

"And the reason you brought us here?" asked Daryth.

"Oh, yes—here!" Alexei moved around the table, holding the torch high. "See that chest there?"

The other two joined him. He indicated a large wooden chest near the far wall of the cave. It sat in the center of a smooth circle of floor that was about thirty feet in diameter.

"If we can get into that chest, I will not be crippled any longer," explained the mage.

"I'll see what I can do," offered Daryth, stepping forward.

"Wait!" Alexei grabbed Daryth's collar with one of his clawlike hands, pulling the Calishite back before he stepped onto the smooth expanse of floor. "There are traps!"

"I might have known," grumbled Daryth. "Just how important is the stuff in that chest?"

"It could mean the difference between our escape and our deaths," said the mage gravely.

"What do you know about the traps?"

"The floor is false, for one thing, a deep pit filled with soft dust. You would sink to the bottom and choke to death —a most horrible death.

"And the chest itself has a trap—something in the lock."

"You're sure we need these 'treasures'?"

Alexei shrugged, not wanting to press the point. Tristan didn't say anything. They all knew that Daryth was the only one with the skill necessary to pick the lock and, perhaps, to avoid the trap there. It would have to be his decision.

"Well, I'll have a look at it, anyway," muttered the Calishite. "How do I get over there?"

"We could stretch the table across the pit," offered the prince. Indeed, the boards were just about the right length to extend from the edge of the pit to the chest in the center.

"Everyone's got a way to get me killed," grunted Daryth. Nevertheless, he turned to lift one end of the solid platform.

Alexei held the torch as Daryth and Tristan wrestled the heavy tabletop into position. At one point, they dipped a corner of it onto the surface of the floor. It met no more resistance than if it had touched water, and sent a cloud of fine dust into the air.

Daryth took the torch and carefully walked to the chest. He knelt and examined the mechanism of the lock for several minutes. Tristan was acutely conscious of the torch burning lower, but he didn't dare say anything to break his friend's concentration.

Slowly, the Calishite drew the narrowest of the wire probes from his glove. Clenching his jaws in concentration, he stuck it into the keyhole, holding it at a sharp angle instead of pushing straight in.

The tiny click was barely audible to Tristan, but in the torchlight he saw a gleaming silver needle stick suddenly forth from the lock. It stopped, less than an inch from Daryth's hand. Even at this distance, the prince could see a greenish substance smeared on the end of the needle.

Daryth bent over the lock again, and it was only a matter of moments before the clasp released and he threw back the lid of the chest.

"*These* are supposed to save our lives?" he asked, incredulous. He pulled forth three tubes of rolled parchment, wrapped in smooth leather cases. Puzzled, he brought them to Alexei.

"Yes!" the mage said. "I am no longer powerless! Though my hands prevent me from casting spells, there is nothing wrong with my eyes! I have but to read a spell from one of these scrolls, and it will be as if I had cast it myself."

"How did you know they were there?" asked the Calishite.

"Cyndre told me. They were supposed to be for an emergency." His gaunt face twisted into a cold smile. "I would call this an emergency."

"Now, we should move on," urged the prince. "We don't have a lot of light left. Besides, if Cyndre remembers that you know about this place, we might have some unwelcome company before long."

"You are very right," agreed Alexei. "Come—this way!"

The mage, obviously filled with fresh confidence, led them from the chamber back to the original cavern. Here they continued to descend, moving much more rapidly than before. But the torch had burned to a tiny stub, and soon even that would be consumed.

"It's going to get dark soon," said the prince, indicating the fading brand.

"Perhaps I can take care of that," said the mage, unwrapping one of the scrolls. He looked it over quickly, setting it aside to reach for another. He apparently found what he wanted, for he began to read to himself, whispering strange words. As he read, a small portion of the scroll in his hands appeared to burst into flames. The bluish fire flickered across the page, burning the letters of each word as it was read, though the parchment itself was unaffected. When he finished, one section of the scroll was blank.

But the stub of the torch glowed with a cool, white light

that was far more brilliant than the fading flames had been.

"That's nice, for a start," admitted the Calishite.

Alexei nodded and tucked the scrolls under his arm. They started down the cave, and their progress improved even more, since now they had adequate illumination for the path.

But still they went down. Several times they even had to scale small cliffs as the cave began to drop even more steeply. Tristan grew more and more concerned about their distance from the surface; they had to be a half-mile below Caer Callidyrr, not to mention a similar distance under the surrounding sea. Was there any safe way out?

Only when his companions stopped in amazement did Tristan notice that they had entered a large chamber. He could not suppress a low whistle of surprise.

This vast cavern dwarfed the room with the chest. The rays of illumination from the light spell could not hope to reach the far corners.

But they didn't have to, for this chamber was filled with its own source of illumination. The floor of the area was covered with huge mushrooms, some towering higher than Tristan's head. Several of these fungi shed a pale green luminescence. Close to the men, it was almost invisible, but across the chamber the area was lit in a ghostly green glow.

A mist of water hung in the air, and they could hear—and faintly see—the plume of a cataract spilling into the cavern. It fell hundreds of feet, splashing down the far wall from an unseen source to an invisible destination. Mosses and molds lined much of the cavern walls, giving the place the look of a dark jungle.

"This is amazing," said Daryth, awestruck.

"I can't believe all these plants can live this far underground," added the prince. "With no sunlight."

Alexei turned to them, concerned. "This was not here, years ago, when I last saw this place. I do not believe a lush garden such as this could have sprung into being without some kind of help."

"You mean gardeners?" asked Tristan.

"Precisely. And we would do well to avoid them. They must be here with Cyndre's knowledge and approval."

They found wide avenues laid, as if by plan, among the huge fungi. They followed the straightest of these across the center of the chamber, moving as silently as possible. The eerie green glow began to seem sinister, but that was their only illumination now, as Alexei had quickly stuck the glowing brand under his robe.

The ground was spongy underfoot, and they realized that the floor of the cavern was lined with thick loam and covered with moss. Someone had put a lot of work into creating this wealth of underground plantlife.

They were near the center of the cavern when they saw them: a dozen small, dark-skinned figures that swaggered into the path before them. Each was about four feet tall with a scraggly beard and evil, glittering eyes. They looked much like ordinary dwarves, except for their dark skin and wide, staring eyes.

As the companions stopped suddenly, another band of the creatures moved from among the mushrooms to block their route to the rear. They were surrounded, since their size made passage among the fungi impossible.

Tristan stepped forward, taking care to make no overt gesture. "Hello," he said. "We were . . . admiring your garden."

One of the dark dwarves spit onto the ground and pulled a sturdy axe from his belt. The others, he saw, all held weapons ranging from hammers and shortswords to a number of hefty axes. The creatures moved in, muttering in a tongue the prince didn't understand.

Still, Tristan was reluctant to draw his sword. For one thing, they were badly outnumbered.

The decision was taken out of his hands, however, when one of the dwarves threw his axe, aiming for the prince's head. Tristan ducked quickly, and the weapon sailed harmlessly by. But the rest of the band howled in rage, and charged—a furious mass of little people, brandishing their weapons with bloodthirsty intent.

The prince whipped the Sword of Cymrych Hugh from its scabbard, and the dwarves paused, momentarily dazzled by the gleaming weapon. And then he heard Alexei.

"Sorax, Frigius Newll—Ariith!"

He felt a blast of something to his left, and the air grew suddenly frigid. A dull blue light flashed in the cavern. It was not bright, but it etched expressions of terror into the faces of the dark dwarves. Most of the dwarves before him gasped or shrieked for a split second, and then collapsed, stiff as icicles. Their flesh turned a pale blue, and frost instantly began to condense on their exposed skin and the metal fittings of their weapons and clothes. A cone-shaped explosion of magic had frozen everything in its path, clearing the way for the men's escape.

Tristan heard howls of anger behind him, followed by the clash of steel—Daryth was protecting the rear of the party. Several of the dwarves before him had avoided the effect of the spell, and instead of running in terror at the awesome display, they charged with even greater intensity.

Tristan's sword split the first one nearly in two, as the prince danced to the side to avoid a hammer blow aimed at his kneecap. He whirled to stab the hammer-wielder in the throat, continuing his motion through a full circle. The whistling arc of his sword lifted the head of a third dark dwarf, and the path before them lay open.

"Run!" he cried, urging Alexei forward as he ran to Daryth's side. The mage hesitated, and then did as he was told while the two men with sword and scimitar slashed and stabbed at the angry attackers.

"Let's go," grunted Tristan as the dwarves fell back to regroup. The two men turned and sprinted after Alexei as the howling mob of their enemies burst into pursuit.

"There's gotta be a hundred of 'em back there now!" panted Daryth as they caught up to Alexei. The three men soon reached the far side of the cavern where, true to the mage's memory, the cave continued on.

"There's a bridge a little way up here," gasped the wizard, slowing slightly. "If we can cross it, I have a spell that might be able to knock it down."

"Good," grunted the prince, turning to look behind. Their pursuers were not in sight; their stumpy legs had left them far behind the running humans.

"Here," said the mage, stopping to wheeze for breath as the tunnel widened into a broad ledge. A deep canyon blocked their path, and they could hear the thunder of racing water far below. The ceiling still pressed above, and an occasional fungus growing from the walls shed the familiar green light.

It was not bright, but even so they saw the end of the bridge. But that was all that they saw, for the rest of the span was gone. From the looks of the decayed anchor posts, the bridge had simply rotted away.

They were trapped on the narrow ledge, as a hundred bloodthirsty dwarves came charging down the cavern behind them.

*　*　*　*　*

"I sure wish you could talk!" exclaimed Newt. This is boring. How much farther do we have to fly, anyway? Are you sure you know where we're going? I'm getting tired!"

In truth, Robyn too wished that she could talk—if only for the purpose of telling Newt to shut up.

She, too, was growing very tired. The gray waters of the Strait of Alaron rolled beneath her. It had been below them for many hours—exactly how long, she did not know. The steady tailwind had helped them, but she wasn't sure how much longer she could keep flying.

"There! I see something!" Newt shrieked, suddenly. "Is that it? It has to be it! Oh, please be it!"

Her eyes—the eyes of an eagle—saw it too. Now it was merely a brown smudge in the northeast, lying at the very limits of her vision. Yet the smudge grew more distinct—she saw regions of forest, and hills, and fields. Soon they would be over it.

Alaron.

*　*　*　*　*

Green water pressed heavily against the seabottom. Giant things lay here. The splintered hulls of doomed ships littered the sandy seabed, like skeletons of impossibly huge creatures. Other, living things lay upon the bottom, or burrowed into its sand—squids, blue whales, and darker creatures that never ventured into waters tainted by sun.

A sound came softly into these black waters. It originated in Kressilacc as a slow, pulsating vibration—a deep thrumming that fell far below human hearing, but could be felt though the sea as a heavy command. Sharks and barracuda darted nervously away from the sound. Whales and porpoises clung to the surface, desperately splashing toward shallow water.

For the Deepsong had begun.

Sythissall began the song, seated in his vast throne made from the hull of a Northman longship. His wide gills, two-foot-long gashes in the side of his blunt head, flexed rhythmically in and out. His concubines and priestesses took up the call, and soon all of the sahuagin of the city sat or floated, motionless except for the flexing of their gills.

The pulsations traveled through the water, along the bottom of the canyon and across its rim, traveling through the darkest, deepest reaches of the sea with growing intensity.

From these enshrouded regions, and from everywhere under the sea, the sahuagin answered the call. The message thrummed deeply through the earth itself, summoning the claws of the deep.

Their powerfully muscled legs and wide, webbed feet propelled the sahuagin toward Kressilacc as fast as any fish. Tridents and spears thrust before them, hooked nets trailing from their silver belts, the warriors hastened to answer their king's command.

Each sahuagin was affected by the ancient cadence. Their white, flat eyes grew wider, and the bristling spines on the males stood tall and menacing. Slowly, the sahuagin drove themselves into a frenzy. Sythissall and Ysalla were pleased.

And Bhaal was pleased.

❦ 16 ❦

The dwarves

The mob of dark dwarves howled toward them. Tristan looked into the chasm at his feet—it was easily a thousand feet deep and several hundred across. The ledge they stood upon ended abruptly to either side of them. It was about ten feet wide, and twenty long. The whole area was outlined in the milky green glow of the ubiquitous fungi.

"Damn!" he cursed, turning to look up the tunnel. Daryth stood watchfully in the mouth, which was only eight feet wide. It seemed as good a place as any to meet the onrushing horde. Even if each of them killed a score of the enemy, though, Tristan knew they would still be overwhelmed.

"Hold them for a minute, if you can," said Alexei, unrolling one of his scrolls. He seemed remarkably unconcerned by their situation.

"We'll do that," said the prince wryly. "I don't suppose you have a spell in there that can build us a bridge?"

"I might have something better," said the mage.

Before Tristan could ask what he meant, the first dwarves came into sight, racing down the cave. Their eyes glared wildly, and their shrill battle cries echoed through the chamber maddeningly. The prince stepped to Daryth's side, and they brandished their blades. Apparently remembering the deaths of their comrades back in the fungi garden, the dark dwarves slowed the pace of their advance, allowing their numbers to swell until the entire cavern mouth teemed with them.

Several of the larger ones pushed their way to the front of the mob. Flourishing their broad axes, these few advanced cautiously toward the pair. Because of the narrow confines, only three dwarves could attack at once.

"Dwithus Soarax, Alti!"

Tristan heard the chant behind him. He even saw, out of the corner of his eye, the telltale blue flicker that showed Alexei was reading a spell from the scroll.

The three dwarves paused. But nothing happened.

"Dwithus Soarax, Alti!"

Again came the chant, the blue flicker. And again, Tristan could see no noticeable effect. Daryth whirled lightly backward, suddenly leaving Tristan to hold the tunnel alone. The dwarves raised their axes and charged.

"Dwithus Soarax, Alti!"

Once again came the casting. Tristan swung the Sword of Cymrych Hugh, temporarily halting the rush of the attackers. The force of his swing took him through a complete circle, and suddenly he was hanging in the air, struggling to regain his footing.

He felt a jerk upon his collar, and he was pulled up and away from the dwarves. He almost dropped his sword in astonishment.

Now he looked down and saw the white water, foaming in the canyon below. The ledge fell away, thirty or forty feet below him, and the dwarves rushed out of the tunnel, their cries of rage amplified a hundredfold. Slowly, Tristan realized what had happened.

He was flying!

He twisted awkwardly to look behind him, and the ceiling seemed to tumble toward his feet. He found himself diving into the canyon, but he lifted his head and swooped upward, narrowly missing the jagged face of the gorge. His flight took him past the dark dwarves, and he twisted and turned as several axes flew at him. In another second he was out of range, and he turned to watch the missiles tumble slowly into the depths of the canyon.

The prince tried to stop, and he rolled through several complete spins before he regained control of his movements. Daryth and Alexei were slightly above and ahead of him. The Calishite moved with the same tentativeness that characterized the prince's flight. Alexei, on the other hand, glided with certainty in a circle above them.

Tristan looked up, holding his hands to either side to help him keep his balance. He rose slowly. By moving his hands, he found that he could alter the direction of his flight. He drifted easily to the side and carefully rose to hover beside the mage and the Calishite.

"The flying spell!" said Alexei. "A wonderful escape mechanism. There happened to be several of them on one scroll. I used them all to get us up here—one for each of us." He did not mention that, had there been less than three spells, he would have left his rescuers behind.

The three of them turned away from the frenzied and frustrated dwarves.

The din the dwarves raised faded against the thundering of the rapids as the distance between the pursuers and their quarry increased. In a minute, the men hovered over the entrance to the cavern on the far side.

"I like this," Daryth exclaimed, pulling to a sudden stop beside his companions. Like Tristan, he was quickly learning how to control his movements.

"The spell will last for a limited time," explained the mage, as they hung effortlessly in the air. "So I suggest we make as much progress as we can."

"It beats walking," agreed Tristan.

Alexei dove further into the cavern, followed by the prince and the Calishite. They soared easily over the rough ground. The cave ceiling was high enough that even Tristan and Daryth, who could not completely control their flights, could sail quickly through the cavern without endangering themselves.

They raced through a mazelike network of caves and caverns. Splashing rivulets of clear water ran through many of the caves, while others were filled with pillars of moist stone that stuck up like teeth from the floor or hung like poised daggers from the ceilings. In some places, the teeth and the daggers had joined to form thick columns, more ornate than anything built by man or magic.

The luminescent fungi were common, so that much of the path was illuminated enough to allow them to travel safely. In those caverns where darkness reigned, Alexei simply pulled the glowing piece of wood from beneath his robe, and they carried their own light with them. In those instances, however, they had to slow somewhat—at full flying speed, they did not have time to avoid obstacles as they fell within the circle of light.

Tristan began to thoroughly enjoy the sensation of flight. He felt a freedom of movement he had never known before.

Sure enough, Alexei soon pulled up to hover before them. "We don't have much more time. The spell will only last for a few more minutes—I'd like to find the passage up before we're grounded!"

"Maybe we should land now to be safe," suggested Tristan.

But Alexei suddenly cried out in glee. "There—that's what I was looking for!"

He dove through a narrow portion of cave, brandishing his light before him. Tristan and Daryth followed, pausing at the base of a long shaft. They might have been in the bottom of a gigantic well.

"Hurry!" urged Alexei. The mage immediately started to fly straight up.

Tristan and Daryth followed. They ascended a smooth-sided shaft, perhaps fifty feet in diameter. The cave that had given them access to the base of the shaft seemed, thus far, to be the only entrance. There was not even a ledge they could have landed on along the cylindrical sides.

If the spell wore off while they were here, there was nothing to prevent them from falling many hundreds of feet to the rocks below. Tristan hoped that Alexei knew what he was doing.

On the other hand, they climbed rapidly—far faster than they could have done on foot, and every inch they ascended took them closer to the world of sunlight.

"Here—we're nearing the top," said the mage. In a moment, he swerved to the side of the shaft and came to rest upon a broad shelf of smooth stone. The edge of the shelf was marked by hanging columns of stones; they looked like icicles, or, in a more sinister vein, like the drooling fangs of a supernatural beast.

Daryth and Tristan quickly came to rest beside Alexei.

"We made it just in time," explained Alexei. "The spell could not have lasted much longer."

"Where are we?" asked Tristan.

"Some distance outside the walls of Callidyrr, I should say," ventured the wizard. "Though I don't know exactly where. These caves up here should allow us to emerge somewhere in the countryside of Alaron."

"We have a companion in Callidyrr!" objected Tristan. "We can't leave him there!"

"I'm sorry," responded Alexei, unmoved. "My objective was to get away from the city."

"Pawldo will be all right," said Daryth, apparently realizing there was no safe way back into the city.

Tristan was not convinced.

"The choice was not ours to make," persisted the magic user. "I never expected to find a community of duergar below the castle of the High King. They block our return via the underground route, anyway."

"What did you call them?" asked the prince.

"Duergar—the dark dwarves. They are the bane of the underdark. They're greedy and malicious, and they strive to enslave all the races that dwell beyond the reach of the sun. We are fortunate that we did not encounter a larger party of them, or we would not have escaped with our lives."

"But why would they be under Callidyrr?" asked Daryth. "Does this have something to do with Cyndre?"

"I am certain it does. He draws his allies from all who are evil and brutal—even those who live underground, or underwater for that matter. Allied with him, the duergar can prevent any approach against the castle from below."

"From below?" Tristan was incredulous. "Who would try to move an army around down here?"

"We would."

The voice, from the shadows of the tunnel, caused all of them to jump. Tristan and Daryth whipped out their blades and crouched, while Alexei held the light high. A half-dozen stunted shapes were revealed in its glare, lined up to block their passage.

"They're all over the place," murmured Daryth, recognizing that these, too, were dwarves.

"Yes, but not duergar," said the prince, straightening and

sheathing his weapon. "Is that who I think it is?" he asked, staring at the central figure among the dwarves.

"I mighta known it would be you!" grumbled the dwarf, stepping into the light. The speaker was a female, though her bristling beard gave no clue as to her sex. She wore a shirt of nicked chain mail and carried a heavy battleaxe. Squinting up at the prince, she spit a long stream of tobacco juice from the side of her mouth.

"Finellen!" cried the prince, dropping to his knees and embracing the dwarf warmly.

"That's enough!" she grumbled, though she managed to slap the prince on the back a couple of times.

Daryth, too, put his weapon away and allowed himself to smile. The other dwarves—they could see more than a dozen now —advanced from the darkness with expressions varying from amusement to distrust to boredom. They were all armed and armored, holding their weapons ready for combat.

"I turn my back for one year, and you get yourself into trouble again!" muttered Finellen.

"I'm afraid so. But Caer Corwell is still safe, only because of your stand against the firbolgs at the gatehouse!

"Finellen and her company fought with us against the Beast, Kazgoroth," explained Tristan, turning to Alexei. "They routed a band of firbolg giants and carried the day. A more courageous lot of soldiers we could not have found."

"Yeah, well it doesn't take a lot of brains to fight firbolgs," grumbled the dwarf. "Not like the duergar. So you had a tussle with 'em?"

The prince explained the tale of their escape from the dungeon, while the dwarves listened intently. They chuckled grimly as he described their airborne escape.

"But what brings you here?" the prince finally asked. "This is a long way from Gwynneth, and I can't imagine you taking a ship across to Alaron."

"No need. These caverns you've been flying through are only a small part of the underworld of the Moonshaes. I marched here with two companies of my best troops when we heard of the duergar activity. We thought you were scouts for 'em, at first," she admitted. "You almost got yer livers spitted, 'cept for the wisdom and patience of our leader—that is to say, me."

"Thank you for waiting," said Alexei. "It would appear that we are allies in the same cause."

"After a fashion," admitted Finellen. "Though I try not to worry too much about what happens on top of the world. We got enough problems down here."

"Your mission is to attack the duergar?" asked the prince.

"That's for me to decide. We don't know what they're up to yet—but it seems likely that it's no good. Now, tell me, what got you tossed into the High King's dungeon?"

* * * * *

"What are we going to do? Tell me!" King Carrathal's voice rose a full octave as he paced in his chambers.

"The time to assert your control is *now!*" said Cyndre. "The prince is loose in the countryside. I tell you, he will return to Doncastle—where else can he go? If you move to crush that nest of outlaws you will catch him in your net as well.

"And if you do not," concluded the wizard quietly, "I fear that you will soon have a force in that forest capable of causing you great difficulty."

"Why—how do you know he will go to Doncastle?" whined the king.

"He was aided by O'Roarke's agent. This I have learned from my mirror. His mission to confront you has failed, and he runs away now. The only place he can hope to find safety is Doncastle!"

"But why must we strike now, so quickly?"

"The bandits under O'Roarke have been content to cower in their woods, preying on passing merchants. I have seen this prince, now. And I suspect he will not let that situation persist. Think what those bandits could do if they were led by a man of ambition—such as the Prince of Corwell!"

"But how can I stop them?" asked the king.

Cyndre's voice whispered persuasively. "With the Scarlet Guard, sire. Send the guard—all four brigades—against Doncastle. Think of it, Your Majesty—the prince, O'Roarke—all of your enemies slain with a single blow!"

"But . . ." The king groped for an objection. The plan was tempting, but some vestige of responsibility tried to rise through the magical curtain that held him enthralled. Sending the mercenaries against his own people . . . was wrong! But he was so confused, and now Cyndre's voice, soft and melodious, drew the curtain back across his conscience.

"I have my most trusted lieutenant approaching the town now. We can speak to him, have him work as our agent before the attack begins. Their defenses will be in a shambles by the time we strike!"

"Very well," sighed the king, collapsing onto his huge bed. "Summon your man."

Cyndre smiled, privately, and whispered a soft word. A moment passed, and suddenly another of the black wizards stood in the king's chambers. The monarch sat upright, clapping a hand to his mouth in surprise.

The newcomer was cowled in a dark robe like Cyndre's, but his hood was pushed back to reveal a narrow, bony face with a tight black mustache and beard. His fingers glittered with an array of diamond rings.

"Welcome, Kryphon!" said the wizard.

"Master, Your Highness." The mage bowed to each.

"What news do you have?" demanded the king.

"I shall be in Doncastle shortly. I have a guide who has promised to show me the interesting features of his town. He will also point out the important citizens—the magic user and the high cleric, in particular."

"And the defenses?" prodded Cyndre.

"I can prepare a map and bring it to you by tomorrow. Do you wish me to eliminate the outlaw O'Roarke?"

The king looked at Cyndre for advice.

"No," said the master of the council. "It is best that he be left in command for awhile. His removal would open opportunities for someone with more vision to take control."

"Very well, master. I must return quickly, so that my . . . friend does not discover my absence."

"Make haste then, but report to us tomorrow."

Kryphon nodded silently and pulled his robe over his head. He said a word softly and quickly faded from sight. It seemed to the king that the image of his diamonds remained in the air for several seconds after the mage had gone.

"Sire, this is splendid," said Cyndre. "With this information and Kryphon's sabotage our success is assured!"

"Very well," said King Carrathal, nervously looking away. "We shall send the Scarlet Guard against Doncastle."

"This time," whispered the sorcerer, "there will not be a tree standing when we are through!"

* * * * *

The muscles in Robyn's wings were weak with fatigue, and she found herself gliding often to preserve her strength. Still, her progress was steady. They had passed over much of the farm country of Alaron, and before her now stretched a vast expanse of green leaves—it could only be Dernall Forest.

"Look at all of those lakes! Wouldn't a swim feel good? I think we should land and rest for awhile, and go swimming. Come on, Robyn—we've done enough flying for today!" Newt, who had been silent for nearly a full minute, began chattering again. In answer, Robyn dipped her wings and glided into a shallow dive.

Suddenly the sound of raucous cawing attracted her attention, and she saw hundreds of crows spring into the air from trees around the clearing. Screeching in rage, the black birds darted toward her.

With her druid's knowledge of wild things, she understood their anger. They saw only an eagle, soaring into their nesting grounds—and, like crows everywhere, they took to the air as a flock to chase the interloper away.

Robyn would have to land somewhere else. Wearily, she flapped her wings, trying to climb out of the clearing. She had not fully appreciated her exhaustion, and now she felt the strain as she struggled for height.

With a rising sense of panic, she saw the crows closing rapidly. In moments they swarmed around her, striking with their sharp beaks to pluck feathers from her tail and wings. Twisting desperately, she found that the large body of the eagle was no match for the nimble crows. She shrieked in confusion and pain as the beaks drew blood, and more feathers flew.

Newt and Yazilliclick struggled to protect the druid. The faerie dragon dove among the crows, slashing with his sharp teeth and claws. Yazilliclick darted through the flock, striking with his tiny dagger. But there were too many for them to chase away.

Robyn twisted this way and that, but felt herself slowly driven to the ground. She sensed no escape, and then a sharp beak struck her in the eye. With a shrill cry of pain, she plummeted to the ground and crashed, motionless, in a meadow full of bright red flowers.

* * * * *

"This is the outer perimeter," Evan explained, though Kryphon could see nothing other than the natural forest around them.

"I see." He was amazed at the subtlety of the camouflage.

"Ranks of archers line up all along here," he said proudly, gesturing to a long series of sturdy limbs. "That's my post."

"And here's the town?" asked the mage, as they saw a number of wooden buildings before them. His initial impression was of a small woodland village.

"Just a small part. See the barriers up there in the trees? We can drop those all over to make instant ramparts—hold up an attacker for hours that way."

Kryphon paused, studying the defenses carefully. He began to understand how the king's mercenaries had been repulsed before. The town stretched into the distance all around him. Small blocks of rough wooden buildings stood among a forest of huge oaks.

Doric sidled up behind him as he concentrated, surprising him with an intimate caress. He whirled in rage, but then forced his body to calm. "Why don't you find us a room—two rooms," he said, taking her firmly by the arms. "I want to look around some more. We'll find you later."

"Why don't you come with me?" she whispered, pouting.

"There is work to be done!" he snarled. "Now, go!"

The woman stalked away toward a row of buildings bearing the signs of inns: The Green Meadow, The Raging Boar, and several others.

"Now, this wizard of Doncastle?" Kryphon asked Evan.

"Annuwynn, you called him? Where can we find him?"

"He lives in a fine manor near here," said the outlaw. "I shall take you to him."

Several minutes later, they stood before a high thorned hedge. The bushes were entwined about a fence of stout green saplings that created a sturdy and solid barrier. They could not even see through it.

"Meet us at the Raging Boar," said the magic-user, dismissing Evan. The bandit stopped, surprised and dejected, but saw that the wizard had already turned his back. Head hanging, Evan trudged toward the inn.

The wizard and Razfallow stepped into the shelter of a small aspen grove beside Annuwynn's abode.

"Vanyss—Dwyre," said Kryphon, quickly fading from view. His voice repeated the phrase, for he had not moved, and Razfallow also became invisible.

The assassin looked around nervously. It disturbed him to hold his hand up and see nothing there. He fought a sickening sense of disorientation as he heard the wizard step past him and saw the branches of the hedge rustle where Kryphon examined them.

"Ariath dupius, cancyck!" chanted the mage, and the trees and thornbushes before him curled out of the way, creating an opening several feet wide. The hedge was thick, but a skilled gardener could not have opened a neater arch.

Kryphon took Razfallow's arm. The two could not see each other, and he wished to remain in silent communication with the assassin.

They stepped through the hole in the hedge and immediately felt warm, humid air press around them. The sun now beamed with a stark intensity. Kryphon noticed a variety of plants. Palm trees bore coconuts high above their heads, and spike-leaved jungle bushes sprouted all around them. Vines hung in thick tendrils from the trees, and brilliant wildflowers blazed everywhere. He heard the chattering of many birds—all tropical varieties that were not indigenous to the Moonshaes. The man had created for himself a complete tropical habitat. Smooth stone walkways passed among the wealth of leafy plants. By following one of these, the pair was able to move in absolute silence.

In spite of himself, Kryphon was impressed. It took a great deal of power to control a climate, as this mage had obviously done. He had magically created this tropical garden in the middle of a temperate forest.

A splash of water rose over the bushes before them, and they rounded a curve in the trail to see the wizard, Annuwynn. The mage of Doncastle was a trim, handsome man. His face was thin, but his jaw was squared and powerful, and clean-shaven. He emerged from a wide pool of water to shake himself dry upon the smooth flagstones. His body was tanned to a dark brown, and he was naked.

Annuwynn shook his long black hair and wiped the water from his face. He walked gracefully beside the pool, moving like a stalking wolf, when he suddenly turning to sit on . . . something. An invisible chair caught the wizard as he fell, supporting him easily.

"Glynnis!" he called. "I desire wine."

"Coming, my lord," responded a musical voice. Kryphon discerned the large outline of the wizard's manor, almost concealed by the thick foliage beyond the pool.

Kryphon squeezed Razfallow's elbow. There was no mistaking the gesture. The wizard felt Razfallow slip away, but he could hear no sign of the half-orc's movement.

A pretty young maid, no more clothed than her lord, emerged from the building, carrying a glass that had begun to gather frost in the humid air. She approached the reclining figure of Annuwynn.

But Razfallow got there first. The wizard might have detected some sign of his enemy's approach, but it was too late. Annuwynn's eyes widened, but then his throat suddenly fell open. A wide red wound suddenly sprouted below his chin.

The dying wizard thrashed in his chair. The wizard's fingers twisted desperately—but he would cast no more spells.

The serving maid screamed and dropped the glass. Annuwynn fell backward, his lifesblood spurting onto the flagstones—and onto the assassin. Razfallow crouched and snarled as the blood marked his invisible form. He saw Glynnis's eyes widen, and his instincts took over. With a growl, he thrust the blade into her heart.

The girl stumbled, a look of surprise growing on her face, and then she fell into the pool. The water swirled around her in a crimson pattern as a flock of brightly colored birds broke, shrieking, from the underbrush. Razfallow cleaned his blade and returned to the mage.

They walked silently from the tropical garden. The opening in the hedge rustled and closed behind them.

And the garden slowly grew cool.

* * * * *

The great form lay sprawled among the wildflowers, one wing folded unnaturally over her back. As Newt dove to Robyn's side, the bird flopped and twisted, growing in size. By the time the wood sprite settled beside her, Robyn lay as a young woman. She clutched the runestick in one hand. Yazilliclick reached tentatively forward to take the stick. He placed it in his quiver of arrows, taking care that it would not fall out.

But she was not moving. Yazilliclick moaned slightly as he saw blood running from her nose, but he realized from the slow rising and falling of her chest that she still lived.

The crows, satisfied that the threat was over, circled back to the trees around the clearing, ignoring the human, the wood sprite, and the little dragon.

"Robyn? W-wake up, please!" cried Yazilliclick, thoroughly miserable. He was in a strange land, farther than he had ever been from his home. Who would help him?

Distraught, the sprite jumped into the branches of the dead oak that had been Robyn's intended landing place. His antennae drooped as he tried to think.

Then he saw movement in the clearing—some men were coming! They were hunters, he thought, dressed in brown leather and carrying bows. He counted six of them.

"Newt! Up here! Up here!" He called to the faerie dragon, who was sniffing about the meadow, buzzing several feet off the ground. Newt quickly flew to his side, curious.

"L-look!" whispered the wood sprite.

"It fell over here," cried one, pointing toward the place where Robyn lay. "It was a big one. Maybe it's not dead."

"Don't count on it," said another, trudging wearily behind.

Newt and Yazilliclick remained invisible on the branch while they waited to see what these humans would do.

"Well, I'll be damned!" exclaimed the leader as he pushed through the grass to Robyn's side. "A woman!"

"She alive?" asked the second, staring in amazement as he reached his companion's side.

"Yeah," said the first. "But I don't know for how long."

"Best get her to Doncastle. Maybe the cleric can fix her up. And Lord Roarke will probably want to know about this, too. A woman falling from the sky!"

"Coulda sworn it was an eagle," said the first as he hoisted Robyn over his shoulders and started back toward the woods. Buzzing silently above them, the faerie creatures followed the men and the druid.

* * * * *

"Good luck to you," said the prince, clasping Finellen's gauntleted hand. They stood at the junction of several underground passages. From here, the dwarf would coordinate her attack on the duergar, and the humans would start on the underground trek to Doncastle. They were able to take the subterranean route because Finnellen had given them a detailed map and had told them of a cave near the center of Dernall Forest.

The dwarf shrugged. "Won't need too much—there can't be more'n a couple hundred of them. Isn't a duergar born who can stand toe to toe with a true dwarf!" Her voice grew serious. "But your task sounds a little more difficult than duergar-bashing."

"What—you mean deposing a king?" Tristan tried to make light of his goal, but his mind had grown more clear after several long talks with Alexei. There was no other solution to his woes and the woes of his land. The king and his council of black sorcery had to be removed.

"We should have this problem tidied up in a few days," said the dwarf awkwardly. "Maybe we'll stop in and see how things are going."

"Your help is always welcome," replied Tristan. "We are going to Doncastle now, though I cannot promise for how long. But I will hope to see you again soon, my friend!"

"Now I've got a battle to win," said the dwarf bluntly. "So be on with ye!" The dwarf turned away and resolutely marched toward her troops, who were arrayed in battle formation farther down the cavern.

Daryth, Tristan, and Alexei started up the cavern on foot. The wizard already seemed healthier. Two days of freedom, even spent entirely underground, had done wonders for him. Alexei's vitality had increased immeasurably as they had made plans to strike back at the king.

Tristan was certain that the mage, that all of them, would need every bit of their strength in the coming days.

* * * * *

Ysalla, high priestess of the sahuagin, did not remain in her city as the king mustered his forces. She was a cleric of Bhaal—in her own way, as devout and remorseless as Hobarth—and she was determined to carry out the commands of her god.

Bhaal had commanded her to do something, and so she did it without question. Unlike Hobarth, she had no potent artifact of evil to aid her efforts. But also unlike Hobarth, she had many willing disciples to help her. The lesser priestesses of the sahuagin numbered in the hundreds, and these would do her bidding as she did the bidding of Bhaal.

And so the priestesses swam from Kressilacc, yellow shapes swimming smoothly away from the city, against the crush of green bodies so steadily arriving. The Deepsong drove the priestesses to their tasks as surely as it summoned the sahuagin warriors to theirs.

The yellow sahuagin, brilliantly ornamented with gold and silver trappings, kicked their way along the sea bottoms of the Sea of Moonshae, the straits of the isles, and even the Trackless Sea. There they sought the wrecks of ships. Far out to sea, they discovered lonely hulks; around especially treacherous points and headlands, they found vast nautical graveyards.

Ysalla herself, accompanied by a dozen of her most faithful disciples, went to a place near Kressilacc, a place the sahuagin visited often. Here, a Northmen longship and a Calishite galleon had sunk, still entwined from their surface combat. The treasures of the wrecks had long been plundered—at least, the metal treasures.

But now Ysalla sought a different kind of treasure. She went to the body of a Northman, frozen in death on the sea bottom. The man's yellow beard and wild hair floated around his bloated, horrified face. His eyes, delicacies, had long ago been eaten by sahuagin young.

The High Priestess cast a spell, her voice clicking and shrieking in the deep water, and the body shifted and rose. The eyelids opened over the horrid, gaping sockets, and the booted feet clumsily sought purchase on the sandy seabed. And he stood before the priestess and waited.

One by one, Ysalla and her priestesses call the drowned men back to a semblance of life, or at least animation. The Northmen and Calishites gathered together and followed the priestesses at a slow, drifting march toward Kressilacc.

All across the Sea of Moonshae and around the islands as well, the priestesses of the sahuagin summoned the sailors who rested there, and another army of death—the dead of the sea—came into being.

❧ 17 ❧

Return to Doncastle

It was late afternoon when Devin burst through the front door, red-faced and gasping for breath. As he flopped into a chair, Fiona and Pawldo jumped up in shock. Canthus leaped to his feet with a growl and stared, hackles raised, at the front door.

All was quiet outside, however. Pawldo stroked the dog's raised bristles, and slowly Canthus relaxed. He sat, but did not lie down again, and his eyes and nose remained focused on the door.

"I didn't mean to frighten you," said Devin, finally regaining his wind. "But I have urgent news."

"What is it?" asked Pawldo. His nerves were raw. Tristan and Daryth had entered Caer Callidyrr several days ago, and there had been no word from them since.

"The High King has called for a general muster of the Scarlet Guard. The entire army has been recalled from its posts throughout the kingdom—they gather now in Callidyrr."

"Why? Is there any more information?" The news seemed to confirm Pawldo's worst fears.

"Rumors—perhaps hopeful. It is said that the king fears a usurper, and that this usurper was, until recently, a prisoner in the High King's dungeon. Now he has escaped."

"Tristan and Daryth?" Pawldo asked.

"I hope so," replied Devin. "Could be them, or maybe nobody at all. That is the way of rumors.

"And of course, there are reports of a rebellious army gathering in Dernall Forest," Devin continued. "The king believes the whole country is ready to burst into civil war."

"Well, isn't it?" demanded Fiona.

Suddenly, Canthus leaped to his feet and growled deeply. Pawldo sprang to the front window, peering cautiously around the curtain. His knees nearly collapsed at the sight.

"Ogres!" he whispered, pale. "Coming to your door!"

Devin's face blanched and he sagged into the chair in despair. In the next instant, however, he leaped to his feet.

"This way," he whispered, grabbing Fiona's arm and jerking open the trap door. He half pushed his daughter down the steep steps, but she landed lightly on her feet at the bottom. He turned and knelt, his face inches from Pawldo.

"Get her out of the city. Go to Doncastle—get word to O'Roarke about the army. Hurry!"

"Come with us!" urged the halfling, taking Devin's hand in both of his. "We can make it!"

"No," said the man impatiently. "They know I'm here— they must have followed me. They won't stop searching until they find me. I will buy you some time. Now go!"

Pawldo turned angrily, knowing Devin was right. He pushed Canthus toward the trap door, and the big hound sprang through the hole. The halfling dove into the opening and heard the door close above him even as the front door splintered under the impact of ogre clubs.

Fiona stared in shock. "Where's my father?"

"He . . . stayed behind. He said it was our only chance to escape. Let's go!"

"No! I can't leave him!" She hastened toward the stairs.

Pawldo took her arm firmly, and Fiona stopped in her tracks. From above they heard snarls, and Devin's voice raised in anger. Then there was a sharp cry of pain, followed by low ogre chortles.

Fiona turned to the halfling with deep, wracking sobs. Pawldo held her in an awkward embrace, inwardly cursing the brutality of the king's mercenaries. He couldn't think of anything to say, so he simply stood and let her cry. Finally, she dried her eyes and raised her head. Her chin was set and determined, but her eyes were shot with pain.

"This way," she said softly.

She led him to the back of the underground hiding place, to a wooden wall made of rough-hewn knotty pine. Reaching her hand into one of the knotholes, she twisted something and the door slid away to reveal a narrow passage.

"Our secret escape route," she explained. A torch, flint, and steel lay just inside the door. As the portal closed softly behind them, she struck a spark, and soon the torch was blazing brightly.

The lass led the way, and Canthus brought up the rear. For several minutes they walked silently through a low tunnel. Then Fiona abruptly slowed her pace. Handing the torch back to Pawldo, she advanced forward at a crawl, heedless of the mud that splattered her frock.

Pawldo heard her grunting from exertion, and then he felt a waft of cold, moist air against his face. She had opened a door into some connecting passage.

"It's the city's storm sewer," she explained as he extended the torch. She had lifted a hatch in the floor of their tunnel that led into a larger pipe below.

The pipe was round, perhaps ten feet in diameter. Water lay in pools along the bottom, a foot or more deep in places. He felt cool, humid air flowing past the opening.

Fiona swung through the hatch first, hanging by her hands before dropping to land easily at the bottom of the pipe. There was a slurping sound as she landed in muck. Pawldo and Canthus followed.

Fiona reclaimed the torch, and led the way at a brisk march. Finally, they saw an end to the tunnel, where early twilight glimmered over the bay. Fiona extinguished the torch, and they carefully advanced to the end of the pipe.

Green waves rolled against the shore, about twenty feet below them. The pipe ended in the face of a high seawall. Looking up, the halfling couldn't tell how high it stretched. Smooth, water-worn stone had been built into this barrier, which was now covered with seaweed and moss. Only by jumping far out into the air could they hope to avoid the jagged rocks at the foot of the wall.

"Can you swim?" asked Pawldo.

"I know how. The question is, will we freeze to death before we reach the shore?" answered the girl.

"Only one way to find out," shrugged the halfling. He sprang from the pipe and dropped into the gently rolling sea. The water struck him like a cold shock, and as he rose to the surface he heard Fiona and Canthus join him.

Fiona started to swim along the shore with strong strokes. Pawldo couldn't see much in the twilight, but he sensed that they were moving away from the harbor. His body was already growing numb.

* * * * *

"They brought her in this evening," Evan explained over the mug of ale Kryphon had just bought him. "Cassidy saw something fall and swears it was an eagle. Attacked by crows, you know how they do?

"But then he goes over to get the feathers, and there's no eagle! Instead, some woman's lying there, banged up and bleeding." Evan was certain his remarks would provoke interest.

The mage leaned back in his chair and regarded Evan with an expression of vague amusement. "Fairy tales," smiled the mage, concealing his curiosity. "Surely the man had been drinking?"

"No fairy tale! And it's been done before; druids do it all the time, turn into birds and such."

"You don't say? Then this . . . woman is a druid?" Kryphon's mind whirled with curiousity. A druid in Alaron?

The bandit shrugged. "Who knows? But Cassidy's got the best eyes I know—the best ears, too." Evan lowered his voice. "He told me that someone killed Annuwynn!"

"The magic-user? The wizard of Doncastle?"

"The same." Evan's voice grew serious. "His loss is a blow, no doubt about it. Someone murdered him in his garden, in the full light of day!"

"But surely you have other stalwart defenders. You mentioned a cleric, er . . . what was his name?"

"Vaughn Burne. To be sure, he's a man worth a company or two!"

"Where might this cleric be? I mean, I hope he's safe."

"Oh, I shouldn't worry. He's busy tending to that flying wench I was telling you about. Right down the street from here." Evan sighed appreciatively as he finished his mug, and Kryphon signaled for another.

"I heard they took her to the Black Oak Inn," Evan said.

"Got nice, comfortable rooms there."

Kryphon laid a heavy gold coin on the table—enough to quench Evan's thirst for the entire evening and send him home with change. He patted the bandit's arm. "I have to go for a while. I want you to stay here and enjoy yourself!"

Evan grinned foolishly and hefted the coin. He didn't even notice Kryphon rising from the table.

The mage left the drinking room and climbed the stairs to his room. There he found Doric sprawled languidly on the large bed, wearing only her belt.

"I must seek the cleric," announced the mage, ignoring the look of desire she gave him. In truth, during the days they had been together he had grown altogether tired of the way Doric pursued him—never leaving him a moment's peace. At first, it had been a delightful aspect of their mission. Now, he wished he could send her back to Caer Callidyrr.

"Take me along," she pouted, seeing his lack of interest.

"No—this I will do alone. Once I locate him, I will of course let you help in his removal."

"Stay here for awhile first," she pleaded, moving over on the bed. The sight of her gaunt body and hollow cheeks revolted him, and he couldn't hide the disgust in his eyes.

"Then go!" she screamed. She picked up one of her boots and threw it at him, but it struck the door he had already slammed as he left.

The Black Oak Inn was easy to find. It was an enormous place, with a doorman at the entrance and a thick red carpet lining the floor of the huge main room. The wooden walls and ceiling beams had been sanded smooth, and the tables and chairs were of ornate detail, obviously imported from Waterdeep or Amn.

A servant escorted Kryphon to a table near a low fire, and a serving wench, dressed in a low-cut gown of red and black, inquired as to his desires. Her plump, rounded body—such a contrast to Doric's—intrigued him, and he watched her walk back to the bar. Then he took in the interior of the place.

There were about a dozen customers, mostly in pairs, sitting around the quiet, elegant room. He saw a partially screened-off stairway in the back of the room. The front door and a door to the kitchen were the only other exits.

The barmaid returned with his wine. "I would like to look at one of your rooms," he said. "I'm thinking of staying here."

She shrugged—what did she care where he stayed? And she didn't like the way he was looking at her. "They're upstairs," she said quickly, turning to another customer.

Kryphon finished his wine in several gulps and walked to the staircase behind the screen. The stairway was a fitting addition to the luxurious main room—the same red carpet covered the floor, and an ornate bannister of carved oak ran beside the stairs.

Mounting the stairs quietly, he reached a short hallway on the second floor of the inn. There he found three doors on both sides of the corridor. He pushed the first open, finding an empty room. At the second, he heard two male voices engaged in quiet conversation. He passed that door to the third, where he heard nothing. Testing the latch cautiously, he discovered that it was locked.

"Eriath, gorax," he said softly, waving his hand before the portal and knocking once.

The door swung open easily. Startled, a young woman sat up suddenly in a deep featherbed. Her long black hair lay in disarray about her head, and her face was covered with scrapes and bruises. Yet her beauty was undeniable.

"Who are you?" she whispered. Her right eye, deeply cut, was swollen shut.

"Pardon me—I seem to have the wrong room." Concern etched his brow as he looked at her face. "Are you all right?"

He stepped into the doorway, and she shrank against her pillow in fright. "Yes—I am! Please go!"

Kryphon toyed with the idea of killing her immediately, but laughed off the notion. Even if this was a druid, she was certainly no threat in her battered state. He decided that she would serve him in another, far more satisfying way.

Then the door next to hers opened and two men stepped into the corridor. They looked pointedly at the wizard, still standing in the doorway of the woman's room, before they went to the stairs.

"Excuse me." Kryphon bowed to Robyn and backed out of the room, closing the door. He cursed the men who had seen him, for he could not afford to be observed—especially if something untoward were to happen to the druid.

Yet, Kryphon thought, I can be patient. He was certain that the druid would be here for awhile.

She would keep until tomorrow.

* * * * *

Black-cloaked figures whirled around her, striking with needle-sharp beaks and raking claws. Robyn felt her skin split as it was torn from her body. She felt herself dying.

And then she awakened, soaking wet, from the nightmare. At first, she breathed a sigh of relief. Then, abruptly, her door swung open. She gasped at the tall, bearded man who stood peering in at her. She was not just startled, she was afraid. For she was certain that Vaughn Burne had locked the door earlier when he had left.

The man said something; she answered, and all the while horror was building in her chest. She wanted to scream. He looked ordinary enough at first glance, but she saw something sinister in his eyes.

Then he closed the door and was gone. She sprang from the bed and turned the latch, making sure the portal was secured. Then she darted back to the security of her covers.

It took her many minutes of meditation to relax. She called upon the power of the Earthmother to soothe her, but that power was faint. Finally she was able to push the tension from her body, and she fell into a deep, dreamless sleep.

She was unaware of the invisible sprite sitting upon her headboard. Yazilliclick had been delighted to see her awaken, but he did not want to disturb her. He watched over her alertly as she went back to sleep.

* * * * *

"Did you find her?" Doric asked.

Kryphon shrugged. "I found an old hag, barely alive, and not worth the trouble of killing. It's the cleric we must find!"

The slender woman nodded, disappointed. Then she had a sudden thought. She sat up and examined the sorcerer's face surreptitiously.

He had lied to her!

She knew now with certainty that Kryphon was much more interested in the druid than he was admitting. Had he killed her already, cheating Doric of that pleasure? No, she decided, he looked preoccupied, like he wanted something. Like he wanted . . . the druid!

The knowledge exploded within her in a wave of jealousy, and she almost drew her dagger and thrust it through Kryphon's heart before she regained her self-control.

"What is it? Is something wrong?" asked the sorcerer.

"I feel . . . ill," she replied, trying to mask her rage. She would plunge her dagger into a heart, but it would not be Kryphon's.

"Would you like to come and lie down?" he asked.

"Can you seek the cleric without me?" she inquired coyly.

"Certainly! My purpose tonight is to learn. I will come and get you before it is time to act."

"Very well. I will await you here." Ignoring his look of annoyance, she squeezed his leg. It gave her a little thrill of pleasure to deceive him.

"I shall seek his chapel. Sooner or later he will have to go back there," Kryphon said. Then he was gone.

Doric waited for several minutes, which was as long as she could bear. Then she rose and left the inn, entering the darkened street with anticipation of blood. She fingered her slender dagger and walked quickly toward the back of the Black Oak Inn.

* * * * *

"Lord O'Roarke would like you to join him in the dining room," said the guard to Tristan, Daryth, and Alexei. They had slipped into Doncastle only an hour before, sending word of their arrival, and the bandit lord had wasted no time in sending for them. Their journey through the cavern network had been rough and tiring, but uneventful. Finellen's map had been flawless, so they had made the journey in two days.

O'Roarke and Pontswain were seated together at a long table laden with meats and breads and cheeses. "Welcome," said the red-bearded outlaw.

Pontswain nodded coolly, his raised eyebrows revealing his surprise at their return. "The halfling?" he asked as they all sat.

Tristan told of their entry into the city and fortress, and of their capture and escape—and of Pawldo, left behind out of necessity. He introduced Alexei, explaining how he had joined them.

"A wizard from the council?" scowled the bandit. "How did you come to be in the dungeon?"

Alexei met his gaze. "My former master and I had a parting of the ways." he said tersely. "I have vowed to do everything I can to destroy him—perhaps I might be of some use to you."

"We would not have escaped without him," said the prince. "He knew the secret tunnel that let us out of the castle, and his flying spell saved us in the cave when—" Tristan paused in shock, though no one seemed to notice. His own words reverberated through his mind as he methodically raised food to his mouth.

He shall fly above the earth, even as he delves its depths!
The prophecy of Queen Allisynn came back to him, every word. Could the prophecy mean *him*? No, he reminded himself, for she said his name will be Cymrych. Still, the coincidence was a strange one, deeply disturbing. Forcing his mind back to the present, he heard O'Roarke sending a messenger to get the cleric, Vaughn Burne.

"And so, what is the word from the High King?" asked Hugh. "Other than his presumed distress at your escape."

"He fears for his crown," offered the prince. "In fact, he has been told that I have come here to claim it!"

"Have you?" O'Roarke asked bluntly.

"Of course not!" Tristan's denial was a little forced.

"What are you going to do now?" asked Pontswain.

"The Ffolk cannot survive with such men as their leaders. I will end the reign of this king—kill him, if necessary!"

"I knew you were mad," snorted Lord Pontswain.

"What choice do we have—go back to Caer Corwell and wait for the next group of assassins? Or stay here, waiting for the king to get tired of our presence and send the guard and his wizards down upon us?"

"We've fought them before—and we'll drive them off again!" snarled the outlaw lord.

"Don't deceive yourself," said the prince. "If a concerted attack came against this place, you would be doomed!"

"Our chances are still better than yours. Revolt against the king? With what?" O'Roarke sputtered.

"With your help," said the prince, lowering his voice but holding his tone firm. "Pontswain, if you will return to Corwell and gather the lords, we can have an army here by early autumn. Lord Roarke, muster your men and challenge the king! I promise you, you will be joined by other lords."

"By what right do you order my men to war?" roared the lord, leaping to his feet. "I shall not do this thing!" The prince saw an odd emotion in the lord's face. It was not anger, nor was it betrayal. It was fear.

"Nor shall I," said Pontswain, turning to face the prince directly. Tristan saw no fear in his eyes—just a cool sense of accomplishment as the lord thwarted the prince's plan.

They stopped talking, then, for they were joined by a small, gray-haired man in a plain robe. The top of his head was as clean-shaven as his face.

"This is our cleric, Vaughn Burne," explained O'Roarke to Alexei before turning to the cleric himself. "I was hoping, Patriarch, that you could help this man. He has done my friends a great service, and as you can see he has suffered greatly at the hands of our enemies."

"I shall do my best," said the cleric with a smile. "The power of Chauntea is mightiest for acts of healing."

"Oh, and how fares our other guest?" asked the lord.

"She is resting. She will live. Her recuperative powers are tremendous."

"Did you learn anything more about her?" inquired Hugh.

"As you suspected, she is a druid. Apparently she flew here all the way from Gwynneth in the shape of an eagle.

Tristan followed the conversation with growing interest.

"I would like to meet this druid. Do you know her name?"

"She didn't tell me—she was very weak. But even so," smiled the cleric, "she was very beautiful. And young, with long, raven-black hair."

Tristan leaped to his feet. "I must see her! Where is she?"

* * * * *

Finellen cursed the underground confines that prevented her from deploying all three of her companies. The duergar had chosen their lair well. It had three points of access, but all of these were controlled by narrow chokepoints. As yet, none of Finellen's dwarves had been able to get inside and scout the place.

They had a rough idea of its size from the placement of the entrances, however. Finellen was certain that it didn't contain more than three hundred duergar—and those were comfortable odds for her own three hundred fighters.

The duergar lair was a complex of central caverns surrounded by narrow tunnels. In one tunnel, a deep gorge blocked the pathway, while in the other two, steep upward climbs were necessary to enter the duergar stronghold. Finellen had one of her companies posted at each entrance.

A shiver ran down her spine as the trumpets blared the call to attack. Each of the companies roared to the attack, and she heard the clash of steel down all three caverns. She cursed the responsibility that kept her out of the fighting, waiting with several messengers at this intersection of caves, but she understood the necessity for it. It was difficult enough to control scattered formations in any battle, but in an underground conflict like this one, visual communication would be impossible. Hence, she had to wait here, listening for word of the progress or setbacks of each of her three companies so that she could send help quickly to wherever it might be needed.

The sounds of battle grew faint—a good sign, as that meant the dwarves had crossed the initial barriers of defense in each tunnel. For an agonizing hour Finellen heard little, and she began to hope that the battle was won.

But then the din of clashing steel grew more distinct. Louder and louder, the noise swelled from the tunnels. Now she heard the cries of wounded, and the horrible battle noise of the duergar all around her. There was no doubt what was happening.

Her companies were being forced to retreat.

* * * * *

Robyn could not go back to sleep. Images of the black, sharp-beaked birds tormented her every time she closed her eyes.

"Robyn?"

"Yazilliclick?" She looked around. "Where are you?"

"Oh, I'm so glad you're awake," cried the faerie, popping into sight on the footboard of the large bed. "I was so worried about you, Robyn. Those men brought you here, and I couldn't stop them, but I hoped they'd help you. I think they did—they did."

She held up her hand, but couldn't help smiling. "Thank you for staying with me," she said. "Where's Newt?"

"F-food! He went to get us something to eat—to eat!"

"We'll be lucky to get anything but the bones," sighed the druid, reassured to have friends beside her in this strange place. Then she laughed as she saw the faerie dragon hovering outside the window, trying to hold his altitude and a large haunch of roast at the same time.

She crossed to the window and opened it, lifting the mutton from the dragon as he dove through the opening and collapsed on the bed. "Boy, is that cook ever a sourpuss! You wouldn't believe the things he threw at me while I was minding my own business, getting a little supper!" The dragon stifled a laugh. "I fixed him, though—you should have seen his face when I used my spell!"

"What did you do?" asked Robyn, a little worried.

"I made it look like maggots were crawling out of all his meat. He was sure upset! It was great fun! Now, can we go home? Or find Tristan, or something? I'm bored!"

"N-Newt! Let Robyn rest!" said Yazilliclick sternly.

"I'm afraid I do need to rest before we go," said the druid, sitting back on the bed. "But you—i—"

Robyn gasped as a black shadow soared through the window into her room. A white face grimaced at her, and she had a horrible vision of an undead skeleton, flying here to haunt her.

But the eyes of this apparition were alive, and its red lips were parted in cruel delight. This figure, robed all in black, was a woman. And now she was diving at Robyn's face. Robyn caught a glimpse of thin, bony hands and wild black hair as the woman flew toward her.

But most of all Robyn saw the woman's steel dagger, extended like a claw for her heart. Desperately, she pulled a pillow from the bed and crouched beneath it as the woman fell upon her. Feathers flew as the dagger sliced the cushion.

The young druid used the force of her attacker's momentum to pull her past the bed, kicking her in the stomach as she sailed by. The attacker slammed into the wall as Robyn threw off the covers and sprang to her feet.

Still bearing that ghastly grin, showing her long teeth, the woman brandished her dagger. Suddenly, Newt flashed across the room, scoring a path of bloody claw marks across her cheek. Yazilliclick pulled out his silver dagger and darted into the fray. With a bestial scream of rage, the woman turned toward the faerie dragon.

"Sheeriath, drake!" she hissed, pointing. A stream of stringlike material shot from her finger, wrapping itself around the little dragon, sticking to him and burying the wood sprite as well. They were both stuck fast in the gluey net of a giant spiderweb.

A sorcerer! Hissing like an angry black cat, the woman crept toward her. She waved the dagger menacingly.

"Centius, heerith!" said Robyn softly. Instantly, the blade of the dagger glowed cherry red. With an explosive hiss of pain, the woman dropped her weapon.

"Magius, stryke!" she shrieked. An arrow of light burst from her pointing finger to strike Robyn in the breast, cutting her skin and burning into her flesh. Pain raced through the druid's body as another, and still a third, magic missile crackled into her bleeding chest. The force of the blows smashed her against the outer wall of the room. Robyn leaned heavily against the window, while the magic-user stood with her back to the door.

Newt and Yazilliclick struggled within the bonds of the web, but they were powerless to move. Robyn felt her strength ebb as blood ran across the front of her gown. She shook her head weakly as the woman pulled a little ball of something from her robe. The smell of sulphur filled the air.

"Pyrax, surrass histar," gloated the mage, her eyes gleaming. The tiny ball suddenly burst into flame, drifting lazily toward Robyn.

Sulphur? Fire magic! Desperately, Robyn raised her hands to her face and then dropped them the length of her body.

"Protection, Mother—" she beseeched. Before she could finish the ritual chant, orange flame exploded around her, blanketing her body in fire. The fireball billowed from the window, illuminating the night and incinerating half the room. Doric stood in the other half, cackling as the fire—far hotter than any natural blaze—consumed the bed, the walls, and the floor. The druid could not be seen in the bright heart of the explosion.

But then the magic-user's eyes widened as her enemy stepped from the heat. Robyn's goddess had heard her plea for protection. She had surrounded her druid with a cool barrier, holding the forces of dark magic at bay.

Doric's jaw fell slack as she stared in awe. The druid came closer, and the blazing rage in her eyes made even the supernatural heat of the fireball grow pale in comparison.

Robyn seized the neck of the mage with hands that were strong and calloused from work in the grove. Her grip tightened, and she felt the windpipe of her enemy close beneath her powerful grasp. Robyn's strength was much greater than this frail woman's—for Doric's power to terrorize and destroy came solely from her magic.

Suddenly, Robyn knew that she wanted this mage to die by magic—and carry a final lesson about the power of the goddess to her grave. Robyn had a spell for healing, and she knew that if she reversed the words of the chant, she would reverse the effect of the spell.

"Matri, terrathyl—wrack," she growled, relaxing her grip slightly. Robyn felt the woman's neck twist, tense, and finally snap. The sorceress fell dead.

* * * * *

Flames raged up the side of the Black Oak Inn as Tristan ran up to the building. Panicked patrons rushed from the doors and spilled through the windows in a race to escape.

Desperately, Tristan forced himself into the main room,

pressing against the flow of humanity. He leaped the stairs four at a time and stumbled into the smoke-filled hallway.

Suddenly, one of the doors burst open and someone staggered into the hall, carrying a bundle. Her face was averted to avoid the swirling clouds of smoke, but there was no mistaking the long fall of ebony hair.

"Robyn!" Tristan gasped, stumbling forward to take her in his arms. She looked at him in disbelief. Her face was streaked with soot and covered with bruises and scratches. Yet she had never looked so beautiful.

Tristan seized her in his arms and helped her to the stairs, noting that the bundle was in fact Newt. The dragon was tangled in a strange web, and Tristan thought he saw another tiny figure buried there as well. Robyn collapsed against him.

He helped her down the stairs and they stumbled from the inn together. She tried to drop Newt and Yazilliclick to take him in her arms, but she couldn't get free. The prince, too, tugged at the wailing faeries, trying to dislodge the sticky mess.

"Robyn, you're here," Tristan said stupidly.

She smiled up at him, and tears welled in the corners of her eyes. Once again, he tried to pull Newt out of the way.

But finally they gave up. He took her into his arms, faeries and all, and pressed his lips to hers. She met him warmly, holding him tight as they ignored the stares of the Ffolk who had gathered to watch the fire.

* * * * *

The goddess saw the specter of Bhaal looming on the horizon of the world. She felt the painful trod of his footstep as his presence drew near.

But her feelings were muted, barely there. Nearly all of her might had been expended in the effort to protect her druids—and that had been only partially successful. The druids of Myrloch Vale were not dead, but they were quite helpless. Unseeing, unfeeling, they could only remain within their stone prisons, awaiting rescue or destruction.

The specter of Bhaal grinned, delighting in the despair of the Earthmother. From Bhaal's point of view, things were progressing very well indeed.

The undead army, under the command of Hobarth and aided by the heart of Kazgoroth, had accomplished everything he had hoped—and more. The Moonwell of the Vale was not only in his hands, but the druids had foolishly sacrificed themselves in the effort to protect it.

The sahuagin, under his devout high priestess, were gathering an impressive force of destruction. The dead of the sea, raised by his faithful clerics, would be another army to throw against the Moonshae Isles. Even Cyndre, his unwitting servant upon Alaron, acted as Bhaal desired. His course, whatever its outcome, would almost certainly yield more bodies to Bhaal's cause.

Bhaal turned slightly and took notice of a new force. He relished killing in all of its forms and took pleasure in the underground battle between the dwarves. Bhaal was surprised as the dark dwarves poured forth in ever-increasing numbers, until a vast horde of them charged through the underdark, threatening everything in their path.

The dark dwarves were minions of other evil gods. Bhaal could not count his clerics among their number. But they were bloodthirsty and numerous.

There would be a way, Bhaal suspected, that they could play into his hands.

❧ 18 ❧

Skirmishes

Canthus growled a warning, and Pawldo didn't wait to confirm the dog's suspicions. "Down—hide!" he hissed, but Fiona had already dived into the muddy ditch. He splashed beside her and felt the moorhound settle in next to them.

Thundering hoofbeats pounded along the road as a column of horsemen rode past. Pawldo pressed his face into the mud. After an eternity, the riders passed, galloping into the distance. Pawldo and Fiona crawled out of the ditch, even more cold and miserable than before.

"I wish we could find a horse!" cursed Fiona. The young woman had grown more furious with each passing day. She railed against the king and the ogres and complained about their own situation. "My feet are worn to the knees!"

Pawldo nodded, looking after the riders. "That pretty well clinches it. They have to be going to Doncastle."

For three nights they had been walking steadily toward the forest, spending their days in isolated barns or sheds, traveling only after sunset. They were cold, hungry, and tired. A sense of danger followed them everywhere, for the riders of the Scarlet Guard were out in force. Some patrolled the countryside, but most rode to the southwest, toward the forest—and Doncastle.

They trudged through the night and reached the outskirts of the forest before dawn. "Let's keep going," suggested the halfling. "We can reach Doncastle by nightfall."

Pausing only to drink from a clear forest pool and eat some bread Pawldo had acquired the previous day, they resumed their march.

* * * * *

King Carrathal awakened suddenly with a small cry of
alarm. Biting his tongue, he felt the coach lurching beneath
him. Where was he? What was happening? He pushed the
Crown of the Isles up—it had slipped over his eyes.

The red satin curtains tinted the afternoon sun to the col-
or of blood as it streamed through the window. The heavily
cushioned seat, plush with furs, felt hard and unwelcoming
against him. There was room for a dozen people within the
large compartment, but King Carrathal rode alone.

Oh yes, he reminded himself. The war.

He pulled the curtain aside and leaned out the window.
Beyond the six horses that were pulling the royal coach, he
could see the companies of the Scarlet Guard stretching into
the distance. Fortunately, the weather was cool and humid,
so the path of their march was not very dusty.

The coach shifted suddenly, and the king whirled to see
Cyndre. The wizard had not been there a moment before—
his sudden arrival in the seat beside him sent the monarch's
heart pounding.

"Well?" King Carrathal did not try to hide his annoyance.

"We'll have provisions when we arrive at Cantrev Bounty."

"Good. Did you have to . . . ?" The king looked away.

"No. It seems the fate of Cantrev Lehigh has become common knowledge. I doubt you will find any other lords reluctant to provide your royal due."

King Carrathal did not seem pleased by the news. The
destruction of an entire cantrev, performed with relish by
his ogres, weighed heavily upon his conscience. Certainly
the wizard had made it sound like a good idea. And, in truth,
since then they had had no more difficulties with the other
lords. Food and drink had been willingly provided in the
next village they had used as a bivouac.

The army column marched on, across the central plain of
Alaron. The ogre brigade marched heavily in the lead. Outriders, their red coats visible for miles, protected the flanks
of the column. Several wagons full of supplies trailed the
column, and the king's coach rolled along behind them. At
the very rear, trailing the army by as much as a half a mile,
rumbled another, larger coach.

This one was pulled by eight black horses. In it rode

Talraw, Wertam, and Kerianow—the rest of the Council of Seven. And there, too, would ride Cyndre.

* * * * *

They spent most of the night together, holding each other, gazing at each other. They made the promises and pledges and exchanged the regrets that made them both feel warm and needed.

Tristan could still not quite believe that Robyn was in Doncastle. To go a year without seeing her, yearning for her every day, and then to have her arrive in this secret city, so far from their home—it seemed impossible.

Yet, the warmth of her body and the light of her smile told him that it was true. She said she had come because she feared for him. Tristan listened in awe as she described the vision she had received from the woman in the pool.

He told her about his father—their father, really—and he held her as she cried for the king. Then he recounted his journey to Callidyrr and his decision to fight the king. He explained about the prophecy, his doubts about its meaning. He concluded with Pontswain's and O'Roarke's refusals to join him.

She, in turn, described her own nightmare of death and desecration. Tristan sat numb; she had needed his help so desperately, and he had been . . .

"Don't," she soothed, sensing his guilt. "We each had our own tasks to perform, and we did them. Perhaps yours will see more success than mine did."

"We can hope—and fight! I will return to Corwell to raise an army!" With Robyn here, Tristan's confidence soared.

"But remember," she said. "This is more than the work of one king—even one helped by black magic. This must be the design of some unspeakable god!"

They were interrupted by a knock on the door.

"Who is it?" called the prince, reaching for his sword.

"Lord Roarke sends word, my prince," called a voice. "The halfling has returned from Callidyrr, and he brings news!"

"Pawldo?" asked Robyn. "He's here, too?"

They raced into the great room of the inn, where Daryth and Hugh O'Roarke had been talking for most of the evening. He saw Pawldo settling into a soft chair before the fire-place, and a young girl—Fiona, he suddenly realized—standing awkwardly to the side.

Canthus was there, too. The moorhound gave a bark of joy and bounded to the prince, nearly knocking him off his feet. The dog then pounced upon Robyn with even more enthusiasm, wriggling and wagging his tail.

"Robyn!" cried the halfling, elbowing the dog aside to embrace the druid. "What are you, I mean how did you . . . ?"

"It's good to see you, too," she smiled, releasing him. "I hear you've been keeping my prince out of trouble!"

"When he'll let me," sulked the halfling. "Of course, then he and Daryth go off and leave me to my own devices, not bothering to tell me that they've come back here! So I sit—"

"I am sorry about that, old friend. There were a few complications at the palace."

"That's what Daryth claims, too. At least you two outlaws took the time to get your stories straight. Hanging around with me has done you some good after all!"

Pawldo suddenly looked at Fiona, standing somberly.

"I'm afraid we bring dire news," he began. "Fiona's father brought us word of a mustering of the High King's army. Devin must have been betrayed—his house was attacked, and he gave his life to see Fiona and me to safety."

The others bowed their heads for a moment in respect to the fallen agent. Hugh O'Roarke went to Fiona and took the girl in his arms. "He was a brave man, your father. I know he would be very proud of you."

"He'll only be proud if you and your men *do* something!" she cried in sudden rage. She pulled angrily from his embrace. Her red hair swung around her head, and her eyes flamed. "And I don't think that's likely, as long as you have your little hole in the woods to hide in!"

"The rest of the news," interjected Pawldo quickly, "is that the entire Scarlet Guard marches on Doncastle!"

Hugh looked dully at the halfling. The air seemed to drain from his body and he shrank into a chair to collapse, holding his head in his hands. Suddenly, he looked up at the prince and glared.

"This is your fault!" he growled. "You have brought this

upon my town!"

"Don't be ridiculous!" Robyn said sharply. "There is a doom stalking our islands, plaguing the Ffolk, and it is far more terrible than the acts of this pathetic king. It seems that the danger is now focused upon your town. So fight it! You have brave warriors here! Stop wasting all this time and get ready to defend yourselves!"

"In times past, we had the wizard Annuwynn at our service," Vaughn Burne pointed out. "Now we do not, and we have a killer at large in our city."

"I thought the killer died in the attack on Robyn," said Pontswain. "That sorceress you described to us."

"I suspect that the killer is still out there. The attack upon the druid was much less subtle, more crude than the attack on Annuwynn. I cannot believe that the same sorcerer performed them both." The cleric did not mention his dream—a vision from Chauntea, he was certain—in which he saw the killer as a man who glittered with diamond jewelry.

"Well, find him!" cried O'Roarke. The lord was still for a moment, and then he took a deep breath and looked at Robyn. "You're right. We can defend ourselves—and we shall. I will summon my captains and form a plan. We shall fight them for every tree, every pathway of the forest!

"My prince. It seems I was wrong. Will you join our fight? I could use your skill and experience."

Tristan nodded.

*　*　*　*　*

Kryphon reflected bleakly on the prospect of returning to his bed, where Doric certainly awaited him. And then he thought of the druid. In an instant, he resolved to seek her out instead.

The flames had died down by the time he reached the Black Oak Inn, but he could tell that the druid's room had been, if not the source, very near the heart of the blaze. The fire had been a cruel coincidence, robbing him of his anticipated pleasure.

Fire. He thought again of Doric—whenever he saw fire he thought of the sorceress. She was like her fire magic in many ways—fickle, greedy, and dangerous. And now this fire, by odd coincidence, had robbed him of the pleasure he had hoped to take from the young druid.

Or was it a coincidence? He recalled Doric's sudden weariness. He hurried back to their room. By the time he reached it, he had guessed the truth. Doric's absence only confirmed his suspicions—the wench feared his wrath after she killed the druid. There was no telling where she might be hiding.

After stomping around the room in frustration, the black wizard at last yielded to his own weariness and slept for several hours. After he awakened, he spent several more hours immersed in the study of his spellbooks. He had used up much of his magic in the past few days, and the study helped to replenish arcane energies.

He thought bitterly about Doric. Her betrayal stung his pride and angered him. She did well to hide. Irritated, he summoned Razfallow.

"I am going to seek the cleric at his chapel. You will investigate other places—the inn where O'Roarke stays, for example. If you see him and you have a chance, kill him. If not, find me and take me to him."

The half-orc nodded. He did not like to walk among this town of men—half-orcs were rare upon the Moonshaes—but he would do as he was told. The assassin left, and Kryphon closed his spellbooks and prepared to leave.

It was noon by the time he returned to the cleric's chapel. As he made his way through Doncastle, he noticed that the city bustled with preparations. Many people, mostly the very old, very young, or the infirm, were gathering belongings into backpacks, saddlebags, and carts. These Ffolk were leaving the city, apparently fleeing. For what?

He saw few pedestrians, but many armed men gathering into groups of a dozen, a score, or more. He caught a glimpse of a familiar face as a group of bowmen passed him.

"Evan!" he called, turning to step alongside the group. The bandit, still enamored by the charm spell, turned to him with a broad smile.

"We're off to the fight," he declared proudly.

"Fight?"

"Rumor has it the king's army is marching on Doncastle. My company is headin' into the woods. We'll skirmish them the whole way. They'll have a plenty bloody trek through Dernall Forest!"

"Your captain?" asked the sorcerer. "May I meet him first?"

"Captain Cassidy? He's right over there." Evan gestured to a large open area, a grass-covered city plaza. Kryphon saw more than a hundred bowmen gathered there.

"Tell him that I have important news for him," whispered the mage. "Have him meet me under that tree."

Kryphon stepped into the shadow of a broad, low-limbed oak. He watched the man hurry into the plaza, stopping to speak to a man on horseback. The officer trotted his steed toward the oak tree, an expression of annoyance on his face. He dismounted easily and stalked up to Kryphon.

"What do you want? I haven't time for—" He stopped suddenly as Kryphon began to wave his hand.

"Dothax, Mylax Heeroz." Kryphon repeated the spell that had, thus far, served him very well. He pulled a diamond pendant from beneath his robe and waved it slowly.

The captain paused, confused. He looked suspiciously at the sorcerer. Slowly, his hand crept toward the steel shortsword girded to his waist. His face twisted as his mind wrestled with the magic.

"Captain Cassidy, my friend," said the sorcerer softly. "It is good to see you again."

The officer looked at him uncomprehendingly, but finally gave him a tentative smile. Magic had won over his mind.

"There has been a mistake," continued Kryphon urgently. "The attack comes from the south—you must take your company there! Screen the approaches to Doncastle, but remember—from the south!"

Captain Cassidy nodded earnestly, grasping the mage's hand. "Thank you!" he said sincerely before springing to his horse and racing into the plaza.

Kryphon smiled to himself before turning back to his original path. The chapel of Vaughn Burne was not far.

* * * * *

The cleric knelt in reverence, meditating. His goddess answered his calls for strength, filling him with her life-affirming power. She knew, as did he, that the coming battle would test his might to the limit.

Vaughn Burne felt a slight disruption in the rhythm of his meditation. Immediately he knew that someone, some *evil*, had entered his sanctuary. A dark presence sent a shiver down his spine.

The cleric ceased his meditations and rose to grasp his silver war hammer. He stepped to the thin curtain that separated his meditation alcove from the main chapel and looked out. The front door stood open, but the huge room, with its dozens of benches, was empty.

Or was it?

Vaughn Burne cast a spell upon himself, passing a hand before his eyes. Now he looked at the room and saw it as it truly was.

Along the far wall, an invisible man was creeping stealthily. The intruder had covered himself with magic, and he carried no weapon. The cleric deduced that he was a sorcerer. And his fingers glittered with diamond rings—this was indeed the killer from his dream. The cleric grew angry, knowing that he was looking at the man who had killed his friend Annuwynn—and who now intended to slay him as well.

The cleric did not grow overconfident. He knew that if not for the warning provided by Chauntea, he would probably have been slain at his meditations. But now he had the advantage, and the sorcerer was not the only one who could use magic.

Vaughn Burne whispered another spell and became every bit as invisible as the mage. He stepped around the screen, careful not to disturb the hanging fabric, and crept toward the intruder. Carefully, he raised the silver hammer. The weapon, like him, could not be seen.

But a floorboard creaked beneath his careful step, and across the room the sorcerer froze. His black eyes turned toward the cleric, and seemed to sear into Vaughn Burne's flesh. But the mage surely could not see him!

Suddenly the magic-user reached into his robe, pulling forth a slender, glittering rod—a glass tube, studded with diamonds. He pointed the thing at a spot just to the cleric's left, as if he didn't know exactly where Vaughn Burne stood.

"Blitzyth, Dorax zooth!" he chanted.

A bolt of energy exploded from the rod, crackling like a lightning bolt through the chapel. It sizzled the air and blasted a hole in the wall, sending dust and shards of wood flying into the street. Vaughn Burne dove to the side as the lightning struck, but heat and fire blazed across his chest. He felt as though his lungs were consumed by flame as he tumbled over empty benches and lay still on the floor.

His robe was gone—burned away—and wisps of smoke rose from his skin.

*   *   *   *   *

The duergar spilled from their lair like an army of insects. Their number seemed limitless as they continued to pour forth long after Finellen's companies had pulled away.

The retreat threatened to become a rout, as even the sturdy dwarves—most of them veterans of a dozen campaigns—quailed before the savage onslaught. With the greatest difficulty, the dwarven captain kept her formations assembled, placed a rear guard, and managed to keep the shaken morale of her troops from breaking entirely.

They had discovered a vast nation of dark dwarves—not the tiny outpost she had first suspected. Somehow, the duergar had overcome the natural balance of forces that served to maintain peace in the underdark: they had destroyed or driven away enough of their neighbors to enable them to develop vast resources of precious food. With that food supply secure, there was little that could stand in their way.

Finellen feared for her people, the dwarves of Gwynneth. The retreat of her companies must not lead to the clanholds, or the entire population would suffer an unspeakable fate.

So she directed the retreat away from Gwynneth, away from the caverns that led to her home. She had only one hope—a slim one, at best. She would try to lead the duergar onto the surface, where their strength was weakest. Perhaps if she could lure the pursuing horde under the light of the sun she could face them and die with honor.

That was all she had left to hope.

* * * * *

Alexei was one of the first to arrive at the smoldering chapel. He saw the hole in the wall and smelled the distinctive odor lingering in the air. And he watched in silence as a group of men bore a stretcher from the wreckage.

He heard the thundering of hooves behind him and turned to see the bandit lord gallop in. O'Roarke's face reflected his anger and shock as he dismounted.

"Do you know what happened?" he asked, looking somberly at the stretcher as it was borne from the church.

"I am certain a sorcerer used lightning magic. The damage to the church and that smell in the air is clear evidence. The cleric is not dead, but he is badly hurt."

"How bad?" O'Roarke's grief showed in his eyes, though his voice remained steady.

"He will be crippled and blind, unless you have another cleric here capable of healing him," Alexei said bluntly.

"There are none in Doncastle. This is a serious blow. Now we are left to face the attack without a cleric or a wizard."

"Perhaps not," said Alexei. "Vaughn Burne used his healing magic on me last night." The mage held up his hands. They were still twisted and scarred, but he was able to move his fingers with some control. The grimace distorting his face showed that his dexterity returned with considerable pain.

"He also gave me access to the spell books of Annuwynn. I have been studying them."

"And?"

"I think I can use them."

"You can start by finding whoever did this!"

"That would please me greatly," said Alexei.

"I'll be with the troops at the King's Gate. Let me know if you learn anything," said O'Roarke.

Now Alexei could begin to wreak his vengeance. He would avenge himself upon Cyndre, upon Kryphon—upon the entire council that had turned him out.

And it would start with this agent who had caused so much damage in Doncastle. He had a good idea about the attacker's identity, but he stepped into the chapel and quickly reconstructed the attack to be sure.

The wizard went over to the spot where the spell had been cast. Searching the floor, he found what he sought: little shards of the rod that was used to cast the spell.

And he learned more than he dared hope. The shards were not glass, or even amber—materials most magic-users would have used for the spell. The glittering fragments were unmistakably diamond.

* * * * *

"I didn't like that place anyway!" declared Newt. "All those people running around—you couldn't even get a bite to eat without asking somebody. And they'd *always* say no!"

"I d-didn't like that t-town either," replied the wood sprite. "B-but I miss Robyn—miss Robyn!"

Newt's tail drooped as he settled to an oak limb high above the floor of Dernall Forest. "Why'd you have to say that?" he said wistfully. "I miss her, too! Why do you think she didn't want to come along with us? I know she likes the woods!"

"I-I think it was the prince—her prince."

Newt sniffed. "Well, we'll go back and see her in a few days. But for now we've got a whole big forest to explore!" With that he dove like an arrow through the leafy canopy, searching for something to interest him.

Still moping, the wood sprite darted behind him.

* * * * *

Daryth emerged from the smithy, running a calloused thumb across the edge of his scimitar. It drew blood without the slightest pressure—the man had done a splendid job!

The Calishite started across Doncastle's shady lanes, on his way back to the inn. The food would be good tonight, he hoped. He resolved to eat much of it, knowing that it might be some time before he got to sit at a table again. The Scarlet Guard was very close—all the rumors on the street indicated that the battle would erupt on the morrow.

He stopped short as a familiar figure stepped out of a tavern, directly in his path. Razfallow froze as his eyes met the Calishite's. The half-orc wore a leather shirt-piece with a high collar and a floppy leather hat with a drooping brim. The disguise was obviously intended to mask the half-orc's race, but Daryth looked full into his beastly face.

"Once again, Calishite?" said the assassin, exposing his wicked pointed teeth with an amused half-smile.

"This will be the last time."

Razfallow suddenly turned and walked, and Daryth followed a few feet behind. He had learned the assassin's lesson well when he had studied under Razfallow at the Academy of Stealth: "Never fail to capitalize on an advantage." It was as if the half-orc taunted him with his back, daring him to strike the single blow that would kill him.

Daryth carefully dropped a hand to his scimitar. He could see the gap between the assassin's hat and his shirt-piece, but something compelled him to hold his hand. Perhaps he wanted to show Razfallow that he had outgrown the old lessons, after all. Or perhaps he wanted to prove to himself that he could beat Razfallow fair and square.

At that moment, the assassin chuckled and stepped into the middle of the street. He whirled in a single, fluid motion, and his shortsword whistled through the air toward Daryth's exposed throat.

But the weapon clanged against the scimitar which had, just as quickly, flashed up to parry the blow. Daryth slashed, and Razfallow leaped away. The Calishite advanced in a crouch, carefully planning his cuts, recovering from each in an instant to clash away the assassin's return thrusts.

Thrust and slash. The half-orc suddenly rushed in, and Daryth backed down the street, almost tripping in a rut. He stumbled and saw the shortsword lash at his chest. He desperately parried the blow, a scant inch from his skin. The move cost him his balance and he dropped to one knee, springing backward before Razfallow could strike again.

Slash and thrust. Daryth drove the half-orc away with a dazzling series of blows. His scimitar whirled like a dancer through the air, barely visible even to the keenest of eyes. But somehow, the assassin's heavy blade blocked each attack. The Calishite stopped momentarily, gasping for breath. He saw the sweat beading on the half-orc's face.

Once again Razfallow rushed, but this time Daryth gave no ground. He stood against the probing blade and laid a vicious slash along the half-orc's forearm. His weariness vanished, and now he leaped in, darting and dodging—pushing the assassin steadily down the street. A ring of bystanders moved with the fight.

Now he sensed a delay in Razfallow's response. Weariness was slowing the assassin's parries. Each of Daryth's attacks came closer to landing, and they could both sense the inevitable end of the fight. For the first time, the Calishite saw something approaching fear in his enemy's eyes—and he relished the sight.

Suddenly Razfallow turned and rolled away from Daryth, springing to his feet and leaping into the ring of bystanders. Razfallow seized the arm of a plump woman and jerked her around to serve as his shield.

But the student reacted quickly to his former teacher's trick. Daryth's silver scimitar followed Razfallow's roll, closed the gap as he sprang up, and met his flesh as he grasped the woman. Daryth thrust around the woman's terrified face, driving his weapon into Razfallow's throat. Razfallow stiffened and made a gurgling sound as his shortsword fell from nerveless fingers. Blood spouted from his torn jugular, and his jaw flapped open. Finally, he slumped to the ground and died.

Daryth cleaned his scimitar on the dead man's shirt, ignoring the looks of thrilled horror on the faces of the Ffolk. He turned and walked away.

This had to be a good omen for the battle, he thought.

* * * * *

They ate cold venison and discussed the impending fight late that evening on the high balcony of Hugh's favorite inn. Tristan and Robyn, together with Pawldo, Daryth, Alexei, Pontswain, and Fiona had joined the outlaw leader.

O'Roarke outlined his plan. The King's Gate, northeast of Doncastle, would receive nearly half of the defenders, since it lay in the Scarlet Guard's path of approach. The rest of the defenders would be spread among the other three gates.

"You're not going to keep a reserve?" asked Tristan.

"Don't have the men," said the bandit. "Besides, Cassidy's archers will have decimated them by the time they get to the gate! We will meet them with steel, and they will break!"

"You can't be sure of that!" Tristan argued. "If they don't—if there are too many of them—fall back to the river. Don't sacrifice the entire town on this gamble!"

"That's enough! You are not required to stay here—leave if you wish. But if you stay, you will fight by my plan."

Tristan wanted to grab the man by his leather collar and thrash some sense into him, but Robyn's presence at his side somehow calmed him.

"Of course I will stay," he said.

"Very well." Hugh O'Roarke turned to Fiona. "You must leave Doncastle tonight, if possible. The women and children have fled to secret glens and caves."

"I will not!" cried the young woman, pounding her fist on the table. "I am going to be a part of any fight! My father taught me to wield a sword and shoot a bow. Give me either, and I will stand in your line!"

The bandit sensed the futility of argument. "You shall have a sword. But you are to remain at my side throughout the day. Do you understand?" Fiona nodded.

"You're all mad!" said Pontswain, staring about the table in disbelief. "To even think about meeting this army, and these wizards, with a band of outlaws in the woods!"

"We have no choice!" growled O'Roarke.

"Yes—yes, you do! We all do! We can go to Corwell. The king might not come after us, but even if he does, we can meet him with men-at-arms at a castle!" Pontswain looked around the table, desperately seeking agreement.

Pontswain saw no supporting looks. With a snarl of frustration, he leaped to his feet and stalked from the room.

*   *   *   *   *

Not a single arrow had flown from the underbrush during the long march through the forest. This in itself, Cyndre thought, boded well for their attack. In the past, the approach to Doncastle had been a nightmare of skirmishing archers and sudden ambush. This time, the ogres had led the way to Doncastle, ready to brutally counterattack at the first sign of resistance. There had been none.

"Why did we stop?" The king stuck his head through the

window of his coach, blinking sleepily.

"It is time to deploy for the attack," explained Cyndre.

"Oh. Very well, then . . . deploy!"

Cyndre walked to the center of the vast forest clearing, where he was joined by the other mages and the four captains of the Scarlet Guard's brigades.

"We will attack Doncastle from two directions," Cyndre explained. "Captain Dornthwait and two brigades of the guard will strike the northeast gate. I will precede this attack with a spell—it will clear the way so that the charge should carry you into the city. After Dornthwait has broken in, the rest of you will take your companies into Doncastle. The city is to be destroyed. Take anything you can carry—but burn the rest!

"The ogre brigade of the guard, accompanied by the other wizards, will infiltrate through the forest and strike the city from the northwest. You will wait until the first attack has developed for two hours. By then, the defenders should all have been drawn from your quarter.

"We will attack tomorrow morning, an hour after dawn. Use the rest of the day to get into positions—I want all units ready by nightfall!"

The captains dispersed to organize their units. Cyndre spent the long afternoon checking with each commander to make sure that he understood the role he was to play in the plan. Only the ogre brigade, which had to make a long march through the woods to the northwest, faced a real challenge.

The long night gradually gave way to dawn, and the sorcerer estimated the passing of an hour after sunrise. He felt the mass of the king's legion behind him as he stepped to the forefront and cast his spell—the spell that would, he hoped, give them free passage into Doncastle.

"Seeriax, punjyss withsath—fore!"

The forest before him slowly filled with yellow smoke. There was no wind, but the smoke, trailing a sickening stench in its wake, began to drift toward Doncastle. It thickened, billowing along the ground as it moved, and drifted steadily away from the king's army.

As it passed through the forest, squirrels, birds, and every other animal fell dead. It grew still more, bubbling and seething like a furious living thing. Tendrils of the smoke, tinged with green, reached forward eagerly toward the outskirts of the city. Cyndre knew that ranks of defenders stood, camouflaged, among the trees before him.

But the killing cloud would find them.

* * * * *

The Deepsong thrummed, building in intensity and volume. Throughout the city, along the canyon walls, across the gardens and balconies, the sahuagin gathered, enthralled. Thousands of them focused their might upon the song, and it grew more compelling with each addition.

Gradually, they began to thrash and jerk from the tension. Flailing around with the vast domes of Kressilacc, the sahuagin thrashed the water into a vast, swirling maelstrom, until the momentum of the sea itself carried the song and the singers through its great circle. And still the Deepsong grew.

The dead of the sea marched along the bottom. Shepherded by Ysalla's priestesses, they gathered around the city. Vast ranks of white bone, pallid flesh, and gouged eyesockets shuffled forward under the priestesses' commands. Unknowing, they stood ready to do whatever they were told.

Then King Sythissall raised one webbed, claw-studded hand, and the Deepsong came to a halt. The frenzy of the sahuagin exploded upward as thousands of green, scaled bodies hurled from the city, kicking their way swiftly toward the surface. The swarm bristled with tridents and spears. The mass of sahuagin broke the surface in a frothing mass of turbulence.

Swimming strongly, their spines breaking the surface to roll through the spray in a menacing flood, they approached the coast of Alaron—the Kingdom of Callidyrr.

And the undead started to march slowly across the bottom of the sea. Led by the yellow-scaled priestesses the dead of the sea shambled over every obstacle, every undersea mountain or valley in their path.

Toward the light, and the air, and the land.

❧ 19 ❧

Wind

"An eagle, huh?" The halfling was obviously impressed with the account of Robyn's journey to Alaron. He, Daryth, Tristan, and Robyn stood overlooking the King's Gate of Doncastle. Below them the defenders of the city stood at their posts.

"And a wolf, once," she added proudly. Her skin was clean and smooth again—the scrapes and burns had vanished from her face. Only the garish scar across her eye indicated the hurts she had received.

"I've learned a lot in the past year," she admitted. "But I missed you all terribly." She touched Pawldo tenderly on the cheek, and he turned away in embarrassment.

She squeezed Tristan's hand, and for a moment he forgot everything but the fact that she was at his side again. His confidence grew; Robyn's strength would be a great asset in the coming fight.

They would certainly need all the help they could get, he reflected, looking at the position before them. The King's Gate was not really a gate at all. It was a wide avenue through the forest that granted access to the northeastern quarter of the city. Most of the defenses consisted of deep, muddy ditches before fences of sharpened spikes. Companies of men with long spears barred the gaps between the ditches. Above them stretched bridges that linked a number of large oak trees. Along these spans, O'Roarke had deployed his companies of archers.

In a few places, tall and solid wooden palisades stood among the ditches and ramparts. Tristan and his companions stood up on one of these, a sturdy platform perhaps twelve feet off the ground to the left of the line at the gate. O'Roarke and Pontswain stood at the right end of the line.

"What's that?" Robyn asked, sniffing the air. Her nose wrinkled with displeasure, but Tristan could smell nothing unusual.

"Look!" shouted Pawldo abruptly, pointing toward the center of their line.

They watched as a green mist emerged from the forest before them. It reached forward with snakelike tendrils, probing along the ground into the positions held by O'Roarke's stalwart footmen.

The companions felt, rather than saw, the panic that infused the defenders of Doncastle. The mist looked so completely evil that no one could have doubts as to its nature—including the unfortunate soldiers in its path. Some men tried to hold their posts. The banner of the Black Bear fluttered bravely above a band of spearmen, but the smoke obscured the soldiers, and the companions watched the banner slowly fall until it, too, vanished into the evil mist.

As the magic cloud moved on, they gasped in horror. The sprawling bodies revealed were twisted torturously. The men had died in the greatest agony, their skin seared and scarred.

"By the goddess, what sorcery is this?" gasped Tristan.

"It can only be Cyndre," muttered Daryth.

"Let's get out of here while we still can!" urged Pawldo. "No mortal troops can stand against an attack like that!"

"Wait," said Robyn quietly. Of all of them, she alone seemed calm in the face of the onrushing wave of death.

The companions watched as gas flowed toward the outer fringes of the line, reaching around the base of the palisade where they stood. Already, a gap a hundred yards wide had been opened in the ranks of the defense.

Robyn reached into her robe and pulled out the strangely carved stick, the runestick that Genna had made and Yazilliclick had saved for her. She held the stick in both her hands, running her fingers over the runes engraved in one end. Suddenly, she brandished the stick like a weapon, pointing toward the green tendrils that were inching their way closer up the wall.

The prince gagged as the odor of the gas reached him, and his eyes began to water. Canthus whined and paced frantically about their broad platform. For a moment, Tristan feared that the dog would jump, but then Daryth laid a steadying hand on his shoulder.

Other men saw the effects of the killing cloud and were not so brave or foolish. They turned to run as the yellow tendrils of gas approached. Some held their weapons and stumbled backward, while others dropped everything and fled headlong into the town. Within minutes, the center of the line was gone—killed or routed.

The green smoke expanded to either side and climbed higher into the air. The companions saw defenders trapped in nearby trees as the mist passed around the tree bases and cut off their escape. Then it climbed slowly, inexorably, toward the men who huddled upon the surrounding platforms. Some of these archers, carrying the banner of the Red Boar, jumped to safety and fled before the gas surrounded them. Others stood their posts, seeking targets for their arrows, but died without striking back. As the mist moved on, it continued to reveal grotesque, twisted corpses in its wake.

Then the mist seemed to clear as a slight breeze moved through the treetops. Robyn turned the stick around, and the wind whirled with her. The mist fell away from their platform as the wind increased in force.

Robyn closed her eyes in concentration, holding the stick like a talisman of hope, and still the wind picked up. The mist pressed in from all sides, but the air flowed outward from their platform, keeping that area free of the killing mist.

Tristan and the others watched, spellbound, as the mist pressed in and then fell back, locked in its battle with the clean air of Robyn's spell. The struggle seemed to last an eternity, but finally the mist began to dissipate, falling away more rapidly and then vanishing into the air.

"They're coming," said Daryth quietly. In the distance they could make out flashes of crimson, growing more distinct every second. The military cadence of drumbeats grew audible, and soon dozens of ranks of troops could be seen.

"The Scarlet Guard," confirmed Pawldo.

"Come on!" shouted the prince, suddenly leaping down the ladder and running among the scattered defenders. His companions followed him from the rampart as he drew the Sword of Cymrych Hugh and held it high.

"Men of Doncastle, rally to me!" Tristan cried. "The power of the goddess has broken the wizard's spell. Fight for your town, your people!"

But the battle cries of the Scarlet Guard sounded across the gate, long, ululating howls that would have shaken the morale of the stoutest defenders.

"Maybe this isn't the place to make our stand," suggested Daryth. "Look around."

The prince saw that they would never assemble enough fighters to hold a position as wide as the King's Gate—too many had died under the killing cloud, and most of the survivors had fled.

"The river! We have to try and form a line at the river!"

Then something caught Robyn's eye. "Look! The banner of the Red Boar!"

They saw a cautious face peering from between two houses. It belonged to a frightened looking young man who carried a long pole, from which fluttered the standard of one unit routed by the killing cloud.

"Here, man!" called Tristan. Tentatively, the fellow emerged from his hiding place. "Are there others? The rest of your unit?"

The man gestured toward the heart of the city. "All gone," he mumbled. "They ran—I did, too!"

Tristan could think of nothing else to do. "Come with us," he urged. Rally them to the standard!"

Reluctantly, the man accompanied them, holding the banner high. The Red Boar symbol fluttered faintly in the air.

"Men of Doncastle, of the Red Boar!" called Tristan, waving his sword. "Rally to your standard!" He repeated the cry as they moved along the line, and slowly the routed warriors emerged from the shelter of buildings and alleys. Still, there were pathetically few.

"Now we have to keep them together while we fall back to the river. Daryth, can you—" Tristan stopped suddenly.

He heard a thundering of hooves and saw Hugh O'Roarke mounted upon his galloping charger, bearing down upon them. "What are you doing?" he cried. "Why are you not at the gates?"

"The sorcerers sent a cloud upon us—a mist that killed all who breathed it."

O'Roarke's face whitened in rage. He looked around frantically, desperate for inspiration. "We'll have to hold them here! I'll pull the garrisons from the other gates—we cannot give them entrance!"

"That will make the disaster worse!" argued the prince. "Choose good ground—and fight there! Fall back to the river—make a line! We have a chance to hold there!"

"Never!" cried Hugh O'Roarke. "We cannot give up another inch of ground without a fight!"

"If you pull the men from the other gates, you'll have no position to hold, anyway. A second attack by the king's army, and you'll be taken from the rear!"

But O'Roarke was no longer listening. Tears ran down his face as he looked at the remnants of the Red Boar company. He whirled his horse to put his plan into motion. "Men of the Red Boar! Hear me! We will stop the king's legion . . . here!" He brandished his sword along their line, and a ragged cheer went up from the men.

The bandit lord did not look back as he rode away. He was on his way to pull his men from every other part of the city—to try to hold a line in a place chosen by pride, not judgement.

*   *   *   *   *

The diamond rod identified the enemy, but it would be up to Alexei to find him. Magic would help, but he would have to search with his own eyes. Alexei was surprised by how badly he wanted to find Kryphon, to kill him. Once the man had been his friend—the two had been Cyndre's most trusted lieutenants. Now Kryphon was at the heart of all he hated about the council that had turned him out.

Before he began his search, Alexei cast two spells upon himself—one to detect magical auras, and another that allowed him to see invisible objects. Then he walked to the

King's Gate, the northeast entrance to the city. This was where the greatest block of defenders had gathered—and where the main force of the king's attack was expected.

Alexei walked among the defenders in total concentration. He looked into every rampart and walked slowly down every street in that quarter of the town. He saw Tristan and his companions on the high palisade. He sensed the ominous presence of the king's army, breaking camp somewhere in the depths of the wood.

But he did not find Kryphon.

Nor was there any sign that magic had been used upon the ramparts or barricades—or anything else. Either the mage was concealed very well, waiting until the attack began, or he was somewhere else.

Alexei hurried to the Lord's Gate—the northwestern approach to the city. He wondered when the attack would come—would he be in time?

Though the defenders were not so numerous here, he found ramparts and ditches manned by willing troops who were ready to defend their city to the death. As he walked among the barricades, rumors of a rout in the defenses at the King's Gate began to spread among the troops.

He watched in shock as Hugh O'Roarke himself galloped along the line of the deep ditch, shouting to all the men gathered there.

"Follow me! The King's Gate has been breached—you must fly to the rescue!"

With a cheer for their lord, the troops at the Lord's Gate burst from their positions. They moved at a trot, ignoring any sense of order, eager to join the fray.

A flash of movement attracted Alexei's eyes to the entryway of a small wooden house. He saw it again—a figure moving stealthily along the shaded side of the building. He wore a black robe with a gray hood that flowed over his shoulders like a cape.

Finally the figure emerged. He walked beside an empty ditch, fondling the sharpened points of the stakes that had been hastily erected there. He threw back his head and laughed, and as the hood fell away from his tight, bearded face, Alexei recognized Kryphon.

His enemy stood at least five hundred feet away, between the trunks of two huge oaks. The trees were connected by a solid rampart, twenty feet up. Alexei fastened his eyes to that rampart as he began to cast a spell.

"Xor-thax, teray."

In the blink of an eye, Alexei teleported to the center of the ramp, materializing in one place as he vanished from the other. As soon as he felt the hard wood of the rampart under his feet, the wizard began his next spell.

But the long beams of the bridge creaked under his sudden weight. Alexei did not stop to see if Kryphon had noticed the sound—he ceased his casting and rolled to the side. A moment later, a blast of magical energy exploded in the middle of the rampart. Each of the ends of the bridge, no longer supported, dropped to the ground.

Alexei leaped from the rampart. In mid-air, he uttered the one-word command for one of his simplest spells—a spell that would take effect immediately. Thus enchanted, he floated gently to the ground like a falling feather.

Kryphon had not waited to identify his attacker, and now Alexei saw no sign of him. Then he heard a low voice behind one of the tree trunks. As he settled to the ground, Kryphon reappeared, wrapped in a shimmering green globe of light.

Kryphon's eyes widened as he recognized Alexei, who stood facing him on the ground. "Well, *comrade*," he said, "I am surprised to see that you are still alive!"

"And you, it would seem, have already lived too long."

Kryphon laughed. "We shall see who has lived too long!"

Alexei suspected the nature of the globe surrounding his foe, and it worried him greatly. But it could be an illusion, and he had to make sure. He quickly raised his right hand and pointed at Kryphon's heart.

"Magius, stryke!"

Five hissing bolts of magical energy shot in rapid succession from Alexei's fingertip, each arrowing toward Kryphon's grinning figure. And each sizzled into extinction as it came into contact with the green sphere.

"I am impressed in spite of myself," acknowledged Alexei. Despite his outer calm, his mind whirled through a succession of desperate plans, discarding each as futile.

"That could not matter less to me," sneered Kryphon. He waved a hand before him, preparing to cast a spell.

"Did you have a pleasurable dalliance with Doric?" asked Alexei, seizing upon that old ground as he groped for a plan.

"Bah! She quickly became annoying."

"Did you send her after the druid? She failed, you know."

Kryphon paused, surprised. "She went without my permission. She has been too frightened to return to me, since—no doubt doubly so, if she failed."

Alexei laughed. "She did not return to you because she cannot. The druid killed her!"

Alexei hoped to provoke a strong reaction from his enemy, but he was disappointed. Kryphon shrugged and suddenly knit his brows in concentration. Carefully, he stroked his fingers through the air.

"Sheeriath, drake," he hissed. Alexei dove to the side at his words, and the sticky strings of web missed him by scant inches. He rolled behind a tree, still concentrating.

The globe of invulnerability protected Kryphon from Alexei's magic. His enemy had all the advantages, stalking him while he could do little but scuttle out of the way. And how could he fight back without using his magic? Without using his magic on *Kryphon*, he reminded himself.

The murderous sorcerer crept closer—Alexei could hear the faint tread of his footfalls. He caught a glimmer of the magical screen coming around the tree and knew that his enemy was almost upon him. Overhead, one end of the shattered bridge hung limply. Kryphon stepped closer, and now Alexei saw him. Kryphon's hands were raised in preparation for a final, killing spell.

Alexei raised a hand, weaving a spell of his own. He saw Kryphon's confident grin—the black wizard felt quite secure behind his magical screen.

But Alexei's spell was not cast at the mage. He pulled forth a tiny glass rod, much like the diamond one Kryphon had used to send the lightning bolt against Vaughn Burne.

"Blitzyth, Dorax zooth!"

The bolt of lightning exploded from Alexei's finger as he pointed not at Kryphon, but straight above him. Kryphon's eyes widened in surprise, and he stumbled over the words of his own casting as he leaned back to look upward.

In a split second he saw the section of the heavy rampart swinging over his head. He watched the bolt of lightning crackle into it, severing the few points of support still holding the wreckage to the tree. And he screamed as the mass of twisted wood plummeted through his magical screen, and his skull, and his chest.

But even his death scream was drowned by the splintering and snapping of the broken mass as it crashed heavily to earth. The pile of wreckage creaked and groaned for several seconds before settling—a suitably anonymous gravestone for Kryphon, Alexei thought. The sudden end to the fight left him weak and trembling. He felt a little frustrated at the suddenness of Kryphon's death—he had hoped to savor the moment more.

He leaned against a rough tree trunk, slowly dropping until he was slumped on the ground. He stayed there for several minutes, until the sounds of marching awakened him from his reverie. The empty battlements greeted his eyes, and beyond, as if to mock him, he saw a line of crimson soldiers advancing toward the gate.

Alexei stayed behind the tree and watched. The soldiers, at first glance, seemed very close—but then he realized that it was their huge size that gave this impression. For these were not humans, marching a hundred abreast toward the undefended gate of Doncastle.

This was the ogre brigade.

*　*　*　*　*

The troops of Doncastle made a valiant stand at the King's Gate. One brigade of human mercenaries shattered against the pikes and swords of O'Roarke's men. The Sword of Cymrych Hugh claimed a dozen or more mercenaries. O'Roarke rode like a maniac, directing his charger into the thick of the fighting, flailing about with a great two-handed sword. The man looked like he had been born to battle.

But then the ogres marched into the rear of the defenders. As the rest of the Scarlet Guard charged the broken position, Hugh O'Roarke led a futile counterattack. Dozens of his men fell around him, pushing their leader to safety. At the last, the bandit leader was swept along with his men routing from the fight—those few that had survived the bloody onslaught of the ogres.

The disaster developed swiftly. Within minutes of the first appearance of the monstrous troops, word spread through the ranks that the battle was lost. With no hope of victory, the men of Doncastle were reluctant to face their doom.

They fled through the abandoned streets of the city, away from the enveloping wings of the royal army. In chaos and confusion, the panic-stricken mass poured through the Druid's Gate, into the wilds of Dernall Forest.

Tristan and his companions stood until the line collapsed around them. It was easy to foresee the inevitable result of the attack, so Tristan again decided to keep his friends together and alive rather than staying to make an heroic but fruitless stand.

"Stay together!" he cried, holding Robyn's hand. Daryth and Pawldo flanked the druid, while Canthus raced behind.

Hundreds of men, eyes wide with panic, pressed around them. Robyn was torn from his grasp by the force of the retreat. As he saw her black hair borne away by the mob, he panicked and reached for the Sword of Cymrych Hugh, ready to battle his way to her side, if need be.

But somehow the druid managed to stop moving, standing serenely with her eyes closed, and miraculously the fleeing soldiers avoided her, leaving her as an island in the raging river of retreat.

They started moving again, swept along by the crowd, and suddenly the prince recognized a tousled head of red hair. He pushed through a pair of bedraggled swordsmen and took Fiona's arm.

"Let go!" she cried, and then recognized him. "What happened? I didn't expect to see *you* running away."

"Come on," he said, forcing her back to his companions.

"I can take care of myself!" She waved her shortsword. "I'm staying here to stick this into the king's heart as soon as he gets here!"

"Join us—you'll have another chance!" Tristan said, maintaining his hold on her as they were swept along.

They passed through the Druid's Gate as smoke was

beginning to fill the air. Once outside of the city, Robyn led the way. The troops followed the pathways through the woods, but she took her companions through the thick of the forest. It seemed that she opened a path with a wave of her hand before her.

"They've put the city to the torch," muttered Daryth, looking behind him. The Calishite plainly regretted their flight.

"What now?" asked Robyn. "The rebels can't run forever. Will the king and his wizards try to slay them all?"

Tristan couldn't meet her gaze. "I'm sure that the sorcerer will not rest until every shred of resistance is crushed from the people of Alaron!"

"And then Gwynneth, perhaps—or Moray? Tristan, we can't let this happen!"

"What do you want me to do?" he demanded.

Robyn gestured into the forest. "You can gather that army and fight again! We'll stand with you!"

"She's right!" Daryth's eyes lit. "The men of Doncastle were not slaughtered—they fled. Rally them, and you'll have an army that can stand again!"

"You must!" cried Fiona, her eyes flashing. "My father died to bring word of that army—Doncastle died trying to stop it! You can't let those sacrifices go in vain!"

"There's too many in the king's legions—this force will never be able to stop them!"

"That's not what you said at Freeman's Down," said Robyn, a little sharply.

"And why do you suppose the king only attacked with the Scarlet Guard?" persisted Daryth. "Could it be that his other lords are not so loyal—that a victory against the king might cause them to lose heart?"

"Perhaps even to join the rebel cause?" added the druid.

Tristan looked at his companions, and he knew they were right. He didn't know how he could hope to rally the broken force—but he knew that he had to try.

"Very well," he agreed quietly. "Let's move quickly and get ahead of the troops. We'll pick a place to rally them and see what happens."

* * * * * *

"A splendid battle! A marvelous fight! My, how a victory gets one's blood pumping! Oh, say—look at the flames!" King Carrathal was quite beside himself. In one blow, it appeared that he had crushed the rebellion. He stood outside his coach at the King's Gate, watching the sacking of Doncastle.

"Now, let's get back to Caer Callidyrr—I simply must have a victory feast!" Still beaming, he climbed into the coach. Cyndre, who had just returned from a meeting with his council, followed.

"Sire, I fear the task is not yet done."

"Eh, what's that?"

"The usurper was not found among the dead. However, my man, Kryphon, was. I'm certain another of my mages also died in that city—I would certainly have found her by now if she were alive. This prince has now cost me, personally—and he will pay! There are still potent forces of rebellion here, and we cannot rest until the spark of mutiny has been quelled for good!"

"Search again for the body of the usurper!" shrilled the king. "He must be here! Put out those fires—his body will be burned, and we'll never find it!"

"I tell you, he lives!" hissed the mage.

"And I tell you you're wrong!" shouted the king. He looked at the wisps of smoke rising from all quarters of Doncastle, at the bodies sprawled across the ground. His mind felt startlingly clear—and he hated what he saw.

"Let them go," argued the king. "We have taught them a lesson. We shall return to my palace, and there I will throw a festival such as Callidyrr has never seen."

"No, Your Majesty. We must—"

"What did you say?" King Carrathal's nose twitched slightly. "Did you say 'no' to me—your lord?"

Cyndre cursed. Dark magic rose within him like the bubbling prelude to a volcanic eruption. His smooth voice cracked into a snarl.

"You are a pitiful worm! Everything you have I have given you, and now you lack the gratitude to repay me or even the sense to see the wisdom of my words!"

"I am king! You cannot speak to me that way! Now leave me—I shall give the orders to return to Callidyrr myself!"

Black magic exploded from the mage, hissing invisibly around the monarch. The color drained from the king's face. Then he slumped in his seat, his eyes open but glazed. Dumbly, he stared into the distance. The Crown of the Isles tipped forward, sliding across his face, and then fell heavily to the floor of the coach.

"I shall give the order," hissed the sorcerer. "And it will not be a return to your castle."

*　*　*　*　*

Hobarth, cleric of Bhaal, ate his feasts and drank his draughts with growing impatience. Waiting for some word from his god, he amused himself by animating the bodies of the twelve druids who had fallen in the fight. Marching his undead army into ranks as separate companies, he placed the druid undead in command. Then he marched and countermarched the zombie and skeleton army across the grove of the Great Druid, trampling everything to mud.

All the trees died, dropping their withered leaves to sink into the morass. Only the Moonwell and the twenty stone statues about it retained any semblance of purity.

And then came the word of Bhaal, and Hobarth smiled at his deity's instructions. He ordered the companies of undead to collect the bodies of their fallen comrades—those zombies and skeletons that had fallen under the defenders' claws, weapons, or magic. The undead carried the bodies to the Moonwell and threw them in.

Each twice-killed zombie hit the smooth water with an oily hiss, twitching and thrashing in a froth of bubbles until it disappeared. Each skeleton burst and cracked upon immersion in the sacred waters. And slowly death spread through the Moonwell, fading the pure light of its waters, warming the cool magic of the Earthmother. With each body added, the white waters faded, to gray, and then to sludgy brown. The light died, extinguished entirely.

And the water turned black.

❧ 20 ❧

Fire

The dwarves emerged from the wide cave mouth, tramping slowly into the light of the sun. Their bodies were bent from weariness, and their grizzled heads were bowed by their defeat. Finellen was the last one to emerge. The dark dwarves hated the sun, but she knew they would not be far behind in pursuit of an ultimate victory.

And this they could earn. The dwarven captain's heart burned with pain as she looked at her warriors. The dwarves had formed into lines, awaiting their captain—but there were less than half of the original three hundred left.

"Let's find a place to finish it," she said loudly enough for them all to hear. None of them had any illusions about their inevitable fate—the thousands of duergar that pursued them would not let them escape.

The cave mouth was near the sea, on the western coast of Alaron. They stood upon a rocky headland with many jutting promontories. In some places, high cliffs dropped to the wavebeaten shore. Finellen did not immediately see a place to make her stand, so she turned to the weary dwarves again.

"Let's march!"

Turning to the north, with the sea to their left, the ragged column began to trudge along the coast.

*　*　*　*　*

The companions fled through the forest, following the path that Robyn created, for a day and a night before they rested. Then they collapsed in a dark grove of pines, haunted by the memories of the battle and the rout. For much of their flight, the screams of doomed and dying men had echoed through the woods behind them. They knew that the Scarlet Guard was pursuing the defeated army.

"What are we going to do?" asked Daryth, removing his boots to rub his swollen feet. Pawldo and Fiona had already dropped off to sleep, but Robyn and Tristan sat up on a cushion of needles, resting their aching legs. Canthus stood alert at the edge of the grove.

"I've been thinking about that," said the prince, exhaustion plain in his voice. "Our only chance is to catch as many of the survivors as possible and try to rally them. We'll need to find a town or a crossroads and wait there."

"We've made good time," nodded the Calishite. "I'm sure we've outdistanced most of the men of Doncastle."

Tristan slumped onto his back. Their whole plan seemed so tenuous that he could not dispel a sense of defeat. But the plan was all they had.

They rested for an hour before wearily climbing to their feet to resume the march. Before long they found a track in the woods and followed it to the southwest. Another track joined it, and the primitive road led them into a wide glen in the forest. Here they found a little village surrounded by pastureland. The forest continued beyond, except to the north. There, a lowland of dead trees extended as far as they could see.

"They've been flooded and drowned," Robyn said sadly.

They entered the tiny hamlet. A dozen thatch-roofed cottages clustered, amid their pastures, on the bank of a winding and placid stream. Robyn led the way up the muddy track.

"Where is everybody?" wondered Pawldo. There was not a soul visible. Even the cattle were gone from the fields.

Robyn stopped and listened. Tristan could hear nothing.

"Look!" cried Fiona, pointing to the path from Dernall Forest. A file of men emerged, trudging wearily along the trail. The muddy, broken soldiers fell into the shade of the trees, collapsing in exhaustion. Steadily, the weary men of Doncastle reached the open ground and stopped to rest.

But then a figure emerged from the forest who did not stoop, who did not march bowed by defeat and exhaustion.

"Alexei!" cried the prince, running to meet the sorcerer.

"It is good to see you all—alive," said the mage. "Many were not so fortunate."

"O'Roarke?" asked Tristan.

"I don't know. Maybe he's with the main band of his army."

"Where's that? I thought they would gather here."

"The king's army pursued swiftly," explained Alexei, shaking his head. "Most of the men were forced southward. I think Cyndre wishes to push them out of the forest, where they can be found more easily."

"Where will they flee?" asked Robyn.

"Who knows?" responded the mage. "Southward across the plain, or west to the coast."

"But the island is only so large," Tristan said. "The king's army will corner them eventually. They'll be slaughtered like sheep! We have to bring them together again—make a stand somewhere."

Tristan turned to the assembly of stragglers. Many of them had been following the discussion with interest, but Tristan couldn't read their faces. Would they follow him?

"Men of Alaron!" he began. "Our cause is not lost. The goddess is with us, and the might of the king has been damaged. One of his most powerful sorcerers has joined our cause.

"Rally with me! We'll gather the forces of Doncastle together and create a plan. We will meet and defeat this king. It is not too late!"

"Who are you, someone who wants to get us killed?" asked one man.

"I am Tristan Kendrick, Prince of Corwell!" he proclaimed. He saw surprise and interest in all too few faces.

"Corwell?" snorted the speaker. "By what claim would you command men of Callidyrr?"

"A claim valid for all of the Ffolk. A symbol of our past and future greatness—the Sword of Cymrych Hugh!" He drew the weapon swiftly and held it above his head. Rays of sunlight reflected from the silvery blade, flickering across the assembled men.

A few more looked interested, but most still wore expressions of skepticism or distrust. The original speaker replied for them.

"The stories are true, then—you carry the weapon of our

greatest king. But still, we have no hope of standing against the Scarlet Guard!"

"You—and I—stood against them well at the King's Gate! It was only another man's mistake that led to our defeat!"

He wanted to rail against the men, threaten them—but he knew that tactic would only drive them away. Yet the defeat and exhaustion on their faces signified more than words how hopeless his task really was.

"Look!" cried one of the men, leaping to his feet. They all turned to the north, and Tristan saw it too: a flash of crimson among the dead trees. More and more of the color appeared, and the prince instantly understood what was happening. A company of the Scarlet Guard had moved in an arc around the retreating humans and now moved toward Hickorydale to seal off this escape route.

"The guard! Flee for your lives!" someone screamed hysterically, and the battered survivors stared in disbelief at their approaching nemesis. Several started for the woods.

"Wait!" Robyn's voice, strong and commanding, rang through the clearing. A gentle breeze ruffled her long hair, and she planted her hands on her hips.

"I offer you a challenge—a chance to avenge your defeat!"

"How?" demanded a burly swordsman. Dried blood was crusted on his shirt and arms.

"If I can stop the king's mercenaries—those," she said, pointing to the approaching red line, "will you join us?"

The swordsman laughed. "Sure." Other men nodded, certain they couldn't lose.

Robyn turned and strode across the pasture just north of Hickorydale, until she reached the edge of the dead wood. The troops of the guard were several hundred yards away, advancing steadily in a neat, unbroken line. They pointed their spears before them—a bristling wall of steel death.

The druid took the runestick from her beltpouch and ran her fingers across a portion of the shaft. She touched the runes reverently, holding the stick before her at arm's length. Then she gestured broadly with it, as if marking a line along the edge of the trees.

Tristan watched her, awestruck by her poise and confidence. The group of men stared as well. The prince watched their faces and saw looks ranging from disbelief and skepticism to blind faith and humble prayer.

Then Robyn shouted. The sound carried clearly to the men, though the word she had spoken was unintelligible. The spearmen of the Scarlet Guard hastened their pace, advancing almost within throwing range of the druid.

But they never got there.

A sheet of orange flame sprang up from the ground along the edge of the dead forest. A slight breeze carried it into the trees, and the dry wood crackled into an instant inferno. The fire quickly devoured the edge of the woods and raced northward. The flames and smoke obscured the men of the guard, but the watchers knew that no men could live in that kind of furnace. The spearmen who did not flee to the north most assuredly died in the fire.

The burly swordsman gave a cheer of triumph. "I'm a man of my word," he said. "My sword is yours."

"Might as well die with friends as alone," said another. A few more rose to their feet, followed by most of the rest. Only a dozen or so remained behind. The others, nearly a hundred strong, followed the prince and his companions away from Hickorydale and Dernall Forest toward a destination none of them knew.

* * * * *

"I-I'm going back there—back there!" Yazilliclick announced suddenly. He sat on the grassy bank of a placid stream and looked up at Newt.

"Back where?" asked the faerie dragon lazily. He lounged upon a tree limb that hung over the clear water.

Newt was bored.

"Come with me, Newt! Let's find Robyn—Find Robyn!"

"Find Robyn? That would be fun! Let's go!"

They drifted along through the vast forest, meandering slowly toward Doncastle. It was a full day later before they got close enough to tell that something was wrong.

"S-smoke?" asked the sprite.

"It sure smells, too! I bet Robyn didn't like that much—a big fire stinking up the whole woods! Too bad we couldn't have seen her—"

Newt stopped in shock as they emerged from the trees.

"W-where's the town?" gasped Yazilliclick. "Where's Robyn—Robyn?"

The whole expanse before them was a blackened wasteland of ash and soot. Tendrils of smoke rose from several piles of charred wood. The Swanmay River, winding placidly through the midst of the desolation, was full of scorched garbage and bodies.

"Come on!" cried Newt. "We've got to find her! I bet she's in big trouble somewhere!"

The two faeries raced with remarkable purpose across the wasteland and into the forest. They didn't know where Robyn had gone, but they would look everywhere if they had to. For another day they buzzed hurriedly, discovering pockets of refugees from Doncastle and companies of the Scarlet Guard. But they found no sign of the druid or her friends.

Finally, they reached the western edge of the forest. Before them rolled a belt of green moor, and they could see the gray waves of the Sea of Moonshae beyond.

"We must have missed her—missed her! We have to go back and try again!" wailed the wood sprite.

"Wait!" said Newt, looking carefully at the moor before them. "What's that?" Before Yazilliclick could answer, the dragon darted from the trees toward the objects that were attracting his eye. Newt blinked into invisibility, and the sprite did the same as he reluctantly followed.

They soon saw that these were creatures, but not the humans they were searching for. Yazilliclick wanted to turn back to the woods, but Newt kept going. "They look familiar—I know, they're dwarves! I know lots of dwarves—they're kind of sourpusses, but they can be fun!"

The dejected sprite trailed along as Newt landed in front of the marching column. The dragon suddenly became visible, drawing a startled curse from the leading dwarf.

"Hi, Finellen!" he chirped. "It's me, Newt! Say, have you seen Robyn anywhere?"

* * * * *

The band of rebels grew as it moved southwestward

through the forest. They encountered many small groups of stragglers, and these willingly fell in with them when they saw the size of the large group. Robyn continued to open the path for them through the forest, and they traveled far more quickly than their pursuers.

Tristan overheard some of the men who had joined them at Hickorydale recounting the tale of Robyn's fire spell. The story grew grander each time, until according to the teller, an entire brigade of ogres had been routed.

It pleased him to hear these boastful stories, and it made the men feel better as well. The morale of the entire group increased with each step and each new band of recruits.

But finally they reached the edge of the forest, having been driven nearly to the coast by the knowledge that the Scarlet Guard was in pursuit. Tristan ordered a rest break, and the men collapsed on the grassy moor, still exchanging boasts. He saw that many of the men were unarmed, and he put them to work cutting and sharpening stakes. The makeshift spears would have to do.

"They look steadier already," remarked Robyn.

"Yes. If we can avoid the king's army for a few more days, I think we'll have an army of our own!" said Tristan. "We'll rest here for an hour and then move on—that's our best chance to pick up more recruits."

"You may not even have to do that—look!" The druid pointed to the south, along the coast.

The ragged band of men trudging wearily toward them were obviously also men of Doncastle—several hundred of them. As they drew closer, Tristan recognized two of the men in the lead.

"O'Roarke and Pontswain," he said quietly.

Robyn and Fiona joined him as he walked purposefully toward the approaching band. The bandit leader stopped to wait for them, and his men flopped wearily on the grass.

"Prince of Corwell," said the outlaw, eyeing Tristan with barely concealed hostility. "I see you have gathered some of my men together."

"They are yours no longer, my lord Roarke," Tristan responded evenly. "You lost the right to command them when you led them to disaster in Doncastle. You were indeed the lord of that town, but that town no longer exists. If you wish, we shall ask them who they desire to follow—I am confident it will be me!"

"So you failed to usurp the king, and now you would take my men instead?"

"Don't be such a pompous fool!" snapped Fiona, stepping before the prince to glare at O'Roarke. "He has done more to strike at the king in a week than you have done in your entire life! Now you *must* help him—it's your only chance to make my father's sacrifice mean something!"

"How dare you—" Hugh choked with rage.

"How dare you pretend you are the man to lead them!" barked the prince. "Your stubbornness cost the lives of hundreds of their companions. Your refusal to look at the battle rationally doomed your entire town to burning!"

The prince's words cut into Hugh O'Roarke like a knife. He had carried the guilty knowledge with him since the battle, but no one had dared to throw it so bluntly in his face.

"There is hope of victory yet," urged Tristan. "You and your men can join with me. You can avenge the defeat, stand up to the Scarlet Guard! We will unite and give battle!"

A spark of O'Roarke's old spirit flashed in his eyes, and he looked from his band of exhausted stragglers to Tristan's group, industriously carving spears.

"Let me lead us all to victory," said the prince quietly.

Hugh O'Roarke drew his sword in a swift motion, then knelt and offered the hilt of his weapon to the prince. Tristan took the blade in gratitude and relief. "Rise, my lord, and join us!"

A cheer arose from both groups as O'Roarke's men stood and marched quickly to Tristan's. The small force now numbered over five hundred men.

"Pontswain?" Tristan turned back to the lord, who had stood sullenly during his conversation with O'Roarke. "Will you, too, cast your lot with us?"

"You have no hope—none at all," said the lord, looking in despair at the ragged band. "I will fight and die here now, for I have no choice!

"But know this, my prince! Our deaths—yours *and* mine—mean the death of hope for Corwell. You have chosen to fight your battle here in Callidyrr. It is my own folly that my fight is tied to yours—for now our own kingdom is bereft of leadership!" Pontswain stalked past him toward the gathering of men.

"He's wrong," said Robyn quietly. "There is a strength in these men that you can harness. We can prevail!"

"You're right. I'm beginning to feel that it *is* possible, that maybe we can win. If we can have just a few more days to grow and get a little rest, we'll have an army that can stand up to the Scarlet Guard and thrash it!"

After a two hour rest, they resumed the march, traveling between the forest and the sea. The coastline here was a low bluff that rolled down a grassy slope to the shore. The beach itself was lined with coarse gravel.

They encountered more groups of stragglers along the shore, and all of these joined their ranks. Finally, in their march to the south, they came over a rise and saw a small fishing town spread before them—Cantrev Codfin, according to one of the soldiers.

There were no signs of activity around the village.

"Stay here, with the men," Tristan said to Daryth and O'Roarke. "I want to have a look at this."

"Take some of the men with you," urged O'Roarke.

"We will be safe," Robyn said. "The danger is past here."

Tristan and Robyn walked down the gentle hill into the village. From a distance, they had seen few details, but as they moved closer they entered a scene of grim horror. In the village, sprawled grotesquely, were a hundred or more bodies. Torn and mutilated Ffolk lay motionless in their cottages and yards. There was no living thing left in the village. Humans, dogs, chickens—everything had been slain by those tearing claws.

"What could have done this?" asked Robyn, her face ashen. "Not the ogres. They wouldn't tear the bodies like this, and they would have burned the place to the ground.

"Not even the sorcerers would do this!" Robyn whispered. She was certain, in some mysterious way, that this attack was part of a larger scheme.

"But what—or who—would do this?"

"I don't know," said the druid, but she pointed to the

ground in a soft patch of wet sand. Many prints of feet that were both webbed and clawed crossed the patch. The feet looked familiar to the prince, and he remembered where he had seen them before.

"The sahuagin have come from the sea."

* * * * *

"What's a scatterbrained faerie dragon doing here?" growled Finellen, in no mood for idle chatter.

"Why, looking for Robyn, of course! I should think that would be obvious, even to a dwarf! But what are you doing here? Now that's a good question!"

Finellen was too tired and discouraged to argue. "We flee one battlefield, and look for another—one where we can die with honor."

"Well, that seems like a silly plan. I mean, like you plan to lose the battle or something! Now, wouldn't it be much better to find Robyn and Tristan and do something fun?"

"What do you know of the Prince of Corwell?" demanded the dwarf. "Quickly, Wyrm, speak!"

"Well, I certainly am not in the mood to talk to someone who speaks to me like that! Wyrm, indeed! Why, if you weren't a friend of my friends, I would use a spell on you that would—"

"Tell me!" growled Finellen in a voice that even Newt could not ignore. Yazilliclick, invisible some distance away, actually feared for the little dragon's life.

"Well, it started when we went back to Doncastle. . . ."

* * * * *

By the following evening, Tristan estimated his fledging army's strength at nearly a thousand men. At the same time, reports of more vigorous pursuit by the king's army came to them through stragglers. That afternoon, they were discovered by crimson-coated horsemen. The riders shadowed them for the rest of the day, and the prince knew that it wouldn't be long before the entire army gathered for the attack.

Indeed, as they came over a hill just before sunset, they saw a full brigade of the Scarlet Guard's human mercenaries. These spearmen and swordsmen stood shoulder to shoulder, facing north.

"Damn!" Tristan, in the lead of his force, stopped.

"That's not all," said O'Roarke, stepping to his side. The bandit lord had been cooperative and forceful in getting his troops to march beside the prince, and Tristan had been grateful for his presence. "There, to the north!"

Looking behind them, the prince saw more red-cloaked figures emerging from the forest. These were huge, rumbling shapes—the ogres!

"We're trapped," he said bitterly. The sea rolled to their west, and brigades of the guard stood to the north and south. To the east, the land climbed quickly away from the shore. If the men tried to flee that way, they would inevitably scatter along the rough ground and be destroyed piecemeal. And even that option was eliminated as another row of crimson uniforms appeared along the crest of the high country—the third brigade of the Scarlet Guard had completed the encirclement.

Alexei, Daryth, Pawldo, O'Roarke, and Robyn joined the prince as he groped for a plan.

"My prince, what is that?" asked Alexei, pointing toward the south. Tristan looked past the ranks of spearmen up the steeply sloping headland, to the rocky promontory he had originally seen as a bivouac. There were small figures up there, moving toward a point below them. The mercenaries, apparently, did not realize there was a group behind them.

"Who are they?" asked Robyn.

"I can't tell—but what's that?" Astounded, Tristan watched the tiny figures pry and push at the boulders on their hilltop. Several of the huge rocks broke free, tumbling toward the backs of the king's brigade below them. More and more of the stones were pushed off the crest, tumbling and rolling until they crashed through the line of the Scarlet Guard.

Soon a crashing landslide tore at the side of the rise as an ocean of crushing rock poured down the hill. Whoever was up there had just done them a great service, but they would need to capitalize on the opportunity.

"Charge!" he cried. "To the hilltop!"

His men voiced a ragged cheer and followed as he held the Sword of Cymrych Hugh high above his head. A thousand voices cried for the blood of the guard, and the rebels of Doncastle rushed forward like a tidal wave toward the broken crimson ranks.

The dust from the landslide had barely settled when the men of Doncastle reached the base of the hill. Many of the crimson-coated spearmen had been crushed by the rocks, and the rest had been separated into small groups in their haste to escape the slide.

These groups were easy prey for the attackers. Tristan led the way into one band of perhaps eighty spearmen. The great moorhound growled and snapped at his side, and the men of Doncastle spread behind him. He stabbed and cut and thrust his way into the thick of the enemy, ignoring a dozen painful wounds.

The pocket of spearmen quickly fell under the attack, and the prince saw his men slow the momentum of their charge. "Onward! To the top!" he cried, leaping among the boulders to begin the climb up the rocky knoll.

He paused and looked back. The ogre brigade lumbered forward, and the mercenaries to the east were streaming down to the shore. But his force had broken through the shattered brigade, climbing the hill. They would reach the top before the other guards could join the fight.

And there, grinning down at him through her bristling beard, stood the stalwart Finellen.

* * * * *

A thousand men of Doncastle and one hundred fifty sturdy dwarves stood upon the rocky knoll and watched the sun disappear into the Sea of Moonshae. The rise was a good place to fight—steep sides dropped to the north, east, and south, while a peninsula jutted into the sea to the west. A narrow neck of land, barely fifty feet wide and flanked by towering cliffs to either side, connected the promontory to the mainland. This would be their final redoubt. Cliffs sheltered their position from attack by sea.

Tristan's elation had dimmed, though, as Finellen grimly pointed out that the help of the dwarves came with its own cost: The creeping mass of the duergar army was plainly visible to the south. Already, the leading dark dwarves were probing the base of their rise—though a brief shower of arrows from the archers of Doncastle sent them scurrying back for cover.

The dark dwarves probed and retreated several times as darkness closed in. Each time they tried to force their way up the slope and were called back by their own commanders. It made sense—all of the enemy armies would attack in the morning and Cyndre would not want to allow the dwarves to attack alone—and possibly suffer a bloody repulse—before the rest of his troops were ready.

The ogre brigade had moved down from the north to camp at the base of their hill on that side, and to the east the human mercenaries of the Scarlet Guard had made camp, cutting off escape inland.

The Prince of Corwell knew that his victory over the king's force, if it were to happen, would have to come here. But he faced the fact with grim acceptance: It was far more likely that the battle would lead to the deaths of them all.

* * * * *

The hard ground prevented Alexei from sleeping comfortably, as it had for the last several nights. He awakened well before dawn, chill and stiff beneath his woolen blanket, listening to the sounds of the slumbering camp.

And then he felt something else—a presence not of this camp, but near it. It settled upon him uneasily, banishing all thoughts of sleep. He arose and threw a robe over his shoulders, shivering in the pre-dawn chill. He suspected the nature of his uneasiness, but he stood still for several minutes, staring to the north until he could be certain.

Cyndre was near.

Alexei had studied and mastered the spellbooks of Annuwynn. His hands, while not as limber as they once were, had recovered sufficiently to allow him to use his magic quickly and easily. And now was the time.

A startled sentry saw Alexei disappear from sight. No one saw him reappear several miles to the north on an empty stretch of coastline. His intuition had served him well—he heard the rumbling of wagons and the tread of heavy foot-falls nearby.

Invisible, the mage walked toward the column that gradu-ally materialized out of the darkness. He stepped to the side to avoid a galloping outrider. The man did not slow down as he passed, but his horse gave a startled whinny as it caught the unseen wizard's scent.

Alexei stopped less than a hundred feet from the road and watched the king's army. He saw the ogres tromp past, and then the rest of the Scarlet Guard. The king's coach rolled into sight, and he saw the green aura surrounding it. No matter—he had a different target in mind.

Finally, he saw the eight black horses and the long wagon that carried the council of sorcerers. Many times he had rid-den in that wagon with his companions to serve some whim of Cyndre's. Now, he expected, Wertam, Talraw, and Kerianow were in there. They had done nothing in particu-lar to arouse Alexei's anger, but that was quite unneccessary. Their deaths would anger Cyndre, and that was justification enough for the sorcerer.

"Pyrax surass Histar," he said, pointing at the coach.

The little marble of fire floated from his fingertip, wafting casually toward the council's wagon. He waited until the spot of light touched the door of the long coach.

"Byrassyll."

Light shot through the darkness, casting long shadows over the members of the king's army. Searing heat followed as the fireball expanded to engulf the coach and its horses. The fire was too hot to grant its victims more than the brief-est of tormented screams.

Moments later, the coach and its occupants were nothing but ashes on the ground. Panic spread through the column as troops and outriders scurried to find the attacker.

But he was already gone.

* * * * *

The hand of Bhaal reached forward. Eagerly, the god nudged the players in his game. Things were progressing splendidly, and he relished the approach of his ultimate victory.

The sahuagin swarmed from the surf at a dozen little villages along the coast of western Callidyrr. They emerged awkwardly from the rolling breakers, stumbling onto the gravelly beaches and struggling to adapt their gills to breathing air. But this they did quickly, flexing those wide organs open as they slipped among the houses and harbors of the villages.

They killed quickly, without emotion. Any man, woman or child they met was swiftly slashed to death by claws and razor-sharp teeth, or impaled. The younger bodies were devoured, and any items of gold or silver were plundered. Then the sahuagin returned to the sea.

Searching, they swam along the coast and gathered with their king at a promontory along the shore.

The undead had marched slowly toward this shore for several days, and finally they climbed the sloping bottom toward shallow water, and surf, and then air. Late in the night they joined the sahuagin at that high promontory.

Sythhissal was the first to emerge, striding boldly from the rolling waves, thrusting his chest forward and swaggering toward the one who awaited him on shore.

The enemy, the sorcerer told him, was on top of the hill. When the sun gave them light, the sahuagin, the undead, the dark dwarves, the ogres, and the humans of the Scarlet Guard, would attack and slay them all. Cyndre said that his plan had come together quite nicely.

And Bhaal chuckled as he heard. "His plan," indeed!

❧ 21 ❧

Earth and Sea

"My prince."

Tristan woke instantly, reaching for his sword. He relaxed as he saw Robyn standing beside him.

"I couldn't sleep," she apologized, kneeling beside him. "And then I saw *that*." The druid pointed to the north, and Tristan saw a brilliant fire blazing in the distance. "It just exploded—like a magic spell, not like a normal fire."

The prince stood and looked. The fire was the only break in the darkness. Moonlight reflected off the sea, but that was only a vague distortion of the gloom.

"Have you been up all night?" he asked.

Robyn nodded. "There's something . . . something *else* out there besides the duergar and the Scarlet Guard. I felt it several hours ago, and it has been growing stronger. Tristan, I'm afraid. There's something horrible here—every bit as horrible as the Beast or the undead!"

He held her against his chest, black thoughts running through his mind. She was right, he knew. And their chances had been hopeless enough earlier in the evening. He had brought her to face death with him on some remote and rocky shore. But for what? For a failed, short-lived cause. Damn his foolishness!

"Robyn," he whispered. "I love you—by the goddess, I love you!"

He kissed her and pressed her close, and for a moment joy filled him. He felt a kind of invincible serenity that banished the real world. But all too soon he remembered their situation. He could not let her go.

"I missed you so much when you were gone that I thought

I'd go crazy. I was even going to come to the Vale and see you, if I could have found you—to try and bring you back to Corwell."

She smiled at him through her own tears, and he continued awkwardly. "I can't ask you to turn from your calling—you have a destiny that even I can see, to serve the goddess. But, if you have room in your life for a husband . . ."

She kissed him quickly, almost playfully. "I like the idea of being a queen," she whispered. "A druid queen! Of course, you'll have to win the kingship for me first. . . ." And they said no more for a time. The sky grew pink and then pale blue as the sun climbed toward the horizon.

Then they heard a sentry shout, and another alarm raised from a different quarter. The battle, it seemed, was beginning.

* * * * *

"By the goddess, what are those?" growled O'Roarke.

Daryth looked into the pre-dawn haze and saw movement at the base of the hill. Things that looked like humans emerged from the mist, stumbling forward. But they did not move like humans, nor did they make any noise. Among them, he saw the fishlike figures of sahuagin, their yellow scales ornamented with golden bracelets and headdresses.

"They're dead!" gasped Pawldo, straining past Daryth to get a better view.

"No! That's impossible!" gasped Pontswain. He stared in shock at the shambling forms, with their sightless eyes and grasping fingers.

The things had pasty white skin—where they had skin at all. Many of them were bare skeletons, clacking along like puppets, while others had swelled into bloated blobs of flesh from their long immersion. Patches of rotten flesh fell away from them with each step, revealing white bone or bleached sinews.

Beside the undead, so ominously silent, there suddenly appeared the berserk forms of a thousand charging duergar. Halfway up the slope, they started to howl. The shrill, unnatural sound carried across the battlefield, chilling the hearts of all who stood in their path.

Waving axes and swords over their heads, the duergar pounded their stubby legs across the rocky slope, momentum carrying them up the hill like a tidal wave.

"Now!" cried O'Roarke. As planned, the men of Doncastle all along the south edge of the hilltop kicked loose the piles of boulders they had prepared overnight. The huge stones thumped and rumbled down the hill.

The dead of the sea took no notice of the rocks, except for those struck by the tumbling missiles. Corpses were spattered by heavy boulders, or knocked down and crippled by smaller rocks. Skeletons went down like tenpins, and many rolling corpses added to the confusion as they tumbled into their fellows below.

But this side of the hill was neither as steep nor as rocky as the other side. Daryth and the rest of the fighters pushed as many rocks as they could, but the all-consuming landslide that had tumbled onto the Scarlet Guard the previous day did not recur.

Soon the boulders were gone, and the duergar roared forward in all their fury. They were close enough now for the men of Doncastle to see their wildly staring eyes, their bristling beards, and dark, scowling brows. When their stubby legs finally carried them to the men of Doncastle, their axes and shortswords were met with spears.

Instantly the din rose to hurricane proportions, as the battles cries of the duergar mingled with the hoarse challenges of the humans, the screams of the wounded, and the crashing of weapon against weapon and shield.

Daryth stood upon a wide, flat rock with Pawldo. Eyeless sockets stared blindly upward as the skeletons reached their clawlike hands toward the defenders in an effort to rip them down. The Calishite slashed and gashed with his silver scimitar. He cut the head from a soggy corpse and, with one vicious down-strike, cut a skeleton into two halves that fell, twitching, to either side of the rock.

Pawldo stood at his back, driving back a white, fleshy thing that tried to crawl onto the boulder. He stabbed it twice with no effect, but then kicked it in the head, gagging as his foot sank into the thing's mushy face.

A skeletal hand reached out, grasping Daryth's ankle. The

Calishite stumbled and slipped toward the edge of the rock, but Pawldo's blade cut cleanly through the creature's wrist, drawing sparks from the rock as the severed hand still clung to the Calishite's leg. Daryth staggered back, twisting to catch his balance. He saw Pontswain's face behind him still gaping in shock. The lord had yet to draw his sword.

The howling of the dark dwarves rose to a frenzy, and Daryth saw with rising panic that they had broken through the line of rebels. Screeching insanely, twoscore duergar raced for the hilltop.

But Hugh O'Roarke bellowed, his red beard and hair seeming to blaze like fire, as he led a dozen men to the breach. He wielded a great broadsword in two hands, roaring a challenge every time he killed a duergar. He roared very frequently, and soon the survivors fell back to their own troops. The outlaw lord charged forward and the gap was filled.

But still they came out of the mist as if they had no end.

* * * * *

"When will they come? I'm getting bored! Robyn, go down and talk to them—tell them we want to get this battle started!" Newt scowled at the ogres, standing in a row at the bottom of the hill. Beside the brutes, the sahuagin slithered and seethed across the moor. The fish-men looked not like individuals, but like the giant, scaly surface of some unimaginable beast, so tightly were they packed.

Tristan, Robyn, Alexei, and Finellen stood at the crest, with Newt and the invisible Yazilliclick sitting on the ground before them. Canthus stood, tense and bristling, at the prince's side. They all watched the attack begin. On the other side, they could hear the battle raging between the duergar and the men of Doncastle. The prince wanted desperately to see what was happening over there, but he could not be everywhere at once. He had left O'Roarke in command, and could only hope that the lord was capable of leading the defense. Daryth and Pawldo were fighting at O'Roarke's sides, and their steady swords could not help but strengthen the defense.

He saw a flash of red hair to his side and looked down to

see Fiona's eyes flashing at him. "I will fight!" she stated, daring him to challenge her. Earlier, he had directed to her a place of some minimal safety—the top of the knoll. She clutched her shortsword, looking as able as many of their fighting men, and more determined than most.

"Very well," he said. She would have to take care of herself.

The sahuagin slithered forward, slipping toward the slope and up onto the rocks, though many of the creatures fell backward. They were unused to walking on land, let alone climbing, and this slowed their advance considerably.

But the ogres suddenly charged at the foot of the hill and lumbered easily up the steep grade. The dwarves sent a few more boulders tumbling toward them—but most of the loose rock had fallen from here the day before. The few ogres that fell to the boulders left small gaps in the lumbering line that were quickly filled by a second rank.

"This'll be a pleasure," grunted Finellen, fingering her axe as she trotted to her company. "Let's go, dwarves!"

The stumpy creatures formed a line of their own, a single rank against the two of the ogres, and marched off the crest of the hill toward the charging monsters. The heavy creatures were slowing their climb, now grunting and panting as they pushed upward—and this was how Finellen wanted to fight them.

The sahuagin, Tristan was happy to see, were still slipping backward almost as fast as they advanced.

"The ogres—there are too many!" cried Robyn.

Tristan saw the ogre brigade spread into a line, one rank deep, but long enough to easily envelop both ends of the dwarven line. Finellen had placed her company line abreast to face the attack, but there were not enough dwarves to meet the huge ogres. The orges struggled steadily up the slope, now only two dozen yards away from the dwarves.

Suddenly the dwarves turned and marched to their right. "What's she doing?" asked Robyn.

"She's shifting the line so that only one of her flanks will be enveloped. It'll help, but I don't think it can save them!"

"Tristan, I might be able to help," said Robyn, "since Yazilliclick saved this from the fire." She held up the runestick.

"Let's go!" Tristan cried. Twenty fighters of Doncastle followed them down the hill as they raced toward the left flank the dwarven line.

"Charge! Get 'em!" cried a shrill voice, and Newt popped into view, clinging to the bristled fur of the moorhound's shoulders like a lancer riding into battle.

The ogres broke into a trot, counting on their massive weight to roll over the puny dwarves. As the companions reached Finellen's line, Tristan could feel the ground shaking underneath his feet. For a moment he regretted their rash charge. Now they faced a company of dozens of ogres. The bestial faces of the attackers broke into grins at the sight of the impudent humans.

The prince drew his sword with a flourish and stood with his feet well braced. He sensed brave men to either side of him—but then his jaw dropped as Robyn darted past. She stood alone, not two dozen yards from the ogres. The monsters howled in glee and broke into a run.

The druid shouted something that Tristan could not hear and waved the carved stick at the ground beneath her. She sprang nimbly backward to stand beside the prince.

The rocky hilltop rose and buckled before him. Two hulking forms, far bigger than the ogres, rose from the ground the stand before them. Each was made of black earth and gray rock, molded into a vaguely manlike shape. Robyn pointed, and the two things shambled toward the suddenly tentative ogres.

"Elementals," she said. "The magic of the Great Druid—stored in the runestick. That was Genna's parting gift to me." She could not conceal her awe at the might of this spells. Genna had crafted the strength to call *two* of the mighty elementals into the stick.

He watched, stunned, as the earthen figures plowed into the rank of ogres. Huge, rocklike fists smashed skulls and crushed chests as the elementals stood side by side to meet the charge. The company of ogres fell apart, many of the monsters clustering to fight the elementals, while a few circled around to attack the companions.

Tristan sprang forward and slashed his sharp blade through the forehead of an ogre. The monster dropped like a stone, and Tristan turned to stab another in the chest. The men of Doncastle and Canthus all joined in the melee, moving quickly among the clumsy attackers.

Six ogres stopped, dumbfounded, as a colorful fountain sprang from the grass before them. They stared transfixed at Newt's illusion while the fight raged around them. An ogre with huge, drooling tusks appeared to be in command of the company, snarling and snapping orders. The Prince of Corwell attacked like a berserker, knocking the club from the ogre's hand with his first blow. His second cut deeply into the monster's forearm, raised in defense, and the third spilled the ogre's guts onto the muddy grass.

Tiny arrows sprang from the air to strike ogres in the eyes or lips as Yazilliclick hovered invisibly about. The missiles were too small to do anything except aggravate the brutes, but they distracted and confused the enemy.

One of the elementals tumbled to the ground, but the second continued to smash at the ogres. Their leader down, their numbers shrinking rapidly, the ogres suddenly had had enough. As one mass, the company facing the companions turned and lumbered toward the imagined security of their own army. Tristan's fighting fury diminished, and he leaned on his sword as he gasped for breath.

But then he noticed the commotion to his right. Finellen's dwarves fought bravely—dozens of ogre dead littered the ground. But the dwarves were paying a heavy price, falling slowly back before the monstrous crush.

And then, to his left, he heard cries of pain and shrieks of horror—human shrieks. He saw that the sahuagin approached the crest and had met the thin line of defenders. He stabbed expertly, knocking a sahuagin spear aside and driving the tip into the monster's chest. But as it fell backward, two more swarmed into its place.

More and more of the fish-men crept up the hill. And suddenly the line of Ffolk collapsed as the sahuagin broke through in a dozen places at once.

And the narrow path to the promontory—their only route of retreat—suddenly lay open before the rushing sahuagin.

* * * * *

White, fishy eyes stared emotionlessly from the hilltop. A hundred sahuagin had pushed through the thin file of defenders to gain the highest ground. They stood in a circle, facing outward, holding sharp tridents or captured spears in a bristling ring of weaponry. Pink, straight tongues flicked between their tooth-studded jaws—the only sign of fear or excitement.

Others of the sahuagin pressed upward to gain the breach their first line had created. Men of Doncastle came from all parts of the knoll to fill that line, however, and they stopped the second push. But still the ring of fish-men held the hilltop and could control the outcome of the battle by striking anywhere they chose.

"Fall back to the promontory!" called the prince, and the word flew down the line.

The men of Doncastle retreated before the dark dwarves, before the bloated, rotted undead. They held firm against the sahuagin, lest more fishmen break through and cut off their retreat onto the high peninsula.

"Finellen—let's break that ring!" urged the prince. The sahuagin stood astride their retreat path. The monsters would have to be pushed out of the way before the rebel force could cross the narrow neck of land leading to the promonotory.

"Charge!" cried the dwarf, and her company—now less than a hundred—shouted a hoarse challenge. Their stumpy legs pounded the ground as, axes flailing, they rushed toward the fish-men.

But another challenge came from the prince's left, and he saw Hugh O'Roarke leading a band of his men into the bristling defense. The bandit lord fought like a demon, roaring and crashing about with his broadsword. The sahuagin stabbed and hissed, thrusting at the human attackers, but then the dwarves crashed into the other side of the ring. The creatures fought to the last, but soon the hilltop was greasy with their red, fishy blood.

Tristan caught a glimpse of Pontswain in the middle of a mob of duergar. The lord's blade was bloody, and though his eyes were wide with panic, he struck about him like a wildman, somehow keeping the dark dwarves at bay.

Now the men of Doncastle fell back across the neck of land. Here, where the promontory was barely fifty feet wide, sheer cliffs more than a hundred feet tall dropped to either side of the peninsula. Farther out, the promontory widened, but it was surrounded by high cliffs on all sides.

The rebels filed across the land bridge as the dwarves and small groups of men held the attackers at bay. Tristan stood with Finellen, and Canthus snarled and fought between them. They fought back-to-back against the sahuagin that threatened at any moment to overwhelm them—but somehow, they held them at bay.

The prince's arms had long grown numb, and blood poured across his skin from a number of wounds. He was soaked to the elbows in the gore of his enemies, and his movements had become automatic. Numbly, he lifted his still-gleaming blade and swung, lifted and swung.

O'Roarke and Daryth stood with their men on the other side of the knoll, holding back the dark dwarves and the sea's dead. They, too, fought with automatic precision, adding body after body to the pile.

Finally the bulk of their force had crossed, and the men of the rearguard backed onto the neck of land. Tristan, Daryth, Finellen, and Hugh O'Roarke stood side by side in the center of the line. They fought a mixture of duergar, sahuagin, corpses, humans of the guard, and ogres.

A vicious, drooling ogre lunged at the prince, and fatigue numbed Tristan's reactions. The monster's huge, spiked club whistled toward his head, but then a wide broadsword cracked into the weapon, knocking it off its mark. The ogre bellowed at Hugh O'Roarke, who had stepped forward to deflect the blow. Before he could recover, the lord staggered from the thrust of a sahuagin trident.

Tristan leaped forward and cleaved the ogre's chest into a wide death-wound, seizing O'Roarke's arm as the lord stumbled. But another fish-man stretched forward his horrible claws and pulled on Hugh's arm. Tristan whirled to avoid a duergar battleaxe, and suddenly O'Roarke was gone.

He heard the lord's bellow of challenge as a dozen sahuagin dragged him into their midst, and saw at least two of the fish-man fall dead from the outlaw's dying blows.

And then he felt the earth reel beneath his feet, and the world began to come apart around him.

*   *   *   *   *

Cyndre sat upon the roof of the royal coach, watching the progress of the ogres and the sahuagin. He could not see the other brigade of the Scarlet Guard, nor the duergar, nor undead, but he felt confident the battle progressed according to plan.

His time would come soon, when all were occupied. He waited specifically for a sign of Alexei. Often in a battle such as this, the mage who revealed himself first was the mage who died first.

But Alexei was careful. Cyndre was not overly concerned by this—he knew his own power far exceeded that of his former lieutenant. Soon it would be time to move.

Below him, seated in the coach, the king drooled and gibbered senselessly. His mind was finally broken, and only with great difficulty had Cyndre concealed this fact from the men of the Scarlet Guard. After their victory, however, it would not matter.

Now, he decided. He would find Alexei and kill him. Then he would see that the battle was won in a suitable fashion.

Cyndre gestured quickly, and in the space of a blink he disappeared.

*   *   *   *   *

Alexei idly watched the struggles raging around him. He stood upon the highest rise on the promontory, separated from the main battle by the thin peninsula. From here, he sought signs of visible magic or any other clue as to Cyndre's whereabouts. Safe from the din of the battle and tense with the thrill of his impending vengeance, Alexei dwelled upon images of his former master writhing under the torturous impact of his spells. When would Cyndre appear? For the hundredth time, his eyes searched the battlefield, looking for an explosion of flame or rolling cloud of gas that would give his former master away. Nervousness seized him. Now that the hour of his vengeance was almost at hand, he feared he lacked the power to challenge the mighty sorcerer. He thought briefly about teleporting to someplace far away—but then he remembered his days of torment, his hands crushed and his spirit broken, in the cell. And he vowed to claim his vengeance no matter what.

Suddenly he felt that same menacing presence that had awakened him—and this time it was very close. He knew that his former master was about to act. But where?

Alexei whirled, in time to see Cyndre materialize a scant twenty feet away. The master of the council drew back his hood enough for Alexei to see those pale blue eyes, icy as death. Alexei unconsciously stumbled backward. Face to face with Cyndre, he suddenly felt grave doubts as to his own powers. Desperately, he groped for a spell, an act, with which he might stave off his doom.

"Stupakh!" sneered Cyndre, and in that one word Alexei saw disaster.

A stunning shockwave of magic slammed into him, knocking the wind from his lungs and smashing him to the ground. He lay, flat on his back, unable to move a muscle—but his eyes and ears functioned perfectly, and he could do nothing but stare at Cyndre's slow approach.

Alexei understood what had happened. His mentor had used one of the words of power—a word that stunned its listener into paralysis. Completely helpless, he wondered why Cyndre had not used the power word that would have killed him on the spot. But the black wizard answered his unspoken question as he stopped above Alexei's motionless body, looking down to gloat.

"Well, my pupil, I see you have studied your lessons well." Cyndre absently prodded Alexei's side with a soft-toed boot. "You have caused me much trouble in the past days—and you have slain people who were close to me, who counted upon my protection.

"For this you will inevitably die. But your death, in itself, will not atone for these crimes. It is fitting that you should first witness the elimination of the rebel army—these pathetic fools whom you sought to aid against *me*! Then, you will be taken, alive, to Callidyrr. Only when the altar of Bhaal is ready to receive you will the life'sblood be drawn ever so slowly from your heart.

"Until that time, you will be secured—this time, with no hope of escape." Cyndre smiled coolly. Alexei could look into his eyes from his position on the ground, but he could do little else.

The black wizard began to cast a spell of doom. Each word struck Alexei like a physical attack. It was made more horrible by the fact that he recognized the spell—he knew what would happen.

When Cyndre uttered the last word to the spell, his soul would be torn brutally from his body, condemned to an imprisonment of infinite suffering, until the sorcerer decided to release him by granting him his death.

* * * * *

Robyn held tightly to the runestick. She had used three of its elements—wind, fire, and earth—the three she understood. The fourth, water, remained, but the young druid did not know what would happen when she called upon it, and so she held the stick as a talisman and little else.

Unafraid but practical, she stayed back from the melee with the ogres—her club would be little threat to the brutes, while one solid hit from an ogre could kill her.

She held Fiona's arm to prevent the lass from charging into the melee. "That sword will only make an ogre mad," she pointed out. She was surprised when Fiona listened to her and paused in her headlong charge.

"If you want to fight," suggested Robyn, "take that blade and stand with those who will meet the sahuagin—we are thin there, and could use you."

"I will!" declared the red-haired girl, eager to accept the assignment. She climbed up the broken hillside to join the men who were now lighting brands and torches in anticipation of the fish-men's onslaught.

Robyn stepped carefully backward across the churned ground, moving up the slope. A panorama slowly appeared. Right before her eyes, the Prince of Corwell wielded his sword in a glittering pattern of swirling steel. He danced this way and ducked back, all the while turning to keep the enemy from his back. And one after another, mighty ogres fell, slain by a single lightning thrust.

She reached the top of the knoll, moving as if in a daze. All around her, the madness of the battle swirled. Humans of the Scarlet Guard fought to gain the crest on the east. Dark dwarves and the horrible dead creatures of the sea were slowly pushed back to the south. And the ogres and sahuagin pressed against men and dwarves to the north. She saw the fish-creatures pushing through the line. One slipped toward her, its jaws gaping, its dull eyes somehow looking both passionless and consumed by bloodlust. And then a man of Doncastle stabbed the thing and it fell, twitching and gasping like a fish on a hook.

She saw a lone figure atop the rise on the promontory—Alexei! The wizard fell suddenly, disappearing behind the crest, and she felt sudden fear. Her numbness vanished, and she raced across the neck of land, up the gentle slope to the top of the peninsula.

She froze in shock as she reached the crest of the rise. She saw Alexei, sprawled flat on his back. She instantly realized that the black robed figure leaning over him must be Cyndre. Gasping for breath, she called upon her druid magic.

She stopped and spread her arms, speaking to the grass and the air. "Thesallest yu, rotherca—to me!"

The droning and buzzing of tiny wings instantly surrounded her. Robyn swung her arms together, pointing to the sorcerers, and the swarm of wasps, mosquitoes, bees, and biting flies snarled as a single entity in the direction of her command.

Cyndre, locked into the meditation of a casting, did not sense the approaching swarm until hot stingers pierced his skin in a dozen places. With a scream, the black wizard recoiled, flailing about himself and staggering back.

Robyn ran forward, pointing the insects away from Alexei as Cyndre tried to break free of the cloud. She had to keep him from casting his spell!

She stopped suddenly again to kneel on the grass. "Mother, your children are born. Give them growth!"

Instantly, snakelike weeds and stout saplings erupted from the ground around the wizard. He screamed again, struggling to break free of the entwining vegetation, but the plants held him fast. The spell had done what she commanded—it had immobilized the wizard momentarily while she searched for an idea.

Suddenly, she felt a tremor beneath her feet. The hilltop shook slightly, and she stumbled. The ground moved again, and she fell to her hands and knees. It seemed as if the earth was stretching.

A shock wave lifted her off the ground and she thumped onto her back. She saw only sky, but she heared a ripping sound, like a sheet being torn in two. Quickly she rolled, remaining on all fours.

A jagged fissure raced across the hilltop, tearing open the sod to reveal a chasm of unfathomable depth. Cyndre saw the fissure too, and the wizard screamed with a shriek of unnatural horror.

For the fissure was racing directly toward him.

Like the gaping maw of an unimaginably huge monster, the earth split across the entire hilltop. The last spot in the tear was the center, where the clump of vegetation held Cyndre firmly. Alexei lay pale and paralyzed beside it. Finally, the thicket ripped in half as the ground tore open. Cyndre, still bound, kicked and struggled as the bushes and saplings slowly leaned into the crevice. Clumps of dirt broke and fell, and slowly the roots of the weeds broke free. For a breathtaking moment the plants hung by a few, frail tendrils—and then those broke free as well.

The wizard reached desperately, grabbing a corner of Alexei's robe. The paralyzed wizard's eyes bulged as he felt himself dragged toward the crevice with his former master. Robyn dove for Alexei's hand, but could not reach him before he disappeared into the yawning chasm.

Cyndre's scream rose from the fissure like the cry of a demon, chopped short as the opening slowly closed.

Suddenly, Robyn had an idea. She lay with her face pressed against the earth, uncertain if the inspiration was her own or had emerged from the ground itself. Quickly, she sat up and pulled the runestick from her pouch. The fissure had almost closed, but a split in the earth still gaped nearby. She threw the runestick and held her breath as she saw it fall into the hole. Then the fissure snapped shut.

Slowly, Robyn climbed to her feet. She walked gingerly

toward the place where the earth had opened, but there was no sign of the fissure in the grassy turf. Cyndre, Alexei, and the thicket of plants that had trapped the sorcerer were gone.

Then she felt a deeper, more frightening rumble—a fundamental distress in the body of the goddess. Awed and frightened, she dropped to her knees and prayed.

* * * * *

Across the battlefield, the frenzy of the combatants died away as the ground shook. Fighters near the sheer cliffs were thrown to their deaths like drops of water shaken from the back of a dog. Everywhere, ogres, humans, dwarves, and sahuagin fell to their hands and knees, hugging the ground for support. Only the undead, mindlessly attacking, stayed upright—and the rumbling earth sent the entire mass of them tumbling down the slope.

The sea raged against the cliffs below the battle. Gray mountains of water rose to smash the rock, tearing it away. And still the waves rose higher, lashed against the land by an unseen force. The ground convulsed again, and a great slab of cliff broke away, carrying a hundred sahuagin back to the sea. Another tremor shook the neck of land where the prince had held the line. Slabs of earth broke away from both sides of the bridge, cutting its width in half and carrying dozens of screaming ogres, guardsmen, and duergar to their deaths.

"Back!" cried Tristan, sensing the imminent danger. Daryth and Pawldo sprang away from the line of bodies that marked their battle, dragging the prince with them. Canthus, too, leaped back from the collapsing ground. In seconds, the men of Doncastle fled toward the safety of the promontory, tripping and stumbling in their effort to run across the shaking ground.

As the mountainous waves crashed against both sides of the neck, the land bridge collapsed, leaving the Ffolk of Tristan's force atop a small island that had been a peninsula just moments before. The gray water roared through the gap, still striking at the shore of the mainland.

The Prince of Corwell stood in awe, ignoring the pitching

ground. The only sound was the deep, supernatural rumbling of the earth and sea. Even the duergar had ceased their howling.

The rumbling grew more pronounced, and Tristan watched as the enemy troops began to sidle away from the cliff, at first hesitantly, but then furiously. Ogres, dark dwarves, humans, and sahuagin all turned in panic and fled.

But they were too slow.

The sea water pounded relentlessly against the base of the cliff, and suddenly great chunks of the rock face began to fall away. With a rumble that drove the prince to his knees, the rocky knoll collapsed into the sea. Tons of earth, rock, and bodies fell headlong into the churning surf. And still the earthquake pounded the land.

The sahuagin clung to the trembling rocks only briefly, slipping and scrambling down the bluff. Many scaly bodies broke upon the jagged rocks, but many others sprang into the air and hit the water in smooth dives. The fish-men that survived the fall swam frantically away from the crashing cliff, seeking the safety of the deep sea.

Next, the land beneath the ogres gave way. The huge creatures clawed and scratched to reach solid ground, but more and more of the cliff gave way, dragging the entire ogre brigade to its doom. Ogre bodies plummetted into space, bouncing and spinning lazily through the air on the long fall to the water. Each ogre crashed into the foaming surf with enough force to smash any vestiges of life that still lingered in its body after the crushing slide from the bluff.

The dark dwarves scattered like rats, fleeing in every direction—but the ground in every direction gave way beneath them. Hundreds of the little figures clung desperately to the lip of the land, only to be shaken loose by another tremor. The dark dwarves fell like tumbling stones, howling all the way to the water. Even their hoarse shrieks could not be heard above the rumbling of the land.

The human mercenaries of the Scarlet Guard clung to their formations, retreating in blocks of humanity, spears and swords bristling against the ogres and dark dwarves that tried to run them down in their own panic.

But even this discipline could not save them. The land

gave way under a huge block of men. The entire formation slid from the lip of the precipice, down the muddy side, and vanished into the churning surf. More mud and rock broke above them, burying the mercenaries completely. One by one, the other companies of red-cloaked men fell, until the last of them broke and ran in panic away from the sea.

Even this escape was too late, as the water raged against the dwindling hilltop, chewing away the remaining clumps of high ground. The land collapsed and fell faster than the men could run, and the last of them tumbled to his doom in a maelstrom of water, dirt, and rock.

Fissures snaked into the land, and the slopes of the knoll followed the crest into the sea. Greedily, the devouring waves churned deeper inland, taking still more of the land, until the collapsing earth outdistanced the fleeing remnants of Cyndre's army, carrying them all into the gray, devouring waters.

At last, as the earth's violence abated, only one element of the king's army remained: a black, shiny coach with red satin curtains and a team of nervous, prancing horses. A sheet of cliff fell away, leaving the carriage standing at the brink of a vast bay that had suddenly eaten into the coast. The horses, staked in place, whinnied and bucked in panic. The carriage swayed alarmingly, and then a wheel slid from the brink. Another soon followed, and then the coach pitched headlong, pulling the helpless horses with it. The vehicle tumbled and spun through the air, until it too crashed into the water and disappeared.

Finally, the land ceased its heaving. The men of Doncastle stood upon a small island, surrounded by sheer cliffs. Fully a half mile of open water separated them from the newly defined shore. Where the rocky knoll had been, there was now a wide bay. The mountainous waves sank quickly, until the sea was an expanse of rolling gray swells—placid on the surface, but in constant motion.

And eternal power.

* * * * *

"Did you guys see that?" Newt blurted. "Boy, it was really something. I hope you were looking, 'cause you'll probably *never* get a chance to see anything like that again!"

"I hope we never do," said the prince simply. He sat on the ground—not trusting that it was entirely solid—with Robyn and Canthus. Daryth, Pawldo, Fiona and Finellen had gone to take stock of their situation. Pontswain, too, had survived the battle. Now he sat, alone and brooding, on the edge of the cliff, as if annoyed that his predictions of disaster had been wrong.

Newt and Yazilliclick suddenly popped into sight beside them. The dragon hovered while the wood sprite landed beside Robyn, his antennae twitching nervously as he stared at the prince.

"Don't worry," soothed the druid. "He's a friend."

"I-I know! I fought for him—for him! But he looks so scary—scary!"

Tristan laughed, and the tension flowed from his body. "Thanks, little one—your arrows really kept those ogres wondering!"

Daryth, Pawldo, and Finellen rejoined the group sitting on the grass. Fiona came up to sit in silence. For the first time, Tristan thought the lass looked tired. Her hair hung in tangles about her face. She wore a bloody bandage about her wrist, and the skin of her legs and face was chafed and bruised. Still, her eyes retained that fiery spark.

Pontswain, too, joined them, though he avoided meeting the prince's gaze. He stared around the battlefield and the vast, blue bay where the enemy army had once stood. His expression passed between disbelief sullen brooding.

"The cliff is steep, but we can get down it in a couple of places," Daryth said. "More serious is the water—but there's a few strong swimmers among the men. If we can't attract a fishing boat or something, we can send them to the mainland to get a boat or two."

"How many men do we have left?" asked the prince.

"About three hundred," said the Calishite. Tristan felt a wave of sadness for the deaths. He remembered O'Roarke's sacrifice with a particular pang.

"And seventy-nine of my dwarves," said Finellen, staring at the ground. She looked up with an expression of fierce determination. "But that's more than I ever thought would live through this fight. My lad, you've got some very powerful friends."

The prince looked at Robyn and took her hand. She slid to his side and leaned against him. They drew strength from each other.

"The prophecy," she said softly. "Do you remember what you told me?"

Tristan shook his head. "I haven't given it a thought."

"'Wind and fire, earth and sea, all shall fight for him, when it is time for him to claim his throne.'"

He sat up straight, remembering the magic of Robyn's runestick. "The wind drove the gas away, in Doncastle. And the fire—that routed the Scarlet Guard at Hickorydale."

"And I saw those earth-guys come out of the ground and pound on the ogres!" said Newt. "They were really something, too—but not like the earthquake! Did you see that? Boy, you should have if you missed it!"

"And the earthquake," finished Robyn, "was the sea pounding against the cliffs, carrying away the land!"

Tristan still shook his head. "It's an amazing coincidence, but it can't be me! Remember, the prophecy starts out: 'His name shall be Cymrych.'"

Finellen snorted in amusement. "Have you ever heard of anybody named Cymrych?" she asked.

"Not in my lifetime, no."

"Well, neither have I—in your lifetime, that is. Now, I don't mix with humans much—nothing personal, you understand— but one thing that comes from living four centuries is a little bit of knowledge."

Tristan was surprised to learn the dwarf's age.

"Used to be, when I was a youngster, half the humans around Gwynneth were named Cymrych—all after Cymrych Hugh, of course. Got so you couldn't tell the western Cymrychs from the southern Cymrychs from the—well, you get the picture.

"From what I gather, the names were changed—altered slightly so that you could tell which branch of the family you were talkin' about."

"Altered to what?" asked the prince.

"All kinds of things. Cymrych—" She took time to pronounce the word carefully. "Kim-Rick became Kimball, Cambridge, Kincaid . . ." Finellen paused. "And Kendrick."

"So your name is Cymrych, in a sense!" said Pawldo, clapping the prince on the back. "Congratulations, Your Majesty! How about a knighthood for your faithful halfling companion?"

Tristan laughed, but he was too dazed to answer. He had wanted to lead the Ffolk into a period of unity and strength. But an hour ago he had been certain that he would be dead by now. The transition was too sudden for his mind to grasp.

"Look!" cried Fiona, suddenly leaping to her feet. She stood at the edge of the precipice, pointing downward. "What's that?"

The prince sprang to her side, staring down the hundred-foot cliff into the green waves rolling below. A circle of whiteness, a shimmering whirlpool, marked the surface of the water, swirling in a growing pattern and calming the waves around it.

"It's her," Robyn said mysteriously.

The circle of water suddenly exploded upward in a foaming geyser, spewing higher and higher from the surface in a fountain of gushing water. Twenty, forty, eighty feet it spouted upward, and still it climbed. There was no sign of anything but frothing, turbulent water. But Tristan understood who Robyn meant.

Finally the fountain reached a level with them, and here it stopped its climb. For a full minute they stared, amazed, at the display. The surviving men and dwarves gathered around their leaders, standing in a semicircle at the top of the cliff, wondering at the portent of this fabulous exhibition. The fountain was not twenty feet away from them, though it rose straight from the water, so sheer was the drop here.

And then the fountain tipped and sprayed them all in a shower of unnaturally warm brine. The watchers stumbled back from the cliff, sputtering and wiping spray from their eyes. When they could see again, the fountain was gone. It had sunk without a trace into the rolling green swell.

But before them, sitting on the wet grass at the edge of the bluff, was an object that had not been there before—an object of gleaming, iridescent gold. Droplets of water clung to its shining surface, capturing and reflecting the rays of the sun in a thousand brilliant colors.

It was a plain object, for all its precious metal: a circlet of gold, with eight points rising along its circumference. It was less than a foot in diameter.

"The Crown of the Isles," whispered Robyn, kneeling.

Tristan's knees grew weak, and he sank to them before the golden circlet. Robyn gingerly picked up the crown. She closed her eyes and breathed a short, silent prayer, and then she placed it upon the head of her prince. Tristan was struck dumb, and he could not speak. Instead, he climbed carefully to his feet, conscious of the precious weight upon his head, and he turned to the men of Doncastle.

Their cheer sounded like a challenge to battle. "Long live the king! Hail to King Kendrick!" The cry echoed across the placid bay, off the shore of the mainland, and back to them, where it grew in volume and enthusiasm. Robyn seized him and kissed him. Tristan felt giddy with joy.

But then he gently broke from her embrace, looking tenderly into her tear-streaked eyes. He looked over the cheering men saw Daryth's and Finellen's beaming faces. And he looked out to sea, across the rolling gray swells that separated him from Corwell. Robyn sensed his uneasiness and clung to him as she spoke.

"You're right," she said, reading his mind. "The danger is not past. Come with me to free the druids of the Vale."

"Of course—as soon as we get a boat."

"I'm coming, too!" said Pawldo.

"And me," nodded Daryth.

"This is the first sensible plan you've suggested on this journey!" said Pontswain, visibly brightening at the prospect of returning to Corwell. He stole a surreptitious look at the golden crown, and his eyes flashed with desire.

"I've got to go that way, anyway," groused Finellen. "I suppose I could stop and see the grove."

"We're going home?" Newt was beside himself. Even Yazilliclick jumped to his feet and clapped his hands.

Robyn looked at Fiona, inviting her to join them.

"My place is here in Callidyrr," said the young woman. She brushed the filthy hair back from her face and smiled. "Someone has to announce the news of the new king! With these men of Doncastle, I will see that Caer Callidyrr is ready to receive you when you return!"

Robyn's throat tightened and she looked away, her eyes scanning the vast surface of the sea. The placid water looked somehow ominous, as if it masked a threat they had yet to understand. I'm frightened, she thought with a shiver.

But she kept her fears to herself.

* * * * *

Bhaal snarled his frustration across the realm of Gehenna. He crashed his clublike fist against the mountainside, breaking away chunks of stone that tumbled free to fall for eternity down the never-ending slope. The plane was wracked by explosions of steam and lava, as the realm itself shared the displeasure of its god.

But Bhaal's anger was fleeting. He held no doubts as to his ultimate triumph. Hobarth and his army of death still occupied their strategic position. The Moonwell at the heart of the Vale had grown thick and black, filled with corpses. His domain of death was strongly established on Gwynneth.

And now, there was much death in the sea.

The bodies of ogres, dark dwarves, humans, and even sahuagin floated against the rough shore or drifted along the rocky bottom of the sea. There were thousands of inanimate corpses, bodies waiting only for Bhaal's command.

Most of the sahuagin still lived. Now the fish-men dove and darted among the bodies of their former allies in a feeding frenzy. The vibrations of the Deepsong still thrummed in their breasts. Bhaal did not want this power to fade.

Ysalla kicked away from a bloated ogre corpse. Other priestesses fed upon it, tearing at the back and shoulders with their sharp teeth. The high priestess had claimed those delicacies, the eyes, before withdrawing.

Suddenly she paused, her arms and legs fluttering in the water like fins, holding her stable. She heard the command of her god and obeyed.

Her sharp, screeching spell frightened the other priest-

esses away from the ogre. When she finished, the eyeless sockets of the ogre suddenly gaped upward. The body lurched awkwardly before settling to its feet on the bottom. The other priestesses hastened to follow their mistress, and more ogre bodies and dark dwarves and red-cloaked humans of the Scarlet Guard slowly filled the ranks of the army under the sea.

Bhaal saw his armies and was pleased. He would bring them together, he decided, upon Gwynneth. The new king's home would be the first land to die completely.

And slowly, but with grim and unshakeable purpose, the army of death began to march across the bottom of the sea.

THE AUTHOR

Douglas Niles is a Wisconsin native and former high school teacher who now writes and designs games for TSR, Inc. His game designs include THE HUNT FOR RED OCTOBER™, a boardgame based on Tom Clancy's novel of the same name, ONSLAUGHT™, DRAGONLANCE® adventure modules, and the ADVANCED DUNGEONS & DRAGONS® BATTLESYSTEM™ game, which won the 1985 H.G. Wells Award for best miniatures rules. He has written numerous interactive books and nearly two dozen role-playing modules. This is his second novel.

He lives in Delavan, Wisconsin, with his wife Chris, children Allison and David, and a 180-pound Saint Berlabrador named Yukon.

Explore the FORGOTTEN REALMS™ Fantasy Campaign Setting!

From the fog-enshrouded moors of Moonshae to the pristine peaks overlooking Bloodstone Pass; from Waterdeep, City of Splendors to Thay; from the Pirates of the Inner Sea to the kingdoms of Calimshan in the South—these are the lands of the Forgotten Realms.

The FORGOTTEN REALMS Fantasy Campaign Setting is the most elaborate and detailed presented by TSR, Inc. to date. An entire new line of novels, AD&D® adventure modules and sourcebooks, and other exciting accessories have been created for gamers adventurous enough to explore the ultimate adventure game setting.

The FORGOTTEN REALMS Boxed Campaign Setting
Ed Greenwood and Jeff Grubb

The cornerstone for AD&D adventures set in the Forgotten Realms, and the basis for all novels and sourcebooks in the series, this set includes four-color maps of the world and almost 200 pages of vital information, both on the Forgotten Realms themselves and on setting up AD&D campaigns in this fabulous land.

AD&D® Sourcebooks:

WATERDEEP AND THE NORTH
Ed Greenwood

Waterdeep, the largest city of the northern realms, home to half a million humans, dwarves, elves, and halflings, is a city of power and evil, intrigue and wealth, ruled by unseen and mysterious lords. FORGOTTEN REALMS creator Ed Greenwood takes you on a grand tour of this, the mightiest city of the Realms.

MOONSHAE
Doug Niles

Exploring in depth the islands off the Sword Coast, home to *Darkwalker on Moonshae,* this sourcebook provides further detailed information on the Realms and adapts adventures found within this novel to an AD&D game campaign.

EMPIRES OF THE SANDS
Scott Haring

The arid, inhospitable countries on the southeastern corner of the continent of Faerun are the subject of *Empires of the Sands,* a 64-page sourcebook. Players wanting to explore this section of the Realms campaign setting can decide whether they prefer to seek their fortunes in the mercenary, Machiavellian country of Amn; the merchant state of Calimshan; or the anarchic land of Tethyr.

THE MAGISTER
Ed Greenwood and Steve Perrin

The Magister is the first word on magic in the FORGOTTEN REALMS campaign setting. It provides thorough coverage of new spells and magical items and instructions for generating new magical items.

AD&D® Adventure Modules:

UNDER ILLEFARN
Steve Perrin

An introductory campaign base for new players of the AD&D game or for experienced players starting a new campaign in the Forgotten Realms. An earthquake rattles the small town of Daggerford, south of Waterdeep. Can your characters handle what the earth brings forth?

DESERT OF DESOLATION
Tracy and Laura Hickman,
Phil Meyers, Peter Rice, and John Wheeler

This epic trilogy outlining the power and mystery of tremendous magical forces is set in the great dust desert of Raurin. For characters of intermediate level.

THE BLOODSTONE PASS SERIES
Michael Dobson and Doug Niles

Only the powerful need apply. A great danger is growing in the North, in the ice-blasted desolation that is Vaasa, and threatening to engulf the shattered nation of Damara. Can your characters stem the tide in this epic four-volume series?

SWORDS OF THE IRON LEGION

An evil power is training armies in a lonely stretch of the Forgotten Realms, and a band of tough-guy player characters—namely the Iron Legion—is the only thing that can keep the power from taking over. *Swords of the Iron Legion* is a series of short adventurers, each by a different author, and each incorporating BATTLESYSTEM™ rules.